C

BY
I D Jackson

To
Diana
Best Regards
Ian Jackson
x

PERCY
PUBLISHING

Dead Charming
Copyright © 2014 I D Jackson
All rights reserved.

Enquiries should be addressed to
Percy Publishing
Woodford Green,
Essex. IG8 0TF
England.

www.percy-publishing.com

1st Published December 2014
1st Edition

ISBN: 978-0-9929298-3-1

Cover Design Copyright © 2014 Percy Publishing
Percy Publishing is a Clifford Marker Associates Ltd Company

Dedication

For Tom, Anna and Susie
Bright lights in a dimly lit world...

*Good and Evil cuts through the heart
of every human being and who is willing
to destroy a piece of his own heart?*

Aleksandr Solzhenitsyn

Chapter 1

TWO YEARS AGO

When it all started Tony Jones was twenty-eight and his wife Emma just a few months younger. Childhood sweethearts, perhaps destined to be together, they'd met in Miss Holloway's class at King's Road Primary, sitting next to each other on their first day and then all the way through school. Tony's cheeky grin and rough-shorn dark hair captivated Emma at first sight and they became the centre of a tight-knit group of young friends with the world at their feet. They became inseparable, even when they moved on to Stretford High and faced the pressures of puberty. Although they were not romantically involved at school, neither Emma nor Tony developed an interest in anyone else of the opposite sex. Tony spent time with his friends playing football and Emma spent time with hers talking about clothes and playing music, but they always found time for each other. Perhaps it was the proximity of their houses, only three doors apart on Royston Road in Firswood, or perhaps the fact that their parents were friends and their fathers worked in the same joinery business, but everyone was sure that Emma and Tony would end up as a couple.

On their last day at Stretford High they finally kissed: not a peck on the cheek or even a friendly kiss on the lips, but a passionate and determined embrace in the dark of the School Prom night, and the two of them cemented an unbreakable bond.

***

Their daughter Jade, the product of their love and now two years old, was playful and pretty, and Emma put her dark hair in bunches or plaits and dressed her in brightly coloured dresses so that other mums might see how special her baby was.

If they stopped to think about it, Tony and Emma would have described themselves as normal, ordinary even. They weren't wealthy, thought little of fame or fortune and had few friends to intrude on their leisure time, choosing instead to pour their love and effort into their daughter. When asked, Emma proudly described her husband as solid and reliable, and it was true: Tony was a practical sort of man who wasn't easily fooled and could usually spot a rogue a mile off. That was until Joe Reed charmed his way into their lives. Nobody could have guessed how Reed would affect them and how their world would change forever.

Tony was working for an insurance company in Manchester. He was doing well and the company was thriving. He'd been in sales for about five years, joining Peterson Insurance Brokers a year or so previously as another step up the ladder. He and Emma were comfortably off and when Jade arrived they'd started saving for the future, putting away Tony's ever-growing commission, as well as ten percent of his salary.

Soon he began to do so well that Emma didn't have to work and gave up her nursing career to concentrate on Jade, while Tony spent all of his time providing for them. The couple considered themselves lucky. Life was good and they were as happy as they could be.

Tony could remember clearly the first time he spoke to Joe Reed. It was a Friday in June; Reed had come for an interview and was waiting outside the company director's office. He was the only one sitting there, and as Tony knew that Mr Peterson saw possible new recruits in batches, he realized he must be the final candidate. Tony was known for being pretty friendly and seeing him alone he sympathized with how nervous the guy was probably feeling. Reed was wearing a dark suit that had seen better days, and his shoes were dirty and almost falling apart. Tony's instinct was that he wouldn't be getting the job: Garry Peterson insisted that his sales team look their best at all times; he saw scruffiness as a sign of weakness and he gave guys like this short shrift, so this candidate was on a loser straight away.

"Alright?" Tony said as he approached.

When Reed turned to look at him it was Tony who suddenly felt nervous. Reed's face somehow didn't fit with the unkempt clothes he was wearing and he stared at Tony openly confident, gaining eye contact and not letting it go. Tony stopped in front of him and started to feel the passing of the seconds as if he were being interviewed himself. Reed's bright grey eyes held Tony's for what seemed like an age.

"Who's top dog?" he asked without preamble.

Tony replied instantly, feeling almost as if he were being accused of something. "Not me!"

Despite the age of his clothes, Reed's grooming was immaculate. He obviously spent a great deal of time making sure that his short straight black hair was gelled into the perfect position to enhance his piercing eyes. His skin was bright and fresh as if he'd just jumped out of a hot shower and the teeth in the smile he flashed at Tony were white and even.

"Marcie Edwards gets the best clients, so her team does the most business," Tony admitted, adding, "You'll like Marcie - she's a star."

Reed nodded, remaining silent but still holding eye-contact.

Veteran salesman for Peterson Insurance though he was, Tony felt somehow rooted to the spot. Recovering, he extended his hand. "I'm Tony Jones."

"Joe Reed," the newcomer responded, offering a small but powerful hand in return.

"Well, good luck, Joe," and Tony walked away with the press of Joe Reed's firm handshake still alive in his palm.

When Tony got home that evening Emma was waiting for him with a lasagne and a bottle of beer. He'd missed Jade's bedtime and Emma was keen to hear about his day. Looking after Jade as a stay at home mum had its advantages, but Tony knew that his wife sometimes felt cut off from the outside world, so the couple had fallen into a ritual of sitting at the kitchen table and talking through the events of Tony's day, picking apart the results and the people. Tony found it relaxing after the pressure of work and hoped it helped Emma feel part of what was going on. Tonight he told her about his meeting with Joe Reed and she was intrigued.

"Do you think he'll get the job?" she asked.

"Definitely! He'll be good too."

Emma was bemused. "I thought you only said hello to him."

"Yes, but there's something about him - something different. I think he'll be amazing," Tony replied thoughtfully.

That night Tony lay in bed with Emma's head on his chest and her arms wrapped around him and couldn't help feeling that his career would be taking a turn for the better. The family was doing well and Tony was already more than happy with their financial position. He knew that his wife would like a larger house than their current three-bedroom semi-detached, and she wanted a brother or sister for Jade. At present they shared the company Audi, so she was longing for a car of her own too. She often felt very isolated when her husband was at work, but if she wanted to see her mum or go to the shops she had to take a bus, or even a taxi. Tony longed to give Emma everything he possibly could, especially because from the moment he'd set eyes on her he'd always had the feeling that he was punching above his weight. She had achieved better qualifications than he had, going on to Higher Education and a degree in art history, and she was very attractive too – tall and slim, with long dark hair and amazing dark brown eyes. Everyone who met Emma loved her from the start. When sleep eventually came, Tony was looking forward to the weekend with his family and didn't have a care in the world.

***

"Morning, Tony!" said Garry Peterson enthusiastically. "I love Monday mornings: gives us a full five days to make sales."

He'd said almost the same thing on every Monday morning since Tony had started working for him.

"This week should see the team close that twelve month contract with Adidas," Tony told him. "Ken Bolt, their Operational Director is coming in at eleven. Is the boardroom free?"

"I'll make it free," Garry beamed. "Who's the lead on it?"

"Doing it myself; I don't want any confusion," said Tony, full of confidence.

"Good plan! By the way, you've got a new starter this morning. He's coming in for an induction with Becky at ten o'clock, and you'll get him tomorrow morning."

"Who is he?" Tony asked, already knowing the answer.

"He's potentially the best salesman I've ever interviewed," said Garry. "His name's Joe Reed and he's got plenty of experience."

"Sounds good," said Tony, smiling to himself.

"I'm giving him to you rather than Marcie because I think he'll fit in with your team. Good luck with Adidas. You know where I am if you need any help."

"I won't, but thanks," said Tony, grinning broadly at Garry Peterson's back as he walked away, already greeting Marcie with his *I love Monday mornings* speech.

When Tony arrived for work on Tuesday at his usual time of eight-thirty Joe Reed was already sitting at the desk next to his. When he saw Tony he stood up and made an effort to meet him half way across the office, extending his small, delicate hand with a smile on his face that would have lit up a mineshaft.

"Remember me?" he asked, "Joe Reed, I'll be in your team."

"Hi Joe," Tony smiled. "We start at nine," he added.

"I'm always early," said Reed. "Fancy a smoke?"

Tony smiled again and shook his head, turning round the way he'd come, and the pair went outside.

Joe Reed acted as if they'd been friends since the day they were born. He was charming, easy to talk to and right from the beginning there were no uncomfortable silences. He was cheerfully self-confident, smiling a lot and lacing his conversation with compliments, and his enthusiasm was infectious. Looking sharp in shiny black shoes, he was wearing an elegant dark blue suit, cut in at the waist and fitting his slim six foot frame like a glove.

"First day, new suit?" asked Tony.

Joe laughed. "Garry said he only wanted smart people in his company, so after the interview he gave me an advance on my commission to get a new suit and shoes."

Tony was astonished. "That's unusual! Garry's a tight bugger. How did you manage that?"

"He offered," grinned Joe, "I think of it as the first sale of my new job!"

When the two men went back inside Tony introduced Joe to the rest of the team and he smiled at them and shook hands with enthusiasm. Tony noticed that Reed made people feel shy and nervous in his presence, and Tony himself somehow felt as though he was in Joe Reed's team rather than the other way round. He sat down with him to show him the ropes and introduce him to his client list but Reed didn't seem that interested, declaring that he'd be giving them all a quick call later to introduce himself. Tony had to make an effort to keep eye contact with him as his concentration seemed to be fixed on something else across the room. When Reed went to make coffee, Tony followed his gaze straight to Marcie and realised he had been more interested in her than in listening to his new team leader. Grinning to himself, Tony knew he had his hands full with Joe, but he was excited that he was on his team. By the end of that first day Reed had closed three deals from his introductory calls to clients, which was amazing and showed his massive potential. Tony and Joe had lunch together and somehow Joe was there every time Tony went outside for a smoke or visited the water machine. Tony Jones was hooked and already felt as though they would be really good friends.

***

"This is Joe Reed," Tony said to Emma as he walked into the kitchen that evening. Joe smiled more broadly than ever, kissed Emma on both cheeks and gave her a hug. She smiled uncertainly, pulling away a little uncomfortably.

"Sorry, Joe Tony didn't mention he was bringing anyone home. Have you eaten?" Emma was suddenly and acutely aware that she wasn't wearing any make-up, her hands moving unconsciously down her body to smooth her denim skirt.

"I could murder a beer," said Reed, his grin fixed firmly in place.

Tony went to the fridge and chose a bottle each whilst Emma retrieved glasses from a cupboard. Joe watched her as she poured the drinks and taking his, drained half the glass at the first attempt.

"Fantastic!" he grinned. "A great new mate with a beautiful wife prepared to cook for me, plus a cold beer; life doesn't get much better."

Emma and Tony glanced at each other and both blushed.

Emma started telling Joe about Jade and how advanced she was at walking and talking. Joe laughed in the right places and smiled throughout, nodding in agreement as he revealed that he also had a two year old daughter co-incidentally called Emma. When the time came for him to leave, Joe and Emma seemed to have hit it off and she returned his hug with warmth when he made his farewells.

"See you tomorrow for more pain." Joe said to Tony.

"Ok Joe, see you then."

"Thanks for the dinner and the drinks, Emma."

Emma smiled. She'd never met a man like Joe Reed and was startled at how he made her feel. His grey eyes seemed to penetrate to the very core of her being; she wanted to look away, but he held her almost transfixed. All she could manage was, "See you soon, Joe - it was good to meet you," which seemed inadequate, awkward even, especially given the fact that she could feel an inescapable heat moving from between her legs and into her stomach, slowly lighting what felt like a furnace.

Tony and Emma went to bed about half an hour later and when she was drawing the curtains Emma spotted

Joe still sitting in his car a little way up the road. The engine of the ancient Ford was running and through the back window she could see he was engrossed on the telephone. He'd mentioned that his marriage was in difficulty and she wondered if maybe they were having a row and he didn't want to go home yet. Despite herself, when the thought crossed Emma's mind that Joe and his wife's problems might be terminal an involuntary smile played across her lips. The vague feeling of guilt that followed prompted her to climb into bed next to her husband and squeeze his body, her hand quickly finding Tony's weakness, which instantly responded.

***

The next day Emma dressed herself and Jade in matching outfits, preparing to head for the supermarket. All morning thoughts of Joe Reed and the effect he'd had on her slid tantalizingly through her mind. Buttoning her daughter's blue polka-dot dress, she laughed openly at her own foolishness. There was no harm in it, she thought; fancying someone else was a natural part of life, and fun too. Nothing would ever come of it, she wouldn't allow it; she was happy with her life and she was committed to Tony. There was a sudden ring on the doorbell and Emma quickly finished strapping Jade into her buggy and hurried down to answer it. There on the doorstep was a smiling Joe Reed.

"I just wanted to say thanks again for the hospitality last night," said Reed leaning through the door to kiss her cheek.

Emma's blush rose from her chest to her neck and quickly flooded her face.

14

She stood rooted to the spot, somehow unable to get her tongue working as he made his way past her and into the hallway to marvel at Jade.

"You must be Jade," and he made a mock of shaking the tot's chubby white hand. "Isn't she beautiful."

Emma found herself responding with a huge smile. "She's a madam today."

Joe turned to Emma, who realised that he hadn't taken his hand from her waist since he arrived.

"Going out shopping or for pleasure?" he asked, and his grey eyes glinted.

"Shopping," said Emma unable to suppress a giggle as she spoke.

"I've got an appointment not far away," said Joe. "I thought I'd pop in on my way past."

His hand was still on her waist, but she was loath to wriggle and escape him. Something about his eyes and the easy way that he moved and spoke made Emma feel weak at the knees.

"Got time for a coffee?" she asked, pointing vaguely towards the kitchen.

"Not a chance," said Reed, quickly removing his hand and retreating backwards out of the hall and over the threshold. "Tony's a slave-driver and he'll want me back at the grindstone as soon as I'm done here."

The mention of her husband's name jolted Emma back to reality and she had a sudden urge to close the door.

"Ok," she said, "I'll let you get on then."

He smiled. "I'll stay for that coffee next time I'm passing."

Emma couldn't think how to reply; she wanted to tell him not to bother, but something was stopping her and the words caught in her throat. She just watched as he turned, walked down the drive and jumped into his car. Aware of the lingering fragrance of his aftershave, she touched her cheek where he'd kissed her and realised as he drove away that she could still feel his hand on her waist.

Chapter 2

Over the next few months Tony and Joe became good friends. He was everything that Garry had predicted, exceeding Tony's personal sales tally and even overtaking Marcie as the company's top business winner. The two men were soon spending more time together after work, drinking and playing pool at the pub near the office. He often came round to the house in the evening and sometimes even at weekends. Tony was pleased to see that Joe and Emma were becoming good friends too, confident that all this was helping create a more effective team at work.

Then one night he and Emma had an argument over Joe coming to the house so often. She said she enjoyed his company but just didn't want him round all the time; she didn't like her and Tony spending less time together, and she missed their talks after work. Tony didn't understand her sudden change of heart, arguing that Joe only visited so often because he'd split with his wife and he didn't like being so much alone in the flat he rented. Eventually accepting Emma's suggestion Tony reluctantly let Joe know and he seemed to accept it in good spirits and said he would come to the house less often.

As it turned out he didn't ever come to the house with Tony again.

***

Not long before Christmas Tony was thrilled to learn that Emma was pregnant and the couple began looking at four bedroom houses in Didsbury, a more affluent suburb of Manchester. With the extra commission that Tony was making he was able to buy his wife a new Vauxhall and she seemed to be always at her mum's or out with Jade. Despite all this, she was becoming increasingly moody and withdrawn and the couple began arguing more often than they ever had before. Tony put it down to Emma's hormones playing havoc with her body and tried to be as understanding as possible, but it seemed that the harder he tried the more emotional and unreasonable she became. This was a new side to Emma that he had never seen before.

"What's the real problem?" Tony asked after another silent meal one evening.

Emma looked at her husband with tears welling in her eyes.

"You'd know if you bothered to stop and look at what's staring you in the face!"

New Year saw changes at work too. Marcie didn't come back after the Christmas break and had apparently left the company. When Tony called she broke down in tears, telling him there were certain people at work she didn't get on with, and she didn't feel she was getting the support she needed. Tony had noticed her sales figures and the figures for the rest of her team decreasing over the last two or three months, but since his own team was doing increasingly well he hadn't taken too much notice, thinking it was just a passing phase. Marcie had been at the company when Tony arrived and he looked up to her as a kind of mentor, so her sudden and unexpected departure came as a real shock.

"Come on, Marcie," he urged. "We've been mates for years and this just isn't like you. What's *really* going on?"

"It's nothing to do with you or the work, Tony. I'm just not happy in that environment any more - I've had enough."

"Enough of what?"

"Just leave it, Tony"

"Have you got another job to go to, is that it?" he asked. "You and John can't survive on just his wages, what with the kids and all."

"Don't worry," she said acidly. "I won't be taking any of the clients if that's what you're worried about. In fact, I won't be working for a while."

"Why?" Tony asked bemused.

Her voice was cold. "Just take it on board, Tony I've left, and that's all there is to it."

"Well we'll all miss you Marcie," said Tony with genuine regret.

Tony could hear her starting to cry as she said, "Just watch Joe," and put the phone down.

Tony looked at the receiver for a second. This was out of character for Marcie: what did she mean by '*just watch Joe*?' Tony knew that she and Joe were friends and also knew they had closed some good business together, so why suddenly turn on him? The only explanation could be that she somehow imagined Joe would take over her team and she had trouble letting go. He went into the sitting room to talk it over with Emma, telling her that Marcie had left and how puzzled he was about her reasons.

"I suppose that's the nature of sales," offered Emma. "If you're not doing well and your figures are suffering, the pressure can get to you."

"I guess so," replied Tony. "It just seems to be more than that, and she says she's not going to work at all for a while. I'd never have thought she was that emotional."

"Well, it just shows we never really know anyone," said Emma and Tony guessed she was referring to him too.

"What's that supposed to mean?" he asked, a little irritated.

"Just what it says,"

Tony ignored her remark and relayed what Marcie had said about Joe.

"So what do you expect me to say?" she retorted angrily, pushing past him and racing upstairs.

Tony followed her, hearing the bathroom door slam. "Emma," he called through the door, "what was that about?"

There was a silence for a few seconds before she replied, "Nothing, I just want a bath."

"As long as you're ok?" answered Tony, feeling more than a little confused.

***

The next morning when Tony arrived for work there

was no sign of Joe at his desk, which was surprising as he usually arrived first. Tony made himself a coffee and at nine sharp had his daily meeting with the rest of the team. Across the office floor Garry's door opened and Tony was surprised to see his boss and Joe coming out together laughing. Garry beckoned him over, called him inside and invited him to sit down.

"What happened with Marcie?" asked Tony, taking one of the uncomfortable leather seats in front of Garry's huge desk.

"She left. She didn't say exactly why, but I think she had some personal problems that were getting in the way of her work."

"I spoke to her last night and she was pretty upset."

Gary looked across his desk, somehow making Tony feel as if the fact he had called Marcie was a breach of some unwritten company rule about talking to ex-employees.

"She didn't say much," confessed Tony. "I don't think she's going to work for a rival company and take the clients or anything."

"She brought in some good business over the years. Faded towards the end, though. Must have thought it was time to quit while the going was good. We all have to move on some time," he added.

Tony answered carefully as it sounded like the comment was a general one, rather than aimed specifically at Marcie.

"I'm working on that big construction company over in Prestbury this week."

"Isn't that one of Joe's new accounts?" asked Garry.

Tony stared at him in astonishment. "No, Garry. I

cold-called that one myself," he said. "I'm the only one who's been involved at all."

He was a touch angry that someone else was getting the credit for his hard work, even if it was Joe, but Garry ignored his employee's reply.

"I've decided to give Joe Marcie's old team."

Tony looked at him in silence across the desk, the anger rising in his guts. Joe hadn't been with the company more than six months and Garry's description of Marcie, coupled with his relegating her achievements to *old team* led to his realizing for the first time that all salespeople were expendable in Peterson's eyes and that he thought he could replace anyone with a mere click of his fingers.

"Ok," lied Tony, hiding his anger as he stood up to leave.

"You're alright with Joe aren't you, Tony?" asked Garry. "He's a big asset and I want you to help him find his feet as team leader."

"Joe doesn't need my help, Garry. He's capable of looking after himself."

"Well, help him if he asks!"

Tony left Garry's office in time to see Joe having his first meeting with his new team. He was cracking jokes and making everyone laugh, and it seemed certain he'd make a fantastic team leader. He glanced up as Tony passed and the grin that he threw out was laced with what Tony couldn't help thinking looked like nothing less than naked ambition.

A disturbed Tony left the office early that day and arrived home to find Emma in tears in the bedroom. This wasn't the first time lately that he'd come home to find his wife crying, and he sat next to her on the bed and put his arm around her shoulders. Instinctively she turned and pressed her head into his chest. "I'm so sorry!" she sobbed.

"There's nothing to be sorry for," said Tony, trying to cheer her up. "You'll feel better soon I'm sure, it's just our new impending financial burden causing problems already."

She pulled herself away. "You don't know the half of it."

"No, I'm sure I don't," Tony said soothingly. He truly felt for her, unable to imagine what she was going through with her emotions apparently permanently on the edge. Eventually, after some gentle persuasion she settled her head back into his chest.

"It'll be just fine," he said.

The couple stayed in the same position for a few minutes until Emma's tears subsided and then Tony pulled a tissue out of his pocket and gave it to his wife.

"Well, I've had an interesting day," he said, trying to take her mind off her emotions.

"Why, what happened?" she asked, blowing her nose.

"Garry called me into his office to tell me that he'd asked Joe to take over Marcie's team - and I'm supposed to help him become a good team leader."

Emma remained silent.

"I wouldn't mind," went on Tony, "but any of the existing members of that team would've been a better choice as far as I'm concerned. I don't even know if Joe has ever managed salespeople before."

Emma let out a fresh burst of sobs.

"It's ok, Honey," he said, assuming she was worried about his own position. "I'll stop earning commission from Joe's sales that's true, but I'll get another team member in the next few weeks."

Emma was now almost hysterical with tears. She pulled away from him and sat up, her mascara running down both cheeks and into her lip gloss.

"Tony I need to tell you something," she said and dropped her eyes.

Her tone created a coldness that spread over Tony's body and he could feel the beginnings of fear growing in his stomach.

Emma remained silent.

"What?" Tony asked instinctively, knowing that what she was about to say he wouldn't want to hear. "What is it?"

Emma remained silent.

The silence continued for several seconds more until, still looking down and with her tears now dry, Emma almost whispered, "Joe Reed raped me!"

Tony sat motionless for a moment, stunned by a mixture of shock, anger, disgust and dread. Unable to comprehend what his wife had told him, his brain relieved the pressure hysterically through laughter, and as he laughed Emma's tears began to flow freely again. Tony went on and on laughing while she stood up and walked out of the room, went into the bathroom and quietly closed the door behind her.

The laughter abruptly ended with Tony's face becoming hard and cold and he sat on the edge of the bed looking down at his feet. His mind was blank: he couldn't understand why Emma had said that Joe raped her. He noticed that his shoes were slowly becoming wet, and then vaguely realised that tears were streaming from his eyes and dropping onto them like rain. He tried to stand, but his body felt as heavy as stone and his throat was tight with anger and anxiety. "No, Emma, no!" he shouted.

Then he sat for a long time alone on the bed, crying and wondering how and when Emma could have seen Joe Reed when he wasn't there. Joe was often out on appointments, probably more than anyone else, and Tony guessed that he must have been visiting the house whilst he was at work.

Eventually Emma came back and stood for a while in the doorway, staring at her husband across the now darkened room. Eventually she came over to the bed, switched on one of the bedside lamps and sat down, leaving a distance between them. She'd stopped crying, but sobs still escaped her like hiccups and she was shaking all over.

After a long silence Tony spoke, his mouth dry. "How did it happen?"

"He started coming round in the afternoon, not long after you first brought him home for tea," she said quietly.

The lack of emotion in her voice somehow had a calming effect on Tony and he wanted to hear the full story. "He said his marriage was on the rocks and would I talk to him about it," she explained. "He asked me not to say anything to you because he reckoned he was embarrassed to talk to someone he respected so much."

"Go on," said Tony evenly.

"I suppose he'd been round about ten times and I don't know how it happened, except he was crying in the kitchen, saying that his wife wouldn't allow him to see his daughter," she said. "I put my arm around his shoulder - you know, to comfort him and somehow…"

"Somehow what?" asked Tony after a short silence.

"Somehow we were kissing," she said quietly.

The pain in Tony's chest was growing and he didn't want to hear another word, but he had to know the truth.

"So what happened next?" he asked.

"I threw him out," she said. "I was shocked with myself and felt awful. After that I didn't see him for a couple of weeks and then he called round with a bunch of flowers saying he wanted to apologise, so I let him in."

"And?"

"Once he was inside the house there were no apologies; he dropped the flowers on the floor and pinned me to the hall wall kissing me, and his hands were everywhere. I tried to push him off, but he was too strong and he said, *let yourself go Emma, you know you want this as much as I do.*" She lowered her head before continuing. "I started kissing him back."

Beginning to feel dizzy, Tony got up, left the room and went downstairs to get a drink from the fridge. He took out a bottle of beer and opened it, feeling as though he were watching himself move around the kitchen from a position somewhere on the ceiling. The room was starting to spin and he sat down at the table with his head in his hands. Emma had followed her husband and was sitting opposite. She hadn't switched on the kitchen light, and the faint glow from the lamp in the hall created almost a halo around her head as she spoke.

"He lifted me off the ground and started to climb the stairs," she said. "I'm ashamed to say that I didn't stop him."

Tony was speechless, his throat tightening with emotion.

"He pulled off my clothes and we were on the bed kissing. Then I realised what I was doing and I didn't want it. I tried to push him off, but he was on top of me and I could feel him pushing against me."

She got up and went to the cupboard for a glass before returning to the table and pouring some of Tony's beer into it; then she drank it down in one long draught.

"I told him to stop and get off me," she went on, "but he wouldn't take any notice, just started giggling to himself. He towered over me, straightening his arms and pinning down my wrists. His eyes were blazing, Tony – I was so scared!"

"Did he say anything?" asked Tony quietly.

"He said *quiet now bitch!*" said Emma, embarrassment flushing her cheeks, "He put his hand over my mouth and I felt him push himself inside me."

Tony's face was streaked with tears. "And what did *you* do?"

"I thought he was going to hurt me. There was nothing I *could* do! He was so strong that I stopped struggling. I stopped… and I let him do what he wanted," she said, starting to cry again.

Tony sat staring at his wife across the table. She looked like someone else.

"What happened then?" he asked in a whisper.

A long silence followed and Tony became angry as he watched her crying tears reserved for herself. He took her by the shoulders and shook her, repeating his question.

"What happened then?"

"When he'd finished," she screamed in her husband's face, "he rolled me over and fucked me in the arse! Ok? Are you happy now?"

Tony rocked back in the chair, realizing after a few moments that his jaw had dropped and saliva was gathering on his chin. He wiped it with the back of his hand, and half whispered his next question, the impossible truth beginning to dawn on him, turning sharp pain to deep despair.

"When did it happen?"

Emma's tears started to flow again and she was shaking with emotion.

"About two and a half months ago."

***

There was no real sleep for Tony or Emma that night as they lay together in the dark. When seven o'clock finally came Tony put on his suit and tie ready for work as usual. He picked up his briefcase from the hall and a knife from the kitchen, not really planning to do anything with it, but wanting to take it with him anyway. Then as he drove he formed a wild idea of waiting for Joe Reed in the car park, and imagined himself slitting his throat. He waited in his usual parking space and eventually Reed's old Ford rolled in through the barrier and parked a few spaces away to the left. Tony got out of his car at the same time that Joe did and started to walk toward him. Joe Reed was smiling.

"You fucking bastard!" said Tony, and he took the

knife from his pocket. "What the fuck did you do to Emma?" he screamed, but he was too late.

Reliving the moment later, he realized that he should have kept quiet - simply smiled back and plunged the knife into Reed's chest. Seeing the knife come out was ample warning for Joe Reed and the one punch he aimed at Tony's jaw was enough to send him sprawling to the ground. He stood over him laughing.

"She's got a lovely tight arse your missus, Mate. If I were you, I'd screw it every night."

Then he jumped back into his car and drove away. Tony Jones never saw him again.

Chapter 3

Marcie Edwards had never had her bum pinched before. She didn't consider herself to be the type of woman that had her bum pinched. Becky Davis, the very blonde and extremely attractive Training and HR Manager, probably had hers pinched on a weekly if not daily basis, but Marcie was above all that. Garry Peterson, Managing Director at Peterson Insurance Brokers where she worked, had even dubbed her 'Marcie the Merciless' after some sixties sci-fi character she'd never heard of, which made everyone snigger at her expense. Apparently this was due to Marcie's ability to squeeze the clients until she had all their business, so she at least took the explanation side of the joke as a compliment.

Marcie had started working at Peterson's about five years before Joe Reed arrived. The only female salesperson in the company, she had scaled her way up the corporate ladder to run her own team of salespeople – no mean feat in an industry dominated by fat, balding executives with big expense accounts, company cars and secretaries doubling as willing mistresses, and Marcie was proud of the fact that she had achieved recognition and even respect in that world. She'd become mother to her second child early on in her career at Peterson's, and she was notorious for almost giving birth at her desk and then taking only two weeks' maternity leave. Marcie knew she had an image as this tough, driven business woman and she enjoyed it.

Joe Reed changed all that.

It must have been obvious to Garry that Joe Reed was going to be good at the job. By all accounts he had plenty of experience, so it came as no surprise to Marcie when Joe was allocated to Tony's team. Marcie was always landed with the wet behind the ears raw recruits straight off the street. The only sort of experience they'd had was serving behind a bar or working in a call centre, and it was her job to train them how to sell, and how to deal with clients for the long term. Garry said that Marcie had the feminine touch and could train a monkey to sell, but all he managed to do with his back-handed compliments was undermine all the hard work, dedication and effort that she had put into building her team.

On his first day sitting with Tony Joe had stared at Marcie across the office until she found it impossible not to make eye contact, and he promptly winked at her as soon as she did so. Marcie laughed; this guy was an idiot! Later on when she was making coffee he introduced himself.

"Hi, I'm Joe Reed," he said. "You must be the amazing Marcie?"

Marcie looked at him for a few seconds, noting the brand new suit and shoes. He was handsome and charming with piercing grey eyes that seemed to be asking unfathomable questions. His black, slicked back hair had too much gel in it and by the afternoon his face had started to show signs of a five-o'clock shadow. He smiled at Marcie and against her better judgement she found herself smiling back.

"Marcie Edwards," she said and took his offered right hand to shake. To Marcie's amazement he quickly pulled her forward slightly, leaned across and then pinched her bum with his free hand. Marcie was shocked, her eyes growing to the size of saucers before trying to laugh off the impertinence of the gesture.

Joe let go of her hand and she ended up rooted to the spot, staring down at the utilitarian blue nylon carpet and feeling like a schoolgirl.

"I think we'll be friends," Joe said as he walked away.

Marcie was surprised by her own reaction and found her face flushing warm pink. Despite herself, she liked his bold approach and felt somehow special that Joe had singled her out for his attention. He was confident and self-assured without being cocky, and his arrogance was endearing and somehow honest and unforced. When he smiled at her he had maintained eye contact until Marcie looked away, his gaze seeming to offer something that she'd never really had – excitement.

Marcie was thirty-seven, married to John Edwards, a low ranking official at Manchester City Council. The couple had two children; Daniel was six and Katy four. The couple were rubbing along ok: no fireworks, but the relationship worked. John was a diligent and conscientious man, who genuinely cared about the city and its constituents and was forever championing some lost cause or other. It might be for a sweet old lady who wanted a pelican crossing, so that she and her friends could cross the road to bingo without getting run down by speeding drug dealers in their black BMW cars; it might be for some guy who thought that collecting bins only once a fortnight was tantamount to a capital offence. John wasn't passionate about any of this; he just approached each problem with a practical and measured eye and more often than not found the appropriate solution rooted in some by-law or other that he'd managed to unearth.

Unsurprisingly, he was also the kind of man who wouldn't be known by name at the news agent's he'd visited at six every morning for the last ten years; the kind of man who went unnoticed at social events and so never went to any, with or without Marcie. He would spend entire evenings in his study, with his prematurely balding head stuck in contract law, or poring over old newspapers looking for inspiration in stories relevant to whatever cause had occupied his attention that day. As for Marcie, she didn't consider herself pretty or even handsome. She wore her dark brown hair shoulder length and the bathroom mirror told her every day that the angular features that confronted her were not especially attractive. At least her wardrobe of designer work suits and shoes, all hard earned from commission, gave her some confidence in her appearance and a sense that she had achieved at least some of her goals. Her career was of paramount importance to Marcie, to the point where she spent the first few years of Daniel and Katy's lives building a financial and material future for them whilst missing out on their childhood.

When Joe Reed began paying her more and more attention she was both flattered and intrigued. Reed must have copied her personal mobile number from a business card and Marcie began receiving text messages from him almost as soon as he started work at Peterson's. Not knowing how to react, she catalogued each message that she received, saving them in a file on her phone. The messages were innocuous, even mundane at first, and exclusively about work - perhaps commenting on a client, or a deal he had put together. Then one of the messages ended with an *x*, which was obviously supposed to be a kiss. Marcie laughed when she saw it, realising that Joe was trying hard to get her attention. She read the message several times over, deciding that the kiss wasn't out of context exactly; all the same, it was unusual enough for her to have noticed it. After that, every message he sent arrived with the ambiguous *x* at the end, sometimes two. Soon the messages started getting more frequent and then more personal. He began to comment on how she looked on a particular day, or how he had noticed her legs as she walked across the room, and he started calling her *Baby Peaches*, which she hated. She knew that she shouldn't have answered them, but it felt sort of exciting and risky to send Joe a message back. She responded to his personal remarks by telling him he was mistaken or a fool and she never reciprocated his virtual kisses. Then one day he sent this.

'Hi Baby Peaches…..I've been thinking about you all night and can't sleep…wanna be my hot water bottle? XX'

Marcie didn't answer: it had all gone too far, and she found herself fretting and sleepless as the realisation dawned that he thought she was interested in him and he obviously wanted to take things further. Part of the problem was that against her better nature, so did she. She sent back a message the next morning, aiming to imply disapproval of the question without putting him off entirely. 'I don't use hot water bottles; I've got central heating, ha ha.' Only this time she ended the message with the text kiss she'd been so carefully withholding and pressing *send*, the deliberateness of it excited her.

Marcie didn't understand what made his brain work. She thought that she was, at best, passable in the moonlight and because she hadn't actually had a conversation with Joe about anything personal she knew that he didn't know who she was. She was sure that he was unaware of even the basic facts about her, such as the fact that she was married with children, although she supposed her wedding ring gave her status away.

She noticed that Joe seemed to be with his manager Tony much of the time, and they would lunch together, smoke together and even go back to Tony's house together, to the point that they acted like comical twins. She realized that Tony must be there when Joe sent the messages, and she even half wondered if they might be having a bet as to whether she would respond, then laughing loudly and slapping each other's backs whilst handing over a fiver to the winner of the latest wager at her expense. But Tony and Marcie had been friends for a couple of years; he treated her as an equal and she knew he respected her opinions, so she dismissed the notion of Joe's attentions being a joke and remained confused.

After Marcie sent the message with the kiss at the end

though, the texts from Joe started arriving almost hourly.

Some weeks later, after literally hundreds of messages back and forth that were becoming more steamy and reckless on both sides, Marcie met Joe unexpectedly in the staff car park one morning. She was running late; Katy had cut her knee falling on the wet patio in the back garden and wanted her to stay home, wrapping herself around her mother's legs. In the man's world in which Marcie operated she knew that five minutes tardiness for her was equal to a day off for one of the '*real*' salesmen. Consequently, she was grabbing her bag from the back seat of the car in her rush to get to her desk when she turned to find Joe standing there smiling. Marcie had been preparing for a dash to the office door and she almost collided with him. The rain, though not heavy, was cold and spreading across the tarmac of the car park and Joe was standing in front of her with damp shoulders and rain water glistening on his gelled black hair.

"Hi, Baby Peaches!" he said.

Marcie was deeply embarrassed at hearing him use his text name for her. She certainly didn't feel like a '*Baby Peaches*', especially with her hair all over the place, now getting wet without an umbrella, and with makeup only half applied in the car's rear-view mirror on the way to the office. To her dismay she felt herself blushing, excruciatingly aware that Joe would be bound to notice the tide of red rising from her chest and neck and into her cheeks.

"You're cute," he said, still smiling.

"I'm late and it's wet!"

Lowering her head so as not to make eye contact, Marcie tried to push past him, knowing all along that the unaccustomed smile on her face, a mixture of embarrassment and excitement would encourage him to press home his advantage. He took a small step to his right to stop her getting past and she looked up at him, their faces only inches apart. When he kissed her the handbag she was holding fell to the floor and she kissed him back. She felt his tongue begin to explore her mouth, her stomach turned over and she pulled away.

"Get lost, Joe!" she said, half laughing. "That's not funny."

"I know," he said. "Not funny at all."

Marcie watched him walk away and into the building, leaving her rooted to the spot; she must have stood there for a full minute staring at the doorway through which he'd disappeared. Dizzy and excited, lost in the romance of kissing in the rain, she couldn't properly catch her breath. It was as if they were secret lovers - the stars of one of the black and white movies she snuggled on the sofa to watch every Sunday, forcing the children to watch them with her. The memory of Joe's exploratory kiss sent tingles through Marcie's body. John had never made her feel like this and she'd certainly never experienced her husband's tongue. On the odd occasion when they did have any intimate contact, it was as if he'd picked up what he thought were the right things to do and say from a car manual and Marcie felt nothing. Sex was a practical affair for John, with producing children the goal, and the couple had already achieved that. Sex for pleasure wasn't on the agenda and Marcie had accepted that simple - and in the circumstances, welcome truth years before. Joe on the other hand had made it clear from his messages that sex was *all* he wanted. There was never any mention of the future or trying to get to know who she was, and standing there in the car park with the memory of his kiss still on her lips Marcie thought, *so what! I need some excitement.* An affair with Joe Reed wouldn't affect John or the family she reasoned, if she was the one in control and could stop it at any given time. Joe wasn't the type to get attached and Marcie thought he would eventually just move on to the next woman - Becky probably. She convinced herself that it would be a bit of harmless fun with no strings, and more importantly no consequences, and for her, now, that was an exciting prospect. Snapping out of her trance and realising at the same time how ridiculous she must look standing stock still in a car park getting wet she ran in to the office.

Then the messages stopped.

Marcie checked her phone constantly but there were no more messages that day. She deliberately bumped into Joe - making coffee, or creating an excuse to go to the car when he and Tony were having a smoke. She smiled at him and tried to make conversation, but he virtually ignored her.

Feeling increasingly desperate to hear something, she sent him a message, 'You ok Joe? xx' When nothing came back, she was driven almost to distraction as she checked and rechecked her phone for any reply, and she lay in bed that night turning over in her mind what had happened in the car park. Perhaps she'd hurt his feelings, or worse still, perhaps kissing her had left him cold and he'd simply lost interest.

When she got up the next morning she sat on the toilet with the lid down, agonising whether to text again. She thought that if she sent another message today without reply she would have made a complete fool of herself and wouldn't be able to show her face in the office again. This time she would be a laughing stock as the stories went around that *Marcie the Merciless* had turned into *Marcie the Matahari*.

In the end she decided that if that were the case there was nothing to lose, as she already looked needy and out of control, so she started to press the keys to construct a message. She considered what to put. Maybe she'd just say how much he was hurting her and how could he treat her like this, but eventually she thought the best option was to try and be funny. 'Hi Joe, my boiler's gone…. have you still got that hot water bottle? ha ha xxx' She sat there turning the phone over and over in her hands, then she opened the file on the handset where she stored Joe's messages and read each one in turn from the first to the most recent for any signs that she had made a mistake. Each text she read only confirmed what she had thought; she began to feel agitated and frustration set in. More silence.

When Marcie eventually made it downstairs to the kitchen table Daniel was playing with his breakfast cereal. His mother had been in the bathroom for almost an hour, leaving everyone to their own devices with disastrous results. Daniel's collar length hair was unkempt and he had on yesterday's white school shirt with a spaghetti sauce stain still visible on the front.

He was obviously not enthusiastic at the thought of school.

"Not hungry, Dan?" asked Marcie.

"I hate school," he moaned.

The fees they paid to Daniel's prep school were astronomical.

"Do you know how hard I have to work for you to go to that school - what I have to give up so you can go there!" she snapped.

Dan just shrugged and Katy started giggling. Katy was still in her pyjamas and her habit of licking the butter off the toast before she ate it meant that her face was glistening wet. John was ignoring everything with his face behind his newspaper, deliberately held up so that he didn't have to get involved with his wife or the kids. Marcie's irritation boiled over.

"Well, if you feel like that, Dan," she shouted, "you can damn well go to St Hughes with the rest of the idiots!" Dan dropped his spoon and started to cry. Katy looked up at her mother stunned, momentarily taking the toast from her tongue, and John slowly lowered his paper so that he could make disapproving eye contact with his wife. Marcie had never raised her voice to the children before and the shame that washed over her was unbearable. She angrily pushed back her chair, and grabbing her bag said quietly, trying to control herself, "Sorry Dan, just eat your breakfast," and then to John, "I'd better go. Sorry, I've got big pressures at work this week."

Conscious of all three of them staring at her, she left the kitchen and walked out to the car, but before she could get there tears of frustration and humiliation were running down her cheeks. She plonked heavily into the driver's seat and put her head in her hands, wondering why she'd allowed herself to be affected like this. Suddenly, her mobile sprang to life with a beep to tell her that she had a message and Marcie rummaged in her bag to find it. 'Hi Baby Peaches!' it said. 'Hope you're ok? Been a bit down lately, will explain all later xxx' She felt a surge of anger. *How dare he text me now!* she thought, and the tears flowed in a rain of self-pity. Slowly she recovered, telling herself that Joe must be having a bad time with his estranged wife, and she suddenly felt guilty at not being more supportive. She conjured up a scenario in which his wife wouldn't let him see his daughter Emma, imagining how devastating that must be for him, and then composed a tactfully worded reply. 'Ok Joe! Hope you're ok too and things aren't too bad at home…see you when I get in xx' An involuntary smile of relief lit up Marcie's face at the thought that there'd been some reason other than the kiss in the car park that Joe hadn't been in touch, and she started the engine and drove in the direction of the office with renewed enthusiasm. 'Meet me at the café on Croft Road and I'll explain xx' came the next message and Marcie immediately performed a three-point turn whilst texting 'Ok…10 mins xx'.

She knew Gerry's Café well; it was where she met her sales team individually if she felt they needed extra support or a friendly ear off the record. It was on a run-down shopping parade boasting charity shops, a Chinese take-away and Everything-Must-Go-for-a-Pound signs in the hardware store. The café itself was okay, producing great cappuccinos and amazing homemade cakes, and when Marcie arrived Joe was already there. He sat facing the door astride a cream Formica table in one of the booths with its shabby green 'leather' bench seats. He was nursing a cup of cold coffee and looked like he hadn't been home the night before, and Marcie couldn't help thinking that this new image of Joe Reed with stubble and a downcast vulnerability was even more attractive. She sat opposite him without speaking and he didn't look up. The waitress came over almost immediately as they were the only customers and Marcie ordered coffee.

"I know," the bored waitress said in a flat monotone. "Cappuccino, no chocolate and an extra shot of espresso," and then without waiting for an answer left her two customers alone.

The couple sat for a few moments longer saying nothing. Marcie began to feel as though she was in a movie.

"You ok Joe?" she asked, breaking the silence.

He raised his head to look at her with tired bloodshot eyes and she caught a slight smell of whisky. He was obviously in an awful place and needed help.

"Just having a bad time with my wife," he said, using his delicate fingertips to push around some grains of sugar that had leaked onto the table top. "She's being impossible - she won't let me even speak to my daughter on the phone."

Despite the fact that he was obviously in distress Marcie's heart lifted at the news.

"With it being so close to Christmas too," he went on. "It's just really difficult to know what to do and how to act. Everything I do and say seems to be wrong. I feel like I'm drowning."

"Have you seen a solicitor?" Marcie asked.

"I haven't got the money for solicitors. Everything I have goes her way already, and anyway," he added, "I don't want anything to affect Emma."

With that Joe suddenly broke down, talking - babbling almost - about his wife and how she didn't care about him or look after him, and how lonely he was living alone in his flat. Feeling genuinely sorry for him, Marcie impulsively offered any advice and support she could give. She had fallen in love with this honest and vulnerable side to Joe that she suspected remained invisible to others because of his apparent bravado and self-confidence.

"Tomorrow night's the staff party," she said, trying to lift his spirits. "At least we can go out and have some fun, eh?"

She hated the office parties and usually avoided such occasions like the plague, but she thought this one would be a chance to get to know Joe better. It was the last day of work before the Christmas break too, so there would be no worries about getting up the next day and she thought she would let her hair down for once.

"I suppose so," he said and for the first time that morning he managed a faint smile.

***

John was surprised the next day when Marcie told him she was going to the Christmas party, as he knew she usually didn't bother, and he was obviously relieved when she told him that he didn't have to come. That day at work was punctuated with the usual pantomime of unwanted gifts and roaming salesmen bothering the women with a sly grin and a sprig of mistletoe, but this year Marcie was more upbeat about the whole thing and even managed to look grateful for the lottery ticket someone had put in an envelope with her name on it for the Secret Santa ritual.

The Christmas do was at The Manchester Metropolitan Hotel in the City Centre. Garry's thinking was that these annual festivities made up for not presenting the staff with a Yuletide bonus, and guilt drove him to throwing a big party. Marcie had made an effort with a black Dolce and Gabbana dress - short, but not too short - black Jimmy Choo shoes, and diamond earrings with a matching crystal necklace. She'd been to the hairdresser in the afternoon and spent an hour on her skin and makeup, deciding at last that she looked as good as she was ever going to get.

"Have a good evening," John said when his wife presented herself in the sitting room. He hardly looked up from his book and Marcie wasn't surprised that he hadn't noticed the dramatic change in her appearance. She sat in silence as she waited for the taxi to arrive, watching John making notes in the margin. She was looking at him now from a new perspective and wasn't impressed with what she saw. A sense of sadness washed over her that she had settled in life for a man who really cared little for her, a man whose thoughts were focused almost entirely on his own interests and well-being. *'Things will change,'* thought Marcie, and when the taxi arrived she got up and left with John barely noticing that she'd even been there.

The hotel was a fantastic choice. Garry and his very

well kept wife Barbara stood in the entrance greeting each one of his staff as if they were the bride and groom at a line-up of their wedding guests. He kissed Marcie warmly on both cheeks, telling her that she was his greatest asset and he was so pleased that she had picked on his company to work for. Marcie was sure she overheard him say the same thing to Becky who came a few seconds behind her, but chose to be flattered by the compliment. Barbara's heavy floral perfume was overpowering as she gave Marcie a practised air kiss and said she was pleased to see her again, which Marcie knew was a lie. Barbara probably hated being there and had more than likely argued with Garry on the way over; Marcie noticed the make-up on her cheeks had been very recently reapplied where tears had probably washed away the original application.

The evening went quickly. Marcie was pleased to find that Joe seemed to have recovered from the emotion fuelled time spent at the café and he was on good form, cracking jokes, dancing badly with everyone and generally being the life and soul of the party. He looked good too, attracting attention and obviously revelling in it. Seeing Marcie was alone and at a bit of a loss, Joe made sure that he looked after her, telling her as soon as he saw her that she looked gorgeous and the new hairstyle suited her face to perfection. Marcie took this as proof that not only had the chat at Gerry's Cafe renewed his interest in her, but that she had earned his respect. Joe was a true gentleman, going to the bar as required and sitting with Marcie at every opportunity, making her laugh with stupid jokes whilst constantly brushing her knee or playing footsie with her under the table.

She felt as though she were at the school disco.

She had never *done shots* but Joe told her it would be fun to join in as everyone was knocking them back, and so she had tequila and Sambuca, both of which tasted awful, but she tried to keep up with Joe. Apart from the shots, the vodka he was buying her seemed to be coming every ten minutes, and by the time midnight came Marcie was pretty plastered. She began to feel sick and threw up in the toilet, watching her recently eaten Christmas dinner disappear down the pan. Dizzy and confused, she found herself bumping against the wall with a stupid grin glued to her face as she re-joined the party. Joe was nowhere to be seen.

"I need to go," she told Garry over the noise of the DJ.

"Ok Marcie!" he laughed. "They'll call you a taxi at Reception."

The room was starting to spin now and she heard Garry call, "Have a good Christmas!" as she tried her level best not to stagger toward the exit.

***

Joe materialized again when she reached Reception. He was smiling. "Whoa! I think someone's had a few too many shots."

Marcie tried to focus on his grinning face as he put his arm round her waist to prop her up.

"Come on," he said, "We'll get a taxi outside."

On the way to the door he paused, exclaiming, "Hang on a minute! I've forgotten my wallet," and

Marcie found herself being helped up the stairs from Reception toward the hotel bedrooms.

She started to giggle. "Where are we going?" she slurred. "To get my wallet," Joe said and forcefully leading Marcie by the elbow they made their way down a corridor before stopping in front of room 116.

"I didn't know you were staying here," said Marcie.

Joe slipped the key-card into the lock and ushered her inside, closing the door behind them.

The room was standard executive style, plain but perfectly equipped for the businessman on his travels. Joe pushed Marcie onto the bed and she started to laugh. "I've never done anything like this before!" she giggled, gasping for air.

"I know you haven't," said Joe, and there was something in the coldly matter-of-fact way he replied that brought Marcie's mind temporarily into sharp focus and the drunkenness momentarily left her.

She tried to connect with him. "I think I've fallen for you, Joe," she said.

Joe Reed was standing over her taking off his shirt, and she watched silently as he slipped out of his trousers.

"Make love to me!" said Marcie, charging her voice with what she imagined was a mixture of raw emotion and sex appeal.

Joe got onto the bed. He started to kiss her and she kissed him back; she was ready for this and she tried to concentrate on his lips, desperate to sober up and enjoy the experience and the magic. His hands were all over her and she felt her zipper come down and then her dress pass over her head. Marcie's bra was pulled open and thrown off the bed and her knickers slipped easily over her hips. She was going to remember this for the rest of her life.

Then Joe Reed bit Marcie's lip.

She thought it was passion and smiled through her shock at the pain. When she opened her eyes, Joe, or the person she thought of as Joe, had undergone a transformation. His grey eyes seemed to have turned black and grown larger, and they were burning with intensity. Marcie suddenly felt very vulnerable and was acutely aware of her nakedness. He grabbed her wrists and held them above her head as he roughly prized her legs apart with his knees and forcefully entered her. Marcie had expected tender and intimate foreplay, creating delicious sexual tension: she had certainly not expected this. She could feel his hot breath on her face as he took total control of her.

"Get off me!" she shouted, but he reacted by slapping her hard across the cheek before clamping her mouth shut.

"I like it rough," he whispered into Marcie's ear, and carried on ramming himself into her.

Excruciating pain shot through Marcie as he ignored her whimpering and struggles. He went faster and harder until she felt him empty himself, and then took his hand from her mouth and flipped her over as if she were a doll. Marcie's head was hanging over the end of the bed and she saw her underwear strewn pathetically on the floor; an all-consuming fear froze her limbs, and she suddenly had her wrists jerked behind her and heard the zip of a cable tie secure them.

"Joe!" screamed Marcie. "What the hell are you doing?"

He punched her in the back of the head. "Shut the fuck up!" he snarled.

Marcie noticed too late the blinking light of a video camera in the corner of the room and went cold as she realised that he must be recording everything.

Joe Reed slipped a clear plastic bag over her head and held it tight. Almost immediately his captive's desperate breathing drew the plastic into her mouth; she could feel her heartbeat begin to pound in her head and she started to panic. Then came pain, a pain that she had never felt before as he pulled her into a kneeling position and entered her arse with what felt like a rod of iron. Marcie tried to scream, but there was no air and she choked on the plastic. Claustrophobia overtook her as the oxygen shrank, and she thought she was going to pass out. She rapidly became more disorientated as she realised that she could see her ordeal reflected in a mirror placed directly in front of her. Joe Reed became like a wild animal behind her, straining his body to get further and deeper inside his victim. With her eyes bursting from an unrecognisable purple face trapped in airless plastic, images of Daniel and Katy jumped into Marcie's mind and rolled across in liquid frames.

She tried desperately to concentrate on her children, tried desperately to focus on their innocent faces, silently praying that she would be spared to see them again. Hope evaporated with the air and her chest tightened, pain spreading through her body like smoke blown across the ground.

It was then that Marcie Edwards lost consciousness.

Chapter 4

His laptop was alive twenty-four hours a day; he didn't want to miss a thing.

The room was dark, with dingy Venetian blinds permanently closed across the sash windows. The sleek laptop sat on a replica oak leather-top desk, and apart from this virtual window on the world he avoided contact with other people whenever he could. A green glass-top reading light and a steaming mug of coffee next to an overflowing cut-glass ashtray were the only other items on the expansive desk-top. The remainder of the room was cluttered with too much cheap furniture, carrying the photographs and electronic image frames that served as a permanent reminder of his desires. The dust rising from the well-worn patterned carpet seemed to hang in the trapped air, giving the chinks of light escaping from the blinds and the glow from the desk lamp the appearance of searchlights dotted about the walls, picking out an occasional blotch of colour in the busy floral wallpaper. The room was fetid with solitude, the tired fabrics accentuating the atmosphere of slow decay that surrounded its only occupant.

The unique electronic sound telling the man that a new video had been uploaded sent him ambling from his position in front of the television, where Jerry Springer was busy enraging a guest for the benefit of his baying audience, and into his worn leather chair. The man sank into his own imprint to stare at the screen.

'Let's see how he did,' he thought.

Pulling a cigarette from a drawer and flicking the lighter with his yellow stained fingers before throwing it back in and slamming the drawer shut, he prepared to click on the new icon on his browser with the tab of *Baby Peaches* highlighted in dark red. The ever patient watcher pulled deeply on his cigarette and blew out the smoke through his nostrils very, very slowly. This was part of a routine to control his growing excitement; he wanted to savour every second of the illicit film that he was about to watch. Despite this ritual effort, his skin began to prickle and he could already feel the body heat suffusing the leather he sat on. In an effort to calm himself he dropped his hands to the side of his chair and let them hang there for a few seconds, trying to relax ahead of the frenzy-inducing scenes he anticipated. Finally he clicked on the icon, instantly revealing room 116 at the Manchester Metropolitan Hotel. The camera was wide-angled, and from a corner position it gave a clear view of the entire bedroom and the door. The empty room took on an air of expectancy and the man deliberately ignored his urge to fast forward, instead taking on the role of the patient hunter in some secret hide, waiting soundlessly for his prey. His mouth was dry and he licked his lips. He drew on his cigarette and concentrated on the detail of the room, drinking in the growing tension. The king size bed dominating the room was neatly made, with the duvet drawn back to reveal pristine white pillows. He could just make out the plastic end of a cable-tie that had been secreted under one of the pillows and he smiled to himself in expectation of its use.

Eventually the door swung inwards and the man watched as Joe Reed came into the room struggling to hold up an obviously drunken woman. *This must be Marcie,* thought the watcher; she looked exactly as he had pictured her from Joe Reed's description. She was slim and tall, her height accentuated by shiny black high heeled shoes, and despite her unsteadiness he could see that she would normally be confident and assured, aloof even. Her shoulder length dark brown hair, obviously freshly coiffured, showed off her angular features and in her own way she was classically beautiful. Joe Reed had done well: he had obeyed instructions to the letter. He was almost holding her up as the door closed behind them and he clicked the lock with his spare hand.

There was no escape.

Reed steered the woman over to the bed and the viewer noticed how long her legs looked in her expensive just over the knee black dress and he relished the noise of her smooth skin shifting under the material as she was led across the room. She dropped, half pushed onto the bed, seemingly exhausted and the man watched carefully as she was manoeuvred so that her head lay at the opposite end to the pillows. He knew that if she looked up she would see herself in the full length mirror that had been specially placed at the end of the bed.

"I've never done anything like this before." Marcie said panting and laughing excitedly.

"I know you haven't," said Joe Reed flatly.

The man pressed pause. He was getting too excited: sweat was beginning to bead on his forehead and he could feel his hands clammy as he took another drag on the almost spent cigarette. Grinding it out in the burgeoning ashtray, he leant back in his chair, cradled the mug of coffee and stared at the screen. Held in suspension was Joe Reed standing in the process of unbuttoning his shirt; *Baby Peaches* was lying facing the unnoticed camera, obviously contemplating with lust and delight the coming experience with someone she trusted, fancied, and maybe even loved! The man lit another cigarette and the smoke wafted around his head, interrupting his steely concentration on the screen for a split second and prompting him into action. He clicked play.

"I think I've fallen for you, Joe," Marcie said as she looked up at him.

Joe Reed smiled down at her, continuing to take off his shirt before moving on to unfastening his belt and taking off his trousers, discarding them where they fell. "Make love to me," she whispered and Joe Reed smiled before lowering himself onto the bed.

The man watching already knew that he would be playing this scene over and over again. Marcie did love Joe Reed, she had asked him to make love to her. She had fallen for his charms, unbeknown to her all orchestrated by the man watching the results of his work on film. He felt satisfied that her pain at the hands of Joe Reed, his willing tool, would be her worst nightmare and his greatest pleasure.

The couple began to kiss passionately with Marcie's

arms stretched around Joe Reed's back. The watcher began to chuckle and then laugh as he saw the woman recoil from the pre-scripted bite to her lip. She searched for her lover's eyes and tried to laugh before the smile quickly faded, her expression betraying the realisation that this wasn't going to be how she expected. There seemed to be a pause of seconds whilst Marcie searched Joe Reed's face for answers and then she screamed.

***

Joe Reed sat on the plastic covered seat at the Formica pull-down table of the caravan that he called home. He had uploaded the video as instructed almost an hour ago and he could feel the silence as a weight in his mind. He knew that he hadn't followed instructions to the letter and was worried. The single berth vehicle was small and damp on a cold January morning. The only window was wet with condensation, allowing a watery light into the otherwise dark space. Joe knew that he couldn't leave yet but he was desperate for coffee, his head pounded and his eyes stung. His instructions were to wait for a reply and he wanted to please. The screen on the laptop went black as the power-save kicked in, and he hurriedly clicked his mouse to bring it back to life. The planned evening with Marcie had started well enough, but had ended off-script and he was hoping that renewed obedience might start to make amends if he replied as soon as he got his message.

This new computer had arrived by courier almost three months ago and already it was showing signs of wear.

Its aluminium shell bore the marks of constant use and the scratches on the top where Joe had ferried it around without a protective case created a curious pattern unique to the machine. Programmes, e-mail addresses and web-sites had been pre-installed, together with the screensaver showing the small terraced house at 63 Cathcart Street, Oldham where Joe had spent part of his childhood. He stared at that house every time the image loaded, and as always he was transported back to the events that had shaped his life.

***

Joe Reed had been born Ed Jerome to Jane Jerome, a prostitute mother, and was the outcome of a ten-minute client and faulty rubber. He was the second product of his mother's profession, his elder sister having succumbed to pneumonia before she was out of nappies. His mother was a drug user who would see her clients whenever she could, even if it meant Ed had to huddle in a corner with hands over ears and eyes shut tight against the horror that his mother must, so he imagined, be suffering. After the client had left it was always the same, a slap or a kick would send him scurrying out of the room whilst his mother scrambled for the workings to feed her all-encompassing habit.

Then one day, seemingly out of thin air, Dan Prince turned their lives around and the young Ed Jerome suddenly experienced stability. Prince began visiting the family almost daily and Jane stopped using drugs. Her clients came to the squalid flat with much less frequency, until eventually they stopped coming altogether. Dan and his mother would talk for hours and

Ed heard laughter in his home for the first time. Jane began to smile and look after herself properly and even got a job at a local pub. Eventually she and Ed moved into a neat, three-bedroom terrace house in Oldham with Dan Prince and his son Declan.

His new brother Declan became Ed's best mate and they went everywhere together. Declan was a loner with no really close friends, and being two years older than Ed he looked after him at his new school; he told Ed what to wear, where to go and who not to talk to and Ed quickly fitted in.

***

The sight of his reflection in the laptop screen pulled Joe Reed back to the present. His black hair was like a sparrow's nest and his eyes were heavy and red. He checked the e-mail icon yet again, disappointed at the continuing lack of contact. Then his thirst got the better of him and he stood up, moving the half a yard over to the sink and picking up the kettle to fill it from the tap. He kept one eye on the screen as he quickly put coffee, milk and sugar into an unwashed cup with a fading Cadbury's Roses logo, and then sat back down in front of the machine with a strangely guilty feeling at having moved from his seat in the first place. The kettle spewed out steam as it boiled, automatically switching itself off, and Joe stood up again and moved to fill the cup. He regained his seat after a few seconds and sat stirring the dark brown liquid slowly and almost hypnotically.

***

It wasn't long before his mind wandered again to 63 Cathcart Street. Ed and his mother had been living with Dan and Declan Prince for only a few weeks when his mother sat him down in their new kitchen to tell him the news, her face alight with a smile Ed had rarely seen. Dan had asked her to marry him and she had said yes. It would mean Ed would have something he had always dreamed of - a father.

The wedding was quickly arranged at a registry office in Manchester, and Ed was apprehensive but excited that day as Dan Prince, his new father-to-be, drove his family for the half hour journey from their home in Oldham for the ceremony in Manchester. Declan sat in the front passenger seat fiddling with the knobs on the radio whilst his mother sat with Ed in the back of the car. Ed loved how his mother smelt of soap and perfume, her new, simple style of flat shoes and skirt and jumper beneath a full length coat somehow giving him a sense of comfort and security. The way she dressed and fussed over him reminded him of the books that he'd read about happy children with loving families, and their simple adventures in a world he had never imagined being part of. He could feel his mother's eyes on him for almost the entire journey, filled with a kindness and understanding that disarmed him and kept him calm. It was as though she were a different woman.

In preparation for this special day in the life of the Prince family, Jane had made a special effort with her shoulder length dark brown hair and had spent over an hour straightening it and applying hairspray to keep it in check. Makeup was unusual for Jane, but today she had applied foundation and lipstick. Ed thought she was beautiful, and he was filled with pride that she was his mum. He could feel his old life being left behind as the few miles drifted by and as he looked out of the window at the passing cars he thought he was the happiest and luckiest boy alive.

Dan Prince seldom spoke and when he did it was almost exclusively to Jane. Ed thought he seemed like a good man, hardworking at a local textile mill and always there to provide his family with whatever they needed. As they travelled along he stared at the back of Dan's shaved head, happy that at last he was safe. Like his son Declan, Dan had few friends and little time for socialising, preferring to be at home. He looked young for his age and anyone would have said at first glance that he was more like twenty-five than thirty-five, but Dan was unimpressed by the flattery and refused to speculate on how he, or anyone else for that matter, looked. He had boxers' features with a flat nose and a full forehead and he was very well built, with hands that could cradle a large melon with ease.

When they eventually arrived at Manchester Town Hall, an impressive Victorian Gothic structure dominating one side of St Anne's Square, Ed bounced out of the car first and stood on the pavement waiting impatiently for the remainder of the party to join him. When they eventually did, the four went inside to emerge an hour later blinking in the bright winter sunshine as a new family in the eyes of the law, and a beaming Ed Jerome became Ed Prince for the journey back to Oldham.

Then everything changed.

***

Ed thought that it was a joke at first. As soon as they arrived back at the house and were through the front door Dan Prince slumped into his customary arm-chair and lit a cigarette.

"Dan," said Jane, "I thought we agreed you were not going to smoke in front of the lad?"

"Don't matter now," said Dan, smirking to himself. "We're all married after that bullshit ceremony. I can do owt' I like and there ain't nothing you can do to stop me. You're my wife now - so 'honour and obey'!"

"Oi!" retorted Jane. "What's got into you?"

Ed began to feel afraid as he watched confusion wash over his mother's face. Dan scowled at him. "Get us a beer!"

He stood staring mutely at this man he thought he had grown to know and respect.

Dan raised his voice. "Get us a bloody beer!" he repeated.

Ed's fear grew to dread, rooting him to the spot, and a tear escaped from his stinging eyes. He looked towards his mother as she reclined on the cream leather sofa, but she only stared back at her son, unwilling to protect him and disobey her new husband. She merely nodded for him to do as he was told. Ed stayed where he was, casting his eyes down to the pink carpet. Suddenly the room seemed very small and the walls were closing in on him. His mind raced back to the car journey and he wondered what he had done wrong. Had he said something out-of-turn? If he had, he couldn't remember what it was and a '*Sorry!*' escaped his lips which was more of a question than repentance.

Dan stood up and seemed somehow taller than Ed remembered. He watched his new stepfather take a step toward him and he looked up to see him releasing his belt.

Dan looked at Jane. "He needs to learn, this lad."

"What!" and she leaned forward in her seat, her face white with shock.

Dan didn't answer. With the belt hanging from his thick fist he said, "Now listen you little bastard, you're here for one reason and one reason only and that's to make my life easier...owt else!" He paused to watch Ed's reaction. "You'll do what you're told and you'll do it when I say, or you'll get the shite knocked out of you...understood lad?"

Jane tried to interject.

"As for you, Bitch, you do as I bloody please. You were some scank whore when I found you. Now look at you! I look after you and you'll be grateful, Lass."

Ed started to cry and Declan, silent till now, slipped out of the room and ran upstairs slamming his bedroom door behind him. Dan's eyes followed the sound of his son's footsteps on the stairs and he only continued when he heard the first thuds of music.

"DO YOU BLOODY UNDERSTAND?" he shouted at both of them.

Ed was suddenly dizzy as he felt his bladder relax.

"He's pissing on the bastard carpet," screamed Dan. "I'll batter him the little shit!"

Ed felt the sting of the first blow from Dan's belt across his back and immediately fell to the floor curling into a protective ball. The blows rained down and he felt the belt lashing his body and legs whilst tears burned his cheeks. After the first few blows his body relaxed and he started to accept the pain as the treatment continued unabated. When the beating finally stopped and Dan's feet retreated he lay still, waiting for whatever was to come next.

"Now clean up that piss and get us a beer," ordered Dan.

Ed slowly got to his feet. His shirt was ripped and his skin was on fire. He looked at Dan who was sweating from the exertion, and any anger he felt was soon overtaken by fear. He looked at his mother for sympathy and began to make a move towards her, but she shook her head and turned her face away.

"Go and get that beer - and get yourself out of those pissed-through clothes!" Dan snarled.

Ed began to sob as he made his way to the kitchen.

***

The sound of a young couple laughing outside the thin walls of the caravan jerked Joe Reed back to the present once again, and he peered out cautiously to see where the voices were coming from. The condensation on the window distorted the figures, but he could just about make them out. They were standing a few feet from the window gazing at each other, seemingly lost to the world going on around them and certainly too engrossed in each other to notice Joe Reed staring at them with a sudden jealousy rising from the pit of his stomach.

They were young, probably not even twenty years old,

and the man was tall and strong with a knot of dark hair and a fading suntan. When he smiled his teeth flashed white and his lover released an involuntary giggle that made Joe Reed's heart leap. He watched enviously as their faces drew closer, the girl's red lips opening slightly to accept a kiss. She closed her eyes first, and Reed thought how impossibly lucky the man was as he drew the woman to him, one hand on the small of her back and the other disappearing into her long mousey blonde hair to pull her head toward his. He pressed his lips onto hers, and Joe saw the woman respond, thrusting her pelvis into the top of her lover's leg with her tongue flicking into his mouth. They kissed for a full minute before parting and then, their faces flushed and their eyes locked, they clasped hands before moving apart and walking off in opposite directions. To the couple that kiss was one of hundreds they would share. For Joe Reed it represented something he never had, nor ever would experience - love.

His heart was beating faster and his hand had involuntarily moved to between his legs when his laptop sounded a PING and the screen revealed the flashing icon to let him know that he had an e-mail. He straightened up and immediately clicked open the message.

"I'm very angry that you didn't carry out my instructions!" it read.

Choosing his words with the utmost care, Joe typed a reply.

"I'm truly sorry, I can explain. I just couldn't do it. I'd got to know her really well and she was my friend. I realise now how stupid I was to disobey you and if I could go back to that room again I would have done it."

"Your instructions were to kill her and force her to watch herself die," came the stark reply.

"I'm sorry," was all that Joe Reed could manage to type.

"Next time you must follow my instructions to the letter," came back quickly, and Joe could sense the anger behind the words.

"I will, I promise," he typed.

"I'll make it easier with the next one."

"The next one?"

There was a few moments pause which found Joe Reed staring dully at the screen.

"Remember Jane was supposed to be your mother? Supposed to look after you but then let someone else abuse you for her own selfish needs? She let you suffer so she could be happy."

"I remember," typed Joe. A familiar feeling of shame washed over him, and he slid down into the chair.

"The woman I choose next will be another Jane. She'll be evil and ugly and she'll have children that she beats and abuses. She'll deserve to be punished. When I find her, you must punish her properly - for both of us."

"Ok I will," he typed, "I promise."

Chapter 5

TWO YEARS LATER

She was ready for this, she felt as though she belonged. The newcomer had dressed meticulously for the role she was sure she'd been born to play. She had chosen a crisp white blouse with a black pencil skirt cut to calf length. The material hugged her figure enough to let people know that she was confident, but not enough to invite any unwanted attention. Her black patent kitten-heel shoes had been chosen to complement her capacious workaday handbag, and the close fitting jacket that finished her look with a single button accentuating her waist gave her exactly the look of professionalism that she was aiming for.

Her features were angular and strong, with high cheekbones and full lips. Long dark hair, clipped at the back to allow the locks to fall behind her ears and beyond her shoulders, framed her classically handsome, rather than beautiful face.

Her warm brown eyes fell on a brass triangular sign on the front of the desk and turning it to face her she stared at the words *Jenny M Foster - Criminal Profiler*. She smiled to herself: she'd made it at last.

Jenny had waited for this moment seemingly each

second of the six long years of study that had finally brought her here. Finishing her Criminology & Forensics with Psychology degree course with the highest marks in the country that year had vindicated her decision to study, and made all the hard work worth it. Landing this job attached to the Manchester Metropolitan Police Serious Crime Squad as their only criminal profiler was a necessary and hard-won stepping stone on a pre-planned path that would lead her career upwards. She was thirty-six, but her enthusiasm and zest for life made her look and even move like a much younger woman. She'd made the decision to study at a late stage, which gave her a major advantage over other candidates that had gone straight to university from school: she had the necessary qualifications, plus plenty of life experience. Jenny had skilfully negotiated the demands of juggling her studies for her degree with holding down a tough position in a property holdings company. The fact that the boss had eventually become her husband was a constant source of amusement to him and satisfaction for her.

Their daughter Lilly, two years old with blonde hair, green eyes and an infectious laugh, was full of personality and a real handful. Leaving her with a child minder would be tough, but she was used to making sacrifices to further her career and this one had always been a given. Her thoughts turned to her husband Peter, who was spending his Saturday looking after Lilly. The child was a miracle, the outcome of a successful pregnancy after several false alarms and devastating miscarriages. Despite the heartache Jenny's assertion that career came before kids meant that when she'd been asked to start earlier than anticipated she'd jumped at the chance to show willing. Now she leant back in the unfamiliar chair and drew a deep breath, she wanted to keep her emotions under control and get her mind ready for the day ahead. She wanted to make a good impression and she was determined to do well. She knew she could make an impact and wanted to show her new colleagues what she could bring to the team. Her mentor Professor Alderman, who had guided her through her studies, had warned Jenny that she might come up against natural resistance within the police force. He had warned that criminal profiling and all the scientific research necessary to put theories into practice on a day-to-day basis would be new to the Manchester Metropolitan Police: hard-nosed detectives would be naturally suspicious. The professor had advised caution, telling Jenny to take things slowly and be prepared to listen, rather than trying to impose her ideas on a reluctant, perhaps reactionary audience. She had heard him out and understood his concerns, but her natural determination told her that she needed to make an impact, and make it quickly.

Opening the small cardboard box that she'd carried in with her, she took out four photographs in identical golden frames, arranging them prominently on her new desk. Lilly was in all of them, first with Peter cradling her moments after she'd been born. The second showed Peter, Jenny and Lilly windswept on Blackpool Promenade, Lilly peeking out from her pram with the proud parents bundled up against a biting March wind. In the third frame Jenny's mum Val held Lilly's hand, with the tot standing unsteadily in shiny black shoes and a dress that flared above her knees. The final image was of Lilly alone and laughing into the camera. The desk upon which the treasured photos now sat looked brand-new and fit for purpose. The ergonomically designed chair moulded around Jenny's slim body, and she took a moment to adjust the height so that she sat proud of the desk. The computer monitor was blank but it sprang into life when she touched the mouse, the bright screen displaying the legend *Welcome Jenny Foster* turning over and over and acting as a screensaver. She clicked a key and was immediately confronted with a security screen that she didn't as yet have a username and password to operate. Jenny smiled: she'd arrived and they'd been expecting her.

Footsteps approached across the office behind her and she turned to face Chief Inspector Mark Ambrose, her new boss. He was in his mid-fifties, with a receding hairline and piercing blue eyes in a long thin face. His freshly shaven chin accentuated a contrasting black moustache, and his broad smile was confident and well-rehearsed. The blue eyes sparkled with genuine warmth at seeing her.

"Hello, Jenny," he said. "I see you found your desk okay."

His accent was thick North Yorkshire and added to his air of solid superiority.

"Yes. Thanks, Chief," she said, giving him a friendly smile.

The Chief remained silent, the warmth in his eyes replaced with a penetrating look that gradually intensified, as though he were dissecting his new recruit.

Jenny feared he was already wondering if he'd made the right decision by risking taking her on.

She had researched Mark Ambrose prior to her interview and had been impressed. He was renowned for expecting total commitment from his team, and commentators said that the old cliché was true in his case - he never asked anyone under his command to do anything that he hadn't done or wouldn't do himself. A stickler for correct procedure, he liked to get involved in an investigation at every level. Suddenly Jenny was acutely aware that his reputation as someone who didn't suffer fools was probably well-founded and here he was, studying her every move. She hoped that greeting him as 'Chief', a title she knew he preferred, would at least show him that she'd taken the trouble to ensure she was properly prepared. She also sensed instinctively that there was no room for nerves, Mark Ambrose was looking for someone he trusted to improve the quality of his team.

"So, where do I start?" she asked.

He watched her for a few moments longer, those sharp blue eyes seeming to take in, decipher and then catalogue everything about her. Jenny knew she would not be keeping any secrets from the Chief.

"Thanks for coming in early," he said, his smile not quite making it to his eyes, which remained fixed on Jenny, pinning her to the seat. "I'm giving a briefing to the team in five minutes. It's in the Tactical Briefing Room."

With that, he turned and walked off, and Jenny was left to watch his neatly tailored back disappear across the room. He was tall, about six foot two, slim and perfectly dressed in a mid-grey suit with spotless black shoes that seemed barely to touch the carpet as he walked. '*So where the hell is the Tactical Briefing Room?*' she thought, glancing round the large office space filled with desks and flashing computer monitors. With not one person of whom to ask directions, she became faintly annoyed that she had little choice but to gather up her handbag and notebook and scurry after the Chief's retreating figure.

***

Two hours later Jenny was back at her desk with four huge boxes full of files and a username and password for the computer system, any first day feel-good factor having well and truly evaporated. Keeping up in the briefing had been a challenge, but the profiler had noted the information for assimilation later. Jenny hadn't been spoken to directly and she hadn't asked any questions, preferring to sit quietly and absorb ideas instead. The Chief's delivery had been thorough, professional and uncompromising. Everyone in the squad had been friendly before knuckling down to the meeting and while the Chief had been shuffling papers, waiting for the room to fill, she'd been greeted with smiles and handshakes along with offers of help and support, and had been made to feel really welcome by the team - in public at least.

She consulted her briefing notes. There'd been two women abducted in and around Whitefield just outside Manchester. The women were both in their thirties, both mothers, and both had shoulder length dark-brown hair. Jenny absent-mindedly played with the ends of her own long brown hair as she read. Photographs of the women had been circulated, together with a life history, transcripts of interviews with any witnesses, photographs of each abduction location and reports from the detectives assigned to the case.

Dawn James, the first alleged victim, had been abducted two weeks ago whilst walking from her home to her mother's house, a journey that should have taken less than fifteen minutes. Since she'd disappeared there'd been a mass of activity, producing boxes of files containing reports and interviews. Following protocol, the Chief had deliberately kept the Press in the dark about the details of the case, so various hacks had run stories on her as a missing person, producing yet another box of sightings and theories. The second woman, Robyn Cox, had been snatched three days ago at about six in the evening, walking along the road between Whitefield and Rawtenstall barely three hundred yards from the take-away where she was due to start work. This second abduction had started a chain reaction in the media, with TV reporters and the nationals quickly linking the two disappearances, and all eyes across the country were now fixed firmly on Manchester.

The Chief was due to give a press conference at midday and before facing the media he was keen to learn if there were any new developments. According to Detective Inspector Sam Bradbury, who was leading the investigation, the main suspect was a man called Joe Reed. Reed had been identified at the scene of the Robyn Cox abduction by a passer-by who recognised him driving a white van away from the site. The witness was a waitress at Gerry's Café in Chorlton and her evidence was considered cast-iron because she had served the same man coffee from time-to-time over a six-month period two years earlier. DI Sam Bradbury went on to explain that Joe Reed was wanted for questioning in connection with at least two serious sexual assaults committed in Manchester around Christmas two years ago. Reed had been at the café with one of the assault victims before disappearing - apparently into thin air. If this sighting was reliable, then Reed had resurfaced with a new twist to his list of crimes. Looking at the notes it all seemed easy and straightforward enough: find Joe Reed and they had their man. Then the Chief dropped his bombshell.

Apparently, according to the original rape investigations, there was no such person as Joe Reed. The suspect didn't turn up on any databases; his DNA was unregistered and his fingerprints didn't match any files at home or abroad. Consequently he was never found and questioned over the assaults. There were no photographs of him and no CCTV images; all the police had was an e-fit from his original victims that was confirmed as the same man by the eye witness who saw him driving the van. The van itself was a nondescript white Luton-style vehicle complete with false number plates. During his previous rape spree 'Joe Reed' had seemed to be able to appear and disappear at will, and was always careful not to leave anything that would lead police straight to him. Basically, this guy didn't exist.

Jenny expelled the air from her lungs and looked down

at the four brown boxes, each with the words JOE REED written in a broad hand on its lid.

"Jenny, have a look through the files, will you," the Chief had said. "See if there's anything we've missed and I'll catch up with you on Monday morning."

All Jenny could think was, '*Great! My first case and I've only got till Monday to make an impression. God, I wish I still smoked.*' Smoking had been her one real vice before she'd fallen pregnant with Lilly, but she'd given up the same day that the test had shown positive and hadn't had a cigarette since.

The large, modern, air-conditioned office was starting to populate with members of the squad returning from the briefing. Most were in groups of two or three obviously discussing aspects of the case, but one of the men she recognised from the meeting was heading directly for her.

At five foot nine or ten he was short for a policeman, with a tanned complexion and deep set eyes.

"Hi," he said, shaking hands across the desk, "DI Sam Bradbury."

Jenny stood up and took his hand, finding it warm and welcoming.

"Jenny Foster," she said, increasing the pressure in her own grip to find the DI responding in kind, resulting in a gratifyingly professional exchange.

"I've been asked to keep you informed of all developments and…you know…look after you a bit for the first few days," he said with a hint of a smile, "which basically means we'll be partners for a while."

"Ok," said Jenny.

Being assigned as a partner on her first day hadn't

crossed her mind and she was taken a little by surprise at the prospect. Obviously the Chief didn't trust her yet.

"What do you know about Joe Reed?" she asked.

"Straight down to it, eh?" responded Sam. "Do you smoke? I could murder a coffee and a fag."

"Sure," she answered, easily convincing herself that this was an ideal way to start a good working relationship. If the Chief needed proof that he had made a good decision, then she'd have to use Sam Bradbury to show what she was capable of and getting him on her side from the start was probably a good strategy.

Once outside, they took a place on a bench after picking up plastic cups filled with what had been described by the machine as cappuccino. Sam offered Jenny one of his Marlboro's, together with a light from his Zippo.

"Thanks," she said, drawing deeply and becoming gratifyingly light-headed almost instantly.

"Reed's a mystery," said Sam continually fidgeting with the filter between his thick fingers. "He turns up from who knows where with no previous, not even a speeding ticket, talks two married women into bed before raping and sodomising them, then disappears into thin air again for two years. He's like a ghost. Have you had a chance to read the files yet?"

It was already approaching midday and the sun was reaching its highest point. Even in her thin shirt Jenny felt stifled by the heat.

"All I know so far is what the Chief told us at the briefing, and I've got four boxes full of files to go through. I'll be up-to-speed for Monday, though."

"That's right," said Sam flicking at the filter. "The

Chief asked you in early to get a head start. Everyone's spooked that a second woman's missing, presumed kidnapped by Reed. It doesn't feel right somehow; feels like there's more to come."

He fell silent, smoking hard, eyeing his new companion with a sideways glance. "So how did you get here?" he asked.

Jenny wasn't prepared to share anything personal with her new partner just yet. "It's a long story," she said, adding "So you've drawn the short straw showing the new girl what's what?"

"It's not all bad - you're easier on the eye than my last partner."

Jenny's head automatically snapped round at the comment with anger flashing in her eyes, only to see a huge grin on his face.

"Have you worked cases like this before?" she asked, without returning his smile. She'd met men like Sam Bradbury and he needed to know that she couldn't be pushed around. Sam looked down at the ground, holding his cigarette between his knees, examining his brown leather shoes.

"I've worked kidnappings, rapes and murders too if that's what you mean," he said. "Most murderers turn out to be sad cases caught up in a moment of madness."

Jenny stubbed out her first cigarette in almost two years and wondered where she could get some perfume spray to disguise the sweet smell.

"And the rest?" she asked.

"Criminals killing each other over an insult or a deal gone wrong."

"So you've never worked a case like this then?"

Sam ignored the obvious challenge to his expertise along with the shiny metal bin with the cigarette logo on the side and ground the spent end into the concrete with his foot,

"This looks premeditated and this Joe Reed guy feels different."

"Different?" asked Jenny, "How?"

"Read the notes from the rape cases," said Sam and meeting Jenny's eyes he added, "I think he likes to play games."

***

When Jenny eventually drew up at home that evening she was two hours later than she'd predicted and she still had an unread box of files stuffed into the boot. Exhausted, she let her head fall onto the steering wheel. She switched off the engine and got out of her black BMW, her heels crunching on the gravel as she took the familiar thirty steps to her door. She pushed the key into the lock and went inside to the sound of the television on low in the sitting room where she dropped into her favourite armchair without speaking to her husband.

"You look exhausted," he smiled. "I put Lilly to bed an hour ago, and she went straight off with her favourite Pooh Bear story."

"Did she ask for me?" said Jenny, her eyes still closed.

"She went off to sleep happy and healthy," said Peter. "I've kept your dinner in the oven, let me put it out for you while you go upstairs and check on her."

"I'm not really hungry. I grabbed a quick burger a couple of hours ago at my desk. Do you mind? Sorry I didn't call to say."

"No worries! I'll pop it in the freezer for another time. It's only spagh Bol."

Jenny yanked herself from the comfort of the chair. She badly wanted to look in on Lilly and put her hand affectionately on Peter's shoulder as she passed.

"Thanks," she said.

Peter had been Jenny's boss at his property management company. She'd worked for him whilst studying and they had slowly fallen in love. He was intensely proud that Jenny had never given up on her ambition to become a criminal profiler, despite her gradually revealed personal difficulties. When his wife came back down she hovered in the doorway.

"It's been a heck of a first day - I'm bushed! I've still got a ton of reading to do, and I feel like my head's about to explode."

"I'll bring some coffee into the study," Peter said smiling.

"There's still a box of files in the boot of the car," she added.

"Ok, I'll bring them in," he replied, his smile broadening.

Jenny settled into her familiar study chair, leaving her computer idle for a bit. She'd spent countless hours in this room completing coursework, preparing for exams and creating lists of targets to be achieved. The utilitarian ash veneer desk had followed her from her father's house to her home with Peter. The fact that one of the metal legs was decidedly wobbly and there was

Sellotape holding the veneer together at one corner where the movers' van had left its mark in no way detracted from the feeling that Jenny and her desk were friends. She wasn't sentimental enough to have gone as far as actually naming her constant study companion, but she loved the desk enough to allow it to sit almost bizarrely out-of-place in a room dominated by dark oak bookshelves and low mood lighting.

Clearing the top of the desk to make room for the box that Peter was standing waiting to put there, she smiled up at her husband gratefully.

"Remember, you've got tomorrow morning too," he said.

"Oh *yes,* it's Sunday tomorrow," replied Jenny, and then winced. "I forgot - we're going to Mum and Dad's aren't we?"

"I'd best get you that coffee," smiled Peter.

"Ok, thanks," said Jenny, and with a sigh she opened the box, pulling out a wad of brown manila files.

Chapter 6

Joe Reed sat staring into space. The only way his mind could deal with the constant torture his surroundings inflicted was to try and shut them out. When he'd received an e-mail three months earlier to tell him he was to move into 63 Cathcart Street, Oldham his blood had run instantly cold, and from that day to this he had nursed an inescapable feeling of dread and terror. This was the house he had shared as a child with Declan and his mother and stepfather, and where all of his worst fears had turned into a living nightmare and then later, deep hatred.

To anybody else it was just an average, tired Victorian end of terrace, sandwiched between its shabby looking neighbour on one side and the main road on the other. The blue and white stone cladding and replacement windows revealed the fact that a previous occupant had carefully improved their future investment, but even these signs of obvious pride were now black with grime and neglect. Inside, the wallpaper was peeling slowly from the walls and the carpets were blotched with stains that the imagination would balk at making sense of. Joe Reed sat stock still on the only chair in what was once the living room and stared blankly at the wall in front of him. He was as filthy as his surroundings, his bloodshot, heavily black-ringed eyes testament to sleepless nights and tortured days.

Everywhere he turned were the memories of those constant beatings and humiliations at the hands of Dan Prince, his stepfather.

A newspaper pushed noisily through the letter-box to join an ever increasing pile of unread mail snapped Joe out of his trance, and the familiar feeling of panic once again set his nerves on edge. He darted a glance towards the door and stood up to peer into the hall, feeling a surge of relief at the sight of a fresh newspaper on the floor. He needed coffee, but that would mean walking past the basement door, and he didn't want to think about who was down there and what he would be asked to do. This time he was certain that he would obey.

The electronic ping that signified a new e-mail came from above and Joe immediately began to climb the stairs, forcing from his mind the image of the two women lying helpless and terrified a few feet below, trussed up like sheep awaiting slaughter. He hurried past the door to the bedroom where his nightmares had been born and nurtured and into a room that was clean and tidy, with a freshly made bed dominating the space. Joe sat at the computer desk that housed his laptop and clicked on the waiting message.

"Get ready," it read. "Now is the time."

Joe Reed found himself heading for the bathroom, and when he emerged half an hour later he looked like a different man. Showered, shaved and dressed in spotless cream chinos, red polo shirt and brown loafers he could have been going out for a night on the town.

Returning to his laptop he typed one word, *Ready*. The reply came back instantly: 'Do it now!'

Joe turned and made to walk down the hall, stopping to stare at the door that led to his mother's old room with memories of Dan, Declan and his childhood as Ed Jerome flooding his mind. The events that had taken place in that room made the beatings seem almost welcome, and his skin prickled as he recalled the full horror.

***

The first time it happened the day had started like any other. It was a Saturday; the rain was dancing off the pavements outside and he and Declan were having breakfast as normal. Declan prepared cereal and toast, while Ed sat at the table just happy to be looked after by his new big brother. He was sore from the fresh set of welts on his back that Dan Prince had administered the previous evening because Ed had forgotten to pick up a copy of his stepfather's magazine on the way home from school. The beatings had become commonplace, and he and Declan often compared the bruises and angry red welts left by Dan's belt. When Jane came into the kitchen and sat down it was Ed's turn to jump up and pour cereal into a bowl and make her a mug of coffee. Then he stood and waited whilst she ate and drank, only to take away the crockery and plunge his hands into the sink to wash up as quickly as possible before turning back to his mother to make sure she was happy for him to leave the room. Dan came in and got his own breakfast and Ed could almost taste the growing tension in the small kitchen.

Usually on a Saturday he and Declan would be told to go and play outside and they knew not to return before tea-time, but today would be different.

Dan turned to his wife. "I think we should have a family day today *Mam*," he said, sarcastically emphasising the maternal reference. "What do you think?"

Jane's face showed her concern but she just nodded wordlessly.

"Make sure you two lads are back for midday! Me and your mam want us all to spend the afternoon together." He turned to Jane. "Don't we, Love!"

"Yes, Dad," said the two boys' almost in unison.

They hurried from the kitchen, scooping up their shoes and coats as they left the house and ran out into the pouring rain. They carried on running past the terrace houses and down to the park at the end of the street, not stopping until reaching the shelter of the underpass linking the park and the estate opposite of neat, one-storey sheltered council housing. The rain was so heavy that each end of the passage was flooded and Ed and Declan were forced to seek refuge right in the centre of the concrete tunnel. Ed was wet through to his shirt, his flimsy coat nowhere near thick enough to repel much more than a shower. Shivering uncontrollably, he took off the soaking garment and threw it angrily to the ground.

"I wish my mum had never met your dad!" he shouted.

Declan shuffled his feet in misery; rain water dripped from his hair and down his face, disguising the fresh tears welling in his eyes.

"I should've said summat."

"About what?" quizzed Ed.

"Everything! Dad always beat us, but now he's got with your mam there's summat different," continued Declan, looking down at the spreading puddle at his feet.

"So what's a family day?" asked Ed, with a nagging feeling of dread growing inside him.

Declan started kicking a coke can from one wall of the tunnel to the other and Ed watched him, waiting for an answer. The noise of metal on concrete in the enclosed space echoed around the walls and Ed had to raise his voice to be heard.

"Declan? Declan!"

Declan stopped his game and crushed the can with his soaked-through stained pumps. "Dad's a bastard!"

"I know," said Ed ruefully. He had hoped for so much more. "I don't know why my mum is like this now and why she puts up with him and his temper."

"She does everything my dad says," Declan replied. "Come on! It's stopped raining - let's knock up some old dears."

He walked off, with Ed picking up his soaking coat and trailing behind him towards the sheltered housing where they would spend the morning tormenting the elderly residents by knocking on doors and disappearing before the knock could be answered.

When they returned to the house just before twelve as instructed, they used the back door to find Dan and Jane in each other's arms on the sofa in the sitting room. The boys stood waiting to be acknowledged.

"What's Family Day, Mum?" asked Ed, gulping nervously.

Jane looked up from her position nestled into Dan's

chest "We're all going to spend the afternoon together," and releasing herself from Dan's arms she stood up.

"Wait in your room," ordered Dan. "Get out of them sopping wet clothes and put your pyjamas on."

After changing the two boys sat huddled on the bed, terrified at the thought of what might be coming next. Dan and Jane had followed them upstairs, turning in to their own bedroom down the corridor. They had sex at a deafening level, their brutish noises culminating in Jane's seemingly endless screams with Dan's grunting vibrating through the house. Ed and Declan held onto each other with no choice but to listen, crying like babies until at last the door to their parents' bedroom was thrown open and Dan came out into the hall naked, his thick-set hairy body glistening with sweat.

"Get in here," he said flatly. "It's family time."

The boys stayed where they were, still crying.

"Now!" he said raising his voice.

Declan patted Ed's back, "We'll be alright," he said and they both got up. Still holding onto each other they made their way down the passage, the few steps seeming to last for an eternity.

Inside the bedroom Jane was dressed in a light pink nightgown. She was sitting on a comfortable chintz armchair next to the bed, as if she were waiting to read the boys a bedtime story. Her face, though, betrayed her concern as they were led into the room.

"Get out of them pyjamas!" said Dan with a grin.

Declan and Ed obeyed, slowly unbuttoning their jackets before letting them and their pyjama bottoms fall to the floor at their feet. Dan laughed and bent down to meet Jane's gaze. She looked first at him then at the two boys, not knowing what to do next. Dan grabbed her chin and kissed her roughly, pressing hard into her mouth.

***

Joe Reed could feel his eyes stinging and the tears rolling down his cheeks. Childlike, he wiped his nose with the back of his hand, the tears for his boyhood seeming to galvanise his resolve, and then he began to descend the stairs. Reaching the door to the basement, he opened it without hesitation and started making his way down to the two captives.

Stopping at the foot of the stairs he could almost taste the terror. The bound and helpless women at either end of the room were staring at him from the mirrors they were lying in front of, and as he went in he could see their eyes move to follow him. He was walking towards the woman who lay furthest away when suddenly the silence of the room was disturbed by a disembodied voice.

"Make the other bitch watch!" it said, spitting out the words like venom.

The occupants of the room stiffened and a look of terror appeared in the eyes of the woman now lying at Joe's feet. He bent down and effortlessly scooped her up, the chain attached to the collar around her neck becoming taut as he repositioned her into a kneeling position with her back against the mirror. The voice came through again, sarcastic this time.

"You'll enjoy watching this, Robyn."

Robyn Cox grimaced with pain, but the gag fixed firmly into her mouth meant that she couldn't speak. Her throat was so dry she could hardly make a sound at all. The weight of her own body pressing on her feet and bending them under her knees was intolerable; it seemed as if the skin beneath the rope binding her ankles to her knees was burning off. Joe Reed left Robyn perched there like a bird as he walked across the room to drag up the second woman, Dawn James, before dumping her back down on the bed. Then he produced a small knife from his pocket and cut the rope that attached Dawn's hands to her ankles: she flaked out motionless, face down.

"Make sure she's awake!" commanded the voice.

Trussed up and carefully positioned to watch whatever fate would befall her fellow captive, Robyn's eyes searched the room. Her gaze darted from one corner to another, expecting to see the owner of the voice orchestrating proceedings, but there was nobody else there. A chill of realisation crept from the base of her spine to set her skin aquiver with goose-pimples.

She was in the hands of monsters.

***

The man sat hot with excitement in his tired leather chair, barely able to control his voice as he spoke into the microphone positioned on his desk. The open laptop showed a split live feed from the basement where Joe Reed was carrying out his orders. One side of the screen was trained on Robyn Cox squirming on her knees against the bonds that were clearly causing her a great deal of discomfort, whilst the other side showed

Joe Reed pulling Dawn James's head up from the bed by the back of her hair and slapping her across the face. Dawn James woke up, or at least her eyes opened, and the man zoomed in on her face, which was turned towards the camera. She was awake, but she was clearly groggy. The gag in her mouth had stretched her face into a grimace and her skin was dirty now and sallow. Her hair, hard with dried blood, lay in spikes across her swollen cheek and when Joe Reed re-positioned her body her limbs remained limp, as light and lifeless as a plastic doll's. The man panned the camera lens out to take in the full extent of the bed with the victim lying waiting for her fate, whilst Joe Reed stood stripping off his clothes. Positioning himself behind Dawn, he put his arm around her waist, pulled her up into a kneeling position and slipped a clear plastic bag over her head.

"Do it now!" the man said forcefully into the microphone.

Chapter 7

Jenny killed the engine and looked at Peter with her best *help me* eyes.

"Do we have to do this?" She almost pleaded.

"Everyone's excited about your new job," smiled Peter. "You'll have a great time. Anyway, it'll be a welcome relief after the last time we were all together."

The radio was on low and Boy George's Karma Chameleon played softly in the background. Jenny fingered the heart dangling from the silver bracelet she always wore, a gift from her father on her sixteenth birthday.

"I know - you're right!" she said.

Their last visit two weeks earlier had been under the shadow of her father losing his elder brother Jim, who had succumbed to cancer after years of struggle, and this celebration might help put a welcome smile on everyone's face.

Peter looked over his shoulder to see Lilly slumped in her car seat, involuntarily twitching her knee when her dream touched on reality.

"What do you think she's dreaming about?" he asked.

"It's probably a nightmare where Darren's trying to saw her leg off again with those plastic tools he's always got with him," answered Jenny. She was smiling now at the thought of how mischievous her sister Candice's son Darren could be.

"Oh come on, let's get it over with! I'll be fine once Dad's finished his fussing," she said, taking the keys from the ignition and opening the door.

Without the benefit of the car's air-conditioning, the heat of the day was an immediate factor. Jenny had chosen her outfit well, with cut-off jeans and a thin cotton top and she felt the heat of the sun warming her exposed skin. She'd spent her entire childhood in this house and she took a second to let the familiar feeling of happiness and security seep into her. The front lawn stretched out in front of the car and the scent of pine trees and lavender from the well-tended borders had an almost instantly calming effect. She wanted to be here; she felt that she belonged to this place.

Her parents were already making their way down the drive from the house. Bob and Val Baker had a seemingly perfect life: Bob had retired, selling an engineering business that now funded a comfortable retirement, while Val hadn't needed to work since her early forties, and spent her time shopping and having coffee with friends, or working voluntarily in the community. Tall - and Jenny thought too thin - with freshly dyed auburn hair, she was wearing a light cotton summer dress and kitten heels. Despite his age, Bob had a thick head of black hair and retained a good physique after many years working with his hands. His sunny disposition meant that he was popular with everyone, but Jenny had always fancied that she was his favourite of their three children.

Ignoring Jenny, her mother opened the back door of

the BMW to fish out her grand-daughter from the toddler seat. Her lean frame ducked inside to wake the child, before unfastening the buckles with well-manicured hands. Smoothing the ruffles in Lilly's yellow dress and taming her unruly blonde hair back into shape, Val couldn't help thinking that the bright white training shoes on the child's dangling feet looked oddly out of place.

"How are you Bob?" Asked Peter already out of the car and shaking hands warmly with Jenny's father.

"If I was any better it would be a sin," replied Bob, grinning from ear to ear.

"How could I be when my eldest daughter's a superstar?"

"Hardly!" said Jenny. "It's just a job, Dad," the mounting embarrassment already showing in her cheeks.

"Just a job?" said Bob, moving to the other side of the car to hug his daughter and kiss her on the cheek and head. "She studies six years, comes first in the country and then lands the perfect position exactly as she wanted and all she can say is, *it's just a job Dad!*"

He and Jenny moved off together, putting their arms around each other's waists, sharing a private joke and giggling like school children as they walked. Peter and Val formed an uncomfortable alliance to follow, with Lilly sitting on her grandmother's hip and protesting to be put down.

The sprawling family house was set in three acres of gardens and woodland in Altrincham, a leafy suburb of Manchester. The mock-rustic façade gave way to six bedrooms, three of which had been turned from their original use as children's safe havens to a lavishly decorated guest bedroom, a gym and an office. Two bedrooms were retained for grand-children, fashioned one for a boy and one for a girl just in case a welcome visitor stayed for the weekend. Downstairs there were large airy living rooms and a huge kitchen where the rest of the guests were waiting. At the sight of the happy, familiar faces Jenny began to relax and beamed with contentment. She took her daughter from Val, and the three newcomers spent the next few minutes greeting family and friends before Bob offered a glass of champagne to propose a toast.

"To my clever daughter!" he said proudly. Glasses chinked and everyone smilingly congratulated an obviously embarrassed Jenny on her achievement.

Jenny's younger brother Glenn tapped a spoon against the side of his glass for quiet.

"No chance!" she said before she was press ganged into action by a chorus of good natured disapproval.

"Ok, ok," she beamed. "It's only a job you know!"

"Great speech, Sis!" said Glenn to a burst of laughter, and was rewarded by Jenny thrusting Lilly towards him.

"Well, I'm glad you're all here," she went on, finding the composure to tolerate the spotlight. "And thanks to Mum and Dad for putting this on."

It was obvious how much work Val had put into making sure this would be a family celebration to remember. The oak floor in the hall had been specially waxed and polished and the freshly cut flowers sitting in vases on every available surface scented the entire house with summer.

"What's happened so far?" teased Candice, Jenny's younger sister. "Have they got you making the tea?"

"Not yet," laughed Jenny. "I'm attached to The Manchester Metropolitan Police Serious Crime Squad in the Police HQ in Manchester. I'm looking at some old unsolved rape and murder cases, trying to give the detectives an idea of the type of person who might be responsible. It's been pretty hectic so far."

Candice was beginning to feel put out by all the attention paid to her sister, and passed her glass from hand to hand.

"Hope it was worth the six years?" she said, smiling unconvincingly.

"I think so; well so far anyway," said Jenny with a determined lift of her chin.

Bob took over, obviously prepared. "When Jenny came to tell us she was going to study to be a criminal profiler, to be honest I didn't think much of it," he said. "But as you all know, she was in the middle of a messy divorce at the time and I decided it might be a good way to take her mind off things." He looked at Jenny with a smile that only a father can produce. "And look at her now! Happy, healthy, with a wonderful daughter and a husband who's stood by her and helped her all the way." Jenny met Peter's eyes and smiled.

"In the end though," continued the proud father, "it's been Jenny's hard work and dedication that's seen her through - I'm not sure where she gets that from!"

Everyone laughed; they all knew how hard Bob had worked to make his business a success. "To Jenny!" he called, eliciting an enthusiastic chorus of "*Jenny!*"

Candice put her glass down with the white wine untouched. She collected Lilly from Glenn her brother to go and attend a not so pressing yell of pain from the children in the sitting room next door. Candice knew that her exit would go largely unnoticed, as Jenny always seemed to be the centre of attention; the golden girl with the seemingly perfect marriage and now the seemingly perfect job. At that moment the melodic chimes of the doorbell echoed around the house.

"I'll go," called Val and returned to the kitchen a few moments later with a huge smile on her face. "It's your Uncle Ronnie!" she said excitedly.

Jenny instantly started towards the door and was met with a long embrace by Val's tall and imposing younger brother. Ronnie had been one of the driving influences behind Jenny's decision to study criminology in the first place. He was a Detective Inspector at Scotland Yard, the Mecca for any would-be detective and his stories of criminals and their crimes had fascinated Jenny for as long as she could remember. It had been Ronnie who had encouraged her to look seriously at profiling, arguing that the police needed all the help they could get now that criminals were using increasingly sophisticated methods to avoid detection.

Ronnie smiled and held Jenny by the shoulders at arm's length. "You're a star!" he said. "That job in Manchester had hundreds of applicants; but it's no surprise to me that you got it."

"Thanks Ronnie," said Jenny, a smile now fixed permanently on her face, and she watched him disappear into the kitchen to say his hellos to the rest of the family.

"I can't believe he came all the way from London," she said to Peter, now standing beside her.

"He's your biggest fan - well, second biggest!" and he squeezed her bottom with a big grin on his face.

"Come on," said Jenny visibly more relaxed. "You're driving, so I might have a drink."

***

Peter and Bob took up their usual places arguing over who barbequed the best sausages, whilst Jenny chatted on the patio to her mum, Uncle Ronnie and her brother Glenn and his wife Wendy. The sun was at its highest and the women wore sunglasses to keep the glare to a minimum, whilst the men basked in the heat. Bob looked over and watched them all laughing as Glenn launched into the repertoire of whimsical, good-natured pokes at life that he knew Jenny and Candice enjoyed.

"It's amazing how Jenny relaxes when she's here, Bob," remarked Peter as he repositioned a dangerously black hunk of meat. "It's as if she reverts to being a teenager again. Her whole attitude changes, it's as if she feels…" and he thought for a moment, "Well, safe."

Bob gave him a searching look. "Is she happy now, Peter?"

"She's still affected by what happened, if that's what you mean."

Bob stiffened defensively. "I know she's not going to just forget it."

"How can she?" responded Peter, expertly collecting a cooked burger from the grill and laying it on one of the buns ready cut by Val and laid out on a large serving plate. "She never talks about it, but I can see the pain in her eyes sometimes."

Jenny's divorce from her first husband Simon had revealed some disturbing truths that her father still found it difficult to come to terms with. Bob had known that his daughter was hiding something from him - he could feel it - but even when she eventually turned up one night in the rain with just the clothes on her back, it had taken weeks before she was able to tell him the full story.

The day she eventually opened up to her father would live with him forever.

He remembered that the house had been cloaked in snow, with the still air biting into his lungs as he struggled through the drift on the drive. When he eventually made it to the front door and into the hall, he found Jenny sitting on the third stair of the grand oak staircase weeping like a child. It was obvious that she'd been crying for some time and there was no light on, though the reflection of moon on snow filtered in, shedding an unearthly glow. Jenny's body was shaking with sobs and the tissue that she held in her hand had already come apart, leaving wet blobs of white on her knees and on the dark pink stair carpet. Over the next hour she revealed to her father the full horror of her marriage to Simon and how he had changed from the man of her dreams to a monster who thought nothing of having countless affairs, before eventually revealing that he had fathered a child with one of his mistresses and told her the marriage was over.

Returning his thoughts to the barbeque, Bob put his hand on Peter's shoulder. "He fooled us all," he said.

His son-in-law nodded in mute reply, watching Jenny walk down the steps of the patio onto the grass, and then over to Ronnie.

Chapter 8

"Thanks for coming, Ronnie," said Jenny happily.

He smiled down at her. "Wouldn't have missed it for the world, are you still off the weed? I could murder a fag."

"Officially." she said, adding ruefully, "but unofficially I have the odd one. Come on, we'll go down to the tree - no-one will see us there."

They made their way to the bottom of the garden to the spot under an old sycamore tree where she and Ronnie had spent many hours talking through how things might turn out once she was qualified and had found the right job.

The tree had been where Jenny had gone to make herself childish promises and where all subsequent big decisions had been wrestled with and problems chewed over through tears and more than once, even despair.

Ronnie produced a lighter and a packet of cigarettes from the pocket of his neat grey slacks and taking two out handed one to Jenny. They lit up conspiratorially from the same flame and fell into the easy union of disassociated smokers.

"I didn't realise you'd already got your feet under the desk?" said Ronnie smiling.

Jenny laughed, "I was supposed to start on Monday,"

she said. "But they asked me to come in a day early and I actually went in for the first time yesterday."

"Saturday? That *is* keen! And is it everything you thought it would be?" he asked, drawing deeply on his cigarette.

"And more! I feel like I was born to do the job."

"And the lads?" he asked, visibly relaxing with smoke curling from his nostrils.

"Everyone's been great so far. Obviously, I don't really know them all just yet, but the ones I've met so far are easy to get on with and very professional."

"How's the Chief?" he asked, knowing how hard a taskmaster Jenny's new boss could be.

Jenny paused to think, tracing the outline of her initials where she had carved them into the tree as a teenager.

"I like him," she said. "He definitely knows what he's doing and leads the team with a straight bat. It's hard to explain, but it's as if he knows what you're thinking before you think it yourself."

She paused again, noticing Ronnie nodding to himself with his head down, a knowing smile playing on his lips.

"He's paired me with Sam Bradbury," she said, blowing out smoke, "one of the DI's."

"Don't know him," said Ronnie. "What have they given you? Something easy to start I hope?"

She played with the filter end of her cigarette. "No chance! That's why the Chief got me in early. It's like I'm in a dream or something. They want me to look at a cold case involving a serial rapist who doesn't seem to exist; only now they think he's added kidnapping to his specialities, so it's pretty urgent. There are two women missing and no leads so the Chief wants me to come up with some input double quick."

A welcome cooling breeze swept through the leaves of the tree. "Straight in at the deep end then?" said Ronnie, a glint of interest in his eye.

"Pretty much. This guy is certainly clever; he's been leading the police a dance for years. He's committed at least two serious offences where he befriended each woman over a period of time, before raping and brutalising them without a second thought. Trouble is, even though both victims' saw him countless times and there are other witnesses and lots of statements, we're no closer to knowing who he is."

"What, no DNA, fingerprints - nothing?" asked Ronnie.

"Oh, we've got all that alright. Trouble is he doesn't show up on any databases; no financials either and nothing on his vehicles. The guy's invisible."

Ronnie's interest was growing. "No employment records either?"

"There's extensive coverage in the files," said Jenny. "Whoever had the task on the original rape investigations seems to have been thorough enough, but just came up with dead ends. He seems to be able to find sales jobs, all commission-based where they either pay cash or cheque."

"So you can trace the cheques then?" Ronnie said, grinding his cigarette underfoot.

"No, he's careful there too," said Jenny. "If he gets a cheque he walks straight into one of those quick cashing places on the high street and converts it into notes.

No trace. He always gives a false address and shows fake ID. The cashiers don't care as long as the cheque clears."

She stubbed out her own cigarette on the tree-trunk and threw the dead butt into her father's ornamental wood.

"Sure we get fingerprints from the cheques," she went on, "but he's always careful to locate cameras and avoid any direct facial shots on the CCTV. So although we have plenty of descriptions, we haven't got an actual picture of him."

She slapped her neck in an attempt to kill a flying insect that had broken off from a cloud in the tree and taken a fancy to her perfumed skin.

"Sounds like a dangerous man," said Ronnie thoughtfully. "Someone like that must think through and plan every part of his life so as not to leave anything material behind that could link him to the crimes. He must be pretty normal in his everyday life otherwise he'd attract attention."

Jenny leant her back against the old tree and turned to face Ronnie. The unmown grass around its base, shaded by the huge branches felt fresh on her bare feet. The sensation of the cool, moist blades seeping between her toes drew her gaze downwards and she spent a few moments savouring the texture.

"He goes under the name Joe Reed," she said. "It's obviously false. I've been wading through the statements from the other three hundred or so Joe Reeds, and anything that sounds or links to Reed and there's nothing to connect any of them to our man."

"Nothing suspicious at all? Seems unlikely."

"There was one Joseph Peter Reed the detectives seemed briefly interested in. About the right age, similar description and lived with his widowed mother. Unemployed with few friends, and seemed to fit the bill."

"Go on," said Ronnie.

"It turned out he had a cast iron alibi. The day our Joe Reed raped the second woman, this Joseph Peter Reed was catching some Christmas sun in Tenerife with his mum and enough witnesses to put any plod off."

"Shame."

"I've been over the statements from the two sexual assault victims. They were encouraged to give first person cognitive accounts of their experiences by a psychologist," said Jenny, and noticing a puzzled look on her uncle's face added, "It's not police work, it's more like therapy. The psychologist asks the victim to write about their experience and they turn it into a story. Doing it that way helps the victim remember more detail and rationalise the crime." She paused, waiting for Ronnie to nod an understanding.

"They're personal and moving accounts, and I'm glad the victims gave permission for the technique to be used in the original investigation," she went on. "Ultimately of course, they were useless in actually catching Reed, but they did show how he went to great lengths to get to know the women first. He was either waiting for the right opportunity, or else he enjoys the sport of making them fall in love with him first."

Ronnie looked at her quizzically, "He makes them fall in love with him? Seems a bit complicated for your average rapist."

"Both victims were married, one of them happily, so she says. He left the first woman pregnant and the second woman a recluse," said Jenny. "He's a real piece of work."

"So why change and start kidnapping? Doesn't seem to fit in at all."

"Tell me about it, he's obviously escalating his activity and getting braver: a bad combination."

"Are you sure it's the same man?" mused Ronnie.

"There's a positive ID from an eye witness."

Ronnie scratched the back of his neck slowly, "What's the Chief's next move?"

"Not sure," said Jenny. "I'll produce a preliminary profile for tomorrow and see if it helps, but now I'm starting to feel guilty having today off. I mean, Sam and the other lads are rushing around all hours looking for this guy, and I'm here being congratulated for doing a good job."

She stopped herself, realising this might be turning into a self-pity rant.

"I know one thing," she said looking worriedly at her Uncle. "He doesn't seem to have any remorse for the women he raped, and I'm really afraid for the women he's kidnapped. I think this change in MO means he's capable of anything."

"Remember your training," warned Ronnie. "Getting emotional won't help anyone. Stay professional and treat the information as facts to be organised and analysed."

"I know," smiled Jenny. "Maintain a professional distance!"

Ronnie laughed. "Come on," he said. "We'll need to

rescue that husband of yours from Val and the washing up."

"Ok, but ask around your end for obvious similarities to any of your unsolved cases," said Jenny. "Reed disappeared for two years after he committed those rapes before turning up again to start kidnapping. I can't believe for a second that he's been an angel all that time, so he must have been elsewhere and I bet he's left a trail."

"Sure," said Ronnie winking at his niece. "I'll talk to a few DI's I know."

***

Arriving back home, Peter lifted a sleeping Lilly out of the BMW whilst Jenny turned her key in the front door and held it open as Peter carefully carried his daughter inside. Following him upstairs, she watched as he got Lilly ready for bed and lowered her little body onto the covers. It was still early, and the parents crept from the room to make their way back downstairs to the kitchen and a welcome glass of wine. Peter opened the fridge, taking out a half empty bottle of white. Jenny collected two glasses from a cupboard and they moved to the sitting room, where they collapsed onto the huge grey settee.

Peter poured. "That went well!" he said.

"I know, even Candy was complimentary in the end," and Jenny drained half the glass in one go.

"Lilly looks like she'll sleep for a week," said her husband.

Jenny smiled, "She loves seeing her cousins. I can't believe how much football she played."

The room was large and well furnished with a sleek black television dominating one wall. Jenny fancied herself as a budding interior designer and the pale grey walls contrasted with the deeper shades of the sofa and carpet, giving the room a feeling of opulence and calm. Fresh lilies stood in an impressive display on the table in the centre of the room and contemporary artwork hung from the three available walls.

Peter cradled his drink in his hands, spinning the wine around the glass. "How was Ronnie?" He asked. "Any good insights into your case?"

"Not really. He seemed as flummoxed as the rest of us." They sat in silence for a few moments before Jenny said, "Here we are, home at nine o'clock and talking about work!" She smiled. "Are we middle aged?"

Peter smiled back, taking the bait, "Not just yet," he said. "Fancy an early night?"

Jenny didn't answer. Putting her glass on the table she took his hand and stood up. Peter felt the tug and stood up too, the smile on his face giving way to desire. He put his hands on her waist and their lips met. Jenny felt familiar warmth grow in her stomach. She enjoyed his lips, exploring his tongue and pressing herself into him. They kissed, lost in each other's embrace and the moments passed slowly whilst they rediscovered their mutual love and understanding. Eventually, they separated, both breathing more quickly with lust growing uncontrollably between them. Peter led Jenny out of the room and they took the stairs, Jenny giggling as she allowed herself to be almost dragged up two steps at a time. Reaching the bedroom they kissed again hungrily, naturally relishing each other's familiar touch and enjoying the closeness of their bodies. Jenny broke off, "I'll use the bathroom first," she said, and Peter flopped down on the bed grinning.

After a few moments he kicked off his shoes and hearing the shower start he absent-mindedly picked up a remote control and the television flashed into life. Peter lay back on the bed, closing his eyes contentedly, happy with his life after two previous marriages had ended in pain and divorce. He'd put these failures down to obsessive work patterns and his drive and energy for success, but he knew in his heart that it was his own nature that had destroyed the trust that any marriage needs to survive. He'd left the second wreckage behind with the thought that he would never find anyone who'd understand him. True, he had met Jenny because she worked for him, but their relationship had quickly blossomed and if he believed in the cliché of love at first sight, then he knew it had definitely happened to her.

Jenny stepped back into the room naked, towelling her hair and Peter caught his breath as he watched her body move.

"Your turn?" she said from beneath the towel.

Peter rose from the bed to pass her in the doorway of the en-suite, pausing to kiss the back of her neck and run a finger up her spine, and enjoying her shudder of delight.

Jenny found a thin nightdress in the wardrobe and slipped it over her head before moving to the bed to wait for Peter's return. She could hear him hurriedly brushing his teeth, and she giggled to herself knowing that his trip to the bathroom would last no more than a few moments. Right on cue he burst naked into the room, almost hurling himself onto the bed, and the pair laughed as they kissed.

Then suddenly Jenny struggled away from her husband's embrace and sprang up into a sitting position. A bewildered Peter sat up too, only to see Jenny concentrating as if transfixed on the TV he'd switched on earlier. He followed her gaze to see what had cooled her enthusiasm so rapidly.

"What is it?" he asked irritably.

Jenny didn't answer but continued to stare at the screen, reaching for the remote to increase the volume. It was the local news and the reader was describing how a woman's body had been discovered dumped at the back of an industrial estate in Bury. It was a live feed from the scene and a white tent brightly lit from outside was visible in the background. The commentator said the Police hadn't yet released the identity of the victim.

"So?" said Peter, becoming more annoyed.

"I need to call Sam," said Jenny, lifting herself from the bed to reach for her mobile on the dressing-table. "See if this is connected to the case I'm working on."

Peter's frustration was beginning to spill over into anger. "What! Right now?"

Jenny ignored the question, already pressing to dial whilst turning to Peter to mouth a '*sorry.*'

Sam answered after just a single ring. "It's probably Dawn James," he said without preamble, his address book ID having identified the caller as Jenny. "Looks like she's been suffocated then dumped."

"Where?" asked Jenny, sounding irritated at the realisation that Sam hadn't been going to call her.

Sam didn't notice. "Chamberhall Street Industrial Estate. The body's been dumped with some rubbish at the back of one of the units. Some homeless guy was looking for a place to spend the night amongst the boxes and came across her instead."

"I'll be there in twenty minutes," said Jenny, already with her head in the wardrobe looking for jeans.

"No need," said Sam. "SOCO are all over the scene, and there'll be a briefing first thing."

Jenny was determined not be left on the fringes of the investigation. "I really would like to see the site," she said. "It'll help with the profiling."

"Ok," said Sam, and hung up.

Peter had slipped under the covers. "Is this really necessary?" he asked, and pointing to the television added, "They look in control to me."

Jenny was pulling a blue sweater over her head and driving her arms into the sleeves. "I've got to see where it happened," she said. "See how he dumped the body."

Peter watched her pull on socks and climb into black ankle boots. Five minutes ago she was relaxed and ready to make love, now she was flying out of the house like a ball of energy.

"They weren't even going to call," she said as she dressed. "I want them to respect me and realize they can do with my help."

"A woman's been found dead," said Peter. "Should you be this excited?"

Jenny was now fully dressed but his question stopped her in her tracks. She looked at Peter and they stared at each other for a moment. Then her face softened as she realized for the first time since she had sat bolt upright on the bed how Peter must feel - abandoned, even rejected.

"Shit!" she said. "Sorry, I just got caught up and didn't think."

She stood for a moment seeing the confusion and hurt in his eyes, but waiting for his approval, waiting for him to say it was ok for her to go.

Despite his frustration, he loved the fact that she was ambitious and the way her excitement seemed to re-charge her energy. He smiled happily, his face relaxing. "It's fine" he said. "There'll be other nights."

"Thanks." She said, feeling a bit like a naughty child.

"If you need to go, you need to go," he said reassuringly.

Jenny smiled back unconvincingly before leaning down to kiss her husband. "I love you," she said holding her face close to his, and she meant it.

"I love you too," said Peter and watched her dart out of the room, ready to get on with the job that was suddenly centre stage in her life.

Peter listened until he heard the front door bang and his wife's car spark to life before he retrieved his own mobile phone from the drawer at the side of the bed. Tapping in his password to bring the handset to life, he smiled at the sight of the three missed calls icon that greeted him.

Chapter 9

When Jenny pulled up at Chamberhall Street Industrial Estate she'd been expecting what greeted her - a myriad of pulsating blue lights, lending the scene an eerie stillness despite the white jump-suited figures coming and going amongst the police vehicles. The last streaks of day had all but faded from the sky, but the air was still warm; it was the kind of summer night when sounds can travel for miles. She could almost hear the echo of the journalists' feet and equipment moving in unison whenever someone who looked more important than just a bobby got within five feet of the barrier that held them back.

This was her first crime scene and she gave herself a moment to calm her emotions at the impending sight of the victim. On the drive over she'd tried to ignore the images that kept crowding into her mind, but now thoughts of Dawn James attended not by a loving husband or family, but by forensic scientists in white suits examining every inch of her violated body forced their way through and set her nerves on edge. She made an effort to control her feelings: the last thing she wanted was to show any weakness to Sam Bradbury, or worse the Chief. During her studies and afterwards whilst completing her forensic training in looking for clues, she'd seen bodies and examined some gruesome photographs, but now she was confronted with a real murder scene her stomach seemed to have pushed itself somewhere up near her throat.

She jumped at a knock on the passenger side window. It was Sam; in the gathering dark she hadn't seen him walk across to her car. She lowered the window and the detective leaned in.

"She's round the back," he said flatly.

"Are you sure it's Dawn James?" asked Jenny, finding her voice surprisingly steady.

"I responded to the call. I'm pretty sure from the photographs we have that it's her. Dental records will confirm it beyond doubt," he said, withdrawing his head.

As soon as Jenny got out of the car she had to struggle with her emotions again, and she was sure that her legs wouldn't carry her weight. She could feel herself shaking from the inside; the nerves prickled just beneath the surface of her skin, making her acutely aware of her movements, and she could feel her own clothes brushing against her body as she started forward. Sam was already walking toward the lights expecting her to follow, but as she did so her feet seemed weighted down, and she found herself making a conscious effort to take each step across the tarmac. The residual heat from the sun of the day was still a factor and she could feel beads of perspiration beginning to form on her face.

Jenny made an effort to clear her mind and find a source of professional detachment. As she drew closer to the scene she remembered her mentor Professor Alderman and tried to imagine what he would say to her as she approached. She thought of his general demeanour, unhurried and unflappable, and was beginning to feel steady and resolute by the time she'd caught up with Sam.

"You'll need to check in with the FDI," he said and guided her to the back of a white transit van marked Police Incident Unit. It was equipped with banks of computers and monitors and it took the sole occupant a few moments to turn and acknowledge Jenny's presence.

The Force Duty Inspector was immaculately turned out in an impossibly smart black uniform. His well-trimmed beard and carefully manicured fingernails signalled his attention to detail.

"Who are you?" he asked without introducing himself.

"Jenny Foster," she replied, without a hint of her recent anguish, and the FDI raised an eyebrow. He hit a few keys on the computer in front of him and Jenny could see that he had all her details immediately at his fingertips.

He gave his prepared speech. "I'm Force Duty Inspector Everett, and it's my job to log all activity at the scene," he said. "What is your function here tonight?"

Jenny paused for a moment, focusing on the question. "I'm profiling the offender."

Everett pointed to a box located on a shelf near the back doors.

"Shoe covers, a paper protective suit, a mouth mask and latex gloves," he said. "You'll have to wait until the Coroner and forensics team have finished with the immediate area around the body before you can get close."

"How long?" asked Jenny.

"They're almost done," he said. "I'll let you know." He turned back to his keyboard and Jenny climbed out of the van to join Sam who'd waited for her outside.

The pair watched as Chief Inspector Mark Ambrose bustled towards them across the car park. Sam seemed to grow half an inch when the Chief spoke to him, almost standing to attention.

"You took the call, Bradbury?" asked the Chief, already knowing the answer. "Did you follow procedure?"

"As soon as I saw her I called it in and waited for the support team."

"You say it's Dawn James?"

"Yes," said Sam. "The body's been placed and she's naked. It's not an accident."

The Chief turned to Jenny.

"Glad you're here," he said. "Have you seen her yet?"

His attitude had softened and Jenny wondered if it was because she was new on the team, or - God forbid! - because she was a woman. Either way she didn't like it: she wanted to be treated the same as everyone else.

"No, I'm waiting for the FDI to give me the go-ahead," she said.

"Ok," he said, eyeing her shrewdly. "Take as much time as you need, I'll make sure they don't move her until you've got all the information you can."

With that he climbed into the back of the van to check in.

Jenny caught Sam's eye and he shrugged, "Looks like you're more use here than me."

"I'm not sure about that," she said.

The Chief's head appeared from the back of the van, "Ok Jenny! You're clear," he told her, and disappeared back inside.

Jenny blew out a deep breath.

"You ok?" asked Sam.

"Yeah, I'm ready," she replied, annoyed that she'd shown him she was anything less than detached, and followed him up an alleyway at the side of the nearest unit. White paper-suited operatives from the forensics team were coming down the narrow passage the other way. There were six or seven of them, all with face masks pulled down below their chins, and all looking exhausted. Jenny didn't know whether to acknowledge their presence or not and was happy to follow anonymously behind Sam as he nodded a silent greeting to each in turn.

Her nerves were creeping back up to the surface of her skin, and she could feel the hairs stand on the back of her neck, sending deep shivers across her shoulders.

As they rounded the end of the passage the pair almost ran into a photographer. He was a short, dark-haired man with an obvious heavy-sweating problem, matting his hair and forming dark patches under his arms that almost joined in the middle of his chest; under the circumstances the light blue shirt he was wearing was a particularly unfortunate choice. He leapt back surprised at almost being upended by Sam, his eyes darting in all directions as he stepped to the side.

"Sam?" he said, nodding a greeting.

"Hi Paul," said Sam. "This is Jenny Foster. Jenny - Paul Short, the photographer."

Foster stilled his eyeballs for a second to fix them on

Jenny before quickly looking away, involuntarily raising his eyebrows.

"So you're the secret weapon everyone's been talking about?" he said.

Jenny was momentarily distracted by the fact that she was obviously the subject of conversation, perhaps even gossip.

"*Photographer* is a pretty narrow description of my job these days," he added.

"I've taken digital video of the body, digital stills and detailed the entry and exit tracks of the offender. I've also asked for a scale drawing of the scene."

"When can I see them?" asked Jenny in a cool professional tone.

"They'll be ready first thing."

"Thanks Paul," said Sam, and they moved on past him.

In front of them was a white tent lit from the inside, and as they covered the few steps to reach it Jenny could see the silhouette of its one live occupant. More reporters, some with TV cameras had made their way to the field at the back of the estate and Jenny realised this was the perspective she'd seen on television. When they both stopped outside the tent she was suddenly acutely aware that she was probably going out to the nation live. Standing on the clear plastic sheeting that obviously marked the perimeter of the sterile scene, the pair silently proceeded to pull on paper suits, fumble with blue plastic shoe covers and snap on latex gloves before fixing on face masks by stretching the elastic stays around their ears. Jenny stepped inside first, with Sam close behind.

She glanced at the body lying on the floor, but couldn't face it yet and immediately turned away. Instead she focused her attention on the figure wearing an identical white paper suit to her own, but with the addition of the word CORONER in thick set letters on the back. He turned as they entered.

"I'm Jenny Foster, attached to the Serious Crime Squad," she said, extending her hand.

He didn't take it. "No offence you understand," he explained. "I don't want to contaminate the gloves just now."

Jenny sensed he was smiling behind his paper mask and she dropped her hand, smiling sheepishly in return and seething at herself for the obvious rookie mistake.

The coroner turned to Sam, "Hello Sam, how's the family doing?" he asked in his broad Scottish accent

"Good thanks, Frasier we should all get together again soon."

The coroner turned his gaze back to Jenny, "Frasier O'Connor," he said by way of introduction, "Chief Medical Examiner with the Coroner's Office."

Frasier was a tall man, and judging by the amount of grey encroaching on his sandy hair probably in his mid-fifties. His leisure time had obviously been disturbed by the call to attend the body, as Jenny noticed he was wearing trainers under the blue plastic protectors with the edges of grey jogging pants peeping from the bottom of his white suit. Jenny found herself faintly annoyed that she didn't already know him.

"What can you tell us?" she asked without further preamble.

"Well she's been dead around five hours I'd say," said O'Connor.

"So, time of death about six o'clock this evening?" asked Sam.

The coroner nodded, his flop of hair bouncing with enthusiasm. "On first impressions, she died from asphyxiation," he continued, leaning down to the body. "But I'll be able to confirm that back at the morgue."

Jenny's eyes followed him down, and for the first time she allowed herself to take in the full extent of the victim's plight. Dawn James was completely naked, lying on her back with her arms folded across her body, one on top of the other. Her eyes were closed and her blackened tongue protruded from between swollen purple lips. Jenny could see ligature marks cutting almost to the bone on both wrists and ankles, and a thick angry red line around her neck. More red lines spread across her cheeks, extending from the corners of her lips. The body was emaciated and covered in bruises and small scratches, and there were what looked to Jenny like carpet burns on her forehead and chin. Comparing her with the most recent photographs supplied by her husband, she had lost a lot of weight and Jenny thought that she couldn't have weighed more than a hundred pounds as she lay there. A bloodless cut stood just below the hairline on the left side of her temple; it was raised and crusty with puss and had obviously remained untreated for some time.

"It would seem she was suffocated with a plastic bag," said O'Connor, as if he were describing the contents of his office drawer. "The type with a draw-string pulled tight; that would explain the fresh mark around her neck….see?"

He pushed the victim's head from side to side to let Jenny see the extent of the marks. Dawn's head moved stiffly and her expression remained fixed, like a doll.

"She wasn't killed here, mind," he continued. "This body's been washed
post-mortem, then wrapped in plastic sheeting before being dumped."

Jenny was listening to O'Connor but her mind felt detached from her body. She couldn't take her eyes off the victim's face. The skin washed and clean was white and smooth as alabaster and her dark hair fell with grotesque neatness onto the skeletal shoulders.

She forced herself to concentrate. "Any sign of sexual abuse?" she asked with an effort to keep the nerves out of her voice.

"It would seem so, yes. But I'll know more once we get her back to the lab," said Connor.

Jenny bent down for a better look at the ligature marks; they were deep and jagged, extending inches up the wrist.

"I reckon she was bound for some time. This cut on her forehead….it looks about two weeks old and it was inflicted with enough force to knock her out," went on O'Connor. "It wasn't cleaned or dressed at the time, which explains the mess it's made of her forehead."

"So that's how he subdued her when she was kidnapped?" asked Sam.

"I can't speculate on that, but it's likely I suppose," replied O'Connor. "She's had two front teeth chipped and the lines on her cheeks probably indicate that she was gagged for a long period too."

"Anything else?" asked Jenny, wildly speculating that O'Connor might say, *yeah, we found the murderer's wallet in her hand full of ID.*

Instead he put his gloved hand on one of the victim's shoulders and the other at the top of her leg and turned her half over.

"Note the lumbar area here."

Jenny shifted to see where the coroner was indicating and could clearly make out the figure *1* burnt into the soft skin at the base of Dawn James' back. It was large, angry and red. The mark stared back at Jenny as if imploring her to realize the pain that Dawn had endured to receive it.

Sam saw it too and caught Jenny's eye with a quizzical look.

"Was she…?" asked Sam.

"Alive when this was done to her?" asked O'Connor, sensing Sam's disgust. "I'm afraid she was, yes. The tissue scarring around the burn looks pretty recent - maybe a couple of weeks old, similar to the cut on the forehead. But again, I'll know more once I get her on the table."

"What did he use to burn her?" asked Jenny, fighting the nausea that was beginning to alter the timbre of her voice.

The coroner traced the scar with his gloved index finger. "It's fairly uniform in width," he said, and the scar tissue flexed like play-doh when he touched it, making Sam wince.

"That's been carved, rather than branded - see!" said

O'Connor, pointing out how the scar extended slightly outside the figure itself. "Note how he's had to stop at the base of the number and at the top too? He's repositioned whatever tool was used several times to create that shape."

The coroner paused, letting his finger rest at the top of the scar. "I suppose it could have been done with the back of a hot knife or something like that," he said.

Jenny and Sam shifted uncomfortably almost in unison.

"I'm just about done here now," said O'Connor, carefully arranging the body in its original position. "If you're finished too, I'll get this moved back to the lab." Jenny continued to stare at Dawn James' lifeless form, suddenly uneasy that the arms placed across the victim's chest had remained stiffly in place throughout the procedure of turning the body. Eventually shaking her mind free, she retrieved a small note book and pencil from her pocket.

"Just a few minutes," she said through another wave of nausea, and began making notes.

The Coroner and Sam stood watching in silence as Jenny scribbled furiously. After a few minutes she stopped writing, indicating that she was finished, and Dr O'Connor summoned the gurney to transport Dawn James to the morgue. Jenny and Sam left the tent and made their way back up the passage to the front of the units. After checking themselves off the scene with the FDI they stood for a few minutes watching the body being loaded into a waiting ambulance. The coroner climbed wearily in behind it. Sam took a packet of Marlboro from his pocket and taking one himself offered Jenny the chance of a smoke, which she gladly accepted.

She drew in the first drag and her body instantly relaxed. Suddenly her knees felt weakened and she found herself examining her shoes, with her other hand rubbing her forehead.

"Tough to see your first body?" asked Sam.

"Not as tough as not seeing her," said Jenny, unable to disguise her annoyance that Sam wouldn't have called had she not called him first.

"I didn't think," said Sam without a hint of apology, and there was a silence between them as they stood smoking heavily.

The night was still warm and with the evacuation of the body most of the police cars and the FDI's Incident Unit quickly disappeared, leaving a few uniformed officers behind to maintain the integrity of the crime scene. SOCO would return to finish their work at the site with the benefit of daylight. The reporters took to their cars and TV vans to file behind the ambulance and follow the body of Dawn James to the hospital morgue where she would face the inquiring scalpel of Dr Frasier O'Connor.

"The coroner mentioned your family?" Jenny said, taking the chance to change the subject amidst the droning engines.

Sam looked at her through a haze of smoke. "Yeah, a wife and two boys, eight and ten," he said almost automatically.

"I've a daughter, Lilly," Jenny volunteered, sensing she wouldn't be asked. "How does your wife feel about you being a policeman?"

Sam looked down at the ground, it was obviously a problem. "Vanessa?" he said. "She likes the overtime money I bring in."

Another silence followed, this one a little more uncomfortable than the last.

"Any leads from the person who found Dawn James?" asked Jenny dropping her cigarette to the floor to stand on it, extinguishing its red glow.

"We've got him down at Bury Station," said Sam. "I didn't need to take him in, but he's homeless and just happy to have a bed for the night. I'm going to speak to him now."

"Mind if I tag along?" asked Jenny.

Sam glanced at her.

"Ok, follow me," he said and grinding out his cigarette underfoot headed off across the car park.

***

Bury Police Station was a mile or so from the industrial estate. Sam had driven quickly, Jenny following close behind, and with the time now fast approaching midnight they encountered little traffic. The station itself was small, old fashioned and in urgent need of a lick of paint. The Duty Sergeant signed them both through, saying that a PC would bring up the witness from the cells. They were ushered in to the only interview room, occupying the two seats at one side of a small, well- used desk. Presently a PC led the witness into the room with a broad grin, "He's all yours," he said.

The man sat down opposite. It was impossible to tell how old he was; anywhere between forty-five and sixty would have been Jenny's guess. He was dressed in filthy jeans with black lace-less boots. Despite the heat he wore a shirt, jumper and a huge thick coat; probably his only possessions and all filthy.

"What's your name?" asked Sam.

The homeless man gazed at them both across the desk and the extended silence made Jenny shift in her chair.

"Got any fags?" he asked eventually in a lazy drawl.

His breath was a mixture of mayonnaise and stale tobacco with a hint of alcohol thrown in and Jenny felt her stomach lurch in revulsion as the odour filled the space between them.

Sam bored his eyes into the man's until he looked away. "Name?" he asked again.

"John," said the man.

"John what?"

"Dillinger," he said, looking past Sam to the door.

"What? The gangster?" asked Sam, becoming irritated.

"I'm not a suspect here," said the witness. "I don't appreciate being locked in a cell."

"They left the door *unlocked*, and you're free to leave at any time. What were you doing at Chamberhall?"

"Looking for a doss."

"Did you see anything other than the body?"

"No, I didn't! I just saw her lying there. She wasn't moving so I walked down to the pub and Edna the landlady called you."

"So you didn't notice she was naked?" asked Sam, leaning forward and raising one eyebrow to ram home the question.

At that moment the witness's body language changed and it was obvious that there was about to be a shift in the conversation. He knew from experience that he could easily move from witness to suspect in any crime at any moment.

Straightening up in his chair, he adjusted his clothing, his shoulders visibly tensing and his head becoming slightly more erect. Sam had his attention.

"No it was going dark behind the units," he said.

"Name?" asked Sam - only this time he meant it.

"John Albright."

"Date of birth?"

Albright reeled off the dates without any more fuss and scribbling the details down on a piece of paper Sam disappeared out of the room. Albright looked at Jenny, and deciding she wasn't a threat returned to his rehearsed slouched position. Jenny couldn't believe he was only forty.

Sam came back a few minutes later breaking the silence. "You're quite well known to the Police aren't you John?" he asked as he sat down.

Albright remained silent, but again snapped upright in his chair, his right leg dancing nervously.

"How old was she exactly?" asked Sam and watched as the bomb went off in Albright's mind, showing immediately in his hairy face.

Sam turned to Jenny. "He's a real nice guy this one," he said nodding over at Albright. "Likes them young. Under fourteen is his preference."

Jenny remained silent, watching Albright squirm in his chair. '*Bastard,*' she thought.

"That was a long time ago," muttered Albright.

"Or you've just got good at hiding your tracks these days?" suggested Sam.

In the silence that followed Jenny watched Albright's shoulders droop; he looked even older now than when the PC had first brought him in.

"Did you see anyone dump the body?" asked Sam.

"No, but I saw a white van parked when I went round the back," said Albright resignedly.

"What time was that?"

Albright pulled up both sleeves to indicate the absence of a watch and shrugged.

"Did you go straight to the pub?" asked Jenny, trying to keep the excitement out of her voice.

Albright shifted in his chair, eyeing his two inquisitors. "Pretty much," he said. "The van left the car-park just after I walked out."

"Do you remember the number plate?" asked Sam nonchalantly.

"No," said Albright. "I didn't look."

Jenny and Sam eyed each other in disappointment.

Albright paused for a moment. "There was one thing though," he said.

"What?" asked Sam.

"The van had red paint on the bumper, like it had been in an accident."

"Ok, thanks," said Sam. Then he gestured to Jenny and they both left the room.

"Take a detailed statement and let him sleep in the cells tonight," Sam told the Custody Sergeant, adding, "And give him a decent breakfast before he goes."

Standing outside the station Sam and Jenny lit more cigarettes and stood in silence for a few moments.

"You'd have thought he'd be happy to help without the need for that performance." said Jenny.

"I used to think the same sort of thing," offered Sam. They smoked in silence for a while longer.

"Look, you'll realise pretty quickly that everyone in this situation is a potential suspect and that no-one wants to get involved," said Sam, "It's natural. Nobody wants to get caught up with the Police, and they definitely don't want to end up on the Nine O'clock News as suspect number one when they've nothing to do with it."

"I'm going to get some sleep," said Jenny.

"Ok, good luck with that," replied Sam, grinding out his own cigarette and moving off toward his car. "See you tomorrow."

***

By the time Jenny pulled in to her drive it was after one and she was exhausted. She looked up to see the bedroom light still on, and she knew that though Peter wouldn't dream of calling her at work, he would have waited up for her as long as he could. She switched off her engine and found herself sitting there for a few minutes. She was sure that the second her head hit the pillow she'd be dead to the world and she wanted a few moments to gather her thoughts.

She realised how important it was to see her home as just that - a home. As with any other job, she needed to leave the stresses and strains behind and use her home as a place of sanctuary. She mentally made herself a promise there and then to try always to leave the troubles of a case she was working on in the car, and not take them through the front door. She wanted to enjoy her marriage, her life and her daughter as a normal wife and mother, and she realised just how difficult that would be if she took her work into her sanctuary. She was already resigned to the fact that the image of Dawn James' body lying naked and broken on the ground behind the industrial unit would stay with her for life, but she was determined that she wouldn't let the *killer* affect her happiness too. "It's just a job," she said out loud to herself. All the same, she knew she sounded like someone trying to convince themselves of something, rather than voicing a certainty.

She forced herself to get out of her car and went up the drive and through the front door. There were no sounds from upstairs and she guessed that Peter must have lost his battle with sleep and ended his vigil. She mounted the stairs and looked in on Lilly, who was sleeping like a starfish. Her skin glistened with childish sweat in the heat of her room and Jenny found herself involuntarily smiling for the first time since she had left the house earlier in the evening, even though her upturned mouth sat uneasily on her face. In the bedroom that Jenny shared with Peter he was lying on his stomach snoring gently. He looked peaceful enough, and she hoped he'd dropped off quickly after she left. The fact that the TV was on with the sound off was a good sign, as he'd obviously succumbed to sleep without realising it.

Jenny undressed in the main bathroom so that she wouldn't wake her husband, and then brushed her teeth and showered before easing herself onto the bed. She avoided Peter's sleeping position before turning out the lights and TV using the switch by her bed and carefully sliding the remote from beneath his shoulder blade. Leaning over, she kissed her husband on the back of his head and closed her eyes ready for sleep, her whole body tense and aching with exhaustion.

***

Jenny bent over Dawn James, her hand reaching out to stroke the woman's cheek and offer comfort. The ice cold feel of the skin didn't seem to bother her, and she leant closer to the face, wanting answers. The woman's lips were red and her freshly made up eyelids looked peaceful. Jenny traced a line around the face looking for memories, searching for answers. Suddenly the eyes snapped open, staring into her own. She could see all the pain and despair, all the horrors that the victim had suffered mirrored in those cloudy blue orbs.

***

Jenny awoke sweating, panic gripping her chest. The nightmare was still vivid in her mind and all she could see was the expression in Dawn James' eyes burning into hers. She realised that her face was wet with tears and her hands were trembling when she put them to her own lips to stop herself crying out. Looking at the clock beside her bed she realised that she'd slept for no more than half an hour.

Almost four sleepless hours later, she was still staring at the red digits of the alarm clock slowly changing the minutes into new hours. The pallid face of Dawn James drifted back into her mind every time she closed her eyes and she was angry at herself; angry that she couldn't stop her job affecting her personally and angry that the murderer had already won Round One. Frustrated and exhausted, she found herself getting out of bed, creeping downstairs and settling into her study to pore over the case files again. The promise to herself to keep her home as a sanctuary against the horrors of her new job had already been forgotten.

Chapter 10

Number 63 Cathcart Street looked quiet from the road. An end of terrace, it was the only house in the street to boast a garage attached to the side, the outbuilding occupying most of the overgrown grass and weeds that served as a garden. The garage had a metal up-and-over green door that hadn't seen a lick of paint in several decades, but it served its purpose: it was easily large enough to hide Joe Reed's van, and he could come and go as he pleased with no interference.

Despite their close proximity, the neighbours seldom saw the occupant of the house and there were no milk or paper deliveries to indicate that anyone actually lived there. The curtains, if windowlene pink sheets nailed up to frames can be described as such, were never open and a cursory glance through the letterbox would have revealed piles of free newspapers and unread junk mail lying in thick dust and grime on the indescribably coloured threadbare carpet. The postman didn't often need to negotiate the two steps from the pavement to the elevated front door, except when he pushed a brown padded envelope through it every two weeks; always the same style envelope and always on a Monday - unremarkable to the neighbours or even the ever changing postman himself, but vital for the occupant of the house. Had the postman stopped to think or care about his round, he might have thought it strange that this house never received a postcard, an electricity bill or even a letter from Readers Digest. But the postal service in Oldham was manned by immigrants, happy to work on short-term temporary contracts for the minimum wage, and they worked hard to hold down their jobs and care for their families. The actual content or quality of the letters and packages they delivered was irrelevant.

The street itself was only around sixty percent occupied, with more than the odd house boarded up or blacked out in the aftermath of an arson attack or rejected insurance claim. Developers and speculators would never choose to move in on this area of Greater Manchester, preferring instead to concentrate on building blocks of architecturally insipid flats in Manchester City Centre, selling them as 'apartments' and offering the lifestyle synonymous with that euphemistic name.

Joe Reed sat inside, untroubled by any such ambition. He felt sick. He'd thrown up where he sat - more than once. Vomit stained his red polo shirt and cream trousers, his brown loafers standing in an acidic pool that had gathered at his feet. The acrid smell as he bent over to add to the mess by emptying the foul saliva from his mouth didn't seem to penetrate his psyche at all. He stared down at the pool, with his dead eyes betraying little thought or emotion. The colour of the carpet on which the single wooden chair stood was defined by numerous stains and patches of filth; the once cream walls were furred with greenish mould, and optimistic spiders occupied every corner of the ceiling. A bare bulb glowed from the light fitting in the centre of the ceiling above Joe's head, bouncing light off the material hastily nailed to the window, and bathing the room in an unnatural pink glow.

The house lay silent as Joe Reed stared at the floor with glassy, unfocused eyes. All he could see was the face of Dawn James as he lowered her to the ground, lifeless behind the industrial units on the Chamberhall Estate. He'd bathed her and washed and brushed her hair before crossing her arms over her chest and wrapping her in plastic to protect her naked body from prying eyes. He'd placed her on the ground very carefully, as if she were a china doll that might shatter at any moment, and then stared at her lying there for a full five minutes before approaching footsteps made him dart down a passage, back into his van and away from the scene. If it hadn't been for the intrusion he thought he might still be standing there now; just watching her, expecting her to move.

When he'd laid her out on the hard concrete, he was sure that she would open her eyes and say something. Shout at him maybe, or at least plead with him; anything but silence. She looked beautiful too, her breasts firm upon her body and her thighs shaping down to her ankles, and Joe Reed was sorry she was dead; sorry that he had obeyed his instructions and let the life flow from her. Even now when he remembered how she felt beneath him as he pushed his way into her he couldn't help but feel his manhood stir inside his rotten trousers. He hated himself for it; hated himself now even more than he had ever hated Dan or his mother or anyone else for that matter.

As he sat, he began to shake, despite the sweltering heat of the room. The hot, trapped air felt like razors in his throat. Each time he took some in it didn't seem to be enough to fill his lungs and he kept it prisoner for as long as he could before blowing it out hard from his nostrils. Looking down he noticed his hands but they seemed as if they didn't belong to him. He couldn't feel his fingers, couldn't imagine how to move them. There were no visible signs that he had ever touched Dawn James; no blood or scratches, but he could see them on her and feel her in his arms, still feel the weight of her body imprinted on his limbs. His thoughts turned in on himself and he felt a deep sorrow, the questions that were ever present in his mind surging forward yet again.

Why do I have to do what he tells me?

Why can't I live a normal life?

Why has nobody ever loved me?

Why can't I love anyone else?

Joe Reed began to cry, and then weep until his whole body shook uncontrollably with the effort. He wept until his nose bubbled and his eyes streamed into the mess already at his feet. He didn't think he would ever stop until finally the tears gave way to huge, gut wrenching sobs that juddered and settled, then juddered again.

An electronic *PING* from the laptop upstairs in the bedroom jerked him out of himself and back into the room. He shook his head to try and free himself of his emotion and stood up. Dizziness immediately set in and he gripped the back of the solitary chair to steady himself. His legs felt like dead weights and he looked toward the open door and imagined the stairs beyond, not knowing how he would find the strength to take them. Another *PING*, this time with an imagined impatience.

Joe Reed lifted one foot and then the other from the gluey mess that surrounded his feet and staggered toward the door, kicking pizza boxes and greying chip-shop wrappers across the carpet as he went. He held onto the door frame for a moment, before almost falling to the banister rail at the bottom of the stairs; like a man finding solid islands in a furious sea. He looked up the stairs that seemed like a mountain to climb, his dizziness making the first few steps shift in and out of focus, the top a distant blur. He collapsed to the floor, but then yet another loud, angry-sounding *PING* brought him to his feet. He started up the stairs, one at a time, gripping the well-worn handrail as though it was the only thing stopping him falling into an abyss. The more stairs he took, the dizzier he felt and half way up he looked back into what seemed like a ravine. On he went again, the effort of taking each step making him breathe harder, compounding his dizziness. At last he reached the top and fell onto the filthy up-stairs carpet, its dust and stench filling his lungs. Feeling as though he'd just completed an epic journey, he raised himself up and staggered down the passage-way and into his bedroom where the open laptop sat waiting on the desk. He slumped into the chair and stared at the screen, then lifted his hand to the mouse and clicked on the new message icon.

The first message read, "Well Done Ed! She deserved all she got. Did you leave her as directed?"

Wearily he typed a reply. "Yes, behind the industrial units on the Chamberhall."

An instant reply came back. "Ok, good! You did well. The world won't miss a bitch like her. Now read the other messages I sent and let me know that you understand them."

Joe Reed typed again a simple, "Ok."

He waited for a few seconds to see if there would be a reply and when he was sure there wouldn't be, he closed down the conversation and clicked on the second message. It was a video file. He double clicked on the icon and waited for it to load.

The film began to play, revealing footage of a woman walking along a road. The woman looked a lot like Dawn James and Joe Reed momentarily froze, thinking that she'd somehow walked away from the industrial estate and was on the way here to his house. He glanced around the room, momentarily thrown into a panic, but then looking back at the screen he slowly realised it was a different woman. Her hair was dark, about the same length as Dawn's had been, and she walked with a spring in her step as if she didn't have a care in the world. The video had been taken on a warm day and the woman wore a red skirt ending just above her knees and a pair of flip flops adorned with glasslike jewels. He could see pink bra straps competing with the shoulder straps of her white vest top, and she looked to be in her mid-thirties, good-looking and confident. He was transfixed as he watched her walk effortlessly along, sometimes obscured by trees and sometimes by the pillar of the car door that the camera was obviously behind. She definitely looked like Dawn

James, and confusion set in as he realised that she also looked like Robyn Cox, who he instantly remembered was still a prisoner in the basement two floors below. But most of all she reminded him of his mother, Jane and he instantly felt hate and repulsion for the woman on the screen. The car was moving slowly behind her on the opposite side of the road with the zoom set at maximum for most of the film. The video lasted no more than five minutes and when it ended he noticed the title *Sharon Daly*.

He clicked next on the third message, which held a number of files.

The first was a 'text only' document with Sharon Daly's personal information, including her home address and the address of a pub called the Rose and Crown in Whitefield where she apparently worked; the second was a week-long account of her movements. The detail of the diary was impressive, with each movement painstakingly recorded with an associated time. The format was hour by hour, set into the days of the week with entries as mundane as 'Wednesday 3pm left the house and walked to the Spar shop on the corner of Derby Street, returning home with two bags at 3.24pm. Bags look full of cans of beer.'

There was also a highlighted entry appearing five times on separate days that read '6.20pm leaves the house and walks down the road entering Whitefield Common at 6.26pm. Walks along the path that skirts the outside of the common until exits the common at 6.34pm. Walks up Glanbourne Street and then onto Manchester Road arriving at The Rose and Crown at 6.50pm. Shift starts at 7pm.'

The third file contained maps of the house and Whitefield Common, sourced through the internet, together with Google Earth images of the house, the common, each road that the journey involved and the pub itself.

The fourth and final file was marked INSTRUCTIONS and set out exactly how and when to intercept the woman whilst she was on Whitefield Common. There were also details of where to park and information about a hole in the fence that Joe Reed should use to get her from the common and into the van without much risk of being seen.

He started to type a message, "What has she done?"

"She's a bitch and deserves to be punished."

"Why does she?" he typed.

The next message was simply entitled BITCH, with a new video attached.

Joe Reed clicked on the icon to start the film.

Sharon Daly was in a Tesco car park with a man, presumably her husband and a boy, probably their son. It was a different kind of day from in the first film. The weather was cooler and Sharon had on jeans and a denim jacket, her hair scraped back into a pony-tail revealing hardened features. Her husband was a big man with a shaven head, wearing a Manchester City replica shirt and faded denim jeans. His massive frame was accentuated by a huge gut that made the shirt he was wearing ride up in the front to reveal his belly button. The son looked about ten or eleven, and wore a replica shirt like his dad's, and also the team shorts and socks. The boy looked dirty; his hair was unkempt and Joe Reed could tell from his body language that he obviously didn't want to be there. Head down, he was a few feet away from his parents, clearly reluctant to join them.

Sharon Daly started shouting at him, and although there was no sound to accompany the action Joe Reed watched with his anger rising as the target of her abuse stood saying nothing, recoiling from the onslaught. Sharon closed the short distance between her and her son and leaned into his face to make her point, grabbing at the boy's arm and shaking him roughly. The man standing behind the pair took over the inquisition and quickly lost his temper. His son looked pitifully small as he stood trembling in the shadow of this giant of a man and repeatedly shook his head without making eye contact. The father looked incensed to the point of madness and grabbed the boy by the scruff of the neck, slapping him on the back of his legs once, twice, three times; each time lifting the boy into the air with the force of the blows.

Sharon Daly stood by barely interested in the plight of her son, it was obviously a regular occurrence and when the man let go of him she barely gave her son time to wipe away his tears before pushing him toward the supermarket doors. The boy stumbled from the force of his mother's push, ending up almost falling over, and the camera zoomed in to catch him wailing with what looked like fear and pain. The film ended on a still of the child's shocked and tear-stained face.

Joe Reed's face contorted and he stared silently at the screen for a few moments longer before he typed a single word, WHEN?

TOMORROW came the reply.

Joe Reed sat back and breathed a heavy sigh. The boy's face still staring back at him from the screen of his laptop reminded him of the look that must have been etched on his own face when he was a child at the hands of Dan, and hatred burned inside him.

Chapter 11

Huddled in her yellow Vauxhall Vectra Paula Tripp had slept very little. She climbed from her makeshift bed in the back of the car and into the driver's seat, rubbing her eyes and feeling every one of her thirty eight years. She yawned loudly, stretching her arms and legs against the onset of cramp and wrinkling her nose against the smell of her own breath. A pizza box on the passenger seat still contained a congealing piece of deep-pan pepperoni, its garlicky staleness competing with the dubious odours consistent with a night spent in the car. Paula's grey trousers were heavily crumpled and there were large patches of dried deodorant under the armpits of her salmon pink shirt. Blonde hair, cut into a sharp bob with an angular fringe, made her blue eyes stand out with a piercingly fierce intelligence in no way dulled by her lack of make-up. Fixing her gaze on the house in front of her, Paula absent-mindedly picked up a polyfoam beaker of coke and put the straw to her lips. Her face puckered with distaste as she sucked in the warm, lifeless liquid, and it was an effort to swallow.

After staking out Jenny Foster at the tiny Bury police station the night before, she'd decided to follow the profiler back to what she assumed was her house. She could have joined the caravan of journalists heading for the hospital morgue, but she didn't see the point; her years of experience told her that no-one there was likely to tell her anything she didn't already know. She also reasoned that she'd be met with a wall of silence if she tackled Frasier O'Connor, the hard-boiled coroner. As always, she'd been pleased with her performance. It wasn't easy to follow someone in the dead of night when there were no other cars on the road, especially when you were stalking them in a shiny yellow beacon that could be spotted from half a mile away. *Stupid choice* she thought, not for the first time, of the brand new car she'd privately started to call her yellow submarine.

Tripp switched on the state of the art black radio fixed to the underside of the glove compartment and tuned in to the police frequency. She listened to the usual assortment of officers already responding to mundane tasks and traffic incidents and glanced at her watch. It was six o'clock, and spots of rain began to spatter on the windscreen. Paula Tripp was well known for her expertise in staking-out a possible story. In her capacity as a journalist on the Manchester Evening News she had achieved everlasting fame as the hack that uncovered the whole truth about a local football celebrity who was supposedly battering his wife. She'd even managed to sell on the story to papers all over the world eager to dish the dirt on an otherwise spotless giant of the game.

Little did her fellow journalists know, but she'd sat outside the target's house for twelve consecutive nights, taking long-lens shots or climbing the walls and creeping through the manicured gardens, careful to avoid the CCTV cameras, to get more intimate shots through the windows. Regularly rifling through the bins wasn't a problem either before her hard-work eventually unearthed the *evidence* she needed to run the story. The fact that the fall from grace of her target was based on skilfully managed rumour, backed up with grainy pictures of the couple arguing in their own front room wasn't Tripp's concern. Once the story went national, the footballer's marriage had broken up pretty quickly, with Tripp and her fellow vultures gloating over this as concrete evidence that the story must have been true. Truth was a commodity that was there to be manipulated rather than proven, and consequences were for others to worry about. Paula Tripp saw herself as a beacon of light in an otherwise black and corrupt world. If there was any dirt on Jenny Foster, she would find it.

She sat there for almost two hours, passing the time listening to the police frequency, with Radio 4 on low as background to catch-up with the day's news. The rain had turned from spots to a curtain of fine summer drizzle; it was already warm outside and the car windscreen steamed up to the point where she needed to switch on her blowers from time to time to clear the glass. The house where Jenny had parked her car in the drive had a name, not a number: the Paddock. This part of Manchester was home to the more affluent members of society and Tripp wondered where the money came from. She didn't need to wait too long for her answer. She had a vantage point through the trees to the front of the house and, as she noted in her diary, at 7.57am the solid-wood, gothic style door swung open and a man stepped out, fully dressed and obviously ready for a day at work. He was wearing a neat blue two-piece suit, blue patterned tie and white shirt, and Tripp fancied she could see his shoes gleaming from where she sat. Eagerly picking up her camera, she took a series of snaps as he walked across the front of the house to where the double garage door was already raising itself in anticipation of his use. The man didn't seem to notice the rain as he sauntered down the smoothly paved path before disappearing inside to emerge a few moments later at the wheel of an expensive looking black Jaguar XJ6.

The car moved slowly as he turned right out of the gravel drive and glided past Tripp's yellow Vauxhall where she'd slid down beneath the dashboard to give the car the appearance of being empty. Paula Tripp sat up and exhaled hard once she was sure the Jaguar had passed. She couldn't believe her eyes: the man was Peter Foster.

***

The yellow Vauxhall had long since driven off by the time Jenny Foster stepped out of the house with a final wave goodbye to her daughter Lilly. The two year old was clinging to the hand of the new au pair who had started working on a trial basis the week before in preparation for Jenny's new job. To Jenny's relief the young woman had proved herself more than capable of caring for the child whilst both parents pursued their respective careers.

Manchester Police Head Quarters off Oldham Road

on the opposite side of the city centre was about twenty minutes' drive from home; Jenny was at her desk before nine, and soon after she got in the Chief came striding towards her across the crowded room already packed with chattering detectives clacking away at keyboards. It seemed to Jenny as if the other officers had been there all night; they even seemed to be wearing the same clothes she'd seen them in yesterday. Jenny herself felt decidedly over-dressed, with the black Chanel trouser suit she'd chosen to wear beginning to feel like a mistake. She'd loved it when she and Peter first saw it in the window of one of the more expensive Manchester boutiques. Once she'd tried it on, her husband was so keen to buy it for her that she'd felt obliged to accept the gift with graceful thanks, along with the feeling that she'd really been given no option. This was the reason why the over-priced garment had been hanging in her wardrobe for the best part of a year, unworn and still bearing its original tags. She'd made the excuse that something so special would only be appropriate for exactly the right occasion. Well, she thought ruefully, this morning wasn't it.

"Morning, Jenny," said the Chief, not stopping for a reply as he dropped a brown folder on her desk. "This is the Coroner's Report on Dawn James." She nodded in answer. "I've scheduled a briefing at midday for all the major players; see what you can come up with to help."

"Ok," said Jenny, fingering the file.

"Are you ok?" he asked. "It can be tough seeing your first body."

"First?" asked Jenny, looking up.

The Chief smiled, "Take your time to look over the notes. Talk to Sam and see if there's anything you can add to the briefing."

As he strode off across the office the dead face of Dawn James and the sights Jenny had witnessed the night before came crowding back into her head. She had eventually managed no more than three hours' sleep, and then she'd dragged herself out of bed feeling light-headed and almost convinced it had all been a bad dream. Since then the profiler's mind had insulated itself against the horror and refused to let conscious thoughts pick at the memory - until now, that was. She opened the folder and saw the first page of the Coroner's Report, with the evocative word *deceased* stamped under Dawn James' name, and then Sam's voice suddenly broke into her train of thought.

"The husband is in an interview room down the hall if you want a word with him. I've taken a formal statement and he says he knows nothing and can't understand why anyone would want to harm his wife. I think he's honest enough. His story's held up as true from start to finish and we've been with him since his wife first disappeared. He's pretty shattered after visiting the morgue to identify the body, so go easy!"

"Ok, I'll have a word with him," said Jenny, almost in a trance. She made her way across the room, down the corridor and into the interview room without remembering a single step of the journey.

Robert James was an unremarkable man. He looked average in every way -height, weight, some hair loss at the temples. When Jenny arrived he was still shaking, gripping onto the handle of a white mug which no longer contained any liquid and staring at the table. The PC standing in full uniform by the door gave Jenny a cursory nod as she came into the room and occupied the chair opposite the obviously devastated husband of the victim.

"Hello, Mr. James, I'm Jenny Foster. I'm a criminal profiler here," she said by way of introduction.

James stood up straight and held out his hand. His face was fixed in a stare that pleaded for her to accept the gesture, as if this sign of normality would somehow keep him from collapsing altogether. Jenny rose from her chair, took his hand in hers and shook it slowly, putting her other hand on Robert's elbow in a futile show of support.

"I'm so sorry for your loss," she said.

The hand-shake lasted a second or two longer than was necessary and then they both sat down noisily, scraping their chairs over the grey paint on the hard concrete floor.

"I told Detective Bradbury everything I could remember," said Robert James and he began reciting the day of his wife's abduction almost robotically. "We got up at 7.30 as usual to get Martin, that's our son, ready for school. Nothing seemed unusual and we…"

Jenny waved her hand stopping him in mid-sentence.

"Yes, I've read the report on the abduction," she said, her mind clearing to focus on the job.

Robert James looked stunned and vulnerable.

"Had anyone been following you or your wife prior to her disappearance, Mr James?" the profiler asked, seemingly unaware that her witness was breaking down as she spoke.

Robert James furrowed his brow. "Following us?" he asked. "Not that I'd noticed."

"No unusual cars in the road? Deliveries you weren't expecting or people you haven't seen before at the school?" asked Jenny.

"Dawn takes…" he stopped to correct himself, "took, Martin to school. I didn't notice anyone hanging around, nothing suspicious anyway, but as I said to Detective Bradbury we live in a busy area, people come and go all the time. I wouldn't notice a new car or a new person particularly." He paused. "Do you think we were targeted? Do you think it was Dawn he was after all along? The other detectives seemed to think the abduction was random."

Jenny watched as Robert James turned his wedding ring over and over on his finger and involuntarily reciprocated by fiddling with the heart dangling from her bracelet.

"It probably was," she said. "Random I mean." She paused. "Had you noticed Dawn's behaviour changing lately?"

"How do you mean?" asked Robert.

"Well, was she acting strangely lately, perhaps more irritable than normal? Was she perhaps more secretive than usual?" asked Jenny.

Robert was becoming defensive. "We didn't have secrets."

"Had you noticed Dawn buying more clothes than usual or wearing a new perfume?" she pressed.

"What are you driving at?" asked Robert angrily.

"Nothing," said Jenny. "I'm just asking whether everything was normal."

146

"Normal?" asked Robert, his eyes searching hers for a definition. "Nothing can ever be normal again."

Jenny realised that her line of questioning wasn't helping. "I think Sam's got your statement," she said, "so you are free to go. We'll arrange for someone to take you home, Mr. James."

Robert looked at her blankly as if each decision presented a new challenge to his mind, and the anger that had shown in his eyes disappeared as quickly as it had surfaced.

"Ok," he said and turned his wedding ring over and over with new purpose.

***

Jenny headed straight outside, fumbling in her handbag for her cigarettes and lighter. She pressed a cigarette between her lips, lit it quickly and inhaled the smoke deeply into her lungs.

"Are you ok?" asked Sam, who was standing a few feet away unnoticed and smoking himself.

Jenny said nothing.

"I feel sorry for the guy," he said.

"I don't think I helped," responded Jenny, not looking at him. "I said you would arrange for someone to take him home. He looks awful."

"Already done," and Sam trod out his cigarette.

He was silently watching Jenny smoke when his mobile rang. After listening for a while, he said, "Ok, I'll be there in ten minutes. Is it ok if I bring Jenny Foster with me?" He rang off as soon as the caller had answered.

"That was the coroner, Frasier O'Connor; says he's got something at his office we need to see."

Jenny ground out her own cigarette in the bin. "Right!"

***

Jenny and Sam only just made it back from the coroner's office in time for the Chief's briefing. The room was hot and clammy and they quickly took the seats reserved for them near the front. The Chief began the session working from notes.

Jenny looked down at her legs while he spoke. She allowed her hands to rest on the obviously expensive black fabric; then her eyes moved down to the black strappy high-heeled sandals that had somehow found their way onto her feet that morning and she began to feel more than a little ridiculous. Sam was in the standard DI issue grey suit that looked like it had never seen the services of a dry-cleaner, the frayed trouser pocket indicating its age. His shoes were brown and well-worn, almost worn out in fact, and Jenny could feel the colour beginning to rise in her cheeks as she realised she was about to become the over-dressed laughing stock of the Manchester Metropolitan Police Force. She began to convince herself that no-one would take her seriously and her cheeks reddened as she imagined how the seasoned detectives would be smirking behind their hands and then later laughing openly with each other about how ridiculous she looked.

The coroner's report confirmed that Dawn James had died of asphyxiation. As he had speculated at the scene, the method used involved the killer employing a draw-string to hold a plastic bag over her head. He also confirmed that she'd been sexually assaulted - sodomised to be exact, and judging by the bruising, forcibly so. There were deep ligature marks almost to the bone around her wrists and ankles, together with marks round the neck consistent with her having been collared. The list of general cuts, bruising and carpet burns filled half an A4 page of the report and it was the coroner's opinion that she had been held, bound and gagged for about two weeks before she was killed, then dumped as soon as she'd died. He also confirmed that the curious number *1* burned into her lower back was caused by the killer applying some kind of hot metal implement directly to the skin. The report speculated that judging from the shape of the point, the implement chosen was probably a soldering iron. O'Connor also stated that the scarring was about two weeks old, which could only mean that Dawn had sustained the injury almost as soon as she'd been kidnapped.

Jenny looked up and slowly gazed around the small room. It was full to capacity with as many people standing at the back as there were occupying seats. There wasn't even enough room to close the door. The detectives, all male bar two, were scribbling attentively as the Chief spoke; their determination to catch a killer was palpable and the atmosphere in the room was growing impatient. The Chief had been talking for too long and the Detectives wanted to get out on the streets and continue the real work of tracking down Joe Reed. The Chief's assurance to her before the meeting began - 'you'll be fine, just tell them what you think' - was advice she didn't need: if Jenny knew anything, she knew her job. She opened the manila folder on her knee to refresh her mind with the bullet points she'd made in the car on the way back from the coroner's office, and when the Chief invited her to begin talking to the group, she rose with confidence and strode to his side. She positioned herself in front of a white board covered with pictures of Dawn James. Dawn's face smiled down happily from a photograph at the top of the board; also in the picture were Dawn's husband Robert and their son Martin, smiling too. Underneath were crime scene photographs from the Chamberhall Street Industrial Estate showing Dawn's now white and lifeless face staring wide-eyed into the lens. Multiple close-up images of her many injuries completed the collage. Jenny's eye followed a line drawn from Dawn's smiling photograph to a picture of another smiling woman with the caption *Robyn Cox* above it in harsh black permanent marker. Jenny remembered the second girl abducted and the thought crossed her mind that the likely future for this victim would produce more stills for the board. She turned to face the audience, realising that Sam had followed her and was standing next to her. She glanced at him, irritated to notice a supportive sort of expression on his face. She cleared her throat.

"I haven't had much time," she began. "I mean, there's not that much to go on at this stage." She paused, gathering her thoughts, focusing her mind on her audience, which seemed markedly less attentive now than a moment earlier when the chief had been talking. As she looked out at the stony faced detectives sitting and standing in front of her, she knew she needed to make an impression, and fast.

"Go on," said the Chief.

"Well, as you know," she said, nodding towards the white-board where a stylised image of Reed's face was linked by dark lines to Dawn James and Robyn Cox, "the suspect calls himself Joe Reed. You've all read the file, studied the e-fit and been hunting Reed for the last two weeks, but that can't be his real name."

She paused, trying to find some focus, she didn't want to just stand there and frustrate her audience, giving them information that they already had; she wanted to make a difference.

"This so-called Reed lives alone," she went on. "He lives somewhere he fits in. We know he's performed successfully in sales jobs, so he's good with people. He'll probably interact well with his work colleagues and neighbours and be liked by them."

The detectives began to look up now and take notes, which boosted Jenny's confidence - she wanted her opinion to be respected, despite her lack of experience. "He's a gregarious and friendly sort of man, but won't stand out as unusual in a crowd. He probably won't draw attention to himself with strangers unless he wants to and he'll appear neat and tidy, clean-shaven and probably decently dressed. He'll take pride in his appearance and will look and smell clean," she said, her description starting to flow. "Women *like* Joe," she emphasised. "Before he raped Emma Jones and Marcie Edwards he'd had a way of getting under their skin and manipulating them. But the way he subdued Dawn James in a blitz attack, surprising her with a blow to the head, is unsophisticated and doesn't fit in with the Joe Reed who committed the sexual assaults two years ago. I think this shows he's lost patience, and rather than taking his time to seduce women and gain their confidence, he now wants more immediate satisfaction."

A hand went up in the audience.

"So he's what? Developing?" asked a young looking detective.

"Yes," said Jenny. "He's more determined, more focused on his task and he's becoming more unstable as time passes. His desires are getting the better of him and he can't think of anything else but the women he's abducting and abusing."

She paused and looked at her notes. "But don't be fooled, he won't make stupid mistakes. He's intelligent, methodical and extremely well organised. He's unlikely to have a job; instead he's fully concentrated on his victims and probably talks to them all the time. He probably lives in an area where not working wouldn't be unusual. He kept Dawn James alive for two weeks, which means that he needs privacy and space, so he probably lives in a house, not a flat. The house needs to have some degree of privacy from the neighbours. We know that Reed's unlikely to be wealthy, so don't think leafy suburbs; he's hiding his victims in plain sight in a built-up area."

"Surely someone would have noticed two women being carried around?" asked the Chief.

Jenny paused for a second. "Yes," she agreed, "I thought about that. He's
probably got a garage where he keeps his van, other-

wise we'd have found it by now, and he must change the number plates each time he takes it out. It could be that the garage connects to the house via a private door. Think Victorian terrace, maybe on a corner or end of a row, the type with a garage attached to the side - or perhaps a small, first-time-buyer type modern detached."

"So basically anywhere in Greater Manchester then?" snorted one of the detectives in the front row.

"I can't be more specific than that right now," answered Jenny. "Except that he's living fairly locally to the industrial estate. He's not going to risk a long drive from the murder site to the dump site. He'll know that a nondescript white van will attract enough attention from the traffic police if they're behind it to check the number plates at least. So I'm guessing that he's living within a fifteen minute radius of the Chamberhall Estate, which means you should concentrate your search within, say, a twenty mile radius."

"That's a huge area to cover," said The Chief. "That twenty mile area is one of the most densely populated in the North of England."

Jenny made no comment on that, merely adding, "Basically, he's highly organised, and he's taking care not to get caught. Whatever his mental state, he's lucid enough to fear justice or perhaps the consequences of his crimes."

Another hand went up. "So he's scared of being caught, but will carry on regardless?"

Jenny rallied. "Yes, he's not going to stop and he's taking sophisticated counter-forensic measures to avoid detection," she said. "He's wearing gloves all the time; he knows about fibres and he's careful not to leave any.

Although he sodomised his victim there was no trace of semen, so he avoided climaxing inside her."

The audience shifted in their chairs, uncomfortable at the reference to sex, and Jenny pressed on.

"Sex is important to Reed. The act of sodomising his victim shows that he wants power over them, shows that he wants them to know he's in control. He binds their hands and feet and gags them, fixing a collar around their neck and keeps them prisoner, probably letting them know their own fate and torturing them with it for days or weeks. He doesn't feed them and only gives them enough liquid to survive. All this shows a need to humiliate his victims and reduce them to something less than human."

Jenny paused again; she was getting too excited, carried away with the moment. She knew she was helping the detectives form a picture in their mind and it thrilled her.

"He might identify with his victims through a traumatic experience in his own past," she went on, turning to the collage behind her. "Look at the physical similarities of the two women. They're similar ages, height and build. Their hair colour and even the styles are the same, and both victims were married with children around the same age. They also share their ethnicity and social class; I doubt these factors are all coincidence."

The room fell silent, Jenny allowing her audience to catch up as notes were scribbled. When she was sure she had their full attention again she continued.

"There is one other thing that's not in your notes. DI Bradbury and I have just come from the coroner's office," she said. "Mr. O'Connor only began the detailed post mortem this morning and he found some items in the contents of her stomach that have a bearing on the case."

"What *items*?" asked the Chief.

"The coroner found notes. Scraps of paper, written on with felt-tip."

Jenny paused for breath, her chest was becoming tight with excitement and she was trying to control her emotions.

"The notes were swallowed by Dawn James just prior to her murder," explained the profiler. "According to the coroner there would have been a build-up of acid in her stomach due to the absence of food. If the paper was ingested and allowed to settle, the notes would have broken down almost immediately."

"What, so he thinks these notes were swallowed just prior to Dawn James being killed?" asked The Chief.

"Exactly," said Jenny. "Given the content of the notes and the fact that the victim's hands and feet were bound and she had a gag stuffed into her mouth, she was unlikely to have written them herself and then swallowed them of her own accord. The coroner agrees that Reed or at least someone with access to Dawn James for the final ten minutes or so of her life must have forced them down her throat."

"What was on these notes?" the chief asked.

"There were twelve in all, probably torn from a single sheet of paper. Some say the same thing, but there are three distinct messages. The first says simply, *HELP ME* the second, *I DON'T WANT TO HURT YOU* and the third…"

Jenny paused, looking out into her audience who were now all on the edge of their seats.

"The third says, *HE'S WATCHING.*"

Chapter 12

The Chief looked stunned; all eyes in the room were on him and he didn't seem to know how to respond. Eventually he managed to find his voice.

"What?" he said. "What does all that mean?"

Jenny turned momentarily to Sam who was shuffling his feet, looking down at his shoes. When he glanced up, her expressive brown eyes were looking straight at him, more alive than he had ever seen them; then she turned her attention back to her eagerly waiting audience.

"The way he left the body of Dawn James is interesting," she said, indicating the pictures on the board. "See here how the body was washed clean with the hair carefully brushed and the arms placed over the chest. These are all signs of guilt, even remorse. The brushing of the hair particularly shows that Reed may have felt sorry for his victim once he'd killed her."

The profiler turned to face her attentive audience.

"There are no post-mortem scrapes or injuries on the victim's shoulder blades or heels, which shows that when he dumped the body Reed was careful not to harm it any further; perhaps another sign of remorse for his actions and maybe something that might go in Robyn Cox's favour."

A silence momentarily hung in the air. "Or not!" said the chief flatly. "He did starve Dawn James, and she was so dehydrated before she died that she was barely functioning."

Jenny realised that she might have speculated too far and looked again at Sam, who remained silent beside her. This time her eyes were not so confident.

"Go on, Jenny," urged the Chief, a slight impatience perceptible in his voice. "What about these notes?"

"There are a number of possibilities, but in my opinion two stand out, Chief," said Jenny thoughtfully. "The first is that he feels so remorseful and sorry for his victims that there's a part of his mind that doesn't want to hurt the women. In that case the notes amount to a kind of cry for help, and this would indicate a deep internal struggle."

Jenny paused, checking the faces of the detectives to see how they were reacting to her theory.

"He could have suffered some kind of psychotic episode and might be showing schizophrenic tendencies, developing two personalities that are battling for control - a *good* Joe Reed and a *bad* Joe Reed if you like, each fighting the other for control and dominating his actions accordingly."

"So the *good* side of the killer is trying to stop the killings?" said the young detective who had spoken up earlier.

The room broke out into nervous laughter and private conversations.

Jenny realised she was in danger of losing her audience and had to raise her voice to be heard. "THE SECOND POSSIBILITY" she almost shouted, and all the heads in the room turned satisfyingly back towards her, "is that Joe Reed has an accomplice. There could be someone forcing him to carry out the killings. This second person would be the dominant partner, acting out his personal fantasies through Reed."

"So in that case, it would've been Reed himself that forced the notes down Dawn James' throat?" asked another detective.

"Yes," said Jenny. "Unless Reed is the dominant one and it was the unknown offender trying to attract our attention."

"There's no evidence of a second killer," said Sam, slightly panicked and speaking for the first time in an attempt to help clarify things. "None of the witnesses who saw the last abduction mention an accomplice, and the slight traces of DNA that we got from Dawn James and the Chamberhall Street Estate all match Joe Reed with no other specific unidentified residue."

"Did we get DNA or fingerprints from the notes?" asked the Chief.

"Only the victim's'," said Sam resignedly.

"Yes, that's true," interjected Jenny. "Plus the witness statements from the original rape enquiries don't mention Reed having an accomplice. In fact they point to him being something of a loner with few friends."

"So what's your best guess?" the Chief asked.

"There's plenty of case history where two killers acting as a team work together to commit murder," answered Jenny. "One partner is usually naturally dominant, with the submissive one becoming almost a victim themselves. Or one partner has some kind of hold over the other, forcing them to commit murder or other crimes."

Jenny glanced at Sam for support, knowing that the Chief and the rest of the assembled company expected her to give an informed opinion that they could use. "Judging by the notes," she went on, "I wouldn't rule out an accomplice just yet."

The chief eyed Jenny and Sam, clearly wrestling with whether the information they'd offered was of any value. He addressed the room. "All the evidence gained from witnesses to the rapes and to the abduction of Dawn James and Robyn Cox suggests that Reed is a loner. Until there's more concrete evidence, we keep our attention fixed on him."

***

Alone with the Chief after the meeting Jenny and Sam fielded questions. Their superior was torn between continuing the investigation on the premise that Reed was working alone, or moving the focus to include his working in partnership with someone else. If Reed and a second person were operating as a team the Chief knew that the scope of the investigation would need to change, and he didn't want to make a mistake now by pulling resources off the hunt for Reed to research a possibly non-existent accomplice.

The chief's office was small, and cluttered with too much light-ash office furniture, all of it well used. Jenny knew that he was married with older children, but there were no pictures on his desk or on the low filing cabinets that seemed to line every available wall. The desk was a mess of papers and half-read files and the wires from the computer hung untidily from the back of the desk before scurrying off under a pile of files left to accumulate on the floor. Jenny couldn't help but think that the Chief was either disorganised and confused, or at least a little autistic in his approach to filing. He looked thoughtful for a moment, allowing the silence to expand.

"Ok!" he said suddenly and decisively, "I'm giving a press conference in half an hour, the media are rife with speculation and they've even come up with a name for this guy - *the Bury Beast.*"

"Not great for Bury," said Sam facetiously.

"I'll put a call in to Dr Phillips. He's a psychology professor I've used in the past," went on the Chief. "You two go over there and see if he has any further ideas about the significance of these notes."

"Ok," said Jenny, enthusiastically.

She'd sat through a series of lectures given by Dr Phillips and she brightened at the thought of meeting him and getting a glimpse of how his mind worked.

"Then," went on the Chief, "I want you to re-interview the alleged rape victims, specifically to see if they recall Reed talking about anyone else in his life that might fit with a possible accomplice."

"I've been over the files in detail," said Jenny. "There was no mention of anyone else in Reed's life apart from a fictitious wife and daughter."

"It's worth a try," said the Chief.

Jenny and Sam stood up together and left him to his thoughts.

***

Manchester University Humanities campus was new and modern with a hotel style reception area and smart furniture. The artwork was huge and inspiring and the students bustling through were young and lively. Seeing the reception desk unmanned, Sam stopped a group of girls in mid conversation, their giggles resonating in the large space. Jenny didn't hear what he was saying, but was soon following him to the lifts.

"Sixth Floor!" he said.

The Sixth Floor Reception was even more impressive than downstairs, boasting plush-looking furniture and a huge display of fresh flowers on the dark-wood reception desk. They were welcomed with professional courtesy by a neatly dressed woman in her forties, her blonde hair perfectly clipped into a sharp bob. She told them that Dr Phillips was waiting and indicated his office, just down the hall. At the door Sam knocked and went straight in with Jenny following.

Dr Michael Phillips PsyD was sitting in an opulent white leather armchair behind an enormous oak desk. The desk was clear except for a leather desk mat.

"I'm DI Sam Bradbury and this is Jenny Foster," said Sam, as Dr Phillips rose to greet them.

"Mike Phillips, please take a seat."

The two seats in front of the desk were also white leather and looked distinctly unused. Jenny took the one to the right hand side. Without preamble and almost before Sam and Jenny had settled into their chairs, Dr Phillips started to talk, his manner brisk and businesslike.

"As you know, Mark rang me to talk about the murder of Dawn James and the cryptic notes found on her body. He told me what was in the notes and also gave me some of the background for your suspect."

Phillips spoke without any hint of emotion and maintained steady eye-contact equally between his two visitors, probably hoping they'd be suitably impressed with his use of their commanding officer's first name.

"I'm due at a lecture in fifteen minutes," he explained, "but until then I'll help in any way I can."

Jenny told the professor her role within the force and Sam filled him in with the parts of the investigation that had, so far, been kept from the media. The profiler talked in detail about how the body had been found and the possible signs of remorse. Finally she came to the notes.

"The notes weren't found *on* Dawn James' body," she said. "They were found *inside* her stomach during the autopsy."

Dr Phillips stood up and walked over to a coffee machine percolating silently on an adjacent cabinet. "Coffee?" he asked.

"No thanks," said Jenny and Sam shook his head.

Expertly decanting coffee into a china cup, he added a drop of milk but no sugar. He was in his fifties, a little over six-feet tall with neat blonde hair, and extremely attractive. His charcoal grey suit was perfectly tailored to his slim, athletic looking physique, and his feet elegantly encased in Italian leather shoes that looked as though they'd never ventured outside. His blue eyes were lively and questioning, contrasting with the expression of calm professional concern fixed on his face. As a student Jenny had valued both the content of his lectures, and the charismatic presence with which he dominated the invariably packed theatre.

"I remember you attending my lectures, Ms Foster," he remarked, stirring his coffee slowly, despite the absence of sugar. "Criminal Psychology Insights if I'm not mistaken. But at that time, if I remember, you were called Jennifer Baker, not Jenny Foster."

"Er, yes...three years ago," she said, feeling smaller in her chair under his piercing scrutiny. "I very much enjoyed them," she added, blushing at the thought that Dr Phillips remembered her from amongst the hundreds of students he must have lectured over the years.

"According to Mark," he said, getting back to the matter in hand, "the most telling note read *he's watching.*"

"Yes, that's right - amongst others," Sam responded.

"Ok," said Dr Phillips. "I'm guessing, Ms Foster, that you have already thought about the psychological possibilities for the note. But," he continued, without waiting for an answer, "one of the most interesting things about psychology, and profiling particularly, is sometimes the inability of the researcher to see the obvious."

"Which is?" asked Jenny.

"He might simply be *being watched,*" he said, resuming his seat and placing his coffee silently, despite the china saucer, on the upper right side of the desk.

Jenny found herself returning Dr Phillips' gaze and recognized a piercing intelligence.

"There are two questions I suggest you focus on," he said, now concentrating his attention entirely on Jenny. "*Watched by whom*? And *why?*"

***

"What did you make of that?" Jenny asked when they got back into Sam's car.

"Strange," said Sam. "He seemed more interested in you than the victim!"

"He acted as though we were two of his students," she said. "I'm not sure he was as big a help as the Chief thought he would be."

"Well he certainly didn't offer much - nothing we hadn't already discussed anyway."

Sam reached for his mobile to call the alleged rape victims. Getting no reply from the number he had for Emma Jones, he arranged an appointment with Marcie Edwards, scribbling notes to verify the address.

"Ok, we'll drive over and see Marcie Edwards first thing tomorrow. She lives alone and doesn't go out much, so she said she was pretty free any time."

"What now?" asked Jenny.

"Report back to the Chief first. Then we need to sit down and go through the post mortem notes and all the witness statements again, to see if we've missed anything."

"Ok," she said, realising that she would need to call Peter to make sure he was home in time to let the au-pair go and see to Lilly. At that moment her mobile rang; it was a withheld number and she answered cautiously.

"Hi Jenny, it's Ronnie."

Caught in the moment, Jenny was briefly at a loss to connect the name with her uncle's voice. "Oh, hi Ronnie!" she said as her memory triggered.

"So, Joe Reed," said Ronnie without pleasantries. "I think I might have a lead on where he's been for the last two years."

Jenny snapped her head round to face Sam, her eyes lighting excitedly.

"Ok, where?" she asked.

"Ireland," answered Ronnie.

***

Paula Tripp had spent the morning following Peter Foster's Jaguar. After spending that uncomfortable night outside Jenny's house in the yellow submarine her intention had been to follow the profiler and get to know her more personally, but the sight of Peter Foster had changed her plans.

Paula Tripp and Foster had history. Three or four times over the previous few years his name had been linked to some questionable dealings in the property market, especially surrounding public buildings in Manchester City Centre. Each time Paula had confronted the businessman with a string of what she thought were well thought out questions about these dealings, he had side-stepped answering them and she'd got into trouble with her boss. Apparently Peter Foster was well connected and her nose for a story told her that he was also crooked.

He'd left his house and driven three miles to a café. It was one of those upmarket places that had baristas instead of waitresses and he'd nursed a single coffee for the entire time and eaten a bacon sandwich, continually wiping the grease from his fingers in what Tripp thought showed more than slight case of OCD.

He'd obviously gone there to meet someone, and was eventually joined by an overweight man in tight fitting beige suit who sat opposite him and ordered coffee. The two men talked quickly, the fat companion using napkins to wipe his sweating brow, despite the air-conditioning. Foster became visibly angry at one point, before handing his companion a small black attaché case. The second man had his back to Tripp when he opened the case, but it was obvious he was pleased with the contents as he stood up almost immediately. Tripp was able to see his face for the first time as he smiled at Foster and offered his hand to shake, a gesture which was ignored with a dismissive wave. The fat man merely shrugged and headed for the door, where Tripp took the opportunity to snap him. She was unsurprised to recognise Benjamin Tully, Chief Planning Officer at Manchester City Council, and mentally added bribing officials to her list of Peter Foster's spurious business dealings. Once Tully had left, Tripp didn't see Peter Foster use his telephone to call or text until a minute before he stood up to leave, when he received and replied to a single text message. He walked out of the café at 9.53, got back to his Jaguar - neatly parked out of sight in a side street - and drove within the relevant speed limits to an underground car park in Manchester City Centre. Tripp was excited: she had a hunch that Peter Foster was up to something. She didn't have any evidence, but her journalist's gut was telling her to stay close, and she shadowed Foster as he took an internal hotel elevator from the car park directly to the Reception of the Midland Hotel. Tripp checked her watch; it was 10.22.

The Midland was a Manchester landmark with its own fine-dining restaurant, health-club, sauna and four star rating. Tripp had learned not to second guess the movements of the subject of a possible story, so she got back into her car and manoeuvred around to take up a position where she could see the main exit of the hotel, as well as the exit to the car park. She doubted that he was using the gym as he hadn't taken a sports bag out of his car, and it was too early for a business lunch. He could be using the hotel as a short-cut across to the Town Hall and the City Centre beyond, but Tripp had a feeling he wouldn't be leaving the hotel for a while and settled into her surveillance routine. This was the part that she loved best about her job, when she had a gut feeling and was following it up.

She called her editor. "Don?"

"Paula?" he answered brusquely.

"I'm on a lead for the Bury murder case."

"Where are you?"

"Not far, but it might take a while."

"Ok."

"Are you running the story front page again tonight?"

"Ambrose is giving a press-conference later, so probably," said Don.

"Well, hold off in case I dig up anything new."

"Dig up?"

"You know me, Boss!"

"What are you up to Paula? I know that tone."

"Probably nothing; just one of my gut feelings."

"Ok, I'll wait till three. If I haven't heard from you, I'll run with whatever we have."

"Ok, I'll call either way."

"Sure," said Don. "Speak later."

The phone went dead and she turned it over a few dozen times whilst she stared at the entrance to the hotel. She'd stopped in the throat of a dead-end alleyway with a Starbucks on one side and a baker's on the other, and after a quick bolt to both, she was back in her car with a caramel macchiato and a couple of hot croissants to keep her company.

**

Peter Foster held the hotel room door open. His companion hesitated for a second making eye contact with him, looking for reassurance but with her nerve endings tingling across her entire body. Peter's confident smile and relaxed posture brought a smile to her lips and she slipped inside the room. She was desperate to tell him how much she loved him, and how happy she believed they could be together. She'd dreamed so longingly of their life as a couple and she wanted to create a scenario that would convince him that they were meant to be together, a world of laughter and bliss where their past unhappiness would fade into insignificance leaving them to embrace each other in the sun of a perfect new beginning.

Peter recognised the look etched onto her angular features. It was a look he'd seen before - submissive, needy and weak. Peter didn't want to hear what the woman had to say, he knew she would plead for their supposed love and once she started to speak, he knew there would be no end and he wouldn't get what he'd come for. He launched himself across the bedroom, catching the woman's face in his hands and driving his lips into hers. He filled her warm mouth with his tongue and felt her initial resistance weaken as she began to respond and press her body into his.

This was too easy thought Peter.

He maintained full contact with the woman's lips and slipped his hands down to her waist, releasing her cream trousers. Then he swivelled her round and pressed his erection into the small of her back whilst almost ripping the black, figure hugging vest-top from her slim frame and hurling her to the bed. She began to giggle and reached to remove her heels.

"Keep them on," he growled, unbuttoning his shirt, "I want you slutty."

The woman forced a smile as she watched Peter slip out of his trousers and toss his boxers across the bed. She wanted him to want her, but she needed more from him too, she wanted a life.

She began to speak as Peter joined her on the bed and began kissing her neck.

"Peter I...," she began before his strong, thick index finger pressed against her lips.

"I know you do," he said and pulled her head back, using her hair to control her movement. He didn't pull hard enough to hurt, just enough to let her know he was in control. Keeping a firm grip Peter positioned himself on top of her, kicking her stiletto clad feet apart so that her knees naturally flexed giving him full control. He pulled her hair still tighter until her face was turned towards the ceiling; still gazing at him, she was forced to look downwards, her eyes bulging larg-

er to cope and reminding Peter of the petrified eyes of
a cow he had once seen just before it was slaughtered.
The smile she saw on Peter's face wasn't the one she
had imagined, the one full of love and respect and
sheer joy at their union. No: this smile she recognised,
full of lust and sexual domination, and she was powerless to do anything but comply.

***

Paula Tripp spent the time in her car worrying about
her weight with every gulp of coffee and every mouth-
ful of croissant. She was skinny and wanted to stay
that way, and these surveillance days were a killer for
her waistline. She spent the next hour and a half listening to a tape - a book by John Sergeant, one of her he-
roes - and stayed sharp by posing herself mental arith-
metic problems. She drifted into thinking about how
famous she'd become if this lead did turn into something useful for the front page, her reveries culminating in accolades at the National Journalism Awards.
Her thoughts were cut short by the sight of Peter Foster
emerging from the doorway of the hotel. She glanced
at her watch: it was 12.30.
Foster stood for a few moments in the shadow of the
doorway and Tripp deduced from his body language
that he wasn't totally comfortable. Then he was joined
by a woman, who slipped her hand into his and led
him round the corner of the building. Tripp already
had her 35mm long-lens in her hand and snapped
them walking away. The woman was tall, probably five
ten, but then Tripp noticed that she was wearing heels
- so more like five eight. She was slim, with long dark

171

hair and a sallow complexion. Her clothes didn't look particularly expensive, but her outfit was well put-to-gether and stylish: cream trousers and a black, semi-revealing top. She had a neat clutch-bag tucked into the crook of her left elbow and was allowing Foster to carry a small pink sports bag for her. They talked for a few seconds, the woman tilting back her head in what looked to Tripp like over-played laughter. She was obviously trying to impress Foster, and when their lips met for more than a furtive kiss it looked as if she had succeeded.

Tripp went on snapping away, capturing a few images every second and knowing that when she reviewed the resulting frames this embrace would be played out in slow motion, showing detail that she could only guess at from this distance. The couple's lips parted and the woman put her head on Peter Foster's shoulder for a second, lifting her chin to whisper something. A smile spread across his face and he leant in for another kiss before she teasingly broke the embrace and slipped her gym bag from his hand. Without another word she walked confidently away and round the back of the hotel. Tripp continued to watch Foster, who was standing stock-still, his eyes fixed on the woman as she walked out of sight. When she didn't turn round to reciprocate his lingering gaze and had finally disap-peared from view, he walked quickly back to the hotel door and went inside.

Tripp threw the camera onto the passenger seat and started her engine; she needed to know who this mys-tery woman was and it was unlikely she'd be able to identify her from the photographs alone. Crossing the steady stream of traffic and edging her way down the side of the hotel, she rounded the corner just in time to see the woman hopping on a tram heading out of the city. Tripp followed closely; she knew that the road ran adjacent to the tram lines as far as they went and that there were only two stops available for the woman to alight. The first stop was difficult to monitor and Tripp found herself having to bump the Vectra on to the pavement to wait for people to get on and off. The garish yellowness of the car, potentially standing out as a beacon to any casual onlooker, was again at the forefront of her mind. She could see the woman sitting about half-way up the tram, texting on her mobile, and she knew she hadn't been spotted as the tram pulled away en-route to its final stop in Hulme.

As predicted, the woman got off the tram at Hulme Station and continued her journey on foot. Tripp parked the car and got out; she'd have to follow at a safe distance and she stayed at least fifty yards behind, in her mind assuming the guise of a fellow passenger who'd used the same tram stop and was now simply walking home. The summer morning rain was long gone and the pavements had quickly dried as if they had never been soaked at all. For the first time Tripp was aware of the sweltering heat of the early afternoon and, excited as she was, the first quarter mile was a breathless slog. Her quarry moved along at a steady pace, having swapped her heels for black ballet-style shoes, swinging her handbag as she went and clearly very pleased with herself.

Eventually the woman turned and made her way through the gated entrance of a recently built block of apartments with small balconies and private parking spaces. "Shit!" said Tripp to herself. She realised that she wouldn't be able to pin down the address if her quarry merely opened one of the communal doors and stepped inside to make her way to what could be any of the apartments in the block. Tripp increased her speed, reaching the gate just as the woman was making for one such communal entry door. The reporter readied herself to run and try to cover the space between her and the door as fast as she could once the woman had passed through in the hope that as in many apartment blocks, the door was heavy and unwieldy and took an age to close. If so, she might be able to slip inside and perhaps follow the woman to her apartment, or at least be able to identify which floor she lived on.

But to Tripp's surprise the woman side-stepped the door and instead took a few steps further right, fumbling in her handbag for keys. She smiled at her luck: the woman was checking her post-box. "Top row, third from the left," Tripp murmured to herself as she heard the metal box clang shut, then watched as the woman disappeared inside the building clutching a pile of freshly delivered envelopes. The seasoned stalker waited three minutes, counting off the seconds on her smart steel Tag Huer bracelet watch, imagining that this was about the maximum amount of time it would take for the woman to gain her apartment from the lobby and be safely inside. Tripp could then go through the gate and consult the mailbox unnoticed.

The reporter waited another slow thirty seconds to make sure and then slipped through the gate and covered the distance across the car-park without incident.

She looked at the boxes: "top row, third from the left," she reminded herself, and her eyes settled eagerly on the identification slip attached to the box in question. It read, *Apartment 28 – C Baker.*

Chapter 13

He played with a silver necklace, running the familiar, thin cold rope through his fingers over and again and his mind filled with images of Joe Reed performing his will exactly as directed. An intense electric warmth coursed through his veins, and he felt his heart almost pounding out of his chest as he mentally replayed the last few moments of Dawn James' life, her milky flesh pressed against the bed and a look of terror imprinted on her face. He watched the air disappearing within the plastic bubble, reducing itself with each breath she struggled to take. Eventually the plastic was sticking to her face and entering her mouth while Joe Reed, his creature, rode her as though she were less than human. The necklace slipped faster and faster through his nicotine stained fingers as his mind reached a frenzy of excitement spilling down into his groin. He wanted more bitches to suffer and he needed Joe Reed to be his weapon again. He could almost taste his urgent longing to see another woman die; *he needed them all to die*. The man felt as though his life had been pre-set to culminate in this moment and he knew he couldn't stop; Joe Reed must kill again, cause more suffering to satisfy *his* need to feel alive, to feel useful - to feel like a man.

Unable to control his own desires, ecstasy turned to a knot of frustration and the man threw the silver chain onto a bare wooden coffee table thick with dirt and populated by old dishes and filthy cups. He exhaled loudly, fouling the air with the stench from his lungs before collapsing onto at well-worn brown leather sofa, soft from years of use. Falling backwards his body disturbed an air so thick that it wisped around the man's shoulders with a cloud of dust floating silently upwards to join thick cigarette smoke, adding to the suffocating oppression. The day was bright and hot outside, and without air conditioning or even an open window the room was suffocating. Globules of sweat stood out on the man's face and forehead and droplets of the same moisture slid through the thick hair on his fleshy arms. He leant his greasy head against the worn and heavily stained sofa top and closed his eyes, desperate for release as his shaking filthy fingers fumbled with the zip of his blue corduroy trousers.

The television remained permanently alive, the screen flickering images and the volume always set to low. Suddenly the half-heard word *strangled* broke into the man's frenzied thoughts, prompting him to open his eyes and tilt his head forward. Reaching for the remote control on the arm of the settee, he raised the volume and quickly pressed to record the footage. He stared at the screen riveted by the sight of a policeman poised to address the camera in full dress uniform, with a crisp white shirt and perfectly knotted black tie, his buttons polished and gleaming in the studio lights. The caption at the bottom of the screen read, *Chief Superintendent Ambrose: Bury Beast Statement.*

The man himself looked assured, confident and in control. There was no hint of a smile or greeting in his eyes or around his mouth as he said, "I am Chief Superintendent Mark Ambrose, head of the Greater Manchester Metropolitan Police based at Central Park, and I have a statement to read regarding the recent discovery of a woman's body in the Bury area of Manchester." The policeman paused as he straightened his notes.

"On Sunday night at around ten o'clock a woman's body was discovered at the Chamberhall Industrial Estate by a passer-by: she had been murdered. The dead woman, who lived and worked locally, has been identified as Mrs. Dawn James, who was thirty-six and married with one son. We are appealing for anyone who was in the area at the time to contact the police - even the smallest detail you may remember could help us catch the killer of this young mother."

Ambrose looked down, again consulting his notes.

"In particular we would like to speak to a Mr. Joe Reed, who we believe could help us with our investigations. I would urge Mr. Reed to come forward, so that we can eliminate him from our enquiries."

At this point the image of Dawn James was replaced with an e-fit of the suspected killer.

"Mr Reed is believed to be in his mid-thirties, with dark, slicked back hair and a tanned complexion; a sketch of the man is on your screen now. We believe that he drives a white Luton-style van, registration number DE08 BXT, though it may be that he changes the registration number regularly. If anyone has any information as to this man's whereabouts, either now or in the recent past, or knows anything about the location of the van, please help the police by calling the incident line number at the bottom of the screen. Any information will be treated with the strictest confidence."

The sketch of Reed was replaced by Chief Superintendent Ambrose. "Joe Reed may be dangerous," he warned, "and should not be approached by a member of the public under any circumstances."

The camera panned to the studio, settling on the young woman interviewer, blonde and well groomed and wearing a mask of anguish and concern. She was clearly ready with questions. "Thank you Chief Superintendent Ambrose," she said. "Can you confirm reports that another woman is missing and possibly being held by Joe Reed?"

The Chief replied slowly and deliberately. "Miss Groves," he said witheringly, "I can't confirm anything other than the information in the statement that I've just read. I would like to add that all enquiries are currently being followed up by a team of dedicated and experienced officers."

The man on the brown leather settee, just another viewer of the millions watching laughed openly and shouted excitedly at the screen. "Stupid drawing looks nowt like him!"

Gloria Groves flicked back her blonde hair and composed herself for her next question. She'd been a journalist and television presenter all her working life and twenty years of experience was telling her that the Chief wasn't going to play ball and was unlikely to give any more information away. All the same, she felt it was down to her to represent her viewers, and she was determined to ask the questions she knew they would want answers to.

"The woman who was murdered - Dawn James - you said that she left a husband and a young son. I'm assuming they've already been offered support and counselling at this terrible time?"

The Chief's face softened, "Yes, a female officer visited the family to break the sad news as soon as we knew the victim's identity. They are being comforted by friends and relatives and all our resources are of course available to them for counselling and support."

"He shouldn't have married the bitch in the first place!" the man shouted at his screen, unable to contain his anger. "That kid'll be better off without her!"

Gloria Groves nodded in response to the Chief's words, her face showing a compassionate concern, well-rehearsed over the years.

"Is it true," she probed, "that Dawn James, a loving wife and doting mother to her son, may have been held captive by the Bury Beast for days or even weeks before she was murdered?"

"Fucking, doting, fucking mother!" screamed the man.

The chief was taken by surprise: this woman was well informed and had details about the case that he had not thought were in the public domain. The question had been asked in such a way that his anger dissipated and he felt his face flush.

"As I said, Miss Groves, I cannot confirm anything other than the facts in my statement."

He paused, realising he needed to give her something more than this stock answer.

"However, I can tell you this," he went on, unscripted and staring straight into the camera lens. "I have absolutely no doubt that Joe Reed is a determined and ruthless man and - as I said earlier - he should not be approached by a member of the public under any circumstances. Anyone with information, no matter how trivial they may think it is, should call the incident number."

The telephone number for the incident desk scrolled endlessly across the bottom of the screen.

The Chief thought the interview was over, but Gloria Groves had other ideas. The interviewer leant across the purple studio sofa to look directly into the eyes of the Chief on the video-link. She stretched her well-toned body to its full length, her tight breasts naturally jutting as she arched her back.

"Should women living in Greater Manchester take precautions, such as not going out alone or after dark, or perhaps even stay indoors as much as possible until this man is caught?" she asked.

The man on the sofa gave a high-pitched laugh, spittle running from his mouth and down his unshaven chin. "Yeah Bitches, stay the hell at home!" he shouted, almost dancing in his seat with excitement.

Chief Ambrose could barely hide his mounting irritation. "*No*, Miss Groves," he said, as if to a wayward child, "I don't think there's any need for women in the Greater Manchester area to lock their doors and become prisoners in their own homes."

"Isn't there?" interrupted Gloria. She knew he had just

allowed his well-prepared guard to slip. "Will you be letting your wife or daughter out after dark on their own tonight?"

The Chief's irritation was turning to anger now and he was unintentionally beginning to show his interviewer how rattled he was.

"Now look here, Miss Groves," he said, forgetting he was live on national television. "You may have your own reasons for wanting to scare your viewers, but…" He paused for a moment, and then quickly regained his composure and launched into a well-practised spiel. "…but fortunately crimes such as these are very rare indeed, and Greater Manchester is a safe place to live. If any of your viewers do have concerns, they can take basic precautions to keep themselves safe by following the advice given on the Crimestoppers website, or they can call the Incident Desk twenty-four hours a day." The Chief caught his blonde inquisitor's eye. "And please do rest assured," he added in his best earnest tone, "that we *are* doing everything we can to catch the killer."

The man on the sofa grinned and shouted at his television, "Like what, Fool?"

Gloria Groves listened to her producer tell her through her ear-piece to wrap it up and go to a break. She turned away from the Chief and his image disappeared, leaving the Incident Room telephone number and the e-fit of Joe Reed.

"Thank you, Chief Superintendent Ambrose," she said, adding pointedly. "I hope we can all rest assured." Then she went seamlessly on with "After the break we have our mystery special guest, who'll be attempting to recreate Gordon Ramsey's famous fish and chip supper live in the studio."

In the incident room at Manchester Police HQ, where the Chief had given his interview by live satellite link, his barely suppressed anger turned to rage and he ripped off his lapel microphone with its battery back-pack still attached and threw it at the ITV cameraman. "What the hell was that?" he shouted at no one in particular. "Is she trying to panic the whole bloody country?"

***

Later that afternoon the Chief, Jenny and Sam reviewed the information received from Ireland following Ronnie's tip. The report ran to several hundred pages of evidence, witness statements and medical reports and made grim reading.

There was little doubt that a suspect matching Joe Reed's description and with DNA evidence to match, had been active in Ireland over a two year period. The report began with details of a victim in County Cork. Reed had apparently befriended the woman whilst working in a car showroom, before raping and sodomising her some months later. A second woman was detailed as a mother of four living in Dublin, who had the unfortunate luck of working with Reed in a busy city centre pub. The report stated that Reed had left the woman strapped naked to a hotel bed. The maid who found her described a horrific scene with blood spattered sheets and the victim barely alive. Scene photographs from both cases were included and showed depressing similarities to the Manchester cases.

But it was the third victim's case file that proved the most shocking.

Veronica Denshaw was a mother of two children, who lived and worked in the small village of Balbriggan on the East Coast of Fingal. Balbriggan boasts a working harbour and sandy beaches, with famously stunning coastal walks overlooking the bay of Drogheda. Its most famous historical building is Ardgillan Castle, set in almost two-hundred acres of parkland and formal gardens on a stretch of elevated coastline between Balbriggan and Skerries. Veronica had worked at the castle for five years as a part time guide, sharing her extensive knowledge of the residence at Ardgillan with a ready smile. From the statement made by the General Manager at the castle it was abundantly clear that not only was she dedicated and hardworking, but loved and respected by everyone she worked with. According to the report, Reed had broken from his usual routine and instead of getting to know his victim and gaining her trust, he'd simply kidnapped her at work. Nor had he kept the woman prisoner as he had his current victims in Manchester, preferring instead to knock her unconscious and take her to a Victorian conservatory within the grounds of the castle, before raping and sodomising her.

Luckily Polly Dougherty, who came across the victim in the conservatory after the attack, was a skilled first-aider. She found Veronica Denshaw with a plastic bag restricting her airway and saved her life by performing CPR and mouth-to-mouth.

Jenny tore herself away from the report. "He nearly killed Veronica Denshaw," she said. "I think he meant to."

"Looks that way," said the Chief.

"Why weren't the cases linked to Reed?"

He shifted in his chair. "It's not as easy as you imagine, Jenny. These crimes happened in the Republic of Ireland and don't appear on our radar."

"But it's up to the Irish Police to notify Interpol if they think an offender may have skipped the country," interjected Sam. "From the reports it looks as though the Garda thought that Reed was still in Ireland."

"So how did Ronnie come across the connection?" asked Jenny.

"Pure luck," replied the Chief. "He told me he asked around after you spoke to him. There happened to be a delegation from Ireland attending a conference at Scotland Yard, and Reed's description rang a bell with one of them."

Jenny found herself making a conscious effort not to brim with pride at her Uncle Ronnie's ingenuity. "The change in behaviour is interesting," she said. "Reed didn't try to get to know Denshaw, he just blitz-attacked."

"True," said Sam, looking up from the report. "He stalked her first though."

"Yes," agreed Jenny. "He's too careful to attack a woman randomly in broad daylight. It seems from the report that her routine took her out to the Victorian conservatory to lock up when the last of the visitors had gone."

"So he waits for closing time, hides somewhere and then makes for the conservatory to wait his chance," put in the Chief.

"Yes, that's likely," said Jenny. "But consider the planning that must have gone into that attack."

Sam was flicking through his notes. "Well, she only worked part-time, and she only locked the conservatory on a Wednesday, the General Manager's day off."

"So he must have been watching her?" asked the Chief.

"For weeks! To be able to predict a potential victim's movements to that degree would have taken lengthy, detailed surveillance. To work out when someone is consistently at the weakest, most vulnerable point in their daily life takes commitment and perseverance."

"But why her?"

"She fits the victimology perfectly," said Jenny. "All three victims in Ireland do."

"You mean they all look similar?" asked Sam.

"Yes, they all have long dark hair. All three are slim and married with children. Plus they all work part-time."

The Chief's face wore a pained expression. "So that interviewer was partly right. Joe Reed sees any woman in Greater Manchester fitting his victim profile as potential?"

"Depressingly, yes," answered Sam. "I don't think the part-time worker detail is all that relevant though."

"Why not?" asked Jenny, slightly unnerved that Sam should challenge what she thought were basic facts.

"It's not a question of them not working full time per se," suggested Sam, "but think about it. The fact that they all work *part* time does provide a convenient pattern that any would-be stalker can start with."

"Yes, I see," said the Chief. "I suppose it would be harder to stalk a woman who didn't have such an obviously cut and dried daily routine - no unexpected overtime, extra commitments and so on."

"Then you think that the part-time worker connection is no more than a coincidence?" asked Jenny, more than a little put out.

"No, not necessarily - just maybe convenient."

Chapter 14

Sam and Jenny drew up at a forbidding looking block of flats, one of the many faceless post-war edifices crammed into more than a mile square of Fallowfield, a small former industrial town squeezed seemingly as an after-thought between Manchester and Oldham. At 9.15 the air was already warm, but the fresh morning sunlight bouncing off the windows of the tired building did nothing to brighten its drab, concrete-grey exterior. Looking up, Jenny thought this a far cry from the leafy suburb where Marcie Edwards had lived with her husband John and their two children, and it crossed her mind that all lives are potentially fragile. Despite our natural human defence mechanisms being pre-programmed to create a safe bubble against people like Joe Reed, there always seems to be someone ready to crash through at any moment, shattering dreams and ruining lives.

The detail of the address told them that the flat they were looking for was up on the fifth floor. "A tenner says the lifts are out," said Sam as he opened the car door.

Depressingly, he won his bet and the pair headed for the five flights of concrete stairs. Once inside the structure the pitilessness of the place became even more apparent. Bare concrete walls entombed the stairwell decorated with gang-style tags and graffiti carefully crafted to instil the dread that Jenny now readily felt. She found herself constantly looking back over her shoulder as Sam strode ahead two steps at a time. Panicking that she might lose sight of him, she found herself almost running to keep up.

"Hang on!" she gasped, pausing for breath when they reached the fifth floor landing.

"Fitness not your strong point?" asked Sam quizzically as he strode down the corridor in search of 516. "Starting smoking again probably wasn't your wisest decision."

Just one knock at the door of the flat that Marcie Edwards now rented was enough to summon her from within her cave-like dwelling. Opening the door to let Sam and Jenny in she said nothing, immediately showing them her back; her act of walking away from them and turning into the sitting room a perfunctory signal to follow. The curtains hanging from the only window and available source of daylight were closed, the chinks between the ill-fitting grey material filtering shafts of sickly light through the stale tobacco smoke lingering in the air. The scattering of furniture was well-used and tatty with no attempt to arrange anything to look pleasant or offer comfort. There were no cushions on the dingy green sofa, no flowers in the vase on the mantle-piece, and the carpet was thin and cheap with a swirl pattern designed to hide the dirt.

Marcie Edwards was clearly just the shell of her former-self: any physical attractiveness she might once have possessed had vanished; her hair was lank and dull and her features gaunt. A television blared out and Marcie made no attempt to turn the sound off, instead she sank into a green velour armchair and placed a cigarette between her thin lips. Lighting it crisply, she opened her mouth in a half-smile in response to the inane chatter of light entertainment, releasing a billowing plume of smoke as she did so. Jenny and Sam glanced at each other, mutely implying that they were probably wasting their time.

"I'm DI Bradbury," said Sam above the din, "and this is my colleague Jenny Foster. She's a criminal profiler with the Manchester Metropolitan Police." Marcie seemed barely to register their presence, let alone acknowledge the introduction.

"Do you mind?" he asked, picking up the remote control from atop a pile of magazines and newspapers sprawled on a glass table-top, and pressing to silence the volume.

Marcie continued to smoke heavily without turning from the screen.

"We wanted to ask a few questions surrounding the events of two years ago," said Jenny.

Marcie ground out her cigarette in a dirty glass ashtray and looked towards Jenny, "Is that all it's been?" she asked, the hardness of her thin face suddenly giving way to a sort of pleading anxiety. Her voice came out as a startled croak as if it were seldom used and needed to be cranked up like an old car to get it going.

"How have you been coping?" asked Jenny.

Marcie cleared her throat, the sound like a faint echo of gravel moving around in the bottom of a bucket.

She brushed her short brown hair with her hand and began to sit up a little straighter. She made an effort to rearrange the folds of the black skirt she was wearing and moved her shoulders to fit more comfortably into the tight black jogging top that clung to her skeletal frame, showing how frail her body had become. Jenny momentarily became aware of her own lithe figure and imagined what it might be like to end up a half-skeleton.

"I'm fine," said Marcie. "The whole thing hit the family harder than me."

She looked over to a sideboard displaying neatly arranged photographs of a contented looking and well groomed Marcie, a man and two children. Jenny went over to examine them, picking up one of the heavy metal frames that featured all four subjects sitting at a table in some restaurant.

The boy looked about six years old, the girl about four, and Jenny assumed the man in the picture was Marcie's estranged husband John Edwards. The photo must have been taken around the time Marcie first met Reed. The children looked happy and their parents were grinning happily too. Looking at the woman in the frame, smiling, attractive and confident, and comparing her with the pitiful shell sitting in front her now, Jenny felt a profound sadness wash over her.

"You look like a happy family," she said encouragingly. "Beautiful children! How old are they now?" She already knew the ages of the children of course, and the fact that Marcie seldom saw them. Marcie and John had split not long after her ordeal with Joe Reed and Jenny knew from reading the file that she had withdrawn into herself, a virtual recluse unable to make even a simple trip to the shops.

"Katy's in proper school now, she got a prize the other day for coming first in a spelling test," said Marcie, retrieving the picture from Jenny. "Daniel's a terror though. He's struggling in class and keeps getting into trouble with the teachers and the other kids."

"Can't have been easy for them," said Sam.

Marcie glared at him. "Nothing happened to *them*!" she almost shouted. "It was me - he..." and she trailed off, her anger disappearing as quickly as it had surfaced.

Jenny looked at Sam and gestured to him to go outside and leave her to it. She felt they were unlikely to get any new information from Marcie, and she could see the pain in her eyes as thoughts of the past opened up old wounds.

"I'll be in the car," said Sam. "Good to meet you, Mrs Edwards."

"It's Ms Riley now," she said pointedly, without looking at him.

"Fancy a cup of tea?" asked Jenny as Sam disappeared out of the room.

"I've only got PG," said Marcie and stood on painfully thin legs before shuffling out of the room with Jenny following her into the kitchen.

Marcie flicked on the kettle and began making tea in two mugs, grimacing at the effort of the task. Jenny sat at the kitchen table, a functional item with a wooden seat either side of the pine oblong that stood with leaves permanently down, full table extension made impossible by the size of the room. She handed Jenny a mug and sat opposite her.

Jenny's eye travelled down Marcie's crossed-over leg, thin and bluish-white where the bone pressed against the skin, her gaze settling on the scruffy trainer that ended it.

"I know this must be difficult for you," she said, taking a slurp of the hot liquid, and suddenly reminded that she hadn't been offered any sugar.

"What, my life?" said Marcie, a look of sorrow etched on her face. "John made me leave the kids; he said I was a tramp and wasn't fit to be their mother or his wife."

Jenny sipped her tea, just letting the other woman talk.

"He never noticed me anyway, always had his head in some book or other trying to get involved in anyone's life but ours. The kids hate me now. He's poisoned their minds against me you see, and he never brings them over here."

She looked around the room and Jenny's eyes followed hers, taking in the stained lino on the floor and the tatty Formica worktops surrounding a cooker that looked like a relic from the nineteen-seventies.

"Not surprising really," Marcie went on, settling herself further into the chair. "He was always a selfish man. I was too good for him really."

Jenny smiled and nodded.

"At least Joe gave me some attention," continued Marcie. "I don't know why he left me there in that room, we could have been together." Marcie looked directly at Jenny to make her point. "We connected," she said with determination.

"How did he make you feel?" asked Jenny quietly.

Marcie paused, staring at Jenny across the sparse table; for the first time her eyes sparked into life and they began to dance. Jenny could see that whatever memories were passing through her mind, they were exciting ones.

"He made me feel alive," said Marcie and then slumped back in her chair, the fleeting excitement shining in her eyes suddenly extinguished like a snuffed candle. "He treated me like a woman," she went on quietly, almost as if she were talking about someone that she had loved and had passed away.

"Go on," said Jenny slowly, trying not to frighten the talk out of her companion.

"He wasn't like John," said Marcie, almost spitting out the name with scorn. "Joe knew how to make me feel special, as if I was the only person in his life; the only one he had eyes for. He made me feel loved and confident and I thought that we would end up together."

"Did he ever tell you that he loved you?" asked Jenny. Marcie leant forward again, an expression of joy on her face. "He didn't have to," she said. "I could *feel* that he did; he didn't actually have to say the words."

"Did he have any other friends?" asked Jenny.

"No, just me. Oh, except Tony of course."

"You worked with Tony didn't you?"

"I liked Tony," said Marcie and then her face turned into a scowl. "But that bitch he was married to. What was her name?"

"Emma?" said Jenny.

"That bitch must have seduced Joe," she growled, then pausing to think she leant closer to Jenny until the smell of stale cigarettes invaded the profiler's nostrils.

"He was so kind, you know?" said Marcie. "That Emma

Jones probably gave him a sob story so she could sleep with him."

"He raped her too," said Jenny quickly without thinking, beginning to be irritated by the self-absorption of this woman.

Marcie stared at her for what seemed like an eternity. She said nothing and Jenny could feel Marcie's eyes burrowing into her, trying to read her mind.

"Rape isn't great," said Marcie eventually, "but to be a victim of a rapist no-one can catch is ten times worse."

"In what way?"

"If you're attacked or robbed in the street you get sympathy," said Marcie her eyes beginning to moisten. "They don't have to catch the man to know what happened." She glazed over for a second, staring into nothing, perhaps recalling a memory before continuing. "When it's rape, no-one *really* believes you. Everyone thinks that you wanted it, that you got what was coming to you."

"I do," said Jenny earnestly, "believe you I mean," she added.

Marcie laughed. "But I don't know you," she said. "And more importantly neither does anyone else in my life." She paused to drink her tea before adding, "When it happens, sure everyone's shocked, sympathetic even. But the longer they can't catch the man the more questions there are: What did he look like? Did you encourage him? Did you fancy him? Why were you alone in a hotel room with him?" She blushed. "In Victorian times if a woman was raped she had to fall pregnant for it to be assumed that she had consented to sex, so even by their skewed standards I'm innocent," and with that she laughed, adding sarcastically. "But not to my loving husband and adoring children - to them I'm no better than a common whore."

The sun streaming through the small kitchen window was beginning to heat the kitchen to unbearable levels and Jenny shifted uncomfortably on the hard wooden chair before rooting a tissue from her bag and pressing it to her cheek.

"It's cooler back in the other room," said Marcie. "This flat isn't fit for a dog." She stood to lead the way with Jenny following.

In the doorway to the tiny sitting room Marcie stopped dead in her tracks.

Suddenly she half collapsed, her legs giving way beneath her and she grabbed onto the door frame for support. Feeling a wave of panic, Jenny instinctively took the woman's elbow to keep her upright. When she followed Marcie's staring eyes to the television screen it was to see an e-fit of Joe Reed almost jumping out at them.

"What the hell?" Marcie breathed.

"It's ok," said Jenny, recovering enough to steer Marcie the short distance between the door and the sofa before allowing her to fall onto its unwelcoming surface.

"That looks a bit like Joe," explained Marcie as the image disappeared, leaving the Chief looking out from the screen irritated and red-faced. "Sorry! It threw me for a moment."

"We're looking for him in connection with another offence," said Jenny. "That's the best image we have."

She sat herself down opposite Marcie on the single sofa chair. "Are you ok, can I get you some water?"

"No, I'm fine," said Marcie, her eyes never leaving the television screen.

"Is it a good likeness?" asked Jenny.

Marcie took a few seconds to answer as Reed's image appeared again, this time with an incident room telephone number to call with any information. "Sort of," she said. "You haven't got his eyes quite right: they're more piercing than that. And the shape of his face isn't quite right either."

"Do you have a photograph yourself?"

"As I said to the police two years ago and ever since, Joe was camera shy; he wouldn't even let me snap him on the mobile."

"Would it be ok with you to work with us? Perhaps make the e-fit a bit better?"

"Sure," said Marcie absent-mindedly.

"It's very important," said Jenny.

"There's the video of course," said Marcie quickly, almost inaudibly.

"Sorry? What video? There's nothing in the file to say that a video of Reed exists."

Marcie reached for her cigarettes, taking one and quickly lighting it. "It appeared a few months ago," she said. "You know - of the office party?"

Jenny was ultra-careful to hide her sudden excitement. "Appeared?" she asked trying to keep any hint of enthusiasm from her voice.

"Well, I don't get out much and no-one comes to visit me," said Marcie, the self-pity oozing from her. "So I sort of follow what's happening to the people that used to work at Peterson Insurance on that." She pointed to a laptop computer lying closed under the television, and until now unnoticed by Jenny.

"You know," Marcie added, "I Google their names."

"Ok," said Jenny, almost unable to contain her excitement. "Can you show me?"

**

Jenny and Sam almost burst into the Chief's office.

"I thought you two were going over the rape witness statements?" he said, obviously unimpressed at the sudden intrusion.

"We've come from Marcie Edwards' flat now," protested Sam.

"You're never going to believe this," said Jenny cutting across her colleague, "but there's footage of Joe Reed that's been posted on YouTube."

The Chief studied Jenny for a few seconds. "Sam, get the team together and let's have a look at this footage," he said. "Jenny, hang on here for a few minutes."

Jenny and Sam exchanged glances as he left.

"So you've settled in ok," said the Chief, as more of a statement than a question. "Don't get ahead of yourself. Your job is a vital one as it is: to collate information and come up with a profile of the offender that officers like DI Bradbury can use to apprehend him."

Jenny hadn't expected to receive a dressing down and was suddenly wary of what the Chief was saying.

She answered flatly. "I know what my job is," she said.

The Chief straightened in his chair. Despite the fact that he was sitting and Jenny standing, she felt suddenly overshadowed.

"That's good," he said. "Your insights could be vital, but to be effective you need to remain detached from the investigation itself. You need to observe and look for details that no-one else is thinking about." He paused, his expression softening and his shoulders dropping to adopt a well-practised almost paternal attitude. "Leave the police work to Sam and the team, they're the professionals," he added, a smile beginning to play around his eyes.

"I am detached," said Jenny becoming defensive, "and I understand that I need to remain objective."

"Good," said the Chief, rising noisily from his chair to extend to his full height, literally filling the space between them. Jenny caught a faint smell of his aftershave, and looking into the now fully smiling face she knew he was making an effort to put her at her ease, but she couldn't help feeling like a small child.

"Let's see this video," he said and held out his hand in a gesture inviting her to go through the door first. Now she was certain that she was being condescended to, and she didn't like it one bit.

***

The tech-room was on the other side of the building and amounted to a floor of computers. Banks of screens populated every inch of space with CCTV images from around the city constantly streaming in. Corresponding human operators concentrated on their tasks, chattering to each other and to unseen outside contacts via microphones attached to their equipment. The Chief strode across the floor towards Sam,

200

who was leaning over the shoulder of one of the operators, his eyes glued to the screen.

"Sergeant?" said the Chief by way of greeting. The young woman operating the computer swivelled in her chair, her back instantly straightening.

"Sir!" she responded.

"What have we got?"

Sam answered for her. "The YouTube video was posted two months ago by Becky Davis, a secretary at Peterson Insurance where Reed was working."

Jenny stared at the computer playing the film. Partygoers filled the screen and the videographer was obviously no professional, the image jumping around as if the camera operator herself was dancing whilst filming. The film was dark, with disco lights offering the only illumination, and faces passed in front of the lens quickly with features often obscured.

"It calms down a bit now," said Sam as the camerawoman stopped dancing herself and began to pan the room.

Jenny recognised Marcie sitting at a table with Tony Jones and a few other party-goers. She was laughing hysterically spilling the drink from her glass down her own dress.

"She's hammered," said Sam flatly.

"She still didn't deserve to be raped," said Jenny impetuously. She felt the stare of the Chief and knew what he was thinking.

"I mean, she was unlucky that Reed was there to take advantage of her," she said, softer this time, trying to sound detached.

"That's Reed," said Sam suddenly. Everyone's attention

switched back to the screen and they all watched Joe Reed walk across the dance floor, his face to the camera.

Jenny was immediately struck by the self-confidence in the way he walked and held his head. Smiling easily at people as he passed them, he knew he was attractive and even on camera he oozed sex appeal. He was wearing a dark grey suit, tailored to his athletic body, a white shirt and striped red tie. The black hair swept back from his face made him look taller than he probably was and he walked with a straight back and lifted chin, aloof and in control. The party, the people, the music, everything seemed to be relegated to the background as he walked through. The other guests, especially the females, watched him go as if he were a god, with Becky Davis the camera operator following him oblivious of the party, as if the camera was magnetically drawn to him. He was walking straight towards the lens now and his presence filled the screen. His eyes, piercing and dominant, caught the recording light and then, suddenly frozen in indecision, he abruptly turned left and quickly disappeared.

"No wonder women fancy him!" commented Sam. "Where can I get some of that confidence?"

"At least we know who we're dealing with now," said the Chief. "Did you say you were bringing in the camera operator?"

"Yes, I sent a car for her; she should be here within the hour," Sam told him. "God knows why she didn't let us have this film two years ago, or at least before she posted it on-line for the world to see."

"Ok," said the Chief. "Jenny, you watch the film until

you're bored, and then watch it another fifty times. I want you to get to know this Joe Reed inside out."

"Sir," said Jenny. She was stunned by the sight of Reed on the film; she hadn't expected to come face-to-face with him - not yet anyway, and not like this.

Chapter 15

Joe Reed spent an uncomfortable hour sitting in his van. He had been told to dress in jeans and a white tee-shirt without logos and to slick his hair back, and now it lay black and glistening above his gaunt white features. He had lost weight and the trousers and shirt hung from his bones at least two sizes too big. He had showered and shaved as instructed; his hands were scrubbed clean and the fingernails along the tips of which he constantly ran his thumb were immaculate. The scent of the cologne he had used liberally on his face and body filled the cockpit of the van and Reed cracked a window slightly to try and breathe fresh air, but there was no breeze and the stifling heat of the day lingered, making the air heavy and every breath an effort.

He had parked next to Whitefield Common, tucked away behind the fence and a good hundred metres from the busy main road that ran along the upper part of the green space. The road he was in was a dead-end with only a few houses, all arranged in a crescent shape at the top. They were tucked away out of sight around a bend behind where he sat, and he had been told that few cars and pedestrians would pass. The two cars that did skirt the van on their way out to the main road paid little attention, except perhaps to curse the parking position. Reed had to duck under the dashboard once when a pedestrian passed leading a small dog, but he was sure the white-haired woman hadn't paid either him or the vehicle much attention and he spent the an otherwise uneventful hour watching the Common through the trees.

Reed was relieved to be away from Cathcart Street and he felt a sense of freedom as he sat waiting here with the evening drawing in. He felt relaxed, at peace even, away from the house where all of his nightmares had gathered throughout his life. He dreaded going back there, and when he drove away from Cathcart Street on his way to the Common, he felt as though he had escaped. His thoughts turned to the woman trussed and waiting in the basement of the house and he felt little sympathy for her. He considered himself to be just as much of a victim as she was - a victim of his circumstances and of the parents who had dominated his childhood and set him on the path he now found himself taking. True, his hands weren't tied and he could, in theory at least, make his own choices, but still he felt trapped by his past. Despite its open doors and easy escape, Cathcart Street with all its memories was effectively a prison, more of a restraint on his freedom than the bonds of the woman who waited in silence and pain for her pitiless end.

Then as he sat there contemplating his next moves it occurred to Reed that he might just drive away, make a call to the Police letting them know where his captive was hidden. The fantasy took shape in his mind, materializing through the fog, and he imagined himself leading a normal life. After all, he thought, he had found work and been successful in the past and he could do it again. Perhaps move south to somewhere quiet where he would never be recognised; Cornwall maybe or one of those villages in Dorset with thatched roofs and white picket fences and ivy creeping up ancient walls with roses around a solid oak door, just like the houses in a jigsaw puzzle that he had completed over and over again as a child. He could find a sales job, make friends and perhaps meet a woman and have a family of his own with smiling, happy children living without the fear of their own memories and unafraid of their lives.

Reed's mind began turning over the myriad possibilities and his fantasies gathered momentum. He invented names for the children and their mother, his wife, imagining their ages and attaching life stories to them. His son would be captain of the football team at an extraordinarily young age, eventually going on to play in the Premier League for Chelsea and winning England caps, whilst his daughter's glittering music career would take her to international fame and fortune with appearances at the Royal Command Performance and private concerts for heads of state across Europe. Reed basked in the thought that he would eventually be recognised as the driving force behind his marvellous offspring, achieving accolades of his own as a fantastic parent, appearing on chat-shows to inspire a new army of motivated, community-minded individuals, all following in his footsteps and ultimately becoming a whole generation of well-adjusted, bright-minded young people.

A smile crept across Reed's face; the feeling of his mouth turning upwards startled him and his thoughts again turned inwards.

When was the last time I smiled?

Why am I here?

What is it exactly that I'm doing?

Suddenly the laptop, open and bright and sitting on the passenger seat sprang into life announcing the arrival of a message, and his dreams of a new life faded in seconds. He stared at the screen, immediately panicking at the thought of this new communication with its inevitable instructions. The imagined urgency brought with it an instant atmosphere of fear and dread and Reed reached quickly over to the machine to click the new message icon.

The man had supplied Reed with a nondescript white Luton-style van, bought in cash from a private seller and driven over from Ireland via the ferry. With its plates changed on arrival at Holyhead it was now virtually untraceable. Prior to delivery to Joe Reed the man had installed a covert camera in the rear-view mirror which could pick up a signal within a quarter of a mile radius, enabling him to track Reed's every move. At that very moment the man could see Reed's face displayed on the laptop beside him in his shabby blue Ford. He had parked opposite a strip of ageing shops on the main road and he watched Reed arrive, make a turn into the road and then disappear to turn around again, stopping half-way up the close as instructed. The man was confident that his presence would go unnoticed. He guessed that after Joe Reed had carried out the planned kidnapping the Police would be focused on the van and so he hadn't bothered with an elaborate disguise. Instead he sat in the driver's seat with the engine idling, as though he were a husband waiting for his a wife to return from one of the shops. The long-sleeved yellow shirt he wore was a mistake in the lingering afternoon heat; wet patches were developing under his arms and his face glistened with beads of perspiration. From his vantage point he could see the front of Reed's van and monitor the comings and goings of any cars and passers-by as Reed sat waiting to carry out the man's plan. The number plates of the cars that came in or out of the road where Reed was parked were jotted down in a small grey notebook, and he carefully took a picture on his phone of a small white-haired woman and her dog who he guessed would have to walk past the van. If any of them saw anything, he would deal with them later.

The man knew that the only CCTV cameras in this part of Bury were at the traffic lights on the north end of the Common and he had instructed Reed to drive all the way around the parkland, avoiding the monitored junction, and leave that way too, thus defeating any official recording of the van's movements. He was excited thinking about the woman that Reed had been instructed to take, and his anticipation of seeing her and perhaps even witnessing the moment that Reed bundled her into the van created the familiar involuntary stirring in his groin that he found so delectable. He was tempted to open the zipper of his cream combat-style trousers and relieve his excitement right there whilst he watched and waited but he held himself in check, knowing that he could recreate the scene in his mind later.

He picked up his lap-top and distracted himself with a message to Reed.

"Are you ready?" he typed, his thick fingers moving quickly over the keys before pressing send.

He watched Reed via the camera image on his screen, and saw him instantly freeze as the message arrived. A smile spread across the man's face as he watched Reed jump to answer.

"Yes," came back the reply.

"Are you shaved and dressed as I told you?" typed the man, already knowing the answer.

"Yes, jeans and a white tee-shirt," came back the reply.

"Good! I'm sending you the picture of the slut we're going to take again, just to make sure you get the right one."

"Ok," came back the instant reply, and the man stopped for a second as he saw Reed's face.

The dread in Joe Reed's eyes almost leapt out of the screen and the watcher could see sweat beginning to form on his forehead. Reed's mouth was moving from side to side and his eyes were staring straight ahead as though he was witnessing the climax of some horror film.

The man typed quickly.

"Just remember who it is that we're punishing here. It's her, it's *Jane*. This woman is torturing her own kid."

"I know," came quickly back from Joe.

The man pressed on. "Jane deserves everything she gets; she deserves to suffer for what she did."

"She deserves to suffer," replied Reed.

"You're doing this so you don't have any more nightmares, so she pays for what she did," typed the man.

"I know," came back the reply. "I just wish things were different, were normal."

The man stared at the screen for a few moments. The tension in Reed's face had relaxed and tears were rolling freely down his cheeks. He made no effort to wipe them away and his face remained impassive, as if he were unaware of his own pain. The man attached the image of Sharon Daly to his next message.

"It's almost time. She'll be reaching the edge of the Common now. Dry your eyes and go and do what we both need, go and make her suffer."

Joe Reed clicked on the icon to display the attachment, and a full-screen picture appeared of Sharon Daly. It was a still from the video that Reed had already seen and her face was contorted with rage as she shouted at her defenceless son.

Heat instantly rose to Reed's face and he brushed away his tears, inspired with fresh determination. He felt his stomach churning with anger and hatred for this woman: this Jane. An all-encompassing surge of emotion flowed through him, sending electric currents of rage to the very ends of his fingers and igniting his mind with purpose.

He typed another message. "Yes- we'll make her suffer."

Chapter 16

Paula Tripp lived alone on the thirtieth floor of one of the newest towers in Manchester City Centre. Having grown up near Tarporley in the midst of the Cheshire plain, Paula was completely new to city life and this apartment was a status symbol she was fiercely proud of. She had come a long way since she left her parents' sprawling dairy farm to join the throng of budding writers and journalists enrolling for a degree in multi-media journalism at Manchester Metropolitan University. Immersed in her studies and with a circle of smart, intelligent friends she became increasingly ambitious, determined to go out there and make a positive difference to a world she viewed as inflexible, and even dishonest. She pored over biographies of the celebrated masters of her craft and despite the cynicism that naturally surfaced as she read about their improbably perfect careers, she envied their success. It was the autobiographies she found it harder to stomach, almost choking on the self-satisfied tone of the authors with their implied assertion that without *them* around, the world would no doubt have been a very much poorer place. Paula often read deep into the night, stoking the fires of her ambition and dreaming of a future which would see her scale the heights of journalism and eventually make her mark on the world stage.

Once qualified, she took on a series of one-off assignments and became a jobbing reporter for newspapers and websites all across Europe, reporting on anything and everything interesting that happened between Birmingham and Newcastle. She travelled a great deal and often her input was accepted but then later discarded and the story together with payment seldom materialised. Tripp realised quickly that she needed a base from which to work - a title at a newspaper, which she thought would be her first stepping stone to the career that she'd been mapping out for herself ever since getting to University. Eventually a local opening came along, but convincing Don Chapman the editor of the Manchester Evening News, one of the most famous and well respected newspapers in the north of England, to give her a job in the first place, let alone recognise that she had any talent had been tough. Paula was convinced he wouldn't be able to identify her in a five man line-up even now eleven years later, as he seldom looked up from his desk no matter how hard she tried to get his attention.

The regular hacks, on the other hand, with their easy smiles and wandering hands had been easy to outwit. All she had to do was flash a hint of cleavage at them or laugh at their inane jokes with her dancing blue eyes flashing the promise of unfettered access to her lithe body. These moves had been more than enough to distract their attention whilst she stepped all over them to get to the top. A few scoops or exclusives, easily won whilst her colleagues were looking the other way, had ensured that at least Don saw her potential in print. This attribute was the only barometer he took any notice of and by the age of thirty-eight Paula had achieved the rank of Chief Reporter and she felt reasonably satisfied. All the same, her old ambitions remained undimmed and the desire for greater success, still burning bright, told her that she could achieve more, much more.

Tripp had spent the afternoon researching the *C Baker* she had followed back to Hulme after the no doubt secret rendezvous with Jenny Foster's husband Peter. She hadn't gone into the office to find information because she wanted to focus on one single task. She knew that the office was a hotbed of potential distractions and that she would inevitably be dragged out to cover some breaking news story unrelated to the Bury Beast case and her search for the elusive C Baker. She saw the tryst between Peter Foster and C Baker as a significant development in the case. She still didn't know how, but she had a feeling that it required her full attention and as an accomplished investigative journalist she would unearth the truth and blow this story wide open.

Paula Tripp had spent a great deal of time and effort on her apartment. Not only was it perfectly equipped for lengthy bouts of concentrated research, but it had exactly the right ambience too. The imported rosewood desk-top was large enough to be able to sit two computer monitor screens at one end and still have ample room to work with a laptop at the other. One of the two screens permanently in situ was tuned in to the twenty-four hour BBC news channel whilst the other played the CNN website live-feed, which meant that she was always aware of any breaking news she might otherwise miss whilst holed up for the afternoon. She also kept a digital radio on low in the background, tuned in to a local station and set to increase the volume slightly for the half-hourly news. To complete her surveillance of live events, her Police frequency radio chattered incessantly, keeping her always on the alert, so if anything happened with the Bury Beast case she'd know straightaway.

Tripp's research efforts now ran to over three hundred pages, each printed and highlighted with marker before being set to one side. She had organised the information into category piles and then by date. Her categories were Jenny Foster, Peter Foster, Joe Reed, and C Baker, Apt 28 Bickerton Rise, Hulme M14 4EQ. The two piles pertaining to the Fosters were packed with information, most of which was education and career orientated and mostly already known to Tripp. The pile regarding the Bickerton Rise address was interesting only to the point of identifying the date of construction, which was a mere three years previously, and the builders of the edifice, a well-known corporation. Her list of the residents of Bickerton Rise was almost complete but uninspiring, with no recognisable names standing out. She had looked at the original marketing for the apartments, and the other occupants were almost a perfect match for the sales blurb: young professional couples, or retirees who had 'down-sized'.

The Joe Reed pile was almost empty save for the web and newspaper reports linking him to the Bury Beast case. Among these were many written by Paula Tripp herself, but still highlighted and catalogued with her usual meticulous care. Truth to tell, she was baffled as to why she and the Police hadn't found this elusive man. When she thought of the resources that had been put to use in concentrating all their efforts on this one person, she could scarcely believe there were still no concrete leads to his whereabouts, and she was amazed at his trick of being able to appear and disappear seemingly at will.

The C Baker pile was even thinner, consisting as it did mostly of papers that simply confirmed C Baker as the current occupant of the address. A Land Registry search showed that the property was owned by a Mr T Boyd and another search that he was a landlord and property developer; his name never appeared with C Baker's in any documents or reports, which probably meant that Baker was a tenant.

Try as she might, Tripp couldn't even unearth Ms Baker's Christian name. Usually it would have been easy to find on the Electoral Roll, but for some reason she wasn't recorded at that address. Either she hadn't lived there long enough, or she preferred not to signal her presence to the world by appearing on the register: either way the result was the same - dead-end.

Hoping her target might be registered *somewhere*, Tripp widened her search criteria and created from the Roll a list of dozens of C Bakers from across Cheshire and Lancashire. She then narrowed down the entries to any C Baker in a household where they weren't the first name on the list. She figured that if this woman wasn't showing at Bickerton Rise she was probably registered at her parents' address. Tripp had further narrowed her likely quarry to Baker households that appeared within the Greater Manchester area, surmising that a single woman would probably be living within an hour's driving distance of her parents' home. If she *was* she was listed at her parents' house she was unlikely to be married, firstly because her name would have changed and secondly her husband would surely have insisted she was registered with him at the family home.

Tripp realised that she had made a great many assumptions, perhaps speculating too far. If she was wrong on any of these counts she knew that C Baker would be impossible to find on the internet and she would need to resort to further surveillance and probably end up having to rifle through the woman's bins.

The final list of Baker households containing the name of C Baker as at least the second resident amounted to seven. Tripp used her skill with search engines to come up with telephone numbers for each household, planning to call the numbers posing as market research and ask if C Baker was at home.

She broke off her research for a few minutes to monitor the screens, but they showed no new developments in the Bury Beast case. Her ears had been constantly tuned in to the radio and the Police frequency, which also told her there was nothing to get excited about, and so she decided to fix herself a drink before making the planned calls to the seven Baker households. It was six pm by now and she thought it a perfect time to catch someone just home from work, but not long enough to have fully relaxed and be too impatient to take a call from a stranger.

Tripp pulled herself upright from the black leather executive chair that she'd chosen as a comfortable seat for long hours of research, and stretched her lithe body to its full length, extending her arms towards the double-height ceiling. She wore a simple black dress flared just above the knee and black suede house shoes, the comfortable type with kitten heels. As she stretched, her own heels lifted from the shoes and her hands clasped together above her head, giving a satisfying extension to her lower back. Exhaling deeply, she shook her head from side to side, expelling the build-up of research cobwebs.

The open plan apartment was tastefully furnished, its off-white walls giving the space maximum volume and airiness. There was one huge corner sofa in the sitting room area, an art-deco coffee table and large designer prints on the walls. Divided from the rest of the room by a low unit, the kitchen area was ideal for chatting to guests while preparing food; the kitchen itself was equipped with state-of-the-art stainless-steel appliances and an elegant matching cooker hood dominated one wall, an artistic 'installation' in its own right.

Paula Tripp's slender hand, its perfectly manicured nails painted a luscious pink, opened the cupboard where she kept a range of expensive glasses for entertaining. Choosing a bohemian crystal tumbler, she half-filled it with ice from the ice-making compartment at the front of her Smeg fridge, then poured a generous shot of Stolichnaya Vodka into the glass before adding a dash of tonic and a slice of lemon. She stood for a moment with her back against the cooking range, moving the ice and liquid around the glass and gazing towards the view from the full length windows that looked out over the city.

It was still light, and dusk had yet to find the skyline. The sun rose and set over the sides of the apartment block, so there was little need for blinds or curtains this far up and Paula Tripp could enjoy an almost uninterrupted view of the city. The 30th floor was the ultimate storey of the building, and as she looked out over the cityscape she smiled to herself, a slight parting of her thin pink lips and a subtle lift of her cheeks betraying a feeling of satisfaction at her own ingenuity. Her nose for a story told her that she was about to break the Fosters wide open and take the Bury Beast story in a direction that would stun her readers and - more importantly - further her career.

Tripp returned to her desk and quickly penned a likely scenario for her call to the seven numbers on the list. The information she was after was fairly straightforward and the calls should end up becoming more like an elimination exercise. First she needed to confirm that the target C Baker at each number was female, match her to the address in Bickerton Rise, Hulme, confirm her Christian name and perhaps even her date of birth, and then get off the phone. Tripp knew that her quarry didn't actually live at the address associated with the number; if her assumptions were right Baker just used it for Electoral Roll convenience - which should make the task easier, as she would be unlikely to encounter the woman herself during the calls. She thought it best to pose as an Electoral Roll moderator calling to clarify that C Baker did actually live at the address. She would say that a routine cross check of the Council Tax database and the Electoral Roll had thrown up an anomaly in the addresses given for C Baker. Of course, the subterfuge could easily be exposed with a quick Google search or a call to the Council Tax or Electoral Roll administration department. For Tripp's purposes the easily assumed genuineness of her questions should produce the required information without the need to go into any detail or arouse too much suspicion, making the need to cover her tracks afterwards irrelevant.

She dialled the first number, careful to use the 141 prefix that would hide her own number and guarantee anonymity. She waited for what seemed an eternity, wrapping and unwrapping the telephone wire around her knuckles in readiness for an answer which frustratingly didn't come. Instead she listened whilst the answerphone repeated a pre-recorded electronic greeting and urged her to leave a message of her own, which she declined by hanging-up. The second number on the list brought the same result, and she gave a sigh of exasperation. This might take longer than she'd expected.

When Tripp dialled the third number on her list she was almost startled to be greeted almost immediately. "Hello, Bob Baker!"

"Hello, Mr Baker," she replied, taking a second to recover her composure before launching into her spiel. "My name is Rebecca Smith. I'm from the Manchester Electoral Ethics Department."

Tripp thought that inventing a genuine sounding body might make it more difficult for the recipients of her call to trace anything afterwards.

"Ok," said Baker, sounding puzzled. "What can I do for you?"

"All it is, Mr Baker," she said, "is that there's been a cross-referral between the Council Tax and Electoral role databases, and there appears to be some confusion over who actually lives at your property and is entitled to vote at elections in your constituency." She was gaining confidence now as she went on. "According to your latest Electoral Roll submission the voters residing at the property are yourself, Robert Albert Baker together with a Veronica May Baker and a Candice Denise Baker."

Tripp paused to rustle some paper. "Is that correct Mr Baker?"

There was a short silence and Tripp could feel Bob Baker swallowing the story without question. When he did eventually answer his speech was slow and awkward, far from the brisk tone that he had used to answer the call. Tripp's blood-pressure rose slightly in anticipation.

"Er, well yes," he said.

Experience told her to stay silent, allowing Bob Baker to dig himself into a hole.

"Candice is *registered* here," he said eventually, "but, she doesn't actually live here at the moment. She's, er, away."

Tripp pounced immediately upon the lie she could hear in his voice.

"Does Candice Baker actually live at Apartment 28 Bickerton Rise, Hulme M14 4EQ? Is that why she's registered for council tax at that address?"

It was obvious from the instant atmosphere oozing

from the handset lodged in Tripp's ear that Bob Baker felt as though he'd been caught out and he began to hesitate like a naughty schoolboy. "I…er…it's just that…" he began.

Seizing her advantage, Tripp said, "Could I ask you to confirm Ms Candice Baker's date of birth please?"

The reporter made a note as Bob Baker reeled off the numbers without any further thought. She now had everything she needed and terminated the call. She carefully let Bob Baker off the hook, telling him that he might be getting a letter from the Electoral Roll asking Candice Baker to register at the Hulme address and that there would be no further action taken as long as Candice changed her registration within twenty-eight days. Bob Baker seemed relieved at the outcome, even wishing her a good evening when she rang-off.

Tripp walked back to the kitchen area to fix herself a second vodka and tonic in an attempt to temper the excitement of the chase that was building inside her. She took the glass, clinking with fresh ice, back to her desk and began looking for Candice Denise Baker, date of birth 10th April 1987. After searching for twenty minutes and printing the relevant pages, she became increasingly excited by the information she found herself collating. She'd always known this story was potentially explosive and her journalistic instincts had told her to follow it up, and hard. Confronted with the information she now had in front of her, she fell back onto the plush leather of her chair, shocked at what she saw on her screen. A random link search between Robert Albert Baker, Veronica May Baker and Candice Denise Baker showed a second child, a second daughter in the family. Tripp literally couldn't believe her eyes as she stared at the name: Jennifer Marilyn Foster nee Baker.

The reporter drew the inescapable conclusion. The woman she had seen coming out of the Midland Hotel after what she imagined must have been a sexual rendezvous with Peter Foster was Jenny Foster's sister.

She could hardly contain herself, getting hit after hit as she launched into searches confirming the link between Jenny Foster and the Baker household. Jenny had spent her childhood and some of her adult life at the Baker address. Bob Baker was a successful and well respected local businessman and together with his wife Val was the centre of a social circle that included anyone who was anyone throughout Cheshire and Lancashire. Even Don her editor was pictured with Bob Baker at some black-tie dinner and he also had significant links with Peter Foster and his property company. In Paula Tripp's mind there was no doubt: Peter Foster was having an affair with his own sister-in-law, unbeknown to his wife and the entire Baker family.

Her excitement at the revelation quickly reached boiling point, her imagination teeming with likely scenarios. She realised that this news in itself would not be instrumental in the search for Reed, but Tripp was experienced and cunning enough to know that information was power, and if Jenny Foster knew nothing of the affair between her husband and her sister the journalist would be able to use it as leverage to get closer to the case. Her mind turned over different methods she could use to manipulate the Fosters to her own ends, and her excitement grew to fever pitch. She saw herself at the very centre of the investigation, privy to crucial facts before other journalists had even started climbing into their cars to head for their press conferences. Tripp mused that because she would be ahead of the game, she could produce scoop after devastating scoop and she would be celebrated not just by her employers at the Manchester Evening News, but by the most credible and powerful media giants of the UK - if not the world.

She sat back in her sumptuous chair, throwing her head back and allowing a long passage of air to escape her lips. Closing her eyes she continued to dream, a smile of pure self-satisfaction spreading across her face when the radio volume increased as the evening news kicked in. Then the words *missing woman* suddenly registered, interrupting her thoughts and demanding her concentration.

In the customary flat tone the news reader informed his listeners that a woman was missing in Bury and had last been seen by her husband before she left for her job at a pub in Whitefield. She had not arrived as planned and the police were keen for anyone who had seen the woman to come forward. The radio bulletin didn't reveal the possible victim's name or an address, but had given a fairly detailed description of the missing woman and a white Luton-style van that the Police were keen to trace. It was clear to Tripp that this must be connected to the Bury Beast case. Women must go missing for a few hours every day for a thousand reasons, so a briefing to the radio station from the police meant that they were concerned that she was the next victim, and they wanted to trace her fast.

Instantly shelving her recent discovery, Paula Tripp picked up the telephone to check in with her editor.

Chapter 17

The first thing Jenny did when she got home was make a bee-line for Lilly's bedroom. The profiler kissed her daughter's sleeping forehead, the guilt of not being there to put her to bed aching in her stomach. She watched Lilly sleep for a few minutes, sprawled across the bed with a film of sweat clinging to her hair and skin. It was still light outside and the black-out curtains gave the room some protection from the last of the day's heat, but the room was stuffy and the air heavy with the little girl's steady breathing. Jenny leant down to kiss Lilly again, perhaps in a subconscious effort to wake her, but her daughter slept on blissfully unaware of her mother's anxious vigil and the words of love that were being whispered next to her face.

Eventually Jenny made her way slowly down the stairs, her muscles feeling weak and useless and her stockinged feet more like work boots as each step jolted up through her knees and hips. Peter was waiting for her at the foot of the stairs. "Are you ok?" he asked.

She brushed silently past him, slowly making her way into the sitting room and flopping into one of the sumptuous grey armchairs. Peter followed closely and sat opposite her, perched anxiously on the end of the sofa and looking concerned. Eventually Jenny broke the silence, still slumped in the chair, and with her eyes firmly closed.

"I'm an awful mother!"

"You couldn't have possibly known that this Joe Reed joker would appear as soon as you arrived at your desk," comforted Peter. "When most people start a job there's a few weeks bedding-in period, but this…" he trailed off.

"What?"

"Well, this is all a bit much isn't it?" asked Peter, an anxious edge to his question.

She opened her eyes and searched her husband's face for the meaning of his words. He looked young for his age, tanned, fit and unruffled as always. His dancing blue eyes were framed by perfectly moisturised brown skin, and she found herself vaguely irritated that there wasn't even a hint of five o'clock shadow to indicate that he was a 'normal' human being.

"All a bit much?" asked Jenny, with a flash of temper as she suddenly came to life. She pitched forward in her seat meeting his eyes full tilt.

"You've no idea," she said sharply.

"Tell me then?" he suggested a little tentatively.

She remained sitting upright for a few seconds, holding Peter's gaze before eventually relaxing her body to ease herself back into the arms of the chair.

"It's the women," she began. "Dawn James and Robyn Cox - they're just like me."

Peter said nothing, just slipped back into his seat knowing that if he kept quiet his wife would open up.

Jenny tugged at her straight dark brown hair. "They look like me, they've even got hair like mine," she said, her face turning into a pleading grimace. "They're mothers like me too. One minute they're looking after their husbands and kids, struggling with part-time jobs, friends and a life, and the next thing they're lying naked on an industrial estate with the life squeezed out of them by a monster."

She was half sobbing out the words now, not even trying to stop her emotions from coming to the surface.

"Who's going to be next? It's all so confusing in real life! Study is one thing; getting degrees and learning about murder and murderers is easy on paper because it's all history. Everything has already happened and when you're asked to look at a case academically you're either right about what happened, or wrong."

She paused momentarily, biting at her lip and with an almost child-like look on her face.

"Can you see what I'm saying?" she pleaded. "There's always someone who already knows how the case ended: there's a conclusion to it all. There's someone who can tell you whether you were right or wrong, and there are no consequences."

Jenny paused again, pouring her silver bracelet from one hand to the other and back again, over and over.

"I mean, I'm telling Sam and the other detectives what I think Reed's like based on his actions and how he's behaving. What if I'm miles out? The consequences are too horrible to contemplate."

Peter broke his silence. "I'm sure your assumptions will turn out to be pretty accurate," he said reassuringly.

She shook her head. "Let's face it, Peter. For all I know Joe Reed could be a black American line-dancer with a death wish, here on vacation."

"Are you scared you might be next?" asked Peter.

Jenny smiled in the same way that she might smile at Lilly when she first asked if Father Christmas was real. "Don't be ridiculous," she said almost spitting out the words. "I'm surrounded by dozens of policemen every day and come straight back home after work." She stopped for a second before adding sarcastically, "Don't worry, *I'm* safe. It's the rest of the female population of Manchester that aren't."

Peter stared at his wife. He realised his question had been a bit stupid, but hadn't expected to be scolded for it.

"I somehow feel part of them," said Jenny, quieter now, deep in thought. "Whether it's because of the physical similarities or because of the hours I've spent studying Reed, I feel as though I'm one of them somehow. As if I've experienced what they're going through." She paused and corrected herself, remembering one of the women was already dead. "Or what they've *been* through.

All I can think about is Dawn James' lifeless eyes looking back at me like glass marbles every time I close mine. I forget about those eyes for a few minutes every day and then I look in the mirror, or look at someone at work and I can see her staring at me."

Jenny's face was contorted with misery as she spoke. She looked beseechingly over at Peter and he could see her pain, feel her anguish.

"Dawn James haunts me, I can see her asking me what I'm doing about it," she said quietly.

Peter was finding it difficult to reconcile this anguished woman with the Jenny he had packed off for

230

her first day as a Criminal Profiler with the Manchester Metropolitan Police. He could see her now almost skipping down the drive to her car with a huge smile on her face, thrilled that after all that hard work and ambition she'd finally made it.

All at once he heard himself saying, "Aren't you supposed to be dispassionate and objective?"

"Piss off!" snapped Jenny instantly, the words slipping too easily, almost instinctively from her full lips and hanging heavily in the air.

Peter's eyes widened: in his position as the Managing Director of his own company he wasn't used to being sworn at, and he certainly wasn't used to it from Jenny. His face reddened, his eyes flashing with involuntary rage.

"Who do you think you're talking to?" he said, his voice gaining decibels with every word. "I'm not one of your bloody copper mates!"

Jenny didn't answer, preferring instead to give her husband her practised stare of indifference as he sprang from his chair and stormed out of the room, thumping up the stairs. She wanted to go after him, tell him she was sorry and try to make amends, but something stopped her, as it always did - her pride.

The sound of her mobile ringing gave her an excuse not to follow him. It was Sam, and there was an unbridled urgency in his voice. "Hello, Jenny? Reed's kidnapped another woman!"

"Who is she?"

"Her name's Sharon Daly, married with an eleven year-old son called Mark. Dominic Daly, her husband, says she does the late shift at the Rose and Crown in

Whitefield, which is walking distance from their house across Whitefield Common. He says she left as usual about six-twenty. Apparently it's her thirty-fourth birthday and her husband and a group of friends had a surprise party planned for her at the pub. So when she left to walk to work he jumped in the car with the son and went over to there to surprise her."

"Ok," said Jenny, her spat with Peter forgotten, "and obviously she didn't arrive?"

"Uh-uh!" said Sam. "Plus, she fits the profile: dark hair, mid-thirties and married with a child."

"Are you at the Daly house now?" asked Jenny. "What's the address? I'll come over and talk to the husband - Dominic you said?"

She scrambled for a pen and paper, and Sam reeled off the address with crude directions. "I'll be there within half an hour," she said and hung up.

Sitting for a moment deep in thought, it occurred to Jenny that if Joe Reed had abducted another woman then the body of Robyn Cox, whom he already held, would be turning up sooner rather than later. With that dreadful prospect in mind, she knew she must concentrate all her mental resources on catching Reed quickly and saving a life.

Jenny made her way to the main bathroom, washing her face, brushing her hair out and quickly refreshing her make-up to boost her morale in preparation for what lay ahead. Crossing the landing, she opened Lilly's door to see her still flat-out, and without stepping inside blew the child a kiss before making her way back to her own bedroom, where Peter hadn't moved. She leant against the door-frame for a few moments watching her husband stare at the television screen. He looked older than he had downstairs, somehow more crumpled.

"Are you ok?" she asked, but he didn't answer, or even look up.

Without another word Jenny took the stairs, hurried out to the drive and got into her car. She knew what she was about to do was cowardly, but she didn't want another argument, not now when she itched to be on her way. She took out her mobile phone, opened the text function and selected her husband as the only recipient.

"There's been a development in the case," she typed quickly. "I need to go out for a couple of hours, will be back as soon as I can." Her thumb hovered briefly over the send button and after a few seconds she added, "Sorry…I love you xxx", pressed *send*, threw the phone on the passenger seat and started the car. The air was still thick and heavy with the heat of the day and Jenny put the driver's window down to its full extent, reversed out onto the road and drove off towards Whitefield.

***

There was little traffic about, and the twenty minute drive via the ring-road link was uneventful. Jenny consulted her phone every few minutes, checking for a response from Peter: none arrived.

As she approached Whitefield, she noticed that police activity seemed to be intensifying every few hundred yards. By the time she turned into Dovecote Way where the Dalys' house stood about half way down, the police cars and vans filled every available space. A *Do Not Cross* plastic line had been erected between lamp-posts and stretched across the road. Reporters, TV vans and the usual knots of ghoulish spectators were being kept behind the line and Jenny had little option but to stop her car in the middle of the road and force her way through the crowd on foot. A sergeant recognised her without the need to fish into her bag for her ID card, and she ducked under the makeshift barrier and made her way towards Number 52. The short, tight fitting grey blazer that she'd put on over a pink blouse needed to be buttoned up to suit the design, and she already felt uncomfortably hot. The end-of-the-day heat clung to the air, and the profiler realised she'd forgotten to spray herself with deodorant. *Bad move Jenny,* she thought as she walked up the short pathway to the house.

The door was open and the front garden was filled with police constables, specials and PCSOs, the later arrivals waiting behind the small boundary wall. Sam was giving instructions to another sergeant and Jenny caught the tail-end of the conversation.

"Ok then, Bill," he was saying. "Make sure you knock on every door, search every alleyway and look under every bush between here and the Rose and Crown. Sharon Daly's normal route is across Whitefield Common into Glanbourne Street, then down Manchester Road and on to the pub. She may have stopped off at one of the fast food places or wine stores still open on Manchester Road, so make sure you cover those too."

He paused for the sergeant to indicate that he understood. "The incident van is on its way. I'll station it at the end of this road. If there are any immediate developments use your radio, otherwise I'll meet you at the van myself in an hour. Clear?"

The sergeant nodded a flop of straw coloured hair and led the army of officers out of the garden and into the road, firing instructions as he went.

"That's a lot of manpower," commented Jenny.

"Well, you know how crucial the first few hours are," said Sam. "If we're going to catch Reed, now is one of our best chances. If he *has* abducted Sharon Daly then someone must have seen something. It's practically broad daylight, for Christ's sake!"

Jenny was worried: she didn't want Dominic Daly or the son Mark any more panicked than they must feel already with dozens of policemen in their front garden. She needed some calm space to talk to them both.

"Have you spoken to the husband and son?" she asked.

"Yes, he's given me a statement - but all he knows is, his wife left the house ok, and then didn't show up at work fifteen minutes later. He called us after walking the route himself without seeing her. He said he just felt there was something wrong."

"Ok," said Jenny. "How sure are you that she's been abducted? She could have decided she didn't fancy a shift at the pub on her birthday and be at a friend's house right now?"

"Unlikely," said Sam. "Dominic made sure he dropped enough hints about the surprise party, and all her friends were waiting for her at the pub. There's no way she wouldn't have turned up."

"How's the son? Mark isn't it?" asked Jenny.

"Very quiet. He says he'd usually have been on the

Common when his mum went through, probably playing football or whatever with his mates. But tonight he was waiting for her to go out so he could go back to the house and join his Dad to go off to the party."

Sam breathed out hard. "I've got a WPC with him, trying to reassure him that everything will be ok, but I don't think he believes her."

"Ok, I'll go inside and talk to them," said Jenny.

The house itself was a neat, three-bedroom semi-detached, and Jenny was sure it would be a nice place to live when there wasn't an army of police around, and the road didn't resemble an Emergency Service car park. Yes, the houses were close together, but the gardens were neat and the road itself tree-lined with mature ash and sycamore every fifteen feet or so, and she imagined that in spring the road would be full of beautiful blossom. Number 52 was well-kept, with UPVC double glazing and newly painted rendering and gutters. The Dalys were obviously house-proud and the interior spoke of a happy family at peace with itself. Just inside the door Sharon and Dominic beamed at visitors from their wedding portrait and continuing into the sitting-room family pictures adorned every spare surface, with a huge portrait of Mark above the Victorian-style fireplace.

The sitting-room was empty, but Jenny could hear murmurings from the kitchen and proceeded down the hall to where Dominic sat at the kitchen table with his son on one side and a WPC on the other. The uniformed officer stood up and met Jenny in the doorway. Jenny spoke in hushed tones. "How are they bearing up?"

"They're both quieter now," said the WPC.

Her face wore a professional look of concern and her brown hair was done up in a neat bun, giving her a faintly school-marmish air and putting Jenny immediately at her ease. Jenny asked her if she could take Mark into the other room so she could talk to his dad, and the woman went over and whispered something to the boy before the two of them left the room.

Dominic hardly seemed to notice as Jenny sat down on a metal-framed kitchen armchair, with the unexpectedly squashy black leather seat settling her further down than she would have liked. She put her black handbag on the table, where the small round feet designed to protect the bottom of the bag had the opposite effect on the glass table-top and she winced as the metal skidded across the surface.

Daly looked up. "I never liked this table," he said. "Sharon's choice. I like wood - it's a much warmer material for a kitchen."

Only now that she was sitting down in front of Dominic Daly did Jenny take in his size. Family life obviously agreed with him, and he'd put on more than a few pounds since he was captured in the blown-up photograph by the door. On the other hand, he'd lost enough of his hair to make shaving off the rest preferable to the alternative pattern baldness. His arms rested on the table with his hands clasped together in front of him. Jenny could make out the name 'Mark' and a date on his left inner arm, and the name 'Sharon' and a different date on his right inner arm. She looked at the broad wedding ring on his fat fingers.

"When did you get married?"

"Eight years ago. Mark isn't mine, well not biologically anyway. I'm his dad in every other sense, though."

"Does he see his biological father?" asked Jenny.

"No," said Daly, adding, "I'm not even sure that Sharon knows who the father is. She was wild when she was younger, a real handful. I'm telling you now that if this Bury Beast guy has managed to kidnap Sharon he's in for a big surprise. She'll murder *him* before he gets the chance to do anything to her."

Jenny felt herself wanting to explain to Dominic that if Joe Reed had taken his wife she didn't stand a chance without help but she resisted, knowing that at least he'd find temporary comfort in holding on to the notion that Reed was in more trouble than Sharon.

"I know DI Bradbury has already asked you some questions," she went on, "but I hope you don't mind us talking?" She continued when it was clear that he didn't. "I'm Jenny Foster, and I'm building a profile of Joe Reed to help the police try and guess his next move and catch him more quickly than they would have done."

"Ok," said Daly tonelessly.

"Then can I ask you first what *kind* of woman Sharon is? Does she have many friends? I know she works at the pub, but does she go to any clubs or regular nights out?" asked Jenny, flipping open a notebook and poising a pen.

"She used to. Not any more though; she spends all her time thinking about what's best for me and Mark. She's great like that! Always got the tea on the table, washing clothes, doing jobs round the house, shopping. You know - she's a real *wife*."

His emphasis on the word sent Jenny's questions in a new direction.

"Do you, or Mark even, help around the house much?" she asked.

"You try and she'd have your guts!" Dominic said, a half smile creeping onto his lips without quite making it to his eyes. "She likes everything just so."

"Ok, thanks."

He looked at Jenny as she stood up to go, his forehead wrinkling into lines that would rival the waves on Bondi Beach. "Is that it?"

"Try not to worry Mr Daly," she said, and put her hand on his huge shoulder and squeezed. "There are more than a hundred officers conducting house-to-house enquiries and more policeman back at Manchester HQ - and they're all concentrating on finding Sharon."

Jenny left the house quickly, nodding to the WPC as she passed the sitting room and noticing that she seemed to have persuaded Mark to sit next to her and watch the television. She found Sam still pacing the garden and talking intently on his phone.

"Nothing on CCTV," he said, the frustration apparent in his voice as Jenny joined him. "There aren't as many cameras here as there are in Manchester, but there are enough and not one has picked up Joe Reed or the van."

Jenny let out a sigh. She'd been hoping that CCTV would at least give them an idea of the direction in which Reed had left the scene. She wondered how on earth he had managed to appear and disappear on a whim.

"Listen Sam," she said. "The victimology of the three

women is so similar they could conceivably even be sisters."

"I know."

"The point I'm trying to make is that Sharon was a housewife, dedicated to her husband and her son. Apart from work, she hardly left the house except to shop."

"Go on," urged Sam, realising Jenny was trying to tell him something of importance.

"Ok, so what are the odds of Joe Reed riding round Greater Manchester on a whim looking for his exact type of woman, finding one, stopping his van there and then, and bundling her inside?" asked the Profiler. "Zero?"

Jenny was happy to be on solid ground. "So he must be stalking them. He must have a method of choosing the right type to be his victim and then following them to get a good idea of their routine."

"Yes, I see," said Sam, realising where Jenny was trying to lead him. "Not just a *good idea* either, but an *exact* schedule of their routine. You're dead right Jenny! If the husband's description of his wife's habits is accurate, there's only one time and place to be able to abduct Sharon Daly successfully, and that's on Whitefield Common between six-twenty and six-thirty pm."

Jenny chimed in, "and in order to know that, Joe Reed must have been watching her every day for at least a week, if not longer."

"The same as the third victim in Ireland," added Sam. "Reed's obviously moved from trying to make a relationship with women he wants to hurt, to stalking them instead," said Jenny.

"Which means?"

"Which means that he's trying to distance himself from his victims," explained the profiler.

"Whereas with the rape victims he knew they would survive, so he felt comfortable getting to know them?" asked Sam.

"Yes, precisely," said Jenny gaining momentum. "With his murder victims he doesn't interact with them at all. Think about Veronica Denshaw in Ireland: he had no intention of forging a relationship with her, but it's clear from the evidence that he was *trying* to kill her."

"And Dawn James was uncared for and half starved to death," Sam added.

"Yes, and so maybe the trigger to going ahead and actually murdering her was the bare fact that she would have died of malnutrition within twenty-four hours anyway," suggested Jenny.

"You mean he can't bring himself to murder straight away, so he keeps his victims captive until he's plucked up the courage?"

"I'm not sure," said Jenny. "But his lack of action and the fact that he keeps the women he's going to murder at arm's length is another sign of guilt and deep regret. Perhaps he just doesn't want to make the same mistake as he did with Veronica Denshaw."

"Another sign?" asked Sam.

"Yes," said Jenny. "I mentioned that Reed's acts of washing Dawn James' body post-mortem and folding her arms over her chest were signs of remorse."

"Remorse maybe," said Sam unconvinced. "But guilt and regret?"

Jenny didn't answer, preferring to show that she was

deep in thought by playing with the heart on her bracelet.

Sam studied her face. "I thought he was one step ahead," he said, "but it seems that he's at least three steps ahead. He must have begun stalking Sharon Daly before he'd even killed Dawn James."

Sam and Jenny stood silently looking at each other. Sam absentmindedly produced two cigarettes and Jenny took one, lighting it from the flame offered. They breathed in smoke at the same time, long and hard, and then suddenly Sam's radio came to life in his jacket pocket. He pulled it out and pressed the intercom. "DI Bradbury," he said.

It was the sergeant he'd been speaking to in the garden earlier - the one detailed to lead the team canvassing the area.

"We've got blood specks on a bush on Whitefield Common, Sir, and one of the lads is talking to a potential witness who was walking her dog."

"Any sightings on the van?" asked Sam.

"She says she had to squeeze past a white van parked in the side road next to the common. She says the van was scruffy, with red paint on the bumper and it was parked about fifty yards from the blood-stains."

"Did she see anyone in it?"

"No," came back the sergeant. "She didn't see it leave either."

"Ok, I'm on my way over!" said Sam, clicking off and returning the receiver to his pocket.

He turned back to Jenny. "It looks like it's definitely Joe Reed. I'll go over to the common and you go home: there's nothing more you can do here tonight."

"What about the stalking angle?"

"I'll put a team on it tomorrow," reassured Sam. "We'll talk to the neighbours of the three victims again, this time with a slightly different tack - see if they remember anything useful. Best thing for you to do now is get some rest and come in fresh in the morning."

Chapter 18

Early next day Paula Tripp made the short journey on foot from her apartment to Central Park, Manchester Metropolitan Police Headquarters. Even at eight o'clock in the morning there was no need for more than a short-sleeved blouse and Tripp wore a matching white summer skirt ending just over the knee to show off her slender legs and a stylish pair of cork-soled wedge heels. She had arranged for one of the staff photographers to meet her outside Central Park to capture Foster's facial reactions. The reporter would then be free to concentrate on asking Jenny Foster the questions that she'd prepared over a hurried breakfast of black coffee and half a grapefruit.

Passing one of Manchester's oldest and most famous department stores she tipped a cheery hello to the burly security guard, who was struggling with a noisy metal shutter. Tripp commented that Kendal's looked like they could afford electric shutters, which produced a rueful smile from the breathless guard. Walking jauntily on, she stopped as usual at Al's Bakery in Deansgate for a second cup of coffee. Al was fit and slender despite his trade, obviously resisting the pastries and cakes he supplied so abundantly to other people. His smile had been an almost daily feature of Paula Tripp's life since she moved to the city, and as with many a routine detail its absence would have seemed like a portent of bad luck. As a creature of habit she would not be able to bring herself to miss him, especially this morning. She ordered and paid for her usual black coffee with an extra shot of espresso, her head spinning as the first sip of the heavy-duty caffeine hit the back of her throat.

Tripp's conversations at Al's were comfortingly normal and homely, with no probing for inside information on the case that everyone was talking about. Al seemed happy to provide Paula with a place of refuge whenever she needed one with no questions asked. Consequently, in addition to her morning visits she would haunt one of the back booths a couple of times a month, nursing a train of black coffees and deep in thought, safe in the knowledge that she would be left to confront whatever demon she was wrestling with, minus a string of questions.

Central Park was only a few minutes' walk away and Tripp glanced at her watch knowing that time was beginning to drain from her window of opportunity. Jenny Foster usually arrived at around eight-thirty and it was now pushing quarter-past, so Tripp took her coffee to go and lengthened her stride to make the remainder of the journey as short as possible.

When she arrived at the huge building, designed to symbolise the ultimate power of establishment and order, the early morning sun had risen to the height of the all-glass portion of the building. Tripp was momentarily blinded as she crossed the car-park, turning left to the entrance which mercifully blocked out the glare of the sun. She still had most of the coffee in her cup and the heat transferring from the polystyrene to her hands, coupled with the instant heat from the glare from the windows brought a reddening to her cheeks which she didn't welcome.

"Morning, Ben!" she called when she spotted the photographer waiting on the steps into the building as arranged.

"Hi, Paula," came the reply. "Is that coffee hot?"

Tripp handed over the coffee without a word and watched Ben first grimace at the lack of milk, but then acquire the taste and slurp a few more mouthfuls before offering the cup back.

She smiled. "Finish it, you look like you could do with it more than me."

Benjamin Pengali was one of the most accomplished photographers on the Manchester Evening News. He was retained by the paper as a freelance paparazzi style "snap-it-sell-it" media stalker of anyone remotely interesting within a fifty mile radius of Manchester. He and Paula had staked out a few z-list celebrities together in the past and Pengali made good company for long boring vigils. Affable and with a ready wit, he charmed his way into venues all over Manchester and Paula guessed he'd been up all night chasing a picture.

"Who were you waiting for last night? Cloud Bar was it?" she asked.

His bright eyes flashed into a smile with his lips following a second later revealing a perfect set of white teeth, too well kept for a mere photographer. He had celebrity written all over him with his beanie in place despite the heat, just offset to show locks of golden curls peeping from beneath. He was tall, lithe and graceful, the perfect clothes-horse for anything tight fitting. The skinny jeans he wore today made his legs look a foot longer than they were, with a white t-shirt pulled tight over his frame, the words *don't look now* shouting in red across the chest.

"Can't say," he answered cryptically. "Not yet anyway." Paula smiled and glanced at her watch. It was eight twenty-six, and she hoped that Jenny Foster hadn't decided to work from home today, or gone straight to some other distraction. Looking up expectantly when she heard the noise of a car humming into the car-park, she saw Jenny Foster's black BMW slowly make the turns around the concrete and park right on cue.

"Here she is!" said Tripp and moved off in Jenny's direction with Ben setting down the remains of the coffee, grabbing his camera and shooting stills as he followed her towards the car.

Jenny had already noticed the pair striding in her direction, and knew she was about to face a barrage of questions. Without ever having been in the media spotlight herself, she hadn't really thought twice about the Chief and Sam running the gauntlet of a crowd of reporters seemingly every time they arrived or left the building. She knew of course that she would be the focus of press attention at some point, but today it hadn't crossed her mind. Her morning already hadn't gone exactly according to plan, with Lilly deciding that her breakfast looked better on the floor than it tasted in her mouth, and being harassed in the car park was the last thing she needed. Peter had laughed uncontrollably, without making the slightest effort to help when she found herself bending down to scoop up the sloppy mess - obviously his idea of punishment for the argument the night before, no doubt still fresh in his mind. Tripp could see Jenny sitting stock still in her car as she approached and she knew she was an unwelcome sight. But then she often was; this kind of reluctance to speak to the press only spurred Tripp on. Relishing the confrontation, she quickened her pace, stopping next to the driver's door with Ben steadfastly snapping away just at her right shoulder. Jenny gave a huge sigh as she accepted her fate, turned off the engine and opened the door.

Tripp was a master of creating pressure in these situations and with the first crack of the door came her opening question.

"Excuse me, Mrs Foster," she said. "I'm Paula Tripp from the Manchester Evening News. Is it true that you and your colleagues are close to making an arrest?"

Tripp knew that the Police were no closer to catching the Bury Beast than they'd been the day or the week before, but she needed a reason for being here and this angle was as good as any.

Jenny felt her car door push against Paula Tripp's leg as she opened it to its full extension and slipped out. Meanwhile she was aware of some unknown photographer, his finger like a trip hammer clicking the camera shutter in a rapid succession of shots, and she felt acutely self-conscious. Thanks to Lilly's breakfast antics, she'd had hardly any time to get ready for work. Her dark hair was scraped back and forced into a utilitarian pony-tail, and she could feel the strands of hair that she'd planned to tidy in the Ladies Room before she went to her desk dancing against her forehead. And then, to top everything, she suddenly realised with a chill of dismay that she wasn't wearing any make-up except foundation, which she was sure would be un-flattering and harsh in the glare of the camera lens. The flowered summer dress with a tailored blue jack-et felt ok, but Jenny wondered with horror if her bare legs and kitten heels would give readers the impression that she wasn't as professional as she should be.

The sun was bright against the glass of the building with Tripp and the photographer highlighted in relief by the glare. The two blurred figures in front of her were all she could see, their bodies and heads bizarre-ly suspended in a bright glow, as if they were wearing halos.

She had no choice but to look Tripp in the face. "No Comment!" she said and attempted to push past.

Paula Tripp and Ben Pengali were veteran stalkers of celebrities though, and not so easily thrown off. Instinctively the pair moved together to halt any pro-gress that the profiler thought she might make and engineered Jenny into position, so that her back was against her now closed car door.

"We've had a report that an arrest is imminent," pressed Tripp. "Is the Bury Beast a local man as you originally thought?"

Jenny felt trapped. She was disorientated by the sun and the sudden physical superiority of her two inquis-itors. She became aware that during the move back-wards Tripp had gripped her elbow and Jenny followed her natural reaction to shrug the hand off. Despite the setback, the reporter stood her ground, the heavily loaded question still hanging ominously in the air. Jenny took a moment to compose herself before looking the other woman directly in the eye.

"I've already said that I don't have any comment for you at this time," she said forcefully, pushing her body forward with more determination and using her heavy black leather handbag to break away from the car and move past the reporter and photographer.

"You will have a chance to ask any questions at the daily press conference at ten am," she informed them.

Her move had been effective: now it was Tripp and Pengali's turn to face the sun and the snapping of the camera shutter stopped abruptly. Ben Pengali knew that any pictures would be useless with such a bright sun behind his subject and Jenny noted with some satisfaction that the camera was quickly relegated to uselessness, hanging limply from the photographer's neck. Tripp though, was determined to press on, despite the sudden brightness forcing her eyes to close. The reporter shifted her weight to stand in Jenny's shadow and reduce the glare.

"I understand that you're new and inexperienced, Jenny," she said, the not-so- subtle use of her Christian name not lost on the profiler. "But, we're the locals, and our readers should be the first to know of any developments."

Then adopting a softer, friendlier, almost conspiratorial tone, she went on, "Our *women* readers are scared Jenny, really scared. There's a monster out there preying on them and they need to know that you're doing everything you can."

Jenny studied Tripp from the benefit of her new position with the sun behind her. She thought the reporter was dressed too young for her age and her makeup was too heavy. The heat had almost baked it onto her face, showing every crack and tag of her skin. Even so, she decided Tripp was probably younger than her, and she could almost feel the ambition and intensity leaking from the reporter. Tripp was slim and her figure was lithe and athletic. Her face was too thin, gaunt even, with high, almost mocking cheek bones and bright darting blue eyes that reminded Jenny of a jackal. She could see through Tripp's flimsy veil of concern and knew that the only person she wanted to benefit from any extra morsel of information was Tripp herself. But what the reporter said next came right out of the blue, her eyes glinting before she settled into an amused silence, watching Jenny's reaction.

"That is, everything you can, given your *personal* difficulties of course."

Jenny's stomach flipped like a pancake, an angry heat suffusing her neck and face.

Tripp knew she'd ruffled more than just a feather and waited patiently whilst her quarry composed herself. Jenny was clearly making an effort to contain her anger and the reporter was surprised when the profiler eventually smiled, ironically at first and then more broadly, apparently genuinely amused.

It was clear that Jenny wasn't taking the bait.

"As I said '*Miss*' Tripp," Jenny emphasised the Miss. "If there are any new developments they will be discussed at the press conference later this morning. Now if you don't mind I need to get to my desk."

With that she turned on her heel, only to be caught

once again by Tripp, her slender hand gripping her elbow like a vice. Jenny turned, anger flashing into her brown eyes. Tripp spoke quickly.

"This is for you," said the reporter, pressing a white A4 envelope into her hand. Jenny stared at the offering.

"What's this?" she asked, swiftly making to give it back.

Tripp placed her hand over the top of Jenny's. "Don't worry, Jenny, it's not a bribe! Just a story you might be interested in, that's all."

"I don't think I would be," said Jenny and pushed the envelope back into her hand.

Tripp continued to hold her by the elbow and quickly slipped the envelope into her open handbag.

"Look," she said, "I'm trying to do you a favour here. Take it and give me a call when you've had a chance to review the information."

Jenny went to retrieve the package from her bag, she was sure she wouldn't be interested in the contents, whatever they were, but before she had the chance to return it, Tripp let go of the profiler's elbow and together with Ben Pengali walked quickly away across the car park.

Jenny stood alone on the tarmac, turning the envelope in her hand. The profiler felt as though she'd been drawn into some conspiracy of which she'd wanted no part. Looking down, her eye caught her watch and realising she was now late, she headed across the car park and into the building.

Once inside, Jenny took the lift to the 6th floor and spent a frantic ten minutes in the bathroom with her brush and make-up bag. She was annoyed that she'd had been caught out by Paula Tripp and her snapping side-kick and her first glimpse in the mirror told her just how unawares she had been taken. She looked nowhere near presentable, let alone at her best. She breathed hard as she stared in the mirror studying the car-crash that now served as her public persona, the thought ever present that pictures would be spread across the Manchester Evening News with her looking like she'd been dragged through a hedge backwards.

The Chief had called her during her car journey to Central Park and had been clear in his instructions. Her task was to go through the piles of correspondence, transcripts of the voice recordings made of calls to police stations across Manchester and print-outs of e-mails from the public that the Bury Beast case had generated. Arriving at her desk she found that the items had already been labelled by other officers in the team who had scanned the missives for pertinent information relating to the case, and in many instances the resulting leads were already being followed up by an army of constables and specials drafted in as support.

The resources allocated to the case were growing, with almost two hundred officers, specials and PCSOs now dedicated to tracking down the Bury Beast.

All regular leave had been cancelled and overtime had become an occupational necessity. There were two women missing, imprisoned somewhere by Joe Reed right now and the clock was ticking to find them. Everyone working on the case knew that Dawn James had been discovered with the number *1* burned into the tender skin at the small of her back.

The numerical factors were causing mounting consternation amongst the ranks as their meaning became clear, and all the team could see was momentum. Jenny had briefed the new officers and the detectives on this fact already and everyone knew that time was against them. Reed must be found before he had a chance to murder Robyn Cox and keep the macabre ball rolling. The Chief had wrestled with the idea of going public and letting the women of Manchester know the type of target that Reed preferred: dark shoulder length hair, aged mid-thirties, probably working, with a husband and children. In the end he had decided that the information would cause widespread panic, especially as the victim profile could be applied to tens of thousands of women. The Chief's latest press conference had concentrated on the video image of Joe Reed at the office party. Reed's starring part in the video and the YouTube link had been sent to all press and media offices in the UK. The play tally of the video was impressive, with over half a million views making it the most watched clip of the week.

The team felt certain that Joe Reed would see the film himself. Jenny had profiled that Reed must be monitoring news channels and the clear image of his face might force him to make a mistake. Some of the detectives even thought that Joe Reed might walk in to a police station to give himself up.

Jenny thought differently. She reasoned that since Reed had abducted Robyn Cox and Sharon Daly practically in broad daylight it was unlikely that media attention or even the prospect of being caught would motivate him into breaking cover. In fact she was convinced that such attention would have just the opposite effect. The telephone on her desk sprang to life and she picked it up without speaking.

"Is this Jenny Foster's extension?" asked a young woman's voice.

Jenny snapped into the reality of the call. "Yes," she said. "This is Jenny Foster."

"I have DI Ronnie George for you," explained the voice and clicked the call through.

"Hi Ronnie," said Jenny, her face breaking into a smile.

"Hi Jenny! How's it going up there?"

Jenny was suddenly torn between speaking to her uncle as a trusted family member, or as a Detective Inspector at New Scotland Yard. Eventually, she decided that her uncle should remain just that: her uncle. "I'm ok," she said. "It's like a madhouse here."

"How did the Ireland information turn out?"

"Good!" said Jenny positively. "It was definitely our man Joe Reed."

"Did he commit murder?" asked Ronnie as though he were asking Jenny if she wanted a cup of coffee.

"Almost. There were three victims in Ireland and he almost managed to kill the last one."

"So a decent pattern then?"

Jenny suddenly wondered why Ronnie had called her at work. He must already know the answers to the questions he was asking; he was the one who'd supplied the information relating to the cases in Ireland.

"Yes, a decent pattern," she replied. "Listen Ronnie, it's great to hear from you, but I'm up to my eyes here."

"Er, ok," there was a momentary pause between them

which Jenny had never experienced before with her Uncle.

The silence became uncomfortable.

"What's the Chief's next move?" he asked, breaking the spell.

"I really don't know,"

"Does he seem in control?"

Jenny could hear an agenda in the question.

"Of course he's in control. When I said it was like a madhouse, I meant there was so much information and so many people involved that it felt…"

"A bit disorganised," put in Ronnie, cutting across his niece.

"Actually the Chief has organised the investigation much better than I would have thought possible," countered Jenny, jumping to her superior's defence. "I've been given a mountain of witness reports to sift through. They'll be keeping me busy for a week by the looks of things."

"Ok, I'll let you get back to it. Call me if you need any advice"

"I will," she lied and clicked off.

What was that? Jenny wondered, staring at the receiver. Unable to provide an answer the profiler put the call from her mind and considered the task at hand.

The weight of the information she'd been given to look through was incredible. The case had clearly captured the imagination of the local people. Her job was not to look for evidence, but to look for any patterns in the correspondence, anything unusual. It was common for this type of offender to try to communicate with the police or the press and Jenny had a long day ahead of her sifting the material and trying to make sense of it. She made a start, but after only a few minutes realised that it would take her a week just to organise this amount of material and she needed help. Spotting Sam talking to one of the new recruits she made the short distance, looking for advice.

"Hi Sam," she said.

DI Sam Bradbury looked up, his forehead was creased and his eyes were dark-ringed from an obvious lack of sleep. He managed a weak smile, but couldn't disguise a hint of irritation at being interrupted.

"How are you getting on?" he asked.

Jenny got her request in quickly, knowing he wasn't in the mood for more than basic information. "I need help to organise all this paperwork."

The irritation in Sam's face vanished as quickly as it had appeared and his features softened, almost sagged. "Jenny," he said almost in a fatherly way, bordering on condescension. "Reed was nowhere to be found last night and I've got a thousand leads to chase up. The public are calling in every second."

He motioned across the room to a line of a dozen female officers wearing headphones and scribbling down information. No sooner had an operator clicked off a call than a light flashed and she was talking to yet another worried Manchester resident.

"I've really got no-one to spare," he said and made to turn back to the officer who was waiting patiently to resume the conversation that Jenny had interrupted.

Jenny caught hold of his arm. "I still need help," she said. "The Chief wants an update at the end of the day and," she pressed an urgency button, "Reed may have made contact already."

Sam stared at her hand on his arm and then smiled at the officer, who was looking more than a little uncomfortable at the profiler's challenge to the lead detective on the case. Then he looked back at Jenny, the smile now fixed in place and called over her shoulder. "Paz?" Jenny followed his gaze to the young Asian boy who answered.

"Yes, Sir?" he replied, immediately crossing the space and standing almost to attention in front of Sam.

"Paz, this is Mrs Foster our criminal profiler. She needs some help organising material generated by the public. Can you give her a hand please?"

Paz looked at Jenny. "Yes of course, Sir!"

"Thanks," said Jenny offering Sam a smile, but he had already turned to the officer to continue his interrupted conversation.

Paz smiled a toothy grin and Jenny thought he must be no more than eighteen or nineteen years old. "Follow me." she said and the pair went back to Jenny's desk, Paz grabbing the back of his chair as they went and wheeling it across the office after her.

"We've got hundreds of correspondents here," she told him without further preamble. "What we're looking for are patterns or anything unusual in the content. The first task is to sort them into four categories: one helpful; two scornful; three neither; four personal. You need to read everything before you put it into a pile and read it fully. Something that may start off helpful could become scornful and that would go into the *scornful* pile. All the thank you and good luck cards and messages need to go into the *neither* pile. That's unless they fit the first two categories. Any correspondence that appears to be from someone that claims to know Joe Reed, Dawn James, Robyn Cox or Sharon Daly or any of their family members needs to go into the *personal* pile. Sound ok?"

Paz's large almost white-less brown eyes caught hers. "That sounds fine," he said. "Like DI Bradbury mentioned, my name is Paz. Well, they call me Paz; my name is actually Sukhwant Patra. It means *'great happiness',*" he added and his toothy smile re-emerged with a vengeance, creasing his entire face.

"Call me Jenny," she replied flatly and began to sort through the papers.

"One more thing," she said stopping momentarily. "Forget the telephone transcripts for now. There aren't many public phones left and Reed will know that we could trace any call made, even if it was disguised by dialling 141 before the number. Concentrate on the posted items and the e-mails that have come from public accounts like yahoo or Hotmail. Anyone can set up an account and lie on the personal information, so they're all but anonymous."

"Ok," said Paz, surveying the piles of paper and almost laughing. "You weren't joking when you said you needed help were you?"

Jenny looked up, thinking that Paz looked more like a schoolboy than a police officer. His long fingers were all that were visible poking out from the sleeves of his grey suit jacket and there was so little of him that the collar of his shirt, obviously 'Size S', hung loosely around his neck with the deep-blue tie starting at the top of his chest rather than tight back to his Adam's apple. His black straw-like hair lay angled down with gel creating a point near his left eye which twinkled as he talked and laughed, the permanent smile of a nervous youth playing across his lips.

"First day?" she asked.

"Well no, not exactly, Ma'am," said Paz, the question bringing a flush to his cheeks. "I've been in records for about three months now."

"Well I hope you're intelligent." said Jenny without a hint of sarcasm. "I need to trust you not to miss anything, so if you're unsure of *anything* - even slightly unsure - you MUST ask!"

Paz's smile evaporated and he focused on doing all he could to convey an aura of professional dedication to his task.

"Of course, Ma'am!" he said solemnly, and began sorting through the pile of papers in front of him.

Chapter 19

Joe Reed sat motionless on his bed staring at his laptop. The screensaver was an image of 63 Cathcart Street taken years before when he was a child and the house was at its best, not the shabby ghost of a place it was now. The photo had been taken on a clear summer's day and everything was bathed in a warm glow of sunlight. Newly installed double glazing, a shiny, freshly painted black door and attractive stone cladding told the neighbours and any passers-by that the people who lived there were doing well and they were proud of it.

The previous evening Reed had bundled Sharon Daly into his van according to instructions and made it back to the house, closely following the route given him earlier by email. The fact that the journey had been half an hour longer than it needed to be, twisting and turning down side streets and alleys hadn't registered as important to Reed, he was just relieved to reach the house safely before carrying his still unconscious victim down to the basement. He'd managed to make the journey without attracting the attention of other road users or any neighbours, and had been free to take his time.

Following more of the usual detailed instructions he

bound and gagged the woman before plugging in and heating a soldering iron. The red light on the handle of the device turned to green showing Reed that it had reached its optimum intense heat and he proceeded to carve a number 3 at the base of the woman's back.

With his left hand bracing the woman to the ground he pressed the hot steel into her soft skin, quickly forcing his knee onto her buttocks to control her spasms, and then slowly traced out the number. The muffled cries of his captive were accompanied by the sizzle of melting flesh as the red hot tip met milky white skin.

Even with the smell of burning fat in his nostrils Reed kept himself detached, remaining emotionless throughout the process; acting as if he were preparing a bird for the oven rather than callously torturing another human being. The woman's eyes bulged from their sockets as she strained to scream against the gag lodged firmly in her mouth. Reed used his weight to control her as he fixed a thick leather collar tightly around her neck before shackling her to a wall. Reed was immune to the woman's suffering and ignored the tears that were flowing freely down her face. Instead, he carefully placed her directly in front of a full-length mirror that lay on its side expressly for the purpose of degrading his victim, a constant reminder of how hopeless her situation was.

The basement was large and well-lit. The only furniture was an iron bed frame standing in the middle of the space, creating a barrier between the victim and the room's other occupant, Robyn Cox. Robyn lay in front of her own personal mirror, suffering in a similar way with her hands and feet bound. She had been cruelly branded with a number 2 at the base of her back and shackled to the wall. The mirror allowed Robyn to see herself at the mercy of her captor twenty-four hours a day, stimulating her imagination to run wild as to her fate. She had already been forced to watch the full horror of Dawn James' death at the hands of Joe Reed, and now every time that she closed her eyes Dawn died again, her final moments played out like an endless video in Robyn's tortured mind. The memory of a maniacal voice that seemed to come from nowhere filled her with dread and haunted every waking moment. The voice had coaxed Joe Reed to visit unspeakable torture on Dawn James as Robyn looked on, and she existed in a state of constant panic in the certain knowledge that she would eventually share the same fate.

Now she saw Reed arrive with his new victim, stumbling a little as he negotiated the stairs with the dead weight hanging limp in his arms. She watched as Reed restrained the woman, and Robyn flinched as he pulled the ropes tight. Knowing what this other woman was about to endure, she herself screamed almost simultaneously with the red-hot tip of the soldering iron beginning to carve into the flesh. Eventually, the acrid smell of burning skin reached Robyn and her throat began to experience involuntary spasms as she almost swallowed the stench.

When Reed had finished restraining and torturing his new victim he quickly left the basement, hardly giving Robyn Cox a second glance as he made his way up the stairs.

Through her mirror Robyn watched him go, her heart

racing. She tried to keep as still as she could, the rise and fall of her chest the only tell-tale sign that she was still alive.

***

There was no television or radio in the house; for communication purposes Reed used the laptop that was permanently switched on in his bedroom. He'd been warned not to use it for anything else and strictly forbidden to click on the prominently displayed Internet Explorer icon. Had he disobeyed his instructions and clicked that icon, or picked up one of the free newspapers delivered twice weekly, but lying in unread piles on the mat inside the front door, Joe Reed would have been conscious of the media frenzy that swirled around him. Every paper and every web-page dedicated to news had run the still image of Reed taken from the video at the Peterson Insurance Christmas party, and every reporter was speculating when he would be caught. They ran story after story featuring Dawn James, often allowing their imaginations free reign. Many of them speculated about how she had died, all fuelled by the appetite of the numerous members of the public who commented on blogs and social media sites, themselves morbidly fascinated by such details. The more thoughtful section of the press focused on the James family and how they were coping, especially in the light of the continued disappearance of Robyn Cox. As for the Coxes, they were endlessly profiled and dissected for public scrutiny, with editorial comment ranging from the absurd to premature gushing tributes to a wonderful mother. The main topic that day was the news that a third woman, Sharon Daly had been abducted from the streets of Greater Manchester and various media outlets began screening safety warnings to all women in the Manchester area. Skilled reporters had put together the common links between the three women and began openly suggesting that any woman between thirty and forty years old, with shoulder length dark hair and married with children might think about staying indoors, or if forced to go out, not to do so alone.

The latest free newspaper to drop through the door of 63 Cathcart Street screamed the headline *Bury Beast!* An image of Joe Reed occupied two thirds of the front page and the editorial was dedicated to a woman described by the writer as 'courageous', who had gone to the lengths of cutting her dark hair short and dying it strawberry blonde, proclaiming that this was the only way to guarantee safety in Manchester.

Alone in the house on Cathcart Street, Joe Reed was oblivious to the media-driven frenzy he had created. Lost in a world of pain and reverie fuelled by the consequences of the instructions that he received and carried out to the letter, he had managed to organise his mind into compartments in order to survive.

When he sat alone and silent, lost in thoughts of his childhood with his mother Jane, Declan his step-brother and his unwanted step-father Dan Prince he was Ed Jerome, a victim of circumstance. Ed was sullen, depressed and inward looking with a sense of injustice that he found hard to bear. He felt as though the whole world was against him; all he wanted was to keep himself to himself and not speak to anyone, ever.

The abuse that Ed Jerome suffered as a child had taken its toll, first at the hands of his birth mother, a drug user whose life had spiralled out of control and secondly from life with his step-father Dan Prince, who physically and sexually abused both him and his step-brother. Unsurprisingly, the man who emerged from that boyhood was defensive, shy, socially inept and extremely self-critical.

In contrast, when he was following orders, working to make women love him before raping them and destroying their lives or abducting them to act out his hatred for Jane, his mother, he was Joe Reed. The name Joe Reed, invented for him to keep him anonymous and safe, he now found useful as a title to a compartment in which he could lock away the horrors of the actions that Ed Jerome would never have sanctioned.

**

The murderer sitting on the bed barely noticed when his fragile, tormented mind eventually gave way to all the pressure. There was no dramatic moment when he fell to the ground clutching at his head as his brain split in two and there was no physical pain, but there came a time when his mind and personality broke apart as surely as if he had smashed his wrist bone clean in two. In that moment alone in the bedroom at 63 Cathcart Street the killer's psyche became like a mirror of itself with Ed Jerome on one side and Joe Reed on the other. When either of the two sides looked into the mirror that he had placed between them like a wall, all it was aware of was a reflection of itself; no longer could one side of this man's personality communicate with the other and Ed Jerome began to think and act independently of Joe Reed, as though they were two people rather than two conflicting sides of the same mind.

Over the next few hours after the abduction of Sharon Daly Ed Jerome became more thoughtful and reflective, feeling sympathy for the women that were trapped in the basement waiting to die. It was true that he remembered all the horrors inflicted by his step-father Dan Prince, but the memories were more diluted now, less intense and he felt as though he should not be defined by that horror. He began finding it more difficult to make a connection between the horrors he'd suffered as a child and the horror he knew was happening in the basement, and the Ed Jerome side of the killer's mind began to grow even more introspective, retreating from reality and unable to intervene.

It wasn't Ed Jerome who was responsible for the death of Dawn James, it was Joe Reed who had suffocated her and left her alone on the industrial estate. Ed Jerome could still see it happening in his mind's eye, like an old movie that he had watched dozens of times, knowing all the dialogue off by heart, but he felt powerless to intervene. Certainly it moved him: he hated the way Reed had shown Dawn James no mercy, but as if assessing a fictional character, he understood why Reed had committed the murder and even sympathised with him.

The women held captive in the basement two floors below him almost never crossed Ed Jerome's mind. He didn't need to feed them or entertain them, or even sympathise with them, and for long periods he almost forgot they existed. Their struggles, pain and fear were all for nothing. To Ed the basement became like the wardrobe in the C S Lewis stories he had read in Mrs Grace's Second Year High School class, with a door he could pass through from time to time - a door leading from one life to another. He was beginning to detach himself from the reality of the women, and his mind began to think of Joe Reed almost as a comic book villain that he could picture as a character outside of himself.

**

Joe Reed on the other hand was angry, an emotional rocket ready to explode at any given moment. He saw the punishment and death of the women stricken in the basement as just and fair retribution for what had happened to Ed Jerome as a child at the hands of Jane Prince and her husband Dan. Reed welcomed the guidance he'd been given, and relished his role in the torture and murder of the women selected for him to punish. Joe started feeling protective towards Ed Jerome, seeing him as a separate entity, someone who needed help and support - a weakling even. Thinking about Ed and how he had suffered, Joe couldn't understand why Ed wasn't as angry and as hungry for revenge as he was. He began to see himself as Ed Jerome's shield against the world. When he thought about Ed being tortured by Dan with Jane Prince complicit there was an immediate reality to the memories that stung him as if he were experiencing it himself. The women deserved everything they got and Reed was determined to make their experience as painful and degrading as he could.

The two minds had effectively erected a wall around themselves, each becoming impenetrable to the other like neighbours separated by high hedges; occasionally muffled voices are heard to confirm their existence, but they remain beyond physical perception. So it became with Joe Reed and Ed Jerome, occupants of a single skull, but remote from each other as distant neighbours.

Chapter 20

Two hours into the process of cataloguing the correspondence from often distraught members of the public Jenny stood outside Central Park, Manchester Metropolitan Police Headquarters drawing deeply on the smoke from her first cigarette of the day.

A smell of freshly mown grass reached her nostrils and she vaguely wondered where an expanse of green could possibly lie, given the concrete jungle that occupied this part of the city. The volume of reading matter had already made her dizzy and after a couple of strong pulls she felt as though she was swaying in a gentle breeze. The door behind her opened and Sam stepped out into the day's sunshine and growing heat, his face still haggard with worry. Jenny offered him her pack of cigarettes and he took one without speaking, using a lighter he produced from his pocket to begin the smoking ritual.

"Sorry I was a bit short with you earlier," he said blowing smoke hard through his flared nostrils. "How's Paz working out?"

"Don't think twice about it," she said before adding, "Paz is great actually, very intelligent and works fast. So thanks for the help. It's appreciated."

"Anything interesting?" asked Sam.

Jenny toyed with the tip of her cigarette before drawing deeply again and allowing the smoke to escape her lips before replying.

"Lots of cranks," she said. "In fact, so many that I had to create a new category for them."

"Sounds about usual," said Sam.

"Obviously I realise that people contact investigation teams with all kinds of weird and wonderful theories, trying to become the centre of attention," mused Jenny. "But there must be letters and emails from a hundred different nutters claiming either to be Joe Reed himself, or to be able to contact Dawn James via their respective spirit guides and tell us where the missing women are right now."

She allowed herself a smile, genuinely amused at her next comment.

"There's even a series of letters from a *J Edgar Hoover of Ashton-Under-Lyne* explaining in minute detail how Robyn Cox and Sharon Daly have actually been abducted by an alien *posing* as Joe Reed and are now cruising around earth in a spaceship."

"Anything credible?" asked Sam.

"The crazy ones are easy to spot, they just slot in bits of information they've guessed at, but there's one interesting character there. A guy called Patrick."

"Interesting how?"

Jenny paused for a moment to make more sense for *herself* of what she was about to tell him. "Well, it's not so much what he says. There are three letters all addressed to the Chief personally congratulating him in a very sarcastic tone on his handling of the case, and there are a couple of lines in the letters that do seem relevant."

"In what way?"

"The writer doesn't give specific details and the letters aren't exactly explosive," said Jenny.

"So what's the significance?"

"It's the *tone*," replied Jenny. "He writes them as if he knows the characters involved personally."

Sam laughed, smoke escaping his nostrils.

"What's funny?" asked Jenny, with an involuntary smile.

"This could be your first '*hunch*'," said Sam. "Are you a detective or a profiler?"

Jenny screwed up her face, letting Sam know that the joke wasn't his best.

"Be careful with this though, Jenny," said Sam, a hardness returning to his features. "If you do come up with anything and then you're wrong, it could throw the investigation off track for weeks."

"I know," she said, becoming defensive. "I'm going to send the letters to Forensics -see if they can extract a DNA sample and identify the sender, just as a routine precaution."

"Have you let the Chief know?" asked Sam, a note of caution creeping into his voice.

"No, I'll wait for the results from the lab. The letters probably mean nothing and I wouldn't want to de-focus the group unless I was absolutely certain they were important."

"Ok, but in my experience a crank is a crank. Remember Wearside Jack? You know - the guy who wrote a series of letters to West Yorkshire Police in the middle of the Yorkshire Ripper case?"

Jenny ground her cigarette into the tarmac. "Yeah,

he turned out to be a nobody called John Humble, if memory serves. He sent a tape too I think, and based on Humble's information the Ripper detectives ended up focusing on Sunderland, rather than Bradford where Peter Sutcliffe actually lived."

"An independent enquiry found that the re-focus probably cost the lives of Sutcliffe's last two victims," said Sam, his cigarette-end joining Jenny's before he added, "Just be careful."

Jenny flashed him a smile. "I'm always careful," she said as she walked back into the building.

***

Returning to her desk Jenny picked up the three letters from Patrick. All three were printed rather than hand-written and all signed with the name *'Patrick'*, each with the same flourish that had initially caught the profiler's eye. The signatures were large enough to encroach into the printed text; they were artistic, extravagant even. Jenny was armed with the benefit of extensive training in graphology, the study of handwriting. The skill told her that the person who had penned the three letters was definitely an egotist and possibly a narcissist, exactly the profile of someone who craved publicity and might go to extreme lengths to try and gain notoriety through the investigation. She turned to Paz who was progressing through the pile of correspondents with an enviable efficiency.

"What do you think of these letters?" she asked, offering her researcher the missives.

Paz stopped what he was doing and took them from her. His earlier youthful attitude now replaced with a measured concentration that put him on an equal footing with any researcher twice his age.

"I'm not sure," he said. "In the first letter he's gushing in his admiration for the Chief; too gushing I think. But in the second one he congratulates him on his professional appearance at a televised press conference, and then slates him in the next sentence for not appearing in the media more often."

He turned to the third letter. "In this one he says that no-one could be doing a better job to catch the Bury Beast than the Chief, except of course someone who had the brains to outwit him!"

"So what does that tell you?" asked Jenny, genuinely looking for affirmation, rather than as Paz instantly presumed setting a test.

The young researcher thought for a few moments longer before meeting her eye.

"He's definitely mounting a challenge to the Chief's ability to run the investigation, but he's stopping short of saying that he could do a better job himself. In my opinion that means he's not trying to add anything to the pot."

He paused, keeping eye contact with Jenny, trying to see if he was on the right track.

Jenny's eyes betrayed nothing but vague interest and he had little option but to continue.

"Ok! So now the letters are becoming more critical of the Chief as each one unfolds, but this last sentence I think is the most interesting…"

Jenny waved her hand to stop him. "Yes, I spotted that too," she said. "The phrase *someone who had the brain's to outwit him* seems too personal somehow, as if he personally knows '*him*'?"

"Exactly," said Paz animated now, his youthful grin spreading across his face. "And that signature, looks like someone wants to get themselves noticed."

"Ok," said Jenny. "Keep sorting through the piles and I'll get these letters and the envelopes to the lab; see if they can come up with a DNA fingerprint and identify the sender."

"Can you do that?" asked the young researcher.

"Of course," said Jenny, resuming the role of sage. "The lab will test the letters themselves for fingerprints and discover the type of envelope and paper used, as well as trying to pin down the manufacturer of the machine that may have printed the copy."

"Impressive," said Paz, his eyes widening with enthusiasm.

"Ink manufacturers use slightly different colour combinations in their cartridges for different printer models, so we might be able to narrow it down to a maker at least," she explained. "Plus, we can extract DNA from the envelope if the sender has licked the seal or the stamp before putting it in a post-box."

"There's the postmark too," said Paz. "The first letter was posted in Oldham, the second in Manchester and the third back in Oldham. Could it mean maybe this guy might be close?"

"Not necessarily," said Jenny. "He could work in Oldham or Manchester and live in Birmingham for all we know. The postmarks can only tell us where he posted them, and we can't assume further than that."

"Of course." Said Paz.

"One more thing. We need to keep all of this, and anything else we may discover, strictly to ourselves."

Paz looked disappointed. He'd planned to share his day's experiences with anyone who would listen.

"It's very important," said Jenny firmly, his hesitation not lost on her. "If we give the team bad information, or worse half a story, it could spell disaster for the entire investigation."

Paz saw the sense. "Yes Ma'am," he said. "Mum's the word."

***

The man sat at his desk, eyes riveted to his computer screen. Despite the window blinds being drawn down, the heat in the room was stifling; a small desk fan was whirring away full-on, but its noisy labours only succeeded in moving the hot air around. The silver chain that had become an ever-present talisman in the man's life was caught at the corner of the slim computer screen and hung loosely, glistening against the plastic of the machine's housing. He concentrated on the images that were now feeding back to him through the discreet CCTV system that he'd had installed inside 63 Cathcart Street before he sent Joe Reed the keys and instructions for moving in. He could see Joe Reed in one of the images now, sitting on his bed staring into space with a vacancy of mind and stillness of action that the man suddenly envied. The man himself could never achieve such a state of calm.

His mind twisted endlessly, with desire and rage occupying every waking hour as he plotted and schemed, dreaming of every new video to be supplied by Joe

Reed. The man was fixated on the impending deaths of the women held captive, and he relished the thought of the scenes of their pain and suffering that he knew would eventually come his way. In the meantime he satisfied himself with the cherished images of Dawn James' last moments that were burned into his brain, every memory easily refreshed with the live version of her slow death available at the click of his mouse.

He wrapped his yellow stained fingers around his half smoked cigarette, allowing the burgeoning ash to fall to the ground at his feet. The threadbare patterned carpet hadn't seen a cleaner for some time and the wheels of the leather chair, more suited to hard-flooring, had created ruts in the once plush fibres now crusted with dirt and ash. The monitor showed images from three cameras in all. One was of Reed, still sitting in the same position and obviously lost in his own world. The second camera focused on the basement, where the man could see Robyn Cox lying motionless and compliant on one side of the room with Sharon Daly, the latest occupant, lying helpless in front of a full length mirror at the other side of the space and writhing against her bonds. The third camera, set up at the kitchen end of the hallway of 63 Cathcart Street, pointed at the front door whilst allowing the entrance to the basement to be visible at all times. This scene was lifeless.

The man studied the image of the two captives helpless in the basement and the smile that crossed his lips expressed not so much amusement as brutish pleasure. With a manipulation of the keyboard the lens zoomed in on the pathetic figure of Robyn Cox with her back to the camera, and as the newly enlarged image came into focus the man could just make out the angry figure *2* burned into her flesh. The number was partially obscured by her hands, which were twisted behind her revealing a thick, deep reddening of her wrists where the handcuffs bit into the soft, tender skin, but the man knew it was there, and the saliva thickened in his mouth as he contemplated Robyn suffering.

Panning the camera he navigated a path up the woman's back, the image now showing the thick leather collar and chain tethering her neck to the wall. Moving the angle of the lens to the left, a full length mirror came into view and in its reflection he could see that the woman was barely conscious. Her bulging eyelids were tight shut and she was involuntarily chewing around a bright red ball-gag which spread her lips wide. It looked as though she was mouthing a silent prayer and the man's excitement grew as he watched. A bead of saliva escaped Robyn's swollen mouth, making its way slowly down the side of her face, cutting through a film of accumulated dirt and ending up dripping into her filthy matted hair. The man watched for a few more minutes, fascinated by the woman's agony, and a warm satisfaction grew inside him knowing that for Robyn Cox every second must feel like an hour. He almost gasped with pleasure when his victim suddenly moaned through the obstruction in her mouth and her body began to shake. She had obviously regained consciousness, and as she woke the realisation of her plight must have rapidly dawned on her. The man imagined the terror seizing her and causing those involuntary spasms, and the hoarse laugh that escaped his lips filled the stale air with malice.

"It's you next, Robyn." He almost panted out the words, a wave of sexual frenzy taking hold of his body, and he too began to shake.

The man zoomed out from Robyn and with the room now returned to full view his gaze fell upon the figure of Sharon Daly, who was still thrashing against her bondage. The watcher laughed, this time with amusement at her struggles.

He wanted to pan in and take a closer look, but he knew that if he succumbed to the pleasure he would become too engrossed and his plan for the day would go unfinished - and his tasks were important. With a great effort of willpower he reduced the CCTV images to his status bar and proceeded to click the WORD document icon on his screen. He closed his eyes and took three deep calming breaths through his nose, holding each one for a few seconds before expelling the carbon monoxide into the hot air through his mouth. Once the ritual had returned his mind to a tolerable equilibrium, he opened his eyes and thought for a few moments before he began to type: *Dear Chief Superintendent Ambrose.*

More than an hour went by as he typed and re-typed a letter, correcting grammar, making certain that his spelling was correct and rewording the letter over and over until he was sure that it conveyed exactly the right message. Once the letter was finished he pressed print, sending the document to an ancient Epson Printer housed on the floor next to the desk. The printer eventually whirred into life and produced the letter on a single page, the man simultaneously reaching into the top drawer of the desk to retrieve a pair of latex gloves from their box. The man snapped the gloves onto his hands and with the rubber protection in place he gathered the document from the printer, careful to hold it by one corner before laying it on a piece of clean blotting paper on the other side of the desk. He picked up his favourite pen, a Silver Cross, and with a flourish of the wrist, quick and expertly practised, he signed the letter '*Patrick*'. The man then folded the paper twice and slipped it into a window envelope that he had ready for the purpose.

Turning back to his computer he clicked the icon to bring up the camera images of his victims, zooming in once again on the desperate figure of Robyn Cox, whose body had ceased shaking and was now motionless. Concentrating the lens on the woman's tortured face, he selected '*print*'. The ancient Epson again called into service laboured to spill out the black and white copy of the still-life picture on screen. The man's thick index and forefinger still encased in latex took the image by the corner of the paper, laying it face down on the blotting paper before writing the words *One, two, buckle my shoe* on the back of the print in the same flourishing hand with which he'd signed the letter, and using the same pen. Then he folded the paper into three and slipped it into the envelope. Next he turned the package over, making sure that the Chief's name and the address of Central Park, Manchester Metropolitan Police Headquarters were clearly visible in the window. He then took a slightly damp sponge from a glass bowl earlier prepared for the task, moistened the leading edge of the envelope and sealed it. Retaining the gloves on his hands the man took a strip of first-class stamps from the drawer and tore one off, proceeding to moisten it with the sponge and place it neatly in the top right-hand corner of the envelope.

The man patted the correspondence and smiled to himself; he couldn't resist tormenting Chief Superintendent Ambrose. He despised the uniformed buffoon and hated the way he turned up on television, trotting out the same old information and making the same old appeal for witnesses. This morning had been the worst performance yet, the policeman's pleading eyes almost begging someone to come forward with the whereabouts of Sharon Daly. He was an idiot, wrapped up in his own self-importance and the man wanted to make Ambrose look foolish in front of the public that he so obviously was desperate to impress.

When Robyn Cox turned up destroyed by Joe Reed in the same way that he had destroyed Dawn James, Ambrose would be haunted by the image in the letter. When the time came for his next appearance on television, the Chief Superintendent would have no choice but to admit to millions of viewers that he was a failure.

***

Jenny was exhausted after ploughing through what she thought must surely be the equivalent of a small post-office mail collection. The difference was that unlike the post-office sorting staff she had carefully opened and read each letter, discussing any detail, no matter how small with Paz her would-be research assistant. Paz had told her at the start of the day that the meaning of his real name, Sukhwant Patra, was *great happiness* and Jenny thought there could never have been a less apt description for how they both felt right now. Paz's neat shirt and tie had been picked and pulled at with frustration through the day and he leant back in his chair, his jacket slung over its back, with the sleeves of his white shirt rolled up above his elbows. Jenny thought he had probably aged about ten years since she had seconded him to the work.

She felt her head throbbing behind her eyes, one of the penalties of letting vanity get the better of her by refusing to succumb to the inevitable march of time leading to, amongst other places, the nearest optician. She rubbed furiously at her temples before roughly smoothing back her pony tail. Just then a WPC looking as though she had just stepped out of the uniform catalogue for devastatingly attractive women police officers, dropped a new batch of email transcripts on to the edge of the desk. She flashed Jenny and Paz a smile set off by her bright eyes and full red lips.

"They're coming in all the time," she said by way of apology and catching the look in Jenny's eye retreated quickly back across the office.

Jenny sighed. "I think I've had enough for one day," she murmured almost to herself, and glanced at Paz whose yawn agreed with her, even if his inclinations didn't.

"I'll stay for another couple of hours," he said. "I'm not doing anything special tonight, so I might as well."

Jenny spent a few moments wondering what kind of life Paz might lead outside work. There was no ring on his finger so he was probably single, probably living, she thought, with proud parents who waited on him hand-and-foot.

She picked up her mobile phone. The incoming message light had been flashing for most of the day and clicking the screen to life she saw that she'd missed calls from Peter and her dad, and one from a number she didn't recognise. She clicked on to the text message icon and quickly scanned through the dozen messages she had received. Two were from Peter asking what time she would be home, as he had a surprise for her; one from her Mum wanting a general update on her life; one from Candice, her sister in her usual cryptic style, and a few more from friends looking for social engagement dates. There was also a message from the number she didn't recognise saying simply *Call me when you can* and a puzzled look crossed Jenny's face. "Anything that I can help with?" asked Paz.

Jenny didn't answer, deciding instead to call the number and see who it was, she might not get time later, and it could be important.

She pressed the re-call button and the ring-tone was almost immediately cut short by a female voice. "Hello, Mrs Foster. Thanks for calling me back."

Jenny didn't recognise the clipped Cheshire accent. "Who is this?" she asked.

"Paula Tripp," said the woman. "Manchester Evening News."

Jenny was struck silent for a moment before eventually managing, "How the hell did you get my private number?" anger swelling in her voice.

Tripp ignored the question. "Have you opened my envelope yet?"

Jenny had almost forgotten meeting Tripp in the carpark that morning and had pushed the envelope into her desk drawer, deciding to concentrate on the case rather than whatever the reporter's envelope might contain.

"Is it directly related to the case?" she asked curtly.

"No," said Tripp. "Well, except in the sense that *you* are," she added attempting to create interest.

Jenny didn't take the bait. "Then I won't be interested," she said. "And one more thing *Tripp*," barbing the journalist's name with scorn. "Delete my personal number and don't call me on it again."

With that she angrily pressed the off button to end the call, and sat and stared at her phone for a second as if it were an alien object newly discovered, rather than her everyday companion.

"Are you ok, Ma'am?" asked Paz, obviously concerned.

"I'm fine," Jenny said, quickly writing her mobile number on a sheet of clean paper. "Call me if you come across anything interesting."

"Thank you, I will," he said as Jenny stood up, retrieving her bag from the floor.

The profiler took out Tripp's envelope from the drawer and gathered up a sheaf of files before wishing her assistant a good night and crossing the office.

The large room was still alive with police officers, some on the telephone, some in small groups deep in discussion, whilst others stared at computer screens. She headed toward the Chief's office glancing at her watch as she went. It was already six, and she hoped to catch her boss to report in as instructed before he left for the evening. She pushed the reporter's envelope into her handbag, meaning to review the contents later. She didn't have time to satisfy her curiosity right now, and anyway it was probably a collection of clippings showing how great a journalist Tripp thought she was. Reaching his door, she was relieved to hear the Chief in conversation and stepped into the office to find Sam sitting in front of the desk.

The Chief looked up. "Come in Jenny," he said. "How did you get on with the letters and emails?"

Jenny sat down in the chair next to Sam. "Not much to report really sir," she said and glanced at Sam, whose face remained impassive. "There are a couple of things I'm looking at, but nothing much interesting at all beyond the wild fantasies of a very worried public."

"Ok," he said. "There's new material every day of course, and I'd appreciate you keeping on top of it. You never know, Joe Reed just might get in touch."

"They often do," replied Jenny almost absent-mindedly.

The Chief turned back to Sam. "If Joe Reed sticks to the pattern, Robyn Cox will become his next victim within a week. It's absolutely vital that we do everything we can to find her whilst she's still alive."

"The thought haunts me," said Sam and Jenny noticed that his face was even greyer now than it had been this morning.

"I'm finding it hard to believe that despite the fact that we have a full, clear image of Joe Reed's face, a description of his van and even a video of him that's gone viral on YouTube, no-one has come forward with a credible address or even area," he said, an air of defeat creeping unchecked into his voice.

"How many sightings have there been?" asked the Chief.

Sam leant back in his chair. "Hundreds, Chief," he said with resignation. "Few of them credible. Joe Reed, average build, dark hair, smartly dressed is suddenly appearing in every cake shop and hairdressers in Greater Manchester, and I'm organising an army of constables, specials and PCSOs to follow up the leads. Whilst we're busy doing that Reed himself is popping up in broad daylight, unnoticed and kidnapping women in the park." His voice was becoming more agitated.

"It's only hard work and research that can save Robyn Cox and Sharon Daly," said the Chief. "Following up the leads, scanning CCTV twenty-four hours a day, listening to the public," and at this point he nodded to Jenny, "are exactly the right thing to do. Manpower and methodical, logical police work will win."

The three colleagues sat silently for a moment contemplating how little they knew. "Joe Reed will put his head around the corner for a pint of milk and we'll be there to catch him. Believe me, it's not just the police force on this one Sam, the population of Manchester has recruited itself on to the team," the Chief added reassuringly.

Jenny wondered if he was right.

Chapter 21

The man studied the CCTV images transmitting from the basement at 63 Cathcart Street. He could see that Robyn Cox, tethered to the wall with her hands bound behind her hadn't moved at all in more than an hour. If he zoomed in he could just make out the tell-tale rise and fall of her breasts, indicating that life still clung to her - but only just. He judged that her prolonged lack of movement meant she had drifted into unconsciousness and suddenly became afraid that she would not wake again, robbing him of the pleasure he would have when he watched her die.

He opened his email client and selected Joe Reed as the sole recipient of his

message. "Get ready, It's almost time," he typed and pressed send.

***

The surprise that Peter Foster had been referring to in his unanswered texts to Jenny turned out to be dinner and a night in a hotel. Hoping to relieve the stresses of the new job, he had planned it to be just the two of them, but Jenny - despite hating herself for it - had become first cool, then full of objections, and finally hostile to the whole thing. The truth was that she felt as though she was being dragged away from the case, and she didn't want to miss any developments. She had called the Chief about it, confident that he would refuse her the time off, but to her surprise he had agreed at once, on the premise that having time away from the case would give her new focus. He argued that she'd been in the job barely a week, and yet that week had seen some of the most intense activity the force in Manchester had experienced for the past ten years. He said he knew how much strain she was under, and that Sam and the team could cope without her for just that short time. In other words, he countered her reluctance with a logic she couldn't deny. Also she knew herself that Joe Reed's MO indicated the unlikelihood of anything further happening for at least a few days. After Robyn Daly was abducted it was a week before the body of Dawn James had been found. Since Sharon Daly had only been missing for a day or so, this gave Robyn a week more of captivity. Jenny tried to talk the Chief round, arguing that Reed might escalate his time-scale, but in the end she had to agree that this was unlikely.

Peter had surprised her when she arrived home the evening before, saying that he wanted to put the unpleasantness of their argument a few nights ago behind them and he'd been bemused by her unenthusiastic response. Despite Jenny's obvious lack of motivation for the trip Peter packed the car early, reasoning that his wife would be more enthusiastic as time went on. Lilly waved a cheery goodbye at the door, holding hands with Jenny's sister whom Peter had recruited to look after her and the house. Candice's son Darren chased after the car with wild enthusiasm as it left the drive, but Candice herself didn't even wave - just stood with her hands on her hips looking sullen as always and watching with indifference.

**

As the Bentley Continental GT in classic midnight blue, hired by Peter especially to enhance the trip, cruised effortlessly east towards Macclesfield Jenny's hostility to the trip gave way to a silent inner panic. As Peter expertly steered the car through the inevitable traffic cones she took a few seconds to study him as he drove. Her husband was lost in concentration, with a boyish gleam in his eyes that betrayed his obvious joy at being king behind the wheel of a machine that she guessed represented at least double her annual salary. His black hair, trademark of a youth she hadn't shared, had given way to a more than modest amount of grey resulting in that salt-and-pepper effect coveted by many middle-aged executives and their well-manicured wives. The piercing green eyes in his tanned face remained fixed on the road, except when occasionally glancing down to admire vehicle's plush interior, and Jenny thought he was probably more attractive now than when she'd first met him a few short years before. He was silently mouthing along to the Michael Jackson classic *Man in the Mirror* that was playing on Radio 2, the station he had chosen, and he'd turned to a volume barely loud enough to register in the car. Eventually he noticed Jenny watching him and glanced away from the road to give her a warm, satisfied smile, which despite her mood she found herself returning without effort. Peter always had the ability to extract a smile from her with merely a glance and ordinarily she felt happy and secure with him, so now it was an effort to wipe the smile from her face and keep up her foul mood. She wanted him to know she wasn't happy that he'd decided out of the blue to arrange a trip she didn't want to take and expected her to just fit in, be enthusiastic even. As a result she'd been forced to abandon her desk right in the middle of the investigation, and now she was angry at the prospect of spending time away with the man she had been in love with since the first time they made eye contact across the office floor. That morning Jenny had tied her hair in a sensible ponytail, chosen a long-sleeved shirt in plain white cotton over black trousers and finished off her look with a pair of flat black shoes. Aware that she was underdressed for a weekend at Shrigley Hall Hotel, one of Cheshire's finest, she thought her lack of effort an appropriate sabotage, certain that Peter would be a little embarrassed by her when the hotel's immaculately liveried concierge held the door open on their arrival. As always, Peter was dressed conservatively, his natural stylishness showing through in his choice of accessories. He lounged in the impossibly sumptuous Mulliner seats in a navy blue shirt with double cuffs and Mont Blanc cufflinks, dark blue slacks and Gucci loafers. On his left hand a Rolex wristwatch could be glimpsed beneath the cuff, as if to trump Jenny's cheap workaday chrome number, worn specifically in protest.

Right now she felt as though they were from different worlds; Peter almost gloating over the sheer opulent excess and Jenny sitting uncomfortably next to him knowing she looked strikingly out of place. She began to feel like a cheap date he'd picked up, expecting sex and all the trimmings once at the hotel, and she found herself despising the car and all that it stood for.

***

Ed Jerome sat on his bed at 63 Cathcart Street, tears beginning to fill his already cloudy eyes. He stared at the screen of the laptop displaying a message addressed to Joe Reed,

"Get ready, it's almost time," it said in stark black font. Ed called out as if he was in the bathroom behind him, his voice apprehensive and shaky.

"Joe, there's a message for you," he said to the empty room.

When Ed turned back to face the screen his features had changed. The tears had disappeared and Ed Jerome was transformed into Joe Reed who stared at the laptop with an expression of fierce determination. Reed's back began to stretch and straighten and his whole body seemed to become larger as confidence coursed through his veins. With his face pulled tight in concentration, Reed pushed his hands through his hair, straightening the black mass, uncovering his forehead and eyes before typing a reply to the message.

"I'll get ready now."

Reed pulled himself to his feet, his body leaner than it had been even a fortnight ago. His jeans were too big for him, sagging around his bottom, and the neck-line of his t-shirt hung lower than his prominent Adam's apple. He'd forgotten about food for days now, and dizziness took hold when he stood up, forcing him back into a sitting position on the bed. Eyesight blurred, he found himself gripping the bed sheets to gain a foothold against the storm overwhelming his senses. Eventually the dizziness left him and he focused his gaze on the laptop.

"I must do this," he said aloud and made another effort to stand, a little more warily this time, allowing his balance to settle before heading off to the bathroom.

When he returned half an hour or so later he was like a different man. He had showered, shaved and dressed once again in the spotless cream chinos, red polo shirt and brown loafers: his killing outfit. Returning to his laptop Joe Reed typed one word, *Ready*.

***

With the road-works safely negotiated and a clear stretch ahead of them Peter Foster pressed his foot down on the accelerator and the power of the car was immediate and thrilling. Jenny ignored the tingle that exploded through her body at the sudden rush of speed and instead smoothed the front of her trousers without looking up. "Macclesfield will be busy," she said.

Peter didn't answer. He was suddenly aware of the smog of antipathy emanating from his wife and his smile evaporated, his grip on the steering wheel becoming perceptibly tighter.

"The hotel's always crazy too," Jenny went on, and continued moving her hands rhythmically over her now creaseless trousers. "Especially at this time of year with all the tourists," she added. She could sense the atmosphere changing, and the car's interior began to seem smaller by the second.

Peter appeared to be thinking for a few moments, letting the tension settle, and then a forced smile spread across his face. "Best not leave the room then!"

"We're not teenagers," replied Jenny quickly in a much harsher tone than she'd intended.

Peter's eyes left the road and settled on Jenny for a second or two. Guilt forced the thought to pass fleetingly across his mind that his wife's hostility went beyond the unplanned trip and he wondered how much she had already guessed. He quickly reviewed the moments before they had left the house and remembered Jenny smiling warmly at Candice, the two sisters sharing a cup of coffee and swapping stories about the children's antics. There'd been nothing unusual - nothing to ring any alarm bells. Perhaps for the first time he took in Jenny's choice of dress for the day; as he watched her he noticed his wife's eyes dart sideways towards him and he suddenly realised that she had no intention of reaching Macclesfield if she could possibly help it. Peter relaxed as he realised that this was the extent of the problem and any other issues were irrelevant.

"Well we can pretend we are," he pressed. "I've even got a starter-cap in the boot that I can wear back to front if you like?"

Jenny's head snapped sideways ready to meet his unintended challenge.

"I can't stand *Shrigley Hall*, she said placing a special mocking emphasis on the hotel's name. "Why can't we go to a normal hotel with normal down-to-earth people that I can at least speak to at the bar?"

Peter laughed returning his eyes to the road. Choosing not to answer her question he hoped that the purr of the engine and the overwhelming smell of leather and polished walnut would do his talking for him.

They continued in silence as the Bentley ate up the miles with consummate ease, the countryside passing quickly whilst Jenny stared out of the window. Peter glanced over at his wife as she sulked in her seat, which she now appeared too small to sit in. Somehow her body had retreated into the leather and she looked decidedly young and vulnerable, like a teenager who'd been scolded by an overbearing parent. He gave a sigh of resignation.

"We can always turn back if you're not going to enjoy it. I mean, time away without work and Lilly to worry about should be fun and exciting, and you look more like you're being driven to face a firing squad."

Jenny shifted slowly in her seat, turning to face Peter with a sudden fire in her eyes.

"I'm not being blamed for ruining this," she snapped. "I just wish that sometimes we could discuss things, rather than you springing them on me as a so-called surprise!"

"Sorry for wanting to spend time with my wife," retorted Peter leaning across to cut short Robbie Williams' version of the classic 'Me and Mrs Jones'.

"We could have spent time together with Lilly as a family," Jenny said more softly. "I don't need big gestures and expensive hotels. I've been working twenty-hour days and I haven't spent more than ten minutes with my daughter awake. It would have been good to have spent the time as a family."

Peter considered his wife. "So if we were home now you wouldn't be in your study reading files and calling *Sam Bradbury* every few minutes for an update?" he asked.

"Of course not," she said, the possible significance of the stress on her colleague's name not lost on her.

They travelled in silence for a few miles more until they reached Knutsford Motorway Services. Peter moved over to the left lane, took the exit and parked at the back of the car park as far away from the building as he could. The tired-looking facility was single story, covered in adverts for coffee and snacks. A few people stood gathered around tall metal bins, smoking, and a scrap of litter caught in the breeze was dancing around some scrubby grass that stretched behind a low fence grey with exhaust fumes. Dozens of people came and went every few seconds, either chattering excitedly on their way in, or looking grim on their way out, doggedly ready to face the motorway again.

Jenny's mind turned to Joe Reed and she wondered if he absent-mindedly wandered into motorway services or coffee shops whilst his captives suffered unknown terrors wherever he was keeping them. She couldn't quite understand how he wouldn't be recognised as a monster and she imagined him standing outside, perhaps striking up a conversation with one of his potential victims. She realised how easy it would be for a charming, good looking guy like Reed to wander over to a woman standing on her own and start a conversation. He might ask for her help, perhaps telling her he had a sick child in his car. Maybe no-one would notice if he knocked her unconscious, bundled her into a faceless van and drove away. Everyone looked so busy, determined to get to their destination and carry on with their lives. Of course, they would be shocked when they eventually turned on the news to find that they might have witnessed a kidnapping, and the story would then probably feature at every dinner party or barbeque until friends and family got sick of listening to it. The reality was that they would probably see nothing and remember less, and Jenny had a sick feeling in her stomach that someone like Reed moved amongst normal people unnoticed, waiting for his opportunity to play out his unimaginable fantasies.

"They're like cattle," she said almost to herself.

"What are?" asked Peter.

"Sorry, I was miles away."

"Thinking about the case no doubt!" he prompted.

"Sorry," she offered again.

Peter tried to imagine what Jenny was seeing.

"As in 'lambs to the slaughter'?" he asked.

"Not really, more like blind and stupid," snorted Jenny.

Peter stared at his wife with new eyes, failing to understand how her mind was working and how her view of the world was being shaped by her new job.

"I'm heading in for a coffee - I'll bring it out. Do you want anything?" he asked.

Jenny was obviously lost in thought, so Peter tried again.

"Coffee?" he said, more pointedly this time and Jenny registered the question with a nod of her head.

"Put a couple of sugars in it," she said and Peter made to get out, but was stopped by Jenny's hand resting on the top of his arm.

"I don't like him you know," she said.

"Who? Reed?" asked Peter.

"It's as if he's infected me."

Jenny's eyebrows drew together, creating a deep furrow between her eyes and a look that pleaded to be understood.

"I'll get the coffee," said Peter and letting Jenny's hand slip from his arm he got out of the car and walked towards the building.

Jenny watched him go and once he'd disappeared she reached into her hand-bag for cigarettes and her mobile phone. She stepped out of the car, lit up and called Sam. "Hi Sam. Anything new?"

"Still running down leads," he told her. "Nothing substantive yet, but we're keeping going."

"Uh-huh," said Jenny, not knowing what to say next and not really knowing why she had called Sam in the first place.

"The Chief says you won't be in till lunchtime tomorrow," he added.

The resulting anger that instantly surged through Jenny was born of guilt rather than malice and she found it difficult to keep her voice steady,

"It's Peter's idea of a stress reliever," she said. "I thought the Chief would've vetoed the idea straight away, but he seemed keener than me!" Then the thought suddenly dawned on her that she was deliberately being kept out of the loop. "Sure there's nothing I should know?"

"Not really. The Chief's probably right; if the profile's accurate Reed will be holding both women for a week yet and you could do with a break. It's still your first week on the job remember?"

"It feels like years," said Jenny.

"Well, it's been a tough initiation."

Jenny reflected on her last conversation with Ronnie.

"I spoke to Ronnie George yesterday," she said.

"That's your uncle?" asked Sam. "The DI who gave us the lead for Reed's activity in Ireland?"

"That's him."

The profiler hesitated, momentarily torn between family loyalty and her respect for Sam and the Chief.

"He was asking me about the Chief."

"Asking what?" enquired Sam, suddenly interested.

"He seemed to be wondering if the Chief could cope with the investigation. He didn't come right out with it in so many words, but I got the feeling he'd been asked to report upwards."

Sam fell silent, obviously processing the information.

"Thanks Jenny," he said at last. "I'll let the Chief know."

"Did I do the right thing? Telling you I mean?" she asked, guilt rapidly descending.

"Spot on!"

"And will you keep me in touch?"

"Sure," said Sam. "If anything happens that I think you should know about, keep your phone on and I'll call you."

"Thanks," she said and rang off.

Jenny lit a cigarette and made a second call to Paz, who also reported nothing new of any interest, and she felt deflated as she clicked off.

Spotting her husband emerging from the building clutching two cups of coffee, she ground the cigarette underfoot and kicked the end under the car before resuming her seat in the opulent Bentley interior. Peter eased himself in beside her, offering her one of the styro-foam cups.

"I do realise you're back on the weed you know," he remarked. "You don't have to hide it from me - I'm not your dad."

She looked at him sheepishly, catching a glint of humour in his eyes. For the first time that day they laughed together and sharing a small moment of humour instantly lifted the tension between them. The rest of the journey passed with Jenny and Peter becoming more at ease with each other as the miles rolled behind them. By the time they eventually arrived at Shrigley Hall Jenny's body language showed her to be relaxed and happy. The couple were pampered with valet parking, bell boys and pleasantly efficient hotel receptionists with practised smiles baked onto their faces.

Eventually they collapsed on to a huge bed and without needing to consult each other made slow, deliberate love in their sumptuous surroundings.

***

Robyn Cox was numb. Her body had been bound for so long that it had lost all feeling and her mind was blank. She barely felt the strong hands on her shoulders shaking her awake as she fell in and out of consciousness. She vaguely heard a man's voice close to her head, but his words seemed distant at first and she couldn't understand their meaning; it was as if they were coming from a different room and echoing down a corridor before reaching her ears. Eventually the sound became closer and then suddenly very real and the voice was clear, *'It's your turn to die!'*

Despite being securely bound, she tried to wriggle against her captor who was now lifting her from the floor before throwing her on to the iron-framed bed. She thought for a second that she might continue downwards into an unexpected softness and be submerged as she had been as a child diving into calm water. She felt the rope tethering her hands loosen and then fall away, followed by the binding around her ankles a few seconds later. Her face was pressed against the mattress and she was grateful for the sudden comfort against her cheek, despite the dank, musty smell.

Her arms and legs felt like lead: there was no pain in them, but they were unresponsive and despite all her efforts she found herself just as unable to move as when she had been bound a few moments earlier. All she could do was lie face-down, semi-conscious in an almost dreamlike state and listen to the voice that echoed inside her head. *It's your turn to die,'* it said again. Robyn could do nothing as rough hands pulled and prodded at her body until eventually she found herself coming face-to-face with another woman. Suddenly Robyn remembered how she had watched someone else die - in this room and on this bed - and she slowly made the connection between the words she had just heard and this woman watching her. The woman looked terrified: tears streamed down a dirty, blood-caked face with a red ball-gag distorting the captive's features.

Robyn felt her own gag being removed. She wanted to cry out, she wanted to plead for her life, tell the man that she had a family and children that would miss her and how much she loved them and loved her life. But there was a rasping dryness in her throat and no words would come, with only a hoarse murmuring and futile movement of her lips to show for her effort.

"Do it now," came a voice, booming through the room and she felt cold plastic on her face as a bag was pulled over her head. Her attacker paused and she heard a belt being unbuckled before the drawstring of the bag was pulled impossibly tight, restricting her breathing. Robyn could not move or even struggle as she felt hands pulling her lower body up on the bed. Suddenly a pain like fire coursed through her abdomen and she breathed hard, exhaling into the bag and then inhaling the plastic itself. Panic gripped her until a moment of desperation produced a final kick backwards against her tormentor.

Eventually, as the air inside the plastic was used up, Robyn's mind began to relax and she submitted to her fate. An inexplicable sense of relief washed over her as the air ran out altogether and breathing became impossible. Tears of sadness rather than pain wet the plastic as it clung to her skin, and images of her husband Colin and Violet their daughter laughing in the sunshine filled her mind before it went blank and she saw no more.

***

An hour or so passed before a knock at the door brought complimentary champagne and chocolates which Jenny and Peter Foster devoured greedily. The self-indulgent luxury sent the pair retreating back to bed to make love again, this time with passion and purpose bringing each other to a noisy climax.

Her previous tensions now a mere wisp of memory,

Jenny luxuriated in the opulence of the room. Heavy silk drapery overlaid the elegantly plain net curtains hanging at the Georgian sash windows. The carpet pile, at least half an inch thick, was tracked with the comings and goings of silk slippers and each piece of furniture, chosen for its softly glowing patina, perfectly complemented the effortlessly stylish décor. The bed where Jenny lay outstretched and naked next to Peter was spread with cool white Egyptian cotton sheets and the huge goose-down pillows yielded extra comfort with each touch. The legs of the four-poster were ornately carved burr walnut, and it occurred to Jenny that some young employee must spend hours each day polishing them, together with the legs of the other beds in the hotel, and this would probably constitute a full-time job.

"This place must be a fortune!" she said to no-one in particular.

Peter took himself off into the bathroom. "Dinner at eight," he said over his shoulder, and Jenny dropped her head to one side thinking she might sleep for a week.

Chapter 22

When a telephone rings between the hours of two and five am it can never be good news and when Jenny's mobile began playing its ring-tone of *'Simply the Best'* at just after four she snapped awake, automatically shaking Peter out of his sleep to share her panic. In the darkness provided by black-out curtains they couldn't actually see each other, but their radar communication system worked fine and neither of them spoke, instead launching an instant search for the mobile, which Peter eventually unearthed from just under the bed. The display told him all he needed to know. He gave a sigh of relief. "It's not Candice," he said and threw the still ringing mobile onto the covers between them before falling back into the goose-down softness of the luxurious pillows.

The only light in the room emanated from the screen of her mobile and Jenny could see Sam Bradbury's name prominently displayed. Gripped by sudden panic, she slid out from between the warm comforting sheets and stumbled toward the bathroom, hitting the answer button and pressing the phone to her ear. "Hi," she said in a whisper before closing the door behind her and flicking on the light switch.

Everything went white for a moment as the instant

light blinded her and she closed her eyes. Then the profiler concentrated on Sam's voice, flopping down onto the toilet seat.

"Sorry to call so early," he said without a hint of apology in his voice, "but there've been a few developments."

"It's fine," said Jenny. "Go on."

"Robyn Cox's body turned up an hour ago," said Sam flatly.

Jenny was instantly and painfully alert. A feeling of intense vulnerability swept over her and suddenly aware that she was naked except for a pair of knickers she wrapped her free arm around herself as shivers coursed through her body. Her voice began to shake. "Where was she found?"

A policeman to his core, Sam knew that Jenny was in shock at the news. Over the years he had delivered bad news face-to-face and by telephone dozens of times and he wanted to give Jenny an opportunity to digest the information.

"Don't worry about that right now," he said. "Get yourself a cup of coffee and call me back."

"Ok," said Jenny, almost robotically.

"There's something else, though," he added. "Has the hotel got a fax number?"

"Sure. I'll find out what it is. Why?"

"That Patrick guy you spotted has sent another love letter to the Chief. You should see that too."

"Right," said Jenny, the promise of usefulness distracting her mind from the horror of Robyn Cox's death. "I'll call you back with it shortly."

"Ok," said Sam and clicked off.

308

Mercifully, Peter had fallen back in to a deep sleep and Jenny used the light from the bathroom to dress quickly and slip out of the room, grabbing as she went her unread pile of manila files. She managed to escape from the dark room without waking her husband; the last thing she wanted now was a confrontation.

She supposed the hotel probably had a business centre and she could use it to talk to Sam and receive the fax he'd mentioned. Four in the morning saw Reception unmanned, but a bemused night porter gave her the fax number she needed and showed her to a spacious room banked with internet-ready computers together with rosewood desks and leather operator chairs.

"Is everything alright, Madam?" he asked.

Jenny suddenly realised how unkempt she must look compared to the usual polished appearance of guests at Shrigley Hall. "I'm fine," she said, mustering her best smile to try and assuage the concerns of the burly night porter. "Thanks for helping me out."

He lingered for a few more seconds and Jenny wondered if he was having second thoughts about her status as a hotel guest. She realised she only had her mobile phone and the manila files, and was even without a key card to get back into the room. "Is there any chance of a pot of coffee?" she asked. "It's Foster, Room 129," she added, deliberately giving him the information he needed to check up on her.

"Of course, Mrs Foster," came the porter's clipped reply and he smartly turned and left the room, his straight back disappearing up the corridor with a sense of purpose.

Jenny rapidly texted Sam with the fax number he

needed to send through the letter from Patrick and called him straight after pressing send.

"Hi Sam," she said. "I've just sent you the fax number for the hotel. What happened tonight?"

Sam sounded defeated as he spoke. "Robyn Cox was found dumped in a park in Rawtenstall," he said. "She was suffocated and strangled, then left naked and wrapped in plastic, similar to Dawn James."

"Any witnesses?" asked Jenny hopefully.

"The body was discovered by a bar manager on his way home from work and he didn't see anyone else. Obviously we'll appeal for witnesses and we're trawling through CCTV footage to try and get a location on the van."

"Is the body numbered?" asked Jenny, the question catching in her throat even as she said the words.

"Same as Dawn James," said Sam. "Only this time it's a number two burned into her lower back. There's no doubt that it's Robyn Cox."

Jenny sat silently for a moment taking in the news, the phone pressed hard against her ear.

"Can you get back earlier?" said Sam, more of a statement than a question.

"I'll leave within an hour," said Jenny, suddenly remembering Peter asleep upstairs. She wondered how she could get him out of bed and motivate him to drive back to Manchester without creating too much of an argument.

"I've just sent that fax," said Sam.

Jenny could hear the machine in the corner suddenly spring into life, quiet and efficient.

'Just like Joe Reed', she thought.

"It's coming through," she said and stood to watch the papers spill out. "I'll call you back when I'm on the road."

"Ok," said Sam. "Let me know what you think of the letter. I think there's no doubt that whoever sent it is either Joe Reed himself or someone very close to him."

The door of the Business Centre opened and the night porter strode in, bringing with him the smell of freshly brewed coffee as he set down a tray on one of the desks.

"I'll review it and give you a call," Jenny told Sam. "Speak later. Bye."

"Was there anything else Mrs Foster?" asked the night porter and Jenny suddenly realised she had nothing to tip him with.

She picked up the bill to sign, vaguely aware that £18.75 was ridiculous for a pot of coffee.

"No, you've been great," she said and turned her back to pour the coffee, imagining the porter's glare as he walked out of the room with just the signed chitty and nothing for his trouble at gone four in the morning.

Jenny added milk and two sugars for energy before she retrieved the fax and settled down to review the contents. The profiler immediately noted the signature as the same flourish she'd seen on the other missives identified during the research compiled with Paz at the station. She opened her file marked '*PATRICK*' and extracted one of the previous letters, using this new one to overlap the previous signatures to be certain that they were exactly the same. The lab results for the original letter, showing that no DNA evidence was apparent, had come back just before she left Police HQ. The lab technicians summarised that the writer must have worn gloves and used a wet pad for the envelope seal and the stamp, thus avoiding any personal contamination of the package.

She realised how careful Patrick must have been when writing the letters and preparing them for the post. He was taking a chance in sending the notes at all, but had used his obvious knowledge of forensic countermeasures to conceal his identity. Jenny was torn between whether this was because he was Joe Reed himself, or a crank trying to insert himself into the investigation. The second page of the fax comprehensively supplied the answer to her dilemma and she held the paper at arm's length as though it might infect her with evil. It showed the image of a woman's contorted face, grimacing against a ball-gag clenched between her teeth.

Even allowing for the graininess of the image after its journey through the fax machine, Jenny could see that tears had made clean tracks on the victim's otherwise filthy face and her hair was matted with blood and sweat. Her stomach flipped, a natural reaction that the novice profiler wasn't expecting, and she gripped the arm of the chair to steady herself as a sudden dizziness overtook her. Nausea came next, hard and fast and Jenny found herself scrambling for the waste-paper bin under the desk to release the remains of her dinner, now reduced to a putrid acid mess that splattered the bottom of the empty bin. "Shit!" she said to herself as she wiped her chin with a piece of Shrigley Hall Hotel notepaper, the only thing she had to hand for the unsavoury task.

Jenny looked again at the grainy image. Sam had added a footnote that read, *Confirmed image of Robyn Cox,* and she quickly realised that this must be one of the final pictures taken of the dead woman. The full horror of the hopelessness and degradation that this innocent mother must have suffered whilst in the merciless hands of Joe Reed hit Jenny hard. She reeled from her own thoughts and found herself biting the back of her hand; desperate, but unable to look away.

Until this moment the notion that Joe Reed was holding his victims captive before killing them was only brought to life through the evidence of rope burns and ligature marks, but the stark reality of this image was different. She could almost feel the gag in her own mouth; the pain etched on Robyn Cox's face penetrated her psyche, and a throbbing pulse to her forehead and a beating in her chest were followed by breathlessness and panic.

Jenny buried her face in her hands, her loose dark hair trailing half way to the ground as she realised that Robyn Cox must have been murdered whilst she herself was making love to her husband or enjoying dinner, unaware that Robyn's life was ebbing away in agony and humiliation. Wracked with guilt, Jenny hugged herself and rocked to and fro; she felt she had let Robyn Cox down, not because she hadn't been able to access the information that would tell Sam and the others where she was, but because she had forgotten that Robyn even existed. The pleasure of the dinner the evening before and the thrill of Peter's touch degenerated into a feeling of deep self-loathing. She slapped the fax face-down on the desk and returned to the waste-paper bin to be sick again, this time only retching up bile that burned her throat as she released the foul liquid through clenched teeth. When the spasms had finally stopped she collapsed head back in her chair, the throbbing pulse in her temple graduating to a full-blown headache. Leaning forward, she drained her coffee cup in a single gulp before shakily re-filling and repeating the process. The caffeine gave Jenny an almost instant rush of energy; she shook her head to free it of the image of Robyn Cox's face imprinted on her memory, and that moment of clarity brought a question to the forefront of her mind.

Why call yourself Patrick? she mouthed, and forced herself to sit up straight and read the letter. Like the others it was typed and addressed to the Chief personally, and it attacked his handling of the case with a liberal use of expletives, this time electronically bold to make their point. It was obviously a taunt intended to show that the writer was in control and that the police were powerless to stop him. There was no hint of remorse in the letter and it was clear to Jenny that the only point in writing and sending it was to infuriate the Chief and sicken the team to distraction. Sam had again added a footnote, informing Jenny that the words *One, two buckle my shoe* had been added in ink on the back of the picture. Jenny thought for a moment and tried to get inside the mind of Joe Reed, trying to make sense of the letter and any meaning. "Why Patrick?" she said to herself again.

Just then her phone rang. Jenny didn't recognise the number, and forgetting that it was still only five am she absent-mindedly pressed to answer.

"Hello, Jenny Foster," said the profiler, adopting her

usual clipped tones when answering an as yet anonymous caller.

"Hello Jenny." It was a female voice she vaguely recognised. "Sorry to call so early, but I'm guessing with all that's happened tonight you're wide awake?"

"Sorry, who is this?" asked Jenny, mildly irritated.

"Paula Tripp, Manchester Evening News - we spoke the other day."

Irritation quickly turned to anger, and the tone of her reply was laced with venom.

"I told you not to call my mobile number!"

Tripp responded calmly; Jenny could even detect the hint of a smile. "I thought you might have called me after you'd looked through the envelope I left with you."

Jenny suddenly remembered their exchange in the car-park of Central Park, Manchester Metropolitan Police HQ and realised that the envelope she was talking about was still among the files lying unopened on the desk next to her. Jenny had planned to have a look through it at some point over the weekend, but Peter had done a good job of putting all thoughts of work out of her mind and she'd forgotten the envelope even existed. She let out a sigh.

"What's so bloody important about it? I've got more pressing things to do than to look through a CV of your dubious accomplishments."

"I told you Jenny," said Tripp seeing her opportunity. "The information is to help *you* personally. It's not directly about the case."

"You never said that," said Jenny as she tore open the envelope. "I'm opening it now and then you can scurry back to your hole."

Paula Tripp remained silent as she listened to Jenny tearing open the envelope and removing the contents, and then smiled at the sudden gasp on the other end of the phone. She could hear the rustling sound of the profiler fumbling with the pictures, and imagined with a certain relish her mounting dismay as she pored over the tell-tale prints Tripp had so carefully ordered. The series began with Peter leaving home and ended with several snaps of him passionately kissing Jenny's sister Candice outside The Midland Hotel in Manchester. The images were dated and timed to show the recipient that this had been a day-time rendezvous which neither party would have relished being made public. "Bitch," said Jenny eventually, and Tripp wondered whether the comment was meant for her or Candice. Jenny stared at the pictures. All thoughts of Robyn Cox, Joe Reed and Patrick were torn instantly from her mind. She couldn't believe what she was looking at: Candice with Peter on her second day on the job, the day after the party at her parents to celebrate her new position. *How was it possible!*

"These are fakes," she said into the phone.

Paula Tripp took a second to let Jenny realise how ridiculous that statement sounded. "I took them myself."

Jenny continued to stare at the last few images, laying them out in front of her. She tried to focus on the two sets of lips locked together in an embrace that according to the time stamp lasted at least thirty seconds. This was no quick peck goodbye and Jenny's nausea grew as the detail revealed a glimpse of her sister's tongue deep in her husband's mouth. She wiped at the tears that had begun streaming down her cheeks, trying desperately to compose herself, and had a sudden urge to get this reporter off the phone and talk to her sister.

"What do you want?" she asked. "It can't be money."

Paula Tripp laughed, "All I want, Jenny, is for us to be friends."

"Get lost!" said Jenny with a vehemence that sent spittle darting across the room.

"Now, now," responded Tripp, a smile still evident in her voice. "That's not the way to talk to your friends."

Jenny tried again, "What *do* you want Tripp?"

"What any friend wants - to get to know you, and especially how you feel about the Bury Beast."

"Including any inside information?" asked Jenny seeing the direction the conversation was taking,

"Why not! People confide in their friends and you can confide in me. You know what I mean, Jenny: you can ask my opinion on the little details that no-one else knows about." She paused, and then added, "I could be like your sounding board; when anything new happens you can call me up and discuss the facts with me."

"And then you report them in the Manchester Evening News?" asked Jenny.

"Or any other paper I fancy."

"Well, the answer's most definitely no!" said Jenny.

The profiler was confused. She couldn't see how these pictures of her husband and sister kissing could force her to reveal details of the Bury Beast case to Paula Tripp.

"Now you listen to me Foster," said Tripp, her voice suddenly bristling with purpose and ambition. "You'll tell me everything I need to know."

Jenny rose indignantly to the challenge. "Why would I!"

"Because if you don't, it won't be the Bury Beast on the front of every newspaper in the country, it'll be you and Peter. Imagine how the public will react when they read about the Manchester Met's new all-singing, all-dancing criminal profiler's marriage falling apart in the middle of the investigation! The nation's press will focus on you and how you can't possibly do your job. Every sordid detail of your marriage, your ex-husband, your slimy second husband's dodgy business deals and all of his affairs will be splashed across every paper in every country in the world." Paula Tripp paused to let the full magnitude of the situation sink in.

"You'll be a laughing stock and the Chief will have you out on your ear so fast your feet won't touch," she added mockingly.

Jenny remained silent. She knew Tripp was right: the Chief would get rid of her under such circumstances, if only to refocus on the investigation. Momentary panic gripped the profiler as she realised with dread that her longed for career would be swept away in scandal and ignominy.

"Think about it," Tripp went on. "I know you're having a wonderful time away with your *loving* husband, but I'm sure you're keen to get back to the office. I'll give you until eleven tonight to call me with the details of Cox's murder the police aren't telling the press." And with that the reporter abruptly rang off.

Jenny sat back in the hotel's plush business centre chair, its normally comfortable back-support mechanism taking a pounding as she rocked back and forth.

The profiler could hardly breathe; anger, fear and pain rocked her body and she seemed unable to exhale the air she was swallowing in gulps. Eventually her lungs could take no more and she almost screamed out a huge breath that doubled her over in agony, her stomach and chest cramping. Tears of pain and rage dripped from her eyes, which were locked tight shut against the prospect of the collapse of her universe. All she could do was scream through clenched teeth until her throat rasped like dry sandpaper. Fortunately the night porter came back for the tray just in time to see Jenny pitching forward out of the chair and to catch her in his arms before she fell to the floor.

"Mrs Foster?" he said anxiously, hauling her dead weight back into a sitting position. "Mrs Foster?"

Jenny's eyes rolled in their sockets, her head and body feeling ready to burst from an inner pressure that continued to build from her core outwards. Spit and bile crept unchecked from the corner of her mouth as she lolled against the pristine black jacket of the night porter. Once he'd settled her into a sitting position he bent to study her face and eyes.

"Mrs Foster?" he tried again, this time taking hold of her chin between a thumb and forefinger that dwarfed Jenny's entire lower face. "Can you hear me?"

"I'm ok," she managed in a whisper, her lips barely moving.

"You stay there and I'll call your husband," he said, taking his hand from Jenny's chin.

The mention of Peter galvanised Jenny into action and her hand shot out, grabbing the porter's sleeve as his hand retreated.

"Don't you dare!" she almost hissed.

He reeled back, shocked both by her words and her sudden recovery as she proceeded to stand up, shakily at first and then with more purpose.

"Sorry," she said. "I don't need a doctor or my husband, I just need some water."

The night porter stared at this strange guest rooted surprisingly sure-footed in front of him, almost challenging him to disobey her as she pulled her hair back from her face and wiped her mouth with the back of her hand.

"Would that be ok?" she asked, and when he didn't move she added, "The water?"

"Of course Mrs Foster," he said and took two giants steps to the corner of the room where a water cooler and plastic cups had been provided for hard-working executives. He handed her the cup and she drained the contents in one gulp as if she hadn't tasted water for weeks before returning it to the bemused man to be refilled.

"Can you cut me a new key-card?" said Jenny as he handed her a second cup of water.

"Of course," he said, but as he made for the door Jenny held him by the elbow. "This never happened, ok?"

The night porter looked at Jenny and a smile crossed his lips as he nodded slowly.

"No problem, Mrs Foster," he said. "Hotel porters are renowned for their discretion."

Then he disappeared from the room, allowing Jenny a few moments to gather her thoughts.

When he returned with the freshly cut key-card Jenny had formulated a plan to get back to the office with a minimum of fuss. She would talk to Candice first before she tackled Peter. She wanted all of the facts and she knew she would get them from her sister rather than her husband. If he'd already cheated on her, lying would be a formality, and the last thing she needed today was to try and distinguish between truth and lies coming from the lips of a man she had trusted never to hurt her, let alone smash her world to pieces.

Chapter 23

Waking Peter and persuading him to leave the hotel for a journey back to Manchester at five-thirty in the morning hadn't been too difficult once Jenny showed him the picture of Robyn Cox bound and gagged waiting to meet her death.

Peter reacted just as Jenny had expected, almost bolting out of bed and diving for the bathroom for a quick shower. Hoping that her husband's state of shock would see them all the way back to Manchester, she stuffed clothes into their overnight bags before taking a shower herself while Peter drank a quick room-service coffee. They hurried down to the foyer to pay the bill and then emerged into the half-light of a new summer day, the scent of freshly-mown grass wafting from the golf course in front of the hotel. The night porter who had helped her earlier and kept her counsel not to speak to her husband about their early morning experiences had transformed himself into one of the liveried doormen. Jenny pressed £20 unseen into his hand and he offered a wink and a smile that made her momentarily blush. Without a word he opened the car door for her and she stepped into the plush interior of the Bentley Continental for the journey back to Manchester.

She told Peter to take her straight to Central Park, asking him not to stop if he could possibly help it as she was understandably keen to get back as quickly as possible. She spent the first half hour of the journey talking to Sam and Paz about the case and the letter from Patrick before steeling herself for a call to Candice to let her know that they were returning early. Jenny was conscious of the fact that as it was not yet seven the telephone would probably wake Lilly or one of Candice's children, but she thought this scant punishment compared to what she was planning for her treacherous sister. After a brief conversation Jenny ended the call without apology, pointedly telling Candice that she was going straight to work without returning home first, but promising to call by her apartment in Hulme for a coffee and quick catch-up on her way home that night. Glancing at Peter during the conversation, she noticed that he'd lost his look of abject horror at the revelation of Robyn Cox's death and had returned to comfortable millionaire driver mode. She was sure that the pair of them thought her too stupid to have found out about their affair, or perhaps they were so arrogant that they didn't care. Either way, Jenny was happy that she'd managed to get out of the hotel without allowing herself to question her husband and spent the remainder of the journey pretending to be asleep so that there was no need to speak.

Despite the pictures of Candice and her husband together flashing painfully through her mind, the profiler managed to drift in and out of sleep as the miles sped by. Peter pressed a button to listen to music, this time choosing Classic FM, and as Jenny wavered in the murky grey between sleep and wakefulness she was aware of the mournful strains of Barber's Adagio for Strings rising and falling around her, permeating her consciousness until she felt almost as though her life were slipping away. The sound of the violins rising to a crescendo broke her grip on the reality of a life she once thought she knew, and seemed to toss her emotions out to sea to be buffeted by strong currents to come.

When she did eventually sit up straight as the Bentley cruised in to Manchester City Centre she returned Peter's smile with an ice-cold stare. His enquiry as to her mood was met with a frosty, "I'm fine," with no further illumination offered despite his repeated attempts at conversation. As she stepped out of the car at Central Park she heard him say, "So, no words of thanks for a wonderful night, or getting up at stupid o'clock to drive you back?"

Jenny stared at her husband through the open door, the unexpected heat of the early morning adding to her sense of claustrophobia and need to get away.

"I'll thank you properly when I get home," she said and even managed a half smile as she closed the passenger door. She wrestled her files - including the pictures supplied by Paula Tripp - from amongst the bags in the boot and marched in to the building. She pretended not to hear Peter call after her that he loved her and was looking forward to seeing her later; his voice sounded alien as he said the words and Jenny knew that she would never feel the same about Peter again. For the first time since they met she felt revulsion for her husband, and she knew her feelings would only grow darker with time. She could already sense herself building a defensive wall against the very man who only a day ago had been the rock of support she believed she would always rely on.

Even as she stepped away from the car Jenny's mind began to work over-time. Despite a whirlwind inner turmoil during the journey, she had managed to keep her emotions to herself as the purr of the Bentley's engine swallowed up the miles, mercifully bringing calm as she half-slept, half-dreamed away the journey. But now, as the heat of the morning became suddenly unbearable and she walked across the car-park toward the sanctuary of Central Park, her mind was full of Peter's forthcoming meeting with Candice. The thought of her husband driving to the home they shared, perhaps encouraging Lilly and her sister's children to play in the garden whilst he wantonly made love to Candice made Jenny's head spin like a crazy washing-machine cycle. She couldn't stop imagining her husband's hands on her sister's breasts, writhing with her in Jenny's bed, mocking Jenny's naiveté as they lay exhausted afterwards.

By now she had reached the steps of the building and clung on to the hand-rail reserved for disabled visitors, her body bent almost double with pain, disgust and nausea. Three detectives she vaguely remembered seeing before suddenly came through the double doors and down the few steps into the car-park. Jenny was forced to try and regain her composure, and she managed a weak smile as they glanced her way, concern stopping them mid-conversation.

"Are you okay, Mrs Foster?" asked one of them, his eyes searching her face for signs of distress.

"I'm fine," said Jenny brightly. "Just caught out by the heat," she added by way of explanation.

The young detective smiled sympathetically. "Air-con's on!" he said reassuringly, but when she didn't immediately move to seek shelter inside he took her elbow, his smile disappearing as quickly as it had appeared. "Are you sure you're ok?" he asked, his face full of concern.

"Yes, yes," said Jenny shrugging off the young man, perhaps a little more brusquely than she had intended, and he took a defensive step back as though he'd been stung by a wandering insect. "I mean, I'll be ok once I'm inside," she added, and forced her legs to propel her up the steps and into the building, all too conscious of the three men watching her. "Shit!" she said to herself, and made her way across the mercifully empty reception area and into the Ladies'.

Jenny stared at her reflection in the mirror: the strain was obvious on her face and she could almost see pain and devastation in her eyes. She took her face in her hands and closed her eyes tight shut, trying to rid her mind of the pictures of Peter and Candice smiling at her through their treachery. After a few moments the profiler opened her eyes and stared into the mirror. *Peter is a prick,* she thought, *but my sister is an evil bitch!* The pain of Candice's betrayal was overwhelming, and fresh hot tears began streaming down her cheeks.

Eventually she wiped the tears away with the back of her hand. She needed to get a grip of herself; she *had* to put her husband and sister out of her mind and concentrate on Robyn Cox and Joe Reed rather than the man who had torn apart her private, personal world. Taking a deep breath and banging her handbag onto the side of the sink she roughly retrieved her make-up bag and proceeded to transform herself into a professional member of the murder team. She applied foundation in angry strokes, before staring into her brown eyes to add eye-liner and mascara. As she did so, she drew deep within herself to find strength to transform the fierce indignation that was now coursing through every nerve in her body into a steely-eyed determination to help the Police track down Joe Reed. She brushed her dark hair until she could see it shine and finally applied lip-gloss before shoving the make-up back into her handbag. Heading for the door, she almost knocked over a startled woman who was just on her way in, and mistakenly stood holding the door open for Jenny to pass through like a whirlwind.

Taking the lift, she headed straight for the Chief's office, negotiating the milling crowd of detectives as she walked across the main office without making eye-contact with a single person, pointedly ignoring Paz as he waved to her from their now joint desk.

She knocked on the Chief's door and went in without waiting for a reply to find him and Sam deep in a conversation which came to a sudden end as the door swished open.

"Hello Jenny," said the Chief cordially. "Glad you could make it so quickly. Sit down and we'll fill you in."

Jenny offered Sam a glimpse of a smile as she settled herself as comfortably as possible for what she anticipated would be a difficult and lengthy meeting. The Chief was stony-eyed and by the haunted look on

Sam's face it was obvious that they had achieved nothing positive in the hours since the discovery of the second victim. The Chief passed Jenny the preliminary post mortem report from the Coroner's Office and Jenny quickly scanned the contents whilst he and Sam waited in silence. Perhaps, she thought, they were hoping she'd spot something they'd missed, give them some fresh hope.

"It's obviously Reed's work," said Sam redundantly, shifting in his chair.

Jenny looked up and the strain in the detective's eyes was obvious.

She went on reading the report, noting the similarities between Robyn Cox's death and the murder of Dawn James. She saw that the ligature marks on the second victim's wrists, ankles and neck were almost identical and that Robyn had a number two burned cruelly into the small of her back - chilling evidence that the sequence of abductions and murders was set to continue. Robyn Cox had been suffocated using a plastic bag in the same way as the previous victim and the evidence of sodomy was clearly defined by the coroner. The body had been washed and prepared for dumping post-mortem and then left in public view wrapped in plastic, just as Dawn James' body had been found. In view of the items found in the stomach of the previous victim, the coroner had wasted no time in analysing the contents of Robyn Cox's stomach prior to a full autopsy. Sure enough, he had found similar notes to those inside the stomach of Dawn James. This time there had been six of them, all written in the same hand as the others, only this time the messages seemed more desperate with four separate pieces almost shouting, *PLEASE HELP ME* in block capitals. The remaining two were more cryptic; one read *Please catch him, he's a murderer,* and the other, *I have no choice.* Jenny noted to herself that the handwriting here was different from the 'Patrick' letters.

Looking up from the report, she found the Chief and Sam staring anxiously at her, obviously hoping for some fresh insight, but her thoughts had turned inexorably to the sort of thing that might be written on such notes if they were lodged inside her own body right now. Jenny felt as though she herself were a victim as she sat there returning the Chief's stare - a victim of her own sister and husband, and a victim of Reed too. All three would be mocking her inadequacies and stupidity at not being able to see the obvious clues right in front of her eyes.

After taking a moment, she closed the report and put it carefully on the Chief's desk.

"Well?" he said, not exactly impatient but interested to hear anything Jenny had to say. "What do you think?" The position of the chairs meant that anyone visiting the Chief's office was forced to confront his humourless blue eyes and long, thin face that grew ever gaunter with each meeting that passed. As ever, he was looking immaculate in his black Chief Inspector's uniform. His hairline seemed to have retreated still further, accentuating his height even from his sitting position. Despite the pressure he was under, his face was clean shaven to show off his black moustache to its full effect, and Jenny could recognise that his authority came from his ability to remain in control in any situation. Given the setback of Robyn Cox turning up dead well before he must have thought she would, she was impressed by his air of control and determination. "There's clearly been an escalation in his pattern of offending," began Jenny. "The timescales between the abduction and murder of Dawn James and the subsequent abduction and murder of Robyn Cox are markedly different." The two men gave her their full attention. "Although the MO remains the same," she continued after a short pause, "there's no evidence from the description of the wounds on the body that the level of violence has increased. So the decrease in the length of time he kept Robyn Cox alive will stem from psychological or perhaps even practical reasons."

"And *will* the level of violence increase?" asked Sam.

"Not necessarily," said Jenny who had quickly assumed her role as expert and was now fully focused on the case rather than her personal anguish. "It's uncommon that an offender such as Reed will escalate the level of violence. I think the way that he kills his victims is central to the reason he kidnaps them in the first place."

"So you think that his time-scale may get shorter, but otherwise he'll stick to his pattern?" asked the Chief.

"Remember Robert Black?" asked Jenny. "The serial killer caught in 1990 bundling a six-year old girl into the back of his van? He started molesting young girls from the age of fifteen and wasn't caught until he'd committed at least four murders over a relatively short period in the 1980's. It was a stroke of luck he was caught at all, thanks to the fact that it was the six-year old's policeman father who stumbled upon Black attempting to kidnap his daughter."

"So," said the Chief, a little irritated by the history lesson. "How is that relevant?"

Jenny paused, picking up the report again and focusing on the notes. "The point is," she explained, "killers have certain triggers that set them off that they don't generally deviate from. In the case of Black he was only interested in girls aged around six or seven, even when he was himself only fifteen. Joe Reed concentrates on targeting a certain type of woman and killing her in a very specific way."

"Do you think it's more like a ritual?" asked Sam.

"I'm not sure," she said thoughtfully. "I'll go and see Dr Phillips at the University again for a second opinion. But judging from the notes found in Robyn Cox's stomach I would say that Reed had suffered a major schizophrenic episode and that may lead him to act more quickly."

"You mean this idea that his good side is fighting his bad side?" asked Sam

"Exactly that," said Jenny. "If I'm right the bad Joe Reed is winning the battle."

"Sam," said the Chief, turning his attention to the DI. "I know you're doing everything possible to find Reed, but I can see what Jenny's driving at. If she's right, he'll be kidnapping another victim more quickly than the last and the next thing we know Sharon Daly will be turning up within a few days." He shook his head, eyes closed, the possibility that they were already running out of time beginning to tell even on his face. "If that happens," he went on, "the whole country will begin to panic."

It had been Sam's idea for Jenny to go with him to a local pub and have a sandwich away from Central Park and the immediate rigours of the case. He said he wanted to fill her in on developments and talk the case over to see if there was anything he had missed. In reality his detective instinct was so strong that he had guessed the moment he saw Jenny that there might be something bothering her beyond Reed and the murders and he wanted to make sure she was fully focused on helping to find the killer.

The Hangman's Gate Pub stood on the banks of the Manchester Ship Canal, once the main arterial route for cargo between Manchester and the main port of Liverpool some thirty-five miles to the south west. The wide waterway was constructed by the Manchester Ship Canal Company, headed by the ambitious Lord Egerton, who personally cut the first sod in 1887. Jenny thought that judging from the condition of the pub, the building could easily have stood for just as long as the canal itself.

They sat at a table-bench in the beer garden that ran down to the water's edge. Jenny chose a table beneath the drooping branches of a willow tree affording some protection from the blazing midday sun. Unfortunately the shade did little to counteract the heat, and Jenny was aware of her slightly damp underarms and the perspiration that had begun to gather and glisten on her forehead. When Sam came striding across the grass in shirt and tie with his grey suit jacket on, Jenny wondered why he wasn't cooking alive.

"Are you keeping that jacket on?" she asked when he sat down opposite her, depositing two cokes and retrieving cutlery and red paper napkins from his jacket pockets.

"I don't really feel the heat," he said. "Well, not till it gets past 40 degrees anyway."

"You should at least loosen that tie."

Sam looked at her and smiled. "Does it bother you?" he asked.

"Does what bother me?"

"Not being in control," he said and swallowed half a glass of coke in one gulp.

Jenny felt her temper begin to flare. There had never been a time since she met Peter and had Lilly and the so called perfect life that she'd felt less in control of anything. "No," she said. "I don't need to be in control, I just think you'd be a bit cooler and more comfortable with your jacket off that's all."

Sam didn't reply, instead reaching into the offending item's inner pocket to produce a packet of Marlboro from which he took two cigarettes and handed one to Jenny.

Jenny took a lighter from her hand-bag and lit hers without offering to share the flame, dropping the lighter purposefully back into the bag. Sam half laughed and shaking his head lit his own cigarette with a lighter he found in his trouser pocket.

They smoked in silence for a few moments.

"What's your opinion of me?" asked Sam.

Jenny was taken by surprise at the question and gave an automatic response.

"I think you're a good policeman," she said.

Her glib answer was greeted by a lift of Sam's eyebrows and a short laugh. "Beyond the obvious," he said.

"I'm not sure my opinion's important," said Jenny, "or necessary."

"Come on," said Sam. "We've stood over a dead body together, which tends to bring people close more quickly than normal. You must have formed an opinion by now. I'm interested to know what it is."

Jenny examined Sam's features, smiling at her from across the table. She couldn't read what he was thinking or where the conversation was leading, but she was sure that Sam wasn't asking such obscure questions to pass the time of day and she knew he expected an answer.

"It's difficult," she said. "You've been with the Force for years, and the Chief even longer, but I'm not sure if you've ever come across someone like Reed. He's ruthless and very well organised and he's two steps ahead of the investigation - seemingly without effort."

"So you think I'm a nice guy, but not up to the job," he said, the smile still playing across his eyes.

"Not exactly," said Jenny, wary that she might be treading on difficult ground. I'm certain you'll catch Reed. They all get caught in the end. He'll make a mistake that will lead you to him, and the Manchester Metropolitan Police will rightly take the credit for bringing him to justice."

"But?"

"Well, it's as if you're learning from the case as you go; gaining experience, benefiting from it even." Jenny trailed off, she didn't like where the conversation was going and she didn't want to say too much.

"That's how these things work," said Sam. "For instance, you have the history of serial killers burned into your brain and think you can use that case history and apply it to Reed and that's all it needs to crack him. But you forget that before Peter Sutcliffe put a hammer in the skulls of his victims, or that before Brady and Hindley the Moors Murderers killed their victims in the 1960's they didn't exist in case history."

"Ok," said Jenny, "I get it. So Reed's a one-off."

"He's unique, Jenny," said Sam. "Reed has already carved his name in case-law history, there's never been anyone like him and there'll never be another one of him."

"No, that's true," said Jenny, "but psychologically he fits a pattern."

"No Jenny," said Sam a firmness growing in his voice. "Remember that Reed was a rapist and conman to begin with. We made an error thinking that he had some kind of plan when he kidnapped Dawn James. We thought that perhaps he would use her to satisfy his sexual appetite. Then he murdered her and broke his pattern. This guy is evolving and he's not working to a plan. If anything his crime spree is extremely random."

"You mean he's changed again because of the time escalation?" mused Jenny.

"It's up to us to try and figure out what his next move will be," said Sam. "We need to get ahead of this guy and the only way to do that is to try to predict who he's going to kidnap next."

"Ok," said Jenny. "Assuming that he's not just going to disappear and create a whole new MO we know what the woman he'll kidnap next is going to look like and we know how old she is. We also know her approximate social status and that she's going to have kids and work in a menial or service industry." She paused before adding, "That narrows it down to about half a million or more women in Greater Manchester!"

"Not all that helpful then," agreed Sam. "We need another detail Jenny, another bit of information that might narrow the field for his next victim. Basically, we need you to find a link between the three victims that no-one has figured out yet; then we might stand a chance."

A waitress appeared with two tuna sandwiches garnished with Italian leaves and a few crisps and put down the plates in front of them. "Table 38? Any sauces?"

"No thanks," said Sam rewarding her with a toothy smile.

"Just give me a shout if you need anything else," she said and headed back up the lawn towards the pub.

"Looks ok!" said Sam, beginning to tuck in.

Jenny stared at the sandwich for a moment or two, and then made an instant decision, almost blurting out the words, "I think I'm being blackmailed."

Sam stopped chewing and reached for a napkin to wipe away any mayonnaise that might escape the corner of his mouth. "Blackmailed? How and by whom?" he asked, alarm creeping into his voice.

"Paula Tripp," said Jenny taking her first bite of the sandwich, which tasted fresh in her mouth and made her suddenly realise how hungry she was.

Chapter 24

The pair ate in silence, Sam occasionally looking up from his food waiting patiently for Jenny to elaborate. She could feel the pressure of his gaze as she slowly chewed through her sandwich. Eventually when they had both finished Sam offered Jenny a Marlboro which she took and lit before inhaling deeply.

"So," he said. "Blackmail? Paula Tripp? Fancy giving me a few more details?"

Whilst Sam smoked and listened Jenny filled him in on that morning's events and how Tripp had called to threaten her. Sam forced Jenny to recall the conversation as word-for-word as she could remember. Jenny did so, without revealing that Peter might be having an affair. Instead, she superimposed the notion that Tripp had discovered something unsavoury about her husband's business dealings and that would be the point of the blackmail.

Relaying the tale, Jenny felt as though she were being unburdened and she found herself expanding into other parts of her personal life which she had not intended to touch on. She told Sam how she had met Peter at work and how difficult her studies had been, even revealing the agony of her many miscarriages before Lilly had blessed the couple with her arrival. Sam remained silent throughout and this spurred the profiler on until at last she realised that he was employing his version of a sympathetic interrogation technique by simply nodding and looking concerned, expertly allowing Jenny to keep talking and tell him all there was to know.

It crossed her mind that she had given too much of herself away to DI Sam Bradbury, and her emotions began to churn again as she realised that she had fallen into the trap of allowing yet another man to edge his way past her defences and put himself firmly in a position of trust. More importantly she realised that she knew almost nothing about Sam outside of work except the bare facts that he was married with two children. She suddenly felt vulnerable and thought that she'd probably made a mistake; the last thing Sam needed whilst pursuing Joe Reed was a neurotic woman in tow - let alone one who so far had contributed very little to helping him solve the case.

She finished talking and began to play the DI at his own game. She kept her silence for what seemed like an eternity, eventually forcing Sam to clear his throat and speak.

"Don't worry about *Paula Tripp*," he said, pouring scorn on the name. "I've had plenty of dealings with her over the years."

"She sounded pretty forceful," said Jenny. "She's desperate to get closer to the case."

Sam smiled. "Believe me," he said. "Once she realises that I know what she's trying to do and I tell her to back off, she'll do just that."

"Are you sure?" asked Jenny.

"And fast!" said Sam by way of answer.

***

The trip over to Manchester University Humanities Campus for her pre-arranged meeting with the suave Dr Michael Phillips would have been easy enough under normal circumstances, and it was now mid-afternoon and the traffic was mercifully light. Today, though, the sun's rays were blasting through the windscreen as Jenny drove and despite the normally effective air-conditioning in her BMW the profiler felt as though she were being baked inside a heat-proof container that was likely to give up its properties at any moment, allowing the extreme sunlight to burn her alive.

Sam had gone straight back to Central Park after their pub lunch, promising to sort out Paula Tripp with a swift call or two on the way back. Jenny's misgivings about Sam and her heartfelt outpourings over lunch made her realise just how much she had begun to rely on DI Sam Bradbury, and her thoughts of Tripp and her threats melted into the background. For the first time since she had met Sam she fully recognised his quality as a rock-like supporter of her and no doubt all of his team's causes, and she had decided to allow herself to trust him to sort out the problem on her behalf. Leaving her car as close to the entrance to the Faculty as possible, Jenny darted across the car park and into the mercifully air-conditioned building. The lift was already on the ground floor and she was quickly at the 6th floor reception desk. She noticed that since her last visit the flowers in the many crystal vases scattered about the opulent reception area had been refreshed with perfect yellow roses, framed with lush green foliage. The fragrance was intoxicating as she stood waiting for the receptionist to end her telephone call. Jenny read the name tag, pinned to the lapel of the woman's smart navy blue jacket: Annabel Masterson. The profiler mused that with the woman's short blonde bob and perfectly applied make-up any other name but Annabel would have seemed incongruous.

"Mrs Foster isn't it?" asked Annabel in a perfectly modulated receptionist's accent.

Jenny nodded and smiled as she signed the visitor's book and was presented with a visitors badge by the efficient woman.

"No DI Bradbury today?" asked Annabel disappointedly, and Jenny noticed that the receptionist's appropriate finger was naked of the tell-tale rings of commitment.

"I'm afraid not. It's just me today. Is Dr Phillips ready for our meeting?"

"Of course," said Annabel. "You know where you're going? He's waiting for you."

Jenny made her way down the hallway, her kitten heels soundless on the deep-pile mid-grey carpet and knocked at Dr Phillips door to be greeted by an immediate, "Come in!"

Dr Michael Phillips PsyD sat at the gleaming oak desk that dominated the spacious room, reclining slightly in his spotless white leather armchair. When Jenny came in he was holding his hands in a prayer-like position and drumming his fingers against each other, the smile on his face not betraying any impatience he might feel at being kept waiting. Phillips' tall, lithe figure seemed hardly to touch the chair as he sat there, but he didn't rise as usual to shake hands. After a brief moment's hesitation at the pointed lack of welcome and protocol Jenny felt herself almost plunge into one of the two matching white leather armchairs reserved for visitors. To her chagrin, the profiler felt the seat pad slowly giving way to her weight, making her feel more insignificant with every millimetre of height lost. She found herself looking up from a position slightly below Dr Phillips' chin line to find herself trapped by his keen blue eyes. Without Sam, who had accompanied her the last time she visited Dr Phillips, the psychologist's stare was solely reserved for her and she almost squirmed under this as yet, silent inquisition.

"Hello Mrs Foster," said the professor.

Do you have any water?" asked Jenny without returning the greeting.

"No problem," and he left his chair and crossed to the polished oak sideboard where he poured some crystal clear water into a glass. Coming to Jenny's side of the desk, he was careful to place the glass on a black leather coaster before returning to his seat. Jenny gulped rather than sipped the cool refreshing liquid, almost gasping when she placed the vessel back on the desk, missing the coaster and allowing the still half-full glass to rest on the desk top. Dr Phillips quickly retrieved it and set it back on its resting place.

Looking around the room Jenny noticed just how extraordinarily neat and tidy the office was. The space was large, comfortable enough for Dr Phillips and two or three visitors. There were no files left out, the filing cabinet situated behind the door encased in oak. Even the doctor's computer lay to the side of his desk rather than on the desk-top itself, thus causing as little clutter as possible, and was housed in matching cabinetry. There was no litter in the desk bin and Dr Phillips' pen and notepad were set at perfect right-angles to each other in front of him.

"So Mrs Foster, how can I be of assistance?" he asked.

"I'm not sure how much the Chief has told you, Dr Phillips," said Jenny.

"Mike, please," he interjected.

"You're aware that Joe Reed has killed his second victim, and that another woman is missing, presumed kidnapped?"

Jenny glanced at the pad Mike Phillips was consulting. All she could see were illegible notes, a practice of writing that he used to disguise from his more intelligent patients who could read upside-down what he was writing about them.

"Mark and I have had a conversation this morning and he filled me in on all of the pertinent details, Jenny," he said, adding, "Do you mind if I call you Jenny?"

Jenny didn't answer, she was getting annoyed. If the Chief had called Dr Phillips and discussed the case with him, why not just tell her that instead of creating this song and dance!

"I thought that you and I could talk about Reed and the case generally," continued Jenny. "What do you think Reed's motives are?"

"Difficult to say," replied the doctor. "As you will be aware, most premeditated killers who aren't interested in financial gain are motivated by sex or an inability to perform sexually. This inability can create tension, leading to frustration and eventually psychotic episodes of extreme violence."

"Reed fits that profile," said Jenny. "He chooses victims that have striking physical as well as socio-economic similarities, which may indicate that he's targeting a particular type of woman that he has an intense hatred for."

"Yes," said Dr Phillips, "or that he loves and cannot attain. Either way I think there is no doubt that the object of his desires lies somewhere in his past. He probably blames whoever this woman is for all the troubles in his life."

Jenny took the glass and sipped some water, purposefully missing the coaster when returning it to the desk. "I know it's a cliché," she said, "but perhaps the woman he's torturing is his mother rather than an ex-relationship."

"Why do you think that?" asked Dr Phillips intrigued.

"Well, it's the women he targeted as a rapist more than when he escalated to murdering them," she explained. "I get the impression from both rape victims' statements that when he was involved with them he treated them more as a mother figure than an ex-wife or girlfriend."

"Go on," said Phillips, his eyes firmly fixed on the glass. Jenny could see how difficult he was finding it not to reach over and replace it on the coaster.

"With Marcie Edwards, he wanted to impress her with his skill in sales and generally at work, which might mean that he was looking for her to be proud of him. With the other rape victim, Emma Jones, he confided his problems in her and she cooked him meals, did some of his washing and looked after him. I think if the object of his hatred was an ex-relationship he would have acted differently, more sexually perhaps?"

"It's possible," said Dr Phillips. "Very possible. What about the victims in Ireland? Do they fit the pattern you've described?"

Jenny realised that the Chief had briefed Dr Phillips extensively. Apart from the immediate investigative team, the connection to the victims in Ireland hadn't been made public. "Somewhat," she said. "There were three victims identified, two of which fit the pattern well."

"And the third?"

"No, the third doesn't fit at all. Reed blitz-attacked the victim and tried to kill her at their first meeting."

"That doesn't seem to fit any pattern we know," said Phillips. "Are the police sure it was Joe Reed?"

"Positive DNA match."

They looked at each other across the desk and Jenny could feel that the doctor was perhaps beginning to take her seriously and treat her as a fellow professional, rather than a student who'd once sat at the back of his lectures.

"Coffee?" he asked, and stood to use the gleaming percolator that sat upon the oak sideboard.

"I'm ok with water," said Jenny, taking the opportunity to stand up too and refill her glass from the water container on the same sideboard. Mike Phillips watched her while he waited for his coffee to brew. He was almost a foot taller than Jenny, his movements slow and deliberate, and he exuded a lazy confidence. Despite his height he wasn't a threatening figure, and Jenny was content to stand with her hip against the sideboard, sipping her water as they talked.

"Have you met many killers?" she asked.

Dr Phillips smiled. "Have you?" he asked in return.

Jenny felt the sting of the put-down, realising that this arrogant academic would never see her as an equal until she had found a way to impress him. She went back to her seat. "Only during my studies," she said defensively, the fleeting moment of camaraderie firmly crushed underfoot by the experienced psychologist.

Dr Phillips set his china cup and saucer to the right hand side of his note pad, taking a few seconds to twist the cup into a position where the blue swallow pattern matched that of the saucer.

"What about the notes found inside the victims? Any thoughts?"

"The notes are perplexing," replied Jenny.

"In what way?" he asked, leaning back in his chair and easily falling into the dynamic of a doctor-patient relationship.

"I think it's clear that Joe Reed is torn between the morality of his actions and his need to carry them through. The notes found in Dawn James' stomach carried an undertone of remorse. The notes found in Robyn Cox seemed more desperate, with four separate messages saying *PLEASE HELP ME* in angry block letters."

Dr Phillips was studying Jenny's face intently as she spoke. It was as if he were ignoring the words she was saying, searching instead for her emotional response.

Jenny was determined to make eye contact with him as she continued.

"The other two notes were directed more at a third party: *Please catch him, he's a murderer* and *I have no choice*, which in line with the notes found in Dawn James' stomach might indicate that Reed is a fully developed schizophrenic, with one side of his personality fighting the other, or even fighting *multiple* personalities for control."

"You've explored the other possibilities of course?" asked Dr Phillips leaning forward in his chair and placing the palms of his hands face-up on the top of his desk.

"Well we had ruled out a partner," said Jenny. "Forensic evidence gathered from the victims clearly shows that only one man was involved with the imprisonment and murder of the women, and eye-witnesses who've seen Reed in his van tell us that he was alone."

"But you doubt that evidence?"

"I'm not sure," said Jenny, surprised that the psychologist had been able to see the indecision in her eyes. She looked away as if to guard against any further scrutiny of her psyche.

"Go on," said Dr Phillips. "The point of your coming here was to clarify your thoughts on the case, and if you want my help I really need to know all the facts."

Jenny was still unsure how much the doctor knew about the case. Given that he was aware of the cases linking Reed to Ireland, she was guessing that the Chief had already told him everything her superior officer thought he should know. But she very much wanted his opinion on the letters from Patrick.

348

"There might be letters," she said, taking the plunge.

Dr Phillips eyes brightened. "Are they from Joe Reed?"

"I'm not sure," she said again, and rooted through the leather document pouch that she'd brought with her, eventually retrieving photocopies of the letters from Patrick.

"I'm probably making a mistake showing you these," she told him. "No details even of their existence have been released to the press; the only other people who currently know of their existence are my researcher, the Chief and DI Bradbury."

Notebook at the ready, and taking the papers from Jenny as though they were ancient parchment, the professor laid them out in chronological order. He slowly scanned each one, making sure he wrote down the details in his illegible script. "Can I keep a copy of these?" he asked.

"Probably better if you don't," said Jenny. "If these letters got into the hands of the press it would be a disaster for the investigation. What are your initial thoughts?"

The psychologist took a moment to think, the grainy black and white image of the second victim Robyn Cox, which might have been taken moments before she died, the focus of his gaze.

"They're obviously genuine. The first three are pretty cryptic and you were right to be suspicious of their authenticity. But this last letter is brazen. The writer's attack on the Chief and his methods shows that he wants a personal battle of wits with the police, and the inclusion of the picture of the victim indicates that he thinks he's winning."

"He is," said Jenny automatically. "What about the inscription?"

"One, two buckle my shoe?" said Dr Phillips. "I remember the nursery rhyme from childhood."

"It's pretty innocuous as a rhyme," said Jenny. "Nothing really that relates to the case, or how the victims are kidnapped or killed." Phillips leant back in his chair, allowing Jenny to continue. "We've run tests on the paper, envelope and stamp and we know that the sender wore gloves and used moist pads instead of his saliva, probably purposefully so we couldn't get any DNA profiling. The letters were posted from three different boxes in the Greater Manchester area, so no clues there."

"Graphology?" asked the psychologist.

"Obviously only from the signature," said Jenny. "As you would expect really - the flourish of the signature shows the writer to be an egotist, perhaps even a narcissist."

"Together with notes found inside the victims, these letters could point strongly to your theory of schizophrenia rather than an accomplice, I would say," suggested Dr Phillips.

"I agree!" said Jenny, perhaps a little more enthusiastically than she had intended. "The writer consistently refers to himself in the first person and never mentions a partner or even uses '*we*'."

"Given the fact that he must have access to the victim to take the picture, and that partners in murder need to trust each other implicitly, I don't think the writer would send the letters without collaboration with his partner" added Dr Phillips. "Plus, of course, the writer has sent the letters specifically to the Chief, each one more inflammatory than the last in the hope that he will spur the police into action. He's probably imagined himself gaining a blaze of publicity."

"Yes, not publicising the letters was a good idea I think," said Jenny. "It puts Reed under pressure by not giving him what he wants. He might start to make mistakes, push himself out into the open, if he imagines he isn't being taken as seriously as he thinks he should be."

Mike Phillips leant forward to meet Jenny's eyes with a steely gaze. "I'm just playing devil's advocate here, but what if you're completely wrong?" Taken aback by the psychologist's sudden change of direction, she could only stare back as he pressed on. "You've sorted out your theories about Reed and who he is and how he acts, and based on these you're going to try and second-guess his possible next move?"

"Yes," said Jenny. "That's the plan."

"Well, now it's time to test your theories against the facts," he said drily. "What if the women are released for exercise, or are allowed to talk and they wrote and swallowed those notes themselves as a cry for help? What if Reed is a perfectly sane and functioning individual who is merely a sadist and enjoys hurting women? He might be helped by one, two or even a gang of accomplices."

Jenny started to stammer a response.

"Look Jenny," said Dr Phillips, slipping back into his former calm and debonair mode, "The truth is that - based on the *evidence* - I can make a case for three or four such scenarios just as compelling as yours."

He paused, searching her face for recognition of his point. "You have, probably correctly, looked at these letters and used them to prove a theory about Joe Reed that you already held. All I'm saying is keep an open mind."

"I do," said Jenny flatly, beginning to get irritated.

"I'm sure you do," said Dr Phillips, the condescension in his voice not lost on the profiler.

"But if I were you," he continued, "I would start again. List all the things you '*know*' about Joe Reed, and then separately all the things that you've either deduced or you're just plain guessing."

"And then, *Dr Phillips*?" said Jenny allowing her temper to begin bubbling to the surface.

"And then, Mrs Foster," replied the psychologist evenly, "I would be able to remain objective about how much of my theory was based in concrete fact and how much was pure conjecture."

Jenny gritted her teeth and smiled. "Thank you for the advice," she said and began retrieving the letters and stuffing them back into her document holder.

Dr Phillips watched her with a slight smile playing on his lips. "There is one other thing that I've just remembered," he said.

"Well?" asked Jenny, taking the bait.

"That nursery rhyme. If I remember rightly, the last line was '*nineteen, twenty my plate's empty*'."

***

Jenny stepped out of Manchester University Humanities Campus and into the baking sun, immediately fumbling around in her handbag for cigarettes

352

and a lighter. The profiler stood with the sun direct and fierce in her face, her anger impelling her to smoke quickly, constantly flicking the ash with her thumb. When she'd finished, she didn't bother looking for the public ashtray receptacle, but instead ground the stub out underfoot almost outside the doors of the building and headed off across the car park to the sanctuary of her car.

The heat of the sun on the windscreen for the last hour made the car feel like a stifling metal can, and Jenny struggled to breathe as the air-conditioning slowly kicked-in. She sat there for a while with the engine running, listening to the cold air streaming from the vents, and staring into the car park where every space was taken up with a gleaming hunk of metal. The bright sun glinted off bonnets and bumpers and she could make out a heat-wave undulating like water at the end of the row where her car was parked.

Suddenly, inexplicably, Jenny Foster found herself screaming.

***

Dr Phillips stood at his window watching Jenny cross the car park and get into her car, moving urgently against the heat of the day. He enjoyed the way her hips swayed in her light grey dress, and he enjoyed watching the tight muscles of her arms and legs contract as she opened the car door and slipped inside. The last thing he saw was Jenny's black patent kitten-heel shoes disappear inside and he was strangely aroused by the image. He continued to watch, expecting Jenny to drive quickly away. When she remained stationary

he supposed she was making a telephone call and proceeded to retrieve a pair of field binoculars from his
desk drawer. He reserved the item to watch his patients
come and go and see them argue with their spouses in
the car park, using the binoculars in an attempt to read
their lips and gain a further insight in to their state of
mind. The psychologist twisted the focus wheel and
directed the lenses toward Jenny's car. Coming slowly
into focus he could see her sitting there alone, screaming her lungs out and thrashing her hands as if she
were fighting off the worst of demons.

Chapter 25

The man sat staring at the video playing on his computer screen. Saliva dripped unchecked from his bottom lip as he watched, the foul liquid having already gathered into a small pool on the desk in front of him. The sound of Robyn Cox slowly dying in front of his eyes coupled with the grunts of Joe Reed as he rode her like a bucking bronco competed with the noise of the small desk fan circulating the blue haze of cigarette smoke hanging thickly in the air. Feverishly chain-smoking as he gazed at the screen with ever widening eyes, he took in fresh detail at each viewing. He clicked back to his video of Dawn James in order to relish the moment when she too died on celluloid, and then replayed the movie over and again, smoking, watching, sweating. He sat for an hour switching between the two films, repeatedly bringing his excitement to a peak. Now he wanted more.

Eventually the man closed both video files and clicked onto an image of Sharon Daly, alone in the basement of 63 Cathcart Street. He zoomed in and there she was - still twitching, still struggling feebly against her bonds. Even after a few short days he could see that his latest captive was losing her strength; he clicked on to watch her intermittently all day, every day and he noticed that she was moving less and less. Just this morning she had tried to wriggle her way free for the hundredth time, perhaps a final attempt before her strength gave out altogether. The man knew that her efforts were futile against the knots and straps of captivity and every time she tried to free herself he laughed aloud, filling the room with an awful sound of malice and evil. For hours now his captive hadn't done much wriggling to amuse him. It was surely time for another victim to join her and then watch as Sharon Daly died at the willing hands of Joe Reed.

The man selected files from his archive of films, images, maps and documents and prepared to send Joe Reed the details he would need to take his next victim. The man had the complete details of three separate women and as he brought the files up on screen he smiled and started pointing at each one in turn as he said slowly to himself, "eeny-meeny-miny-moe, catch a bitch by the toe, when she squeals kill her slow, eeny-meeny-miny-moe." At the final word his finger settled on a file marked Emma Jones. When he opened the electronic zip-file to remind himself of this particular victim he and was almost taken aback by her resemblance to the one particular woman he hated more than he had ever hated another human being.

He had stalked Emma Jones for longer than all the rest, to the point of obsession. He noted with pride that the itinerary of her movements not only ran to several pages, but was also extremely well detailed, right down to her hanging out washing and putting out the family's ginger cat. The man's smile broadened at the prospect of Emma Jones trussed up in the basement, waiting to die at the hands of Joe Reed and his hand shook with excitement as he parcelled up her details into a Zip file. He sent them to Reed there and then with the message, "This bitch is special."

***

It was seven pm by the time Jenny returned to Central Park after breaking down in her car outside the Humanities Campus. When she relayed the conversation between her and Dr Phillips to the Chief and Sam she had been careful not to reveal to her colleagues the fact that she had betrayed their confidence by showing the *Patrick* letters to the psychologist. She only hoped that Dr Phillips would respect a professional confidence by not disclosing his knowledge of the letters to the Chief, Sam or anyone else, especially the press. She knew she had taken a huge risk, and given Phillips' response, she wasn't at all sure that she'd done the right thing.

It had been less than twenty four hours since she discovered that her husband, the man she was supposed to trust above all others, had in fact betrayed her in the most cruel and unforgivable fashion. Yet here she was putting her trust in another man, Dr Phillips - the second of the day after confiding earlier in Sam Bradbury. She hated the fact that she had to trust men, who she knew could and probably would throw her to the lions at the merest hint that they themselves might be criticised. Taking Dr Phillips' advice though, Jenny let the Chief and Sam know that she would be starting to re-think her profile, deconstructing her theories about Joe Reed and then testing each one against the facts.

The Chief welcomed the news, telling Jenny he thought it was the best way to go, given the complexity of the available information and the seemingly changeable nature of Joe Reed, not to mention the letters from Patrick. He congratulated her on her dispassionate approach. Sam on the other hand said nothing, merely allowing a playful smile to pass over his eyes when they met Jenny's. Sam had sent a text earlier letting her know that Paula Tripp had been dealt with and wouldn't be bothering her again, and Jenny assumed the smile related to that episode and thought no more of it.

She did however, want to talk to Sam about how he had persuaded Tripp to drop her threats, and she made a mental note to seek him out first thing the next morning. For now, she wanted to get away for her promised visit to Candice.

***

Jenny sat in her car outside her sister's apartment in Hulme, picked up her phone and began to text Peter. 'I'll be a while,' she typed. 'Is Lilly ok?' and was surprised by the immediacy of the response. 'Lilly's fine, see you later xxx,' read her husband's message. Jenny imagined him Peter sitting there with his phone, waiting for a message from her, or perhaps someone else. The thought crossed the profiler's mind that Peter had guessed she knew about his affair with Candice; maybe Paula Tripp had told him, in revenge for Jenny telling Sam everything and Tripp being warned off by the DI. She yawned, realising that she'd been awake and active since just after four that morning; she felt as though the day had lasted a year, and she was desperately tired. Adjusting the rear-view mirror to check her make-up, she lingered over her reflection. What was it about her? Two husbands had now betrayed her, and she stared into her brown eyes trying to find the answer. Her reflection told her that she wasn't pretty or glamorous in a Marilyn Monroe sort of way but she was striking, with large, warm brown eyes and full lips framed by an angular bone structure that showed them to full effect. She couldn't see a wrinkle in her skin, and as she bared her gleaming white teeth she looked younger than her 36 years. Her nose, the one feature she would have chosen for re-shaping if she was gripped by vanity in later years, caught her eye. Unimpressed, she irritably flipped the mirror back into place before getting out of the car and making her way over to the buzzer labelled with her sister's name, *C Baker*.

Jenny fiddled impatiently with the heart on her silver bracelet while she waited to be buzzed in. When she was eventually admitted she took the lift to the second floor where it opened onto a narrow hallway. The many blonde wood doors were identical, with stainless steel handles and privacy eye-holes. They looked too close together to allow enough living space between apartments as she made her way to the far end where her sister lived in Number 28. Candice's door was slightly ajar, so Jenny walked straight in. "It's me," she called.

"I'm just settling the kids; pour some wine if you like," she heard her sister call back.

She made her way down the small dark hallway, past

another of the blonde wood doors that led to the bathroom and into the main living area. Although the apartment was small, it had in miniature all the hallmarks and features of its larger and more opulent cousins in the city centre. Jenny made straight for the wine rack in the kitchen area of the main room, selecting a Merlot red which she knew was easy to drink, and began searching the drawers for a corkscrew.

The room occupied about half the square footage of the entire apartment and its nod to open-style living meant that it served as the sitting room, dining space and kitchen. The white kitchen units with stainless steel appliances and cooker hood coupled with the solid boards of the maple flooring meant that the room never lost its echo when tasks were being undertaken. As Jenny fiddled with the corkscrew she wondered, as she often did, just how comfortable and practical this living arrangement must be for her sister with two children under five. She poured the red wine into two glasses that she found in a cupboard just as her sister walked in, a dirty nappy in her hand which went straight into the bin under the sink. Candice turned on the taps and plunged her long fingers under the running water.

Jenny picked up one of the glasses. "Claudia still in nappies?" she asked, moving the few steps to the full length window to gaze at the view of the car-park, boundary wall and the road beyond.

"I put a fresh one on her for bed every night, and she instantly goes in the bloody thing," said Candice still scrubbing at her manicured red nails.

Jenny ignored her sister's moaning and watched the

cars intermittently appearing and disappearing as they navigated the road beyond. On the way there she had pondered over how the meeting would go. She imagined herself smiling at Candice, before cleverly directing questions at her sister that would elicit answers to damn her from her own mouth. Now though, despite all the forward planning, when Jenny turned to confront Candice she was filled with angry loathing.

She watched her sister as she nonchalantly dried her hands on a kitchen towel. Her thin frame was a little too tall for the kitchen units and she had to stoop slightly to replace the towel on the side of a drawer case. Candice's long straight black hair had obviously benefited from some attention as the recessed spot-lighting, programmed to shine ceaselessly from above, bounced off its glossy surface. Even with no make-up to speak of, Candice suddenly seemed wildly attractive.

"So?" said Jenny fixing her sister with a steely glare. "Did you sleep with Peter this morning when he got back, or was it a bit early for you?"

Candice visibly wobbled where she stood, gripping on to her wine glass. She let out an unnatural half-laugh and moved quickly to sit down on the red leather three-seater settee that dominated the sitting area. Jenny paused before moving across the room herself. Not wanting to sit next to her sister, she had no option but to occupy a bright red Arne Jacobsen 'egg chair' almost opposite her quarry.

She set down her wine glass on the lacquered surface of the low table between them.

"Was he any good this morning?" she pursued. "After all, he would have been tired."

Candice held her head down so that her long black hair almost covered her face. This was a practised trick she'd perfected in her childhood to deflect her parents' anger when she had been caught out for some transgression or other.

"Well?" urged Jenny, her anger now rising to the surface. "Answer me!"

Candice's face slipped further behind her curtain of hair. Jenny wanted to reach over and start pulling at it. Now she raised her voice almost to shouting level. "Speak to me Candice!" and the sound echoed off the walls.

"Shush!" implored Candice. "The kids aren't asleep yet."

Jenny stood up, quickly moved to the door and closed it. "You can't hide behind your hair this time," she said. Candice responded by straightening her back and deliberately pushing her black curtain aside. "I'm not," she said. "I don't know what you're going on about, that's all."

"Come on," said Jenny. "You know *exactly* what I'm talking about."

"You're just paranoid," answered Candice slurping at her wine. A slight shake of her hand caused some of the liquid to spill on to her chin and she was forced to quickly wipe it away before it trickled onto her pristine white t-shirt.

Jenny's anger boiled over. "Paranoid?" she shouted and roughly pulled from her bag the envelope containing the offending pictures before spilling them on to the gleaming table top between them. "*Now* tell me I'm paranoid."

Candice's face crumpled as she looked at the pictures. She didn't need to handle them as they had landed face-up and she could almost see Peter's tongue invading her mouth. "How did you…," mumbled Candice, her question trailing off in shocked silence.

"You bitch!" screamed Jenny, who suddenly lost any control that remained. Picking up her wine she threw it, glass and all directly at her sister. The missile hit Candice on the left shoulder open-end first liberally splashing her with the blood-red liquid and the glass hit the floor, shattering into hundreds of crystal pieces. Candice stood bolt upright, throwing her arms out sideways and there was a delay of a few seconds before an ear piercing scream left her lips and all hell broke loose.

The door burst open and in ran Darren and Claudia like a mini-whirlwind. Woken by the sudden noise, they burst into floods of tears and ran screaming to their mother. Confronted with the sight of Candice's stained t-shirt, five year-old Darren obviously thought she was badly injured, and launched himself towards her. Claudia had run in barefooted and now crunched on a piece of broken glass and fell to the floor screaming, and with blood pouring from a deep gash.

Jenny jumped up from her chair. "Sorry! Sorry!" she mouthed as she swept Claudia from the floor and rushed to the bathroom. Jenny dropped the toddler into the bath, running cold water over the child's foot; there was a sharp piece of glass sticking out, and a panicking Jenny quickly pulled it out, producing even louder screams from her wriggling charge. She could see now that the glass hadn't penetrated beyond the skin and the bleeding was already beginning to lessen when Candice burst in dressed in just a bra. It had been white before the red wine had soaked through the protection of the t-shirt and created crimson patches over each cup.

"Give her to me," said Candice angrily and wrestled Claudia from Jenny's grasp. "There's a first-aid kit in the cupboard under the sink."

Jenny left the room, pushing past the sobbing figure of Darren in the bathroom doorway and returned a few moments later with the green medical box.

"Make some tea," ordered Candice. "I'll be fine here," she added, opening the box and taking out witch hazel and a roll of bandage.

Jenny lingered for a second watching her sister work quickly, soothing her sobbing toddler whilst attending to the wound. "Honestly, the cut's nothing and I need to settle them again," Candice said without looking up. "Put the kettle on, eh!"

Jenny left the bathroom and after clearing the mess on the living room floor did as she was told, making tea for herself and sipping the hot liquid. She listened as Candice gradually calmed the children and coaxed them back to bed. Eventually returning to the living room wearing a black hoodie, Candice made herself tea and resumed her place on the settee with Jenny opposite. The atmosphere was calmer after the commotion of the children's intervention and Jenny sat back in silence waiting for her sister to talk.

"When Paul left me I thought my life was over," Candice said. "I'd already given up my job at the estate agents to bring up the kids and I felt so alone." Jenny stayed silent. "I mean *really* alone," she went on, realising her sister wanted the whole story. "I even thought of…" she hesitated, "You know - ending it," she said, and waited for a reaction.

Jenny didn't take the bait.

"I didn't start it," said Candice toying with her cup. "It was Peter, flirting with me every time he saw me - touching my arm, making me laugh, showing me attention."

Jenny broke her silence. "Just because a man flirts with you, you don't just go to bed with him," she admonished, "especially when he's your sister's husband."

The pair sat in silence for a few moments, both women cupping their hands around their mugs of tea.

"Why?" said Jenny. "Why pick on *my* husband? Why not go for someone else?"

"I don't know. Like I said, he was always paying me compliments and he…well, he *noticed* me."

Jenny could feel her blood temperature begin to plummet as a sudden realisation dawned, and she began to shake inside. "You said he was *always* paying you compliments," she said hesitantly. "How long ago did it start?"

Candice began examining her feet, moving her toes in a rapid motion that made her fluffy leopard slippers dance. Her black hair fell again over her face, which coupled with her black hoodie made her look not unlike a crow.

"Candice?" said Jenny, her voice beginning to crack. "You have to tell me how long."

The answer, when eventually it came from beneath that curtain of protective hair, was chilling. "About a year," Candice whispered, and at the awful reality of her sister's words the room began to swim.

Jenny started to weep. She had promised herself she wouldn't cry in front of Candice, but that was when she thought her husband had taken advantage of a quickie with her sister. An affair that had been going on for a year was something that the profiler was not prepared for. She set down her mug on the lacquered table and taking her body in her arms cried unashamedly like a child, only breaking out of her tears when she felt her sister's arm on her shoulder. She shrugged Candice off angrily and made a dash for the bathroom, locking the door behind her. She looked at herself in the mirror. Her brown eyes were bloodshot and red raw from too much crying through the day, and now the end of her offensive nose had reddened too. She took paper from the toilet roll and blew it hard, wiping away tears from her high cheek-bones.

"What a fool I've been," she said to herself as she smoothed out the wrinkles that had gathered on the front of her light grey trousers. As she stood there she resolved that these would be her last tears of the day and pulling herself together she unlocked the door, returning to her sister with a new determination.

Candice was sitting where Jenny had left her. Controlling a rising nausea, she sat beside her on the red leather settee. "Tell me everything," she said, making eye contact and placing her hand on her sister's knee. "I really need to know."

Coaxed by Jenny, Candice spent the next thirty minutes revealing all the details of her deception. Apparently she had been able to move in to the apartment because Peter had not only lent her the deposit, but was also paying the rent. Most of the clothes that Candice wore had been bought by Peter and he regularly had sex with her, either here at the apartment whilst the children were at nursery and school or at a hotel in Manchester if he was bored.

Jenny listened as Candice talked - increasingly animated as she grew in confidence. The profiler gained details about times and places, and even pretended to sympathise with Candice's fears that Peter might be taking advantage of her. Candice relayed how she felt used by Peter, as he hadn't as yet kept his promise to tell Jenny and get the affair out in the open.

"I told him," said Candice. "I told him that you had to know, that you had a *right*."

Jenny could contain herself no longer. "What so you could take over as Mrs Foster?" she asked and moved away from Candice and back to the red egg-chair opposite.

"No!" said Candice indignantly. "So the lies would stop."

Jenny watched her sister for a few moments, the black hair now pulled off her face and behind her ears. Her eyes were bright, as though she had tried to do Jenny a favour by convincing Peter to be honest and at that moment Jenny realised just how pathetic her sister had become. "So why?" she asked. "What reason did he give for sleeping with you?"

"He said I was the most beautiful woman he had ever seen," said Candice, her neck stretching with pride as if to make the point. "He said that you'd ignored him and you didn't want him."

"What?" asked Jenny, incredulous at her sister's stupidity.

"He said that all you cared about was your courses and that you always had your head in books studying for your degree rather than paying him any attention."

"Did he," said Jenny flatly

"He said that you ignored Lilly and that you weren't really suited to being a mother," said Candice as though sharing a confidence.

Jenny glared at her sister, she had heard enough.

"Candice," she said, finding an inner calmness. "You're my younger sister and I've always felt as though I looked after you. When you and Paul split I was there as a shoulder to cry on and we spent many nights together whilst I listened to your woes. Remember?"

"I know," said Candice. "I'm so sorry."

"*Sorry* won't cut it this time," replied Jenny with real venom. "You know the pain that divorce brings and the devastation for the children involved. It happened to you, I never imagined, even for a single second that you above all people would be the one who would wreck my marriage."

Candice sat staring at her sister waiting for the final blow.

"From now on Candice, you're not my sister," said Jenny, making sure that she gained eye contact before adding, "and never will be again."

Jenny stood up, collected the photographs from the table and made for the door, stopping as an afterthought to add, "By the way, don't even think about calling Peter as soon as I've left, to warn him that I know about you and I'm on my way home. "Anyway," she added,

"Don't worry, I'm sure he'll be in touch soon enough."
And with that, she marched out of the apartment.

Chapter 26

Jenny was woken the next morning, not by her alarm, but by Lilly throwing herself full length at her mother as she lay on top of the bed. Peter was standing in the doorway, still in his blue pyjamas, obviously just out of bed but still without a hair out of place. "Why the spare room?" he asked

"I was in late and you were already asleep. It just seemed easier."

***

Jenny had driven to her parents' house after her visit to Candice and without telling them why she had spent a few hours in the gathering darkness under her favourite sycamore tree at the bottom of the garden, smoking and drinking non-alcoholic punch intermittently supplied by her worried father. When the pressing for information became too much, Jenny blamed the case and said she needed time alone to think about Joe Reed and his next move. Grudgingly accepting this as a reason for her sudden appearance, her parents had eventually left her alone.

It was one of those summer evenings when a hot day had given way to a pleasantly calm night with a full moon bathing the sky with light. In this ethereal atmosphere Jenny had thought long and hard about Peter and Candice and had made a decision that whilst she would never forgive either of them, their indiscretion wasn't worth destroying Lilly's life. As she looked towards the lighted downstairs of the house she could see her mother and father moving restlessly around, sporadically appearing at the windows to gaze anxiously down the garden to catch a glimpse of their daughter. Realising more clearly than ever that the endurance of her parents' marriage was a rock-bed in her life, she wondered if she would be the same person today if her parents had divorced when she was young. The profiler's thoughts cemented her decision that Lilly was the most important part of her and Peter's life, and she committed herself there and then to sorting out their problems for the sake of her daughter.

***

"Ok, breakfast?" asked Peter.

"Sure," she said and began the game of holding her daughter at arm's length before lowering her so that their faces met, and then blowing gentle raspberries on Lilly's neck making the child scream with laughter. Half an hour later Jenny came into the kitchen with Lilly, who was now wearing a pretty lemon summer dress that finished above her knees, with lemon ankle socks to match and strap-on shoes. Jenny had chosen a blue trouser suit with a white blouse, which she could only hope would keep her cool on what promised to be a swelteringly hot day. Lilly sat in her mother's arms, her blonde curls mingling with Jenny's long, straight dark hair. Mother and daughter watched Peter as he bustled around the hand-painted cream kitchen creating a full English breakfast for the three of them. As Jenny sat there at the oak kitchen table she did her best to reciprocate Peter's smiles and small talk in a natural-seeming way. He cracked eggs and turned bacon, expertly tossing a plain-omelette for Lilly before presenting Jenny with her plate of carbs.

"Thanks," she said and popped Lilly in to her high-chair, strapping her in whilst Peter presented the omelette with a pink plastic fork.

"No problem, what time is Tricia due?"

"Eight o'clock," answered Jenny, and as she forced the food down her throat she wondered if her husband was screwing the au-pair as well as her sister.

Her private anger at the thought manifested itself in the sudden aggressive use of her knife and fork, and she began shoving food into her mouth in roughly cut pieces large enough to demand prolonged chewing.

"Are you ok?" asked her husband.

Although Jenny had made the decision under the tree last night to save her marriage, confronted by the thought, the realisation even, that Candice was not his only extra-marital conquest she hated her decision.

"I'm fine," she said. "What are your plans today?"

"I've nothing on until lunchtime, so I was going to use the time to catch up on some paperwork at home," he said.

She felt her stomach turn over and threw her cutlery loudly onto the plate causing both Peter and her daughter to stop eating and to stare at her.

Waves of panic and anguish flooded through Jenny's slim frame, she couldn't help speculating on Peter's relationship with the au-pair, and forgotten, yet familiar feelings invaded the profiler's nervous system - feelings she thought had died with her previous marriage to Simon.

Jenny had built a strong protective wall after the collapse of her first marriage and Peter had shown enormous patience in his determination to penetrate her defences, spending many hours talking long into the night, understanding her, consoling her and eventually loving her. She had come to trust Peter with every fibre of her being; now as she glared at him over the kitchen table all that seemed to fall apart as she realised that she would never trust him again.

Peter's face contorted with concern and he adopted his familiar role of trying to coax her to talk to him and tell him how she was feeling. Ordinarily, Jenny would have opened up to her husband, slowly at first perhaps, but eventually finding comfort in his ability to listen to her and understand her with compassion and love. But Jenny realised that his attention was no more than a charade which he probably adopted with everyone in his life to control their emotions and have them act how he wanted them to, creating as little fuss and as few problems as possible to disturb his world. Without her quite realising how it happened, Jenny's love had begun to turn to hatred.

The doorbell gave Jenny a sudden excuse to stand up and leave her husband with his plea of, "Jenny, you can't bottle things up, tell me how you're feeling," unanswered and hanging in the air. The timely escape from Peter's searching eyes was short lived though, and the sigh of relief that escaped Jenny's lips as she left the kitchen was replaced with a sinking feeling when she opened the door to the smiling figure of Tricia the au-pair. Jenny hadn't really seen Tricia as a woman before, but had chosen her to look after Lilly based on the child-minder's experience, interview and references. It was true that the two women got on well. They had made an effort to get to know each other better over coffee during the short time she'd been there, but now Jenny realised that she didn't really know her au-pair at all, and as she took in the woman's long blonde hair, full lips and sparkling brown eyes she felt as though she were letting a wolf into a sheep's pen, patting its back as it slipped past her licking its lips with hungry intent.

Jenny didn't speak or step aside to let Tricia in to the house and the au-pair's smile began to fade to be replaced with a quizzical look, her head dropping to one side with her eyebrows simultaneously lowering to show concern for her employer.

"Everything ok?" she asked, putting out her hands as if she knew that Jenny needed to be held.

Responding to the invitation without hesitation Jenny almost fell on to the woman's shoulder and began to sob, her tears instantly mingling with the strands of the au-pair's golden hair. Tricia bore her weight with surprise before closing her arms around the profiler's shoulders, and it was only when the woman uttered the soothing words *there, there* under her breath that Jenny dragged herself free.

"Sorry," she said, her face flushing with embarrassment. "I really don't know what's wrong with me this morning."

"It's ok," said Tricia, the sympathetic look still imprinted on her face. "I read about the latest murder in the paper yesterday. I can't imagine the stress you must be under. That's why I came a bit early, to try and help out. That poor woman and her family, It's all just awful."

"Yes, it is." Tricia moved inside the house and Jenny instantly took in her long bare tanned legs, her bottom encased in Daisy Duke-style denim shorts and her breasts bulging beneath a cream t-shirt.

"Go through," said Jenny, the words sticking in her throat. "Lilly's just finishing breakfast."

Tricia flashed Jenny a smile, obviously convinced she had helped her employer cope with her troubles, and then turned to disappear into the kitchen.

Jenny bit hard on the back of her hand and began tugging so nervously at the heart on the silver bracelet her father had given her at sixteen that the thin chain gave way and snapped in her fingers. Cursing her own clumsiness, she pushed the chain into her trouser pocket and followed Tricia into the kitchen where she had already extracted Lilly from her high-chair and stood with the contented child in her arms whilst exchanging small talk with Peter.

"Peter?" Jenny interrupted.

Peter swivelled in his chair, the smile fading as he faced his wife's intense stare.

"Can we have a coffee in the garden?" asked Jenny.

"Sure," said Peter. "I'll bring two out," and got out of his chair.

"Good," said Jenny forcing a smile for Tricia's benefit. "You'll be ok will you?"

"Of course," said Tricia. "We've got a whole day's play ahead of us," and she smilingly tickled Lilly's neck, making the toddler scream with laughter and wriggle like an eel.

***

When Peter opened the french doors leading to the patio with two mugs of coffee in one hand, Jenny was already occupying one of the four matching chairs at a white painted, wrought-iron table. He set down the cups and faced his wife.

"Smoking at home now?" he remarked, meaning it as an observation rather than an admonishment.

"Wherever I like really," answered Jenny. Drawing deeply on the filter and purposefully inhaling the smoke, she held it in her lungs for a few seconds before blowing it between them, creating a thin grey mist. In the gathering warmth of the morning the smoke hung in the air, dispersing the small flies that had begun to gather around the table. The garden extended to almost an acre, and the natural York-stone patio where Jenny and Peter sat was sheltered by the building. With the garden south facing, the bright morning sun cast a shadow of the house, but then filled the lawn beyond it. At the end of the shadow the lawn fell away to a small wooded area where Peter had erected a structure larger than a shed, but smaller than anything that could be lived in. This was where he spent a great deal of time alone, reading, writing and creating schemes for his business. To the right, the lawn stretched to a sturdy yew hedge which acted as an effective barrier to the neighbours property, and the left side of the garden was planted as a rockery with lines of green beans beyond and stone steps that led to a greenhouse crammed with tomato plants. Jenny's input had been to introduce blazing summer colour: dahlias, fuchsias and buddleia. Golden forsythia spectabilis had taken root and spread out, and geraniums in all shades of pink and red spilled over in pots dotted around the patio. But this was Peter's domain and the neatly striped lawn dominated the space with Jenny's colour an afterthought, relegated to borders and the wooded area at the extremity of the garden.

"So?" he asked, "What's the problem?"

Peter was still in his pyjamas, blue silk with matching slippers. Reclining languidly there, he made the awkward looking seat seem like a padded deck-chair rather than a bone-crunching hunk of hard metal. His hair looked shiny and vibrant despite the liberal sprinkling of grey and as he sipped his coffee Jenny noticed how immaculate his hands were, with perfectly manicured nails and smooth, slender fingers. Jenny reached down to retrieve the brown envelope that she had been sitting on, before laying it on the table between them.

"This is the problem," she said.

She folded her arms across each other, only moving to raise her hand to her mouth to drag nervously on the cigarette as she watched Peter open the envelope, pull out the pictures and begin flicking through them. He took his time, appearing unflustered as he studied each one in turn before he carefully returned the prints to their envelope and laid it back down on the table. Jenny flicked her spent cigarette end toward Peter's pristine lawn,

"Well?" she prompted.

"Well what?" he asked, acting as though the envelope and its explosive contents were irrelevant.

Jenny lit another cigarette and simply stared at her husband whilst she smoked, the atmosphere between them becoming more charged as the seconds turned to a minute, then two minutes. When Jenny flicked her second stub onto the lawn Peter eventually spoke.

"Do you mind?" he said. "Your fag ends will do nothing for the grass."

"You can't just stay silent and ignore it," said Jenny.

"I realise that," said Peter and shifted his weight in the uncomfortable chair, no longer looking relaxed and tanned, but beginning to act like a caged tiger about to strike.

"I talked to Candice," said Jenny. "Last night," she added.

Peter looked up, not quite establishing eye-contact, but it was a start.

"Did you, what did she say?"

"Probably a bunch of lies," said Jenny. "I want to hear it from you."

"It was nothing," said Peter. "Just a bit of fun, that's all."

"You mean *is* nothing," said Jenny through clenched teeth. "As far as my *sister* is concerned it's far from over."

"It is now," said Peter at last making eye contact.

"So what are you going to do Peter?" asked Jenny. "Turn her and the kids out of that flat she's in? The one you're paying for?"

"She pays her own rent," said Peter flatly.

"With a subsidy from you," growled his wife.

A silence again descended on the pair, both staring down the length of the garden at nothing in particular, neither wanting to carry on with the conversation, but both knowing that escape was impossible.

"It's such a mess, Peter," said Jenny at last. "What I want to know is why?"

Peter considered for a second and then stood up, walking over to the nearest part of the expanse of lawn before bending down to rip out a handful of grass which he brought back to the table and laid on the upturned envelope.

"What does the word love mean to you?" he asked.

"What?"

"Come on - indulge me, what does the word love mean to you?"

Jenny flopped back in her chair, puffing out her cheeks in frustration.

"You see?" said Peter. "It's a tough one to define. The truth is that love means something different to everyone." He separated the grasses into their individual strands. "Just hear me out," he continued. "What colour is grass?"

"Don't be ridiculous," said Jenny, irritation beginning to redden her face. "What do you mean what colour is grass?"

"Well if you ask anyone what colour grass is," said Peter, "they'll tell you it's green, right?"

Jenny didn't answer.

"But look at these strands of grass. They're all different shades of green - light green, mid and dark; some are even white and yellow."

"So what?" said Jenny, irritated to the point of submission.

"Well, if you look at the lawn it *is* green," stated Peter, "and that's what love's like."

Jenny lit another cigarette. "Ok, go on," she said. She wanted to understand what her husband was trying to say and decided that she would at least listen,

"Like the strands of grass everyone's idea of what love means to *them* is different, but put it all together and it always looks like love," said Peter, "and like the grass, everyone sees the green and not the detail."

Jenny was reluctant to go along with all this and unwilling to grasp the concept.

"Sorry Peter, what is it you're trying to say?"

Peter gave her a condescending smile, as if he was trying to make Lilly understand that it was a bad idea to pull wings from a butterfly.

"The point is Jenny," he said gently. "If you ask every person on the planet, they'll be able to say that love exists, but my idea of love and their idea of love will be as different as the colours in these strands of grass."

"But my idea of betrayal and your idea of betrayal are the same," said Jenny.

"I'm not sure that's true," said Peter.

"So if I slept with another man that would be ok with you?"

Peter hesitated and Jenny knew he was about to lie.

"I'm just saying that your idea of love and my idea of love are different," he said. "In fact my idea of love might be different to everyone else's on earth."

"You didn't answer my question," said Jenny, smoking

hard. "I thought that by getting married we had defined our idea of love?"

"That's just it," said Peter. "Love can't be defined. If I say that I love you, you imagine that means the way you love me."

"Of course."

"Well, you can't actually define the way I love you, and I'm not arrogant enough to imagine that you love me the way that I love you."

"No that's right," said Jenny sarcastically. "I haven't slept with a member of your family so we must love each other in different ways."

Peter sighed and leant back in his chair, implying that he only wished he'd been able to explain his concept to Jenny in a way she could grasp.

"You're an idiot," she said flatly, adding a third cigarette end to the lawn.

"What time are you leaving?" asked Peter.

"Why, do you want to screw Tricia when I've gone?"

"Don't be ridiculous."

"Sorry!" said Jenny sarcasm oozing from her pores. "I thought that's what you meant with your whole grass speech? You love me but you get to screw anyone you want?"

"Not quite," said Peter.

"Well that's what you're saying isn't it?" she went on, sarcasm giving way to real pain. "That your love is different to mine and you feel a need to have affairs. That I'm not enough for you?"

"I just meant that we see things differently that's all," said Peter. "Whilst me playing away from home is a big issue for you, it's not such a big issue for me."

"And so we just go on as normal?"

"*Yes!*" said Peter, raising the tone of his voice as though his wife had suddenly reached a state of enlightenment. "I slipped - made a mistake - I accept that. But at the end of the day I love you more than anything in the world, Darling."

"*Darling?*" said Jenny with incredulity. "Never call me that again."

Peter fell onto the back foot. "I understand that it will take time for you to forgive me and get back to normal, but I promise I'll do everything I can to make things right," he said earnestly.

Jenny stayed silent, knowing what was coming, knowing that Peter was about to throw himself on her mercy and plead with her to give him another chance and it made her feel physically sick. "Don't," she said as Peter came to her side of the table and dropped to his knees in front of his wife, wrestling her hands from by her sides to hold them.

"Jenny, you're my world, my life," he pleaded, genuine tears beginning to fill his piercing green eyes. "I'm so sorry for what happened. It was a moment of weakness that'll never happen again," and with that he buried his face in his wife's bare legs and Jenny could feel his tears wet her skin.

She looked down at the back of her husband's head, hatred filling her heart.

How could she forgive him for shattering her world into tiny pieces?

As he sobbed in her lap, Jenny thought how ridiculous he looked and how stupid his lies were. She knew for a fact that Candice hadn't been just a fling because her sister had already admitted that the affair had been going on for some time. His lies told her heart that Peter would betray her over and over again without a single thought for her happiness. Jenny struggled to come to terms with the promise that she had made herself under the sycamore tree in her parents' garden the previous night. She still thought that Lilly didn't deserve to live her life with divorced parents, squabbling over who loved her the most and who would have the child on any given weekend. "Peter?" she said pulling at her husband's head so that he would stop crying and look at her. "Peter, come on."

Peter dragged himself up from his knees and slumped back into the chair opposite his wife, acting like a sulky child who'd been caught stealing an apple, but couldn't find a good enough reason to blame the grocer for leaving it out in the open on display. Jenny pulled a tissue from her pocket and handed it to her husband, who blew his nose loudly, taking time to wipe away the moisture from his nostrils.

The pair sat in silence, Peter reaching for Jenny's hand and holding it across the table, above the offending envelope. He pawed at her fingers and spun her engagement and wedding ring as if realising for the first time that they were capable of being removed.

"Don't worry," said Jenny eventually. "We'll try and work something out."

"Thank you," said Peter and began to cry again, only this time with obvious relief.

Chapter 27

Joe Reed sat in his van waiting for the time appointed for him to waylay the woman who had been chosen as his next victim. Reed had let his personal appearance and hygiene routines slip since he had dumped the body of Robyn Cox in Heaton Park. His light blue polo shirt was soiled with sweat around the armpits and collar and his usually spotless cream trousers were greying, as well as suffering from Reed's recently acquired and obsessive habit of rubbing his grimy hands up and down the tops of the thighs. As he sat waiting for his victim he constantly wrung his hands together and stared with shaking eyes through the windscreen. He decided to consult his laptop, and bringing the machine out of sleep mode he saw the image of the woman, her eyes wild as she was caught in mid-pose roughly shaking a baby boy. In the still image the woman's mouth was fixed wide-open at the point of capture, obviously shouting something into the face of the distraught baby, who had collapsed into a crumpled little heap of fear and anguish. A second child, a girl aged about four years old, looked on in horror from her position behind the pram from which the baby had obviously been wrenched.

The baby boy had wild black hair and red cheeks and

Reed thought that he couldn't have been more than eighteen months old. That alone would have been enough to fire Joe Reed's anger - spur him on to take the woman and make her pay for the abuse she meted out to her son, so effortlessly and beyond cruel. This time though, the motivation was different and Reed hated this woman more than he had ever hated a woman in his life.

When Joe Reed had received the most recent Zip file by email he had recognised the prospective victim instantly as Emma Jones, who had been married to Tony at Peterson Insurance, the woman he had befriended and then raped.

When he saw her face again, it was as if he had known her in a previous lifetime and for a second her features had sparked the joy of recognition and he had been happy to see her. Then the whole truth had been laid out for him in vivid detail.

The dossier stated that Emma was still married to Tony Jones; they had moved house and Tony was working for a different company, while Emma stayed at home to look after their two children. Reed remembered that Tony and Emma only had one child, a daughter called Jade and he was surprised to learn that since the last time he had seen either of them - the day when he'd left Tony reeling on the ground in the car park of Petersons Insurance - Emma had given birth to a son, Anthony. Included in the Zip file were a number of images of this Anthony, the Jones's newest addition, and the similarities between Joe Reed and the baby were pointed out in stark detail.

The boy's hair colour was the same and both Reed and

Anthony had striking grey eyes. A time-line had been presented showing without doubt that Emma Jones must have conceived her child at about the same time that she was raped and slowly but surely he came to the conclusion that the baby must be *his* son.

Reed was startled at the revelations and sat for hours sorting through the information in his mind, trying to remember what had happened and the time-scale involved. For a few moments Joe was ecstatic with joy and hope for the future.

Perhaps if he spoke to Emma and told her that they could make a life together she might come with him, and he might start a new life with a real family. On the other hand, he had been informed that Emma Jones was the worst one yet. More like Jane Prince than any of the other bitches. To prove it the man had sent Reed the video of Emma roughly handling and shaking his son, and that idea sent hatred coursing like acid through Joe Reed's veins.

The video had started with Emma Jones leaving her house, pushing a pram with Anthony inside. Jade was walking beside her holding on to Emma's free hand.

Emma looked to be in a hurry as she rushed down the road with Jade forced almost to skip along to keep up. Suddenly Emma brought the procession to a halt and leaned in to the pram, obviously trying to comfort the baby. There was no sound on the video so Joe Reed didn't hear what was said, but Emma was shouting into the pram and occasionally turning her attention to Jade, smoothing her blonde hair to calm her. They started off again, walking even more briskly this time until after a few hundred yards they stopped again.

This time Emma reached into the pram and lifted the baby out. The boy was crying and kicking his legs, but instead of holding the child in an attempt to comfort him as a loving mother would, she began to shake him violently.

The video zoomed in to the faces of the mother and child, Emma Jones was screaming into the baby's face, holding the child by both shoulders and shaking him with increasing violence. Anthony stopped crying at first, a look of shock crossing his tiny face and his body went stiff as his mother shook him for what seemed like an eternity. Eventually, the crying started again, but this time it didn't look like the normal cry of a baby, more like the screaming of a wild animal. Emma realised something was wrong and stopped shaking the child, clutching the baby to her chest in an apparent fit of remorse.

Reed could see that the boy was still screaming in pain and he realised at the same time as Emma that the baby's arm was hanging at an unnatural angle and must be badly broken. Emma Jones gingerly laid the child back in the pram and reached for her bag and her mobile phone, her hands shaking as she dialled.

Then the video ended.

The pain and anguish Reed felt at the thought of his son being abused made him squirm in his seat. The memories of the abuse that *he* had suffered at the hands of his step-father suddenly sliced through him as though it had happened yesterday and he thrust his fist into his mouth, biting down hard, using the pain to control his anger.

***

Through the camera installed behind the van's rear-view mirror the man watched Joe Reed biting down on his clenched fist, and smiled with satisfaction. It had been easy to lead his protégé through to the undeniable conclusion that the abused baby was probably his and the man knew that Reed would react exactly as he wanted him to: with focus and purpose.

The man sat in his blue Ford; the evening was drawing in and since it was some time after Manchester rush-hour most of the traffic had already passed through Bury. The nondescript car was parked about one hundred yards past the entrance to a large supermarket and up a side street, and from this position the man could make out the bonnet of Joe Reed's van sticking out from a narrow alleyway between shops in a tight row of establishments opposite the large store. The man knew there were no windows looking out from the supermarket wall facing the road; the bricks were adorned with colourful adverts for deals involving bread or beans, and the large structure acted as a barrier to the houses beyond as they sat huddled together and dwarfed by the superstore. The shoppers' car-park was also at the opposite side of the store from the road and the well-used entrance and exit were further away again, accessed from a side-road off an adjacent thoroughfare. With most of the shops now closed for the evening Reed was all but invisible except to the cars that occasionally travelled along Whitefield Road.

The man had been studying Emma Jones's movements over several weeks and knew that on any given

Monday his target would arrive just before seven for a Pilate's session in a studio above the row of shops. In order to reach the class Emma Jones would park in the shoppers' car park and then cross the road on foot, disappearing up an alleyway next to the one where Reed sat waiting in his van before rounding the building to take the metal steps at the rear. Emma must have preferred this class to any other because it was a private session between herself and her instructor, and the man knew that when Emma Jones left the road to enter the alleyway she would be alone and invisible until she reached the top of the steps. He had sent Joe Reed strict instructions to wait until his victim had disappeared up the alleyway before he left his van, going along his own alleyway and then confronting the woman on the isolated ground before she could reach the steps up to the safety of the studio.

Now he wiped his mouth free of the errant pastry crumbs from the sausage roll he was chewing on, his dirty, nicotine stained hand dragging across the stubble on his chin. He picked up a green flask and unscrewed the top to pour coffee, made with milk and sugar, when he spotted in his wing mirror a woman walking down the deserted road. The man had chosen this road because it led nowhere in particular; obviously a long disused access road to shops that had been demolished. It was lined on both sides with unkempt hedges that ended fifty yards behind his parked vehicle with a small patch of waste ground clearly well known to fly-tippers, judging by the old mattress and rusty iron that were strewn amongst other rubbish. The woman momentarily slowed when she saw the blue Ford, obviously nervous as to why someone would be sitting in their car at such a spot. She crossed the road to pass the car as quickly as she could. The man turned his face away from the woman as she passed by putting his head out of the car window to fiddle with the wing-mirror. When he turned back she had almost reached the end of the road and without looking back she re-crossed and disappeared around the corner.

Breathing a sigh of relief, he poured his coffee, carefully replacing the lid and tossing the thermos into the back seat. The passer-by hadn't seen his face and the number plates on the blue Ford were false, so even if she'd made a mental note of the numbers they would mean nothing to the police. It was when he looked out of his windscreen that his blood ran cold.

***

Emma Jones parked her car as usual in the shopper's car park of the large superstore on Whitefield Road. She always parked there, but never used the store for her shopping, preferring a smaller supermarket nearer to her house.

If it crossed her mind at all that she was parking illegally she wouldn't have been bothered about the misdemeanour, especially not tonight anyway. Tony had rung to say that he was following up a potentially big sale and would have to work late. Her mother, helpful as always, would only agree to entertain Jade for an hour or so and consequently Emma either wouldn't be able to go to her Pilate's class at all, or she would have to take Anthony with her.

It wasn't a surprise that her mother declined to look after the baby even for an hour. The child had been the subject of arguments ever since Emma found out that she was pregnant. Her husband Tony hated the child and would do anything to avoid seeing him, let alone hold or feed him. She tried to convince herself that Tony would change his mind and come round to loving the boy if only he would give himself the chance, and she devised endless plans to get the pair together - just the two of them - to give father a chance to bond with his son. Only the boy wasn't his son; that at least was a cast iron fact. Anthony had eventually come into the world after a difficult labour, the midwife and paediatrician had declared that second births were always easier and Emma had gone to the hospital at the first squeeze of contractions, convinced that the baby would make a quick appearance. Her husband had packed her into the car, the hope apparent in his eyes that the baby was his and not Joe Reed's, the man who had callously befriended him and then raped his wife before disappearing without explaining his actions or being prosecuted for the crime.

Emma and Tony had made a pact to put the thought from their minds that the baby was anybody else's except Tony's and the fiction had lasted right up to the birth.

The labour itself had lasted a full two days and Tony had been a rock of support, holding Emma's hand, looking suitably concerned and fetching water whenever called upon. He stayed at the hospital for the entire time, fussing over his wife and eagerly questioning anyone that looked remotely medically qualified.

That was until the moment he saw the baby for the

first time when his eyes turned to stone and he left his wife to cope with her new-born. When the baby's head emerged he was seen to have jet black hair. Tony stood back from the birthing bed, tousling his own thick sandy mop and seemed to know instantly that the baby was a Reed and not a Jones. Even though the baby's eyes were closed, he knew with conviction that they would not end up blue like his own. Since that day he had treated the child as if it were an alien.

Emma had told him he was being paranoid and had even enlisted her mother, who was supportive at first in trying to convince Tony that babies' hair and eyes can be any colour when they're born, and that Anthony would quickly change into the son that he'd always wanted. When the baby didn't change and Tony eventually insisted on a DNA test to prove the case beyond doubt, Emma lost even her mother's support: Tony was not the father.

***

Emma retrieved the pram from the boot of the car and set it up before extracting Anthony from his car seat and depositing him into the stroller, being extra careful not to bump his arm, which was encased in a white plaster-cast. She stared at the child in his yellow t-shirt and blue jeans with smart red piping on the pockets. He kicked his legs and smiled at her, pointing to the supermarket doors, obviously excited to go inside where he knew that racks of sweets and chocolate could be found. *'Can't talk yet, but not stupid'*, thought Emma as she bent down and tousled his black hair. Her eyes fell on the plaster-cast and she remembered with shame how she had shaken the boy in anger and frustration, only stopping when it was clear that she had caused serious injury.

She hadn't meant to hurt the child, Tony had told her that morning that he was considering leaving her, saying that he couldn't take the pressure of knowing that Anthony was Joe Reed's child. He told her he would never be able to love the child and that when he looked at Emma all he felt was anger and a sense of betrayal.

Emma had stormed out of the house taking Jade and Anthony with her, but Anthony wouldn't stop crying and she had vented her frustration on the boy in a moment of madness. She'd immediately rung Tony, who came rushing from the house and called the ambulance, telling her to take Jade and go home and he would look after the boy. When the pair returned home that evening Anthony was sporting a full arm plaster-cast and her husband had an angry bruise on his forehead. Apparently he had deliberately head-butted a tree before the ambulance arrived, in order to fool the doctor and nurses into believing that he'd lost his balance on some loose paving and fallen with the boy in his arms and that was how they got their injuries. The story had been accepted and the pair had been treated without suspicion. More importantly to Emma, the time that Tony had spent with Anthony had softened his attitude to the child and when he walked through the door with the boy in his arms Emma felt there might be hope after all, and that they might finally be a family.

Tony hadn't mentioned leaving again. He had become attentive and kind, almost back to his old self, even feeding Anthony over breakfast that morning. The fact that Tony had called this evening to say he was working late to secure a large sale, reassured Emma that he might be starting to feel responsible for his family again and wanted the best for them. A smile crossed her face as she pushed the pram toward Whitefield Road, heading for the alley between the accountants and the dry-cleaners and on to her Pilates class. Anthony would just have to sit in his stroller and watch.

***

Joe Reed spotted Emma Jones crossing Whitefield Road, taking extra care to make sure there was no traffic as she negotiated the kerbs with the stroller. Reed could see his son kicking his legs and sucking on an orange toddler cup held with one small suntanned hand. The other hand he placed awkwardly in his lap encased in a plaster-caste. Reed quickly clicked the mouse on his laptop. He wanted to check if the instructions included the boy, but the laptop screen had turned to black and after a few seconds he realised that the battery must have given out. At the second kerb the stroller jolted violently as Emma Jones tried to tip the front wheels upwards over the steep concrete and Reed watched angrily as the boy began to wail. Once it was safely deposited on the kerb Emma leaned in to the pram, rubbing the child's arm and kissing his forehead, which seemed to calm the toddler and after a minute or so he stopped crying and Emma pushed the pram into the alley. Reed made a quick decision, fuelled by his anger. He got out of the van, a tyre-iron clutched in his right hand.

The man looked on horrified. "Why's she brought the kid with her?" he said out loud. "She NEVER has the kid with her." He quickly gave life to his laptop and stared through the camera link at Reed, who was simply gaping out of the windscreen. "I'll e-mail to call it off. We'll do nowt" the man said to himself. He quickly typed a message to Reed and clicked on the camera image again to check Joe Reed's reaction to the change of plan. The man's dread grew as he saw Reed lift up his machine and turn it over in his hands before closing it and slamming it back down on the passenger seat of the van. "Shit," thought the man, "his bloody battery's dead."

He watched helplessly as Joe Reed got out of the van with what looked like raw determination. The man thought about rushing over to drag Reed away, but then realised that would be a mistake. If he went over now and confronted him, he might end up the one with a tyre-iron buried in his skull.

Reed was a killer after all, the man had witnessed him murdering two women and raping countless others. *'No',* he thought. *Best just to sit and wait.*

***

Emma Jones made her way down the alleyway between the shops, it was familiar enough to her, but it was only now with a stroller to push that she realised how narrow and full of obstacles it seemed to be. Anthony was quiet again and she was making slow, steady progress toward the end of the passage when a figure appeared in the gap. The buildings on either side were tall enough to block out much of the remaining light of the evening and the sun was going down beyond the end of the alleyway, which meant that the figure appeared only as a black shape. Emma thought it must be Janice her Pilates instructor, come to give her a hand with the stroller on the stairs. However, with each step that Emma took towards the figure she noticed that the silhouette was too large to be Janice and after a few more steps fear began to grip her as she realised that the black shape belonged to a man. Moreover the shape knew her name,

"Hello Emma," it said. "It's been a while."

"Who's that?" said Emma, her voice becoming shakier with every word. "I've got a child with me and my husband's just around the corner waiting."

"Who?" said Reed, "Tony? I don't think so Emma."

Emma heard something in the voice that she recognised, but the sudden familiar feeling that washed over her was succeeded by a dread, more real and all- consuming than anything she had ever felt before, and when the voice spoke again, she knew why.

"How's our son?" said Reed and Emma went stiff. The thread of recognition turned to certainty and she knew that the voice belonged to Joe Reed.

"But…how?" was all she could manage.

Reed covered the short distance between them and she saw his face emerge from the shadows. Emma recoiled from those eyes, burning with hatred and purpose.

"Joe?" she whispered.

Joe Reed stared at Emma Jones thinking that she hadn't aged a day since he had left her crying and despoiled on her marital bed. Her long, dark hair shone with vitality, and despite having given birth to his child, her body had kept its youthful shape. Her brown eyes sparkled even in the half-light and Joe searched them for a few moments for some clue as to why she had hurt their son.

"Why did you break his arm?" said Joe emotionlessly. Emma took a moment to compose herself; she knew she was in grave danger. Joe Reed, the man who had raped her and ruined her life had also killed at least two women, maybe countless more and Emma almost lost her balance as she realised that he had probably come to kill her and perhaps Anthony too.

"It's been hard, Joe," she said, swallowing her fear. "Really hard."

"Did breaking his arm make it easier?" said Joe through clenched teeth. Emma recoiled as Reed raised his arm to waist height and she noticed the tyre-iron for the first time.

"No," she stammered, automatically raising her arms in defence, "it's just that..."

"What?" said Reed coiling to strike.

"It's just that," said Emma frantically searching for words that might stop Reed from swinging the tyre-iron and bashing in her skull, "It's just that I still love you!" she blurted out.

Joe Reed looked as though he had been hit by a thunderbolt; any forward movement instantly checked, he froze where he was, his arm in mid- air. "What?" he asked, his voice losing some of its ferocity.

"It's true Joe," lied Emma. "I loved you then and I've never stopped. Every day I think about you - about us - and I wonder where you are and what you're doing."

She searched Joe Reed's eyes, looking for a sign that she was getting through to him.

"You should never have left me Joe," she said. "We could have been together."

It was his eyes that softened first, with his face following, the tension relaxing from his cheekbones and his mouth dropping slightly open. They stood looking at each other with Anthony stock still in his stroller staring up at his parents as though he knew that this was a pivotal moment. The stand-off lasted until Anthony eventually broke the silence when his cup clattered to the floor and both adults simultaneously looked down at the boy. Reed began first to weep and then to wail uncontrollably before letting go of the tyre-iron and dropping to his knees, taking the boy's head in his arms and pressing the black hair to his chest. He looked up, his face contorted with emotion. "This is really our son?" he asked through his sobs.

"Yes," said Emma, with a growing belief that she might yet take control of the situation, "He's eighteen months old now, Joe. He's just like you with his black hair."

Reed cupped the boy's face in his hands. "When he looks at me with those grey eyes, all I can think about is you," she lied. Reed stood and reached out to Emma. He had the look of a lost child, as though if Emma reached out to him in return he would crumble completely.

A voice called out from the end of the alleyway, breaking the spell. "Is that you, Emma?" Janice had come down the stairs from her studio and was standing watching the couple. "Are you ok Emma?" she asked anxiously.

Joe Reed's face became stony again, and he whirled around to see where the voice had come from. Emma took the chance to retreat a few steps back up the alleyway dragging the stroller with her. Reed took a second, glancing between the two women and seemingly undecided what to do next, he shot off toward Janice, who began to scream.

"No!" shouted Emma. "Leave her Joe!"

Reaching the end of the alleyway Reed used his shoulder to knock Janice to the ground before racing out of the passage, and Emma could hear his footsteps running across the yard at the back of the shops until the sound eventually faded.

She pushed Anthony towards Janice who was already regaining her feet, apparently unharmed by the fall. "Call the Police!" she said.

"Who in God's name was that?" gasped Janice, brushing dust from her clothes.

"Just call them." and Emma lifted Anthony out of the stroller and into her protective arms.

Chapter 28

Jenny sat at her desk at Central Park turning Patrick's most recent letter over in her hands as if it might yield some startling new information that would help find Joe Reed. The fact that Reed had botched his attempt to kidnap Emma Jones the previous evening and then again managed to disappear into thin air was nothing short of miraculous. Emma had apparently noticed a van, presumably Reed's, parked in an alleyway close by, but the vehicle had disappeared along with Reed by the time the police arrived - all within two minutes of the call coming in.

The name *Joe Reed* coupled with the phrase *still in the immediate vicinity* had produced a police response unknown in the history of one of Greater Manchester's oldest towns. Residents living on Bury New Road must have been stunned when the air came alive with a wailing chorus of sirens shooting through at break-neck speed, every officer primed to go down in history as the one who apprehended the elusive Joe Reed. Jenny imagined a succession of able, experienced policemen scratching their heads as they completed their extensive search pattern protocols, called up CCTV images and questioned possible witnesses, only to come up with one dead-end after another.

"There's no time left," she said almost absent-mindedly.

Sukhwant Patra - 'Paz' to his colleagues - the researcher who had been allocated to help Jenny sift through paper trails, was sitting opposite and took the remark as a conversation opener. "What for Ma'am?" he asked, looking up from other letters he'd been diligently reading and cataloguing.

"Sharon Daly," she said quietly.

Paz searched the profiler's angular features. Her jaw was set tight, as though she were bracing herself against imminent bad news. Still lost in her own thoughts, she returned Paz's question with a blank stare before gazing ahead into the general office. More than fifty police officers, detectives and researchers were either at their desks or milling purposefully around. Following Jenny's eye-line Paz realised she wasn't alone in her train of thought; the frenetic urgency with which these officers were going about their tasks told of an inner fear infecting the entire team.

"Are you ok Ma'am?" he asked, but Jenny still didn't answer. She was sitting there in a kind of trance, as though her brain needed all the energy that her body wasn't using to concentrate on whatever was on her mind.

"Mrs Foster." When no answer came he tried again. "Jenny!" he said, but this time louder and with purpose.

The profiler snapped out of wherever her mind had taken her to return to the room and she turned to meet Paz's eyes with a withering stare.

"Are you ok Ma'am?" asked Paz again, more cautiously

this time, concern beginning to creep into his voice. "You had me worried there, what did you mean when you said there's no time left for Sharon Daly?"

"You were at the briefing this morning," she said sharply. "Reed has increased both his time frame and his possible use of force to subdue his victims."

"Ok, but he was unsuccessful with Emma Jones."

"Irrelevant," said Jenny with a wave of her hand. "You think because he missed his target last night that he'll crawl under a stone to lick his wounded pride?"

Paz didn't answer.

"No, he'll be even more determined," said Jenny firmly. "Reed sets his time agenda according to his urges, and I promise you that after missing Emma Jones his frustrations will be boiling over."

"So now he's more unstable you think he might be even more dangerous?"

"Yes but that could be an advantage for us," she told him. "If he's out of control he'll make mistakes, rush things. Reed stalks his victims before he abducts them, and judging by the detail needed to intercept Emma Jones and the other women I would say that he watches them closely, maybe even around the clock."

"Yes, that's true," said Paz.

"So what do you think might happen if a victim he's been stalking escapes his grasp?" asked Jenny. "He won't have the time to line up another woman with his frustration at breaking point will he?"

"You mean he could go for anyone?" asked Paz, his brown eyes growing even larger.

"That's a possibility. We might end up with Joe Reed driving around in his van snatching random women off the streets - and then any woman mid-thirties, with long dark hair who fits the victimology could be at risk, simply by being outdoors."

"But, surely we'll catch him before that," said Paz. "Just look around you, some of the best police minds in the country are searching for Reed. We got some interesting new facts about him from last night...it's just a matter of time isn't it?"

"Or," said Jenny thoughtfully, "he might just finish off Sharon Daly and disappear again, perhaps for years, maybe even for good."

Jenny stood up, stretching the tightness from her back, and headed for the door hoping a cigarette and a coffee from the machine might help her find the answers she was looking for. Crossing the busy office floor unnoticed, she slipped out of the double doors, crossed the corridor and pressed for the lift. Normally she would have walked the six flights of steps but she was feeling lethargic, defeated even, and suddenly couldn't face the exercise. The lift seemed to be taking an age to reach her; she kept her eyes fixed on the red digital display indicating that the transport sat stationary on the floor above, and impatience began to set her nerves on edge. Without warning the double doors behind her swished open and Sam was standing beside her.

"Got the same idea as me, eh?" he said, joining her vigil and staring at the lift display.

"Yeah, I need a smoke," she said.

"What time are you seeing Emma Jones?"

"I'll go over to the house in about an hour," she said, without turning to face him.

When the lift eventually put in its appearance Jenny

stepped in first, closely followed by Sam, and with the doors closing directly after the pseudo-female electronic voice had announced they would. Jenny pressed the Ground Floor button and the lift began to descend. Sam stayed silent and began shuffling his feet into a kind of dance routine over and over again. He was staring downwards pushing the heels of his brown brogues together to form a V with his feet before quickly pushing the toes inwards to form the opposite shape. As he performed his dance his heels and toes clicked together creating a rhythm that got on Jenny's nerves, and the walls of the lift seemed to be closing in around her. The journey felt as though it was taking far longer than it should, the floors passing painfully slowly between 6 and 3 where the lift ground to a halt and the electronic voice announced that the doors were about to open.

When they did so, the hall was empty. Sam looked at Jenny, tutting and raising his eyes in recognition that someone had pressed the button and then probably taken the stairs, and the profiler's mood darkened at the prospect of an even longer stay in the lift. The electronic voice soon announced that the doors were about to close, which did and Sam began his dance again, the clicking of his heels and toes becoming like hammers on anvils in Jenny's brain.

"Do you mind?" she said and Sam stopped his dance mid flow, his feet caught in a limbo between moves. "Thanks."

"You got my message about Paula Tripp?" he asked after a pause. "She won't be bothering you again."

"Thanks," said Jenny, suddenly realising that she had

trusted Sam to make the problem go away and hadn't given it another thought.

"What did she say?" asked Jenny, embarrassed that Tripp might have told Sam about Peter and Candice, Jenny felt her cheeks redden.

"Enough," Sam told her, adding after a pause, "If you want to talk I'm available."

Before Jenny could comment the electronic lift voice told the pair yet again that the doors were about to open and Jenny stepped out as soon as there was just enough room for her body to fit between the sliding doors. Sam shook his head and half-grinned as he followed her across the faux-marble floor towards the bright sunlight beyond the main entrance doors.

Without warning Jenny suddenly stopped dead in her tracks as if she'd met an invisible glass barrier and Sam was forced to take evasive action to avoid walking straight into the back of her.

"Jenny!" said Sam, annoyed, and then realised the profiler was staring straight ahead at the entrance doors, her mouth dropping open.

He followed her gaze, his eyes out on stalks and his own mouth dropping open too.

Coming through the entrance doors, shuffling rather than walking, was the unmistakeable figure of Joe Reed. Reed's image had been burned into both of their brains and they'd have been able to pick him out in a Wembley crowd. Here, and standing on his own, they were certain it was Reed without needing any confirmation from the other.

Sam came out of shock first and lunged headlong into a startled Joe Reed, sending him sprawling onto the hard floor. The DI then expertly flipped his captive over before grasping flailing wrists to pull Reed's arms behind his back and apply handcuffs retrieved quickly from the trouser pocket of his suit. Sam kept one hand on the handcuffs whilst the other applied pressure to the back of Reed's neck, immobilizing his quarry. Jenny, the Desk Sergeant and a handful of other uniformed police in the foyer had been watching like wide-eyed statues, seemingly unable to move.

"Give me a hand will you Sergeant," said Sam without looking up. The instruction seemed to break everyone's concentration at once and four officers immediately swamped Reed, hauling him to his feet.

"What do you want me to do with him?" asked one of the officers. The three stripes on the arm of his uniform set him apart from the other policemen who were holding Reed's arms as though he might vanish into thin air in front of them.

"Put him in a cell," said Sam, and then turned to Jenny. "Get the Chief!"

***

Ten minutes later the Chief, Sam and Jenny were standing in a room reserved for interview conferences watching Joe Reed on the other side of a one-way mirror.

Reed had been brought up from the cells and with the handcuffs removed he was sitting upright in the only chair on one side of a bare table. His small, delicate hands were palm down on the white plastic surface; Jenny could see that his feet were crossed over each other and she was bemused at his posture. All

Jenny could think about was Sharon Daly, where she was being held and the condition that she might be in. If Sharon wasn't already dead and Reed was sitting calmly in Interview Room 1 unable to feed her or give her water, she wouldn't last long trussed up and forgotten.

"He seems fairly relaxed," said Jenny. "Has he said anything?"

"Only that he wants to help," said Sam.

The Chief was incredulous. "You mean he walked in and said that?"

"Yes! Jenny and I were on our way outside when he just appeared in the doorway. I was worried he might cause havoc - be armed even - but when he was searched in the cell there was nothing in his pockets, not even a pen-knife."

"Nothing?"

"Nope! There's no weapon, no ID, no wallet, not even ten pence in change."

"Do you think he tipped off the press before he walked in?" asked Jenny. "There must be a hundred reporters outside, everywhere from Manchester to Peking."

"Well someone did," said the Chief, a palpable annoyance in his voice. "I'll go out and give a statement shortly and perhaps we'll find out then."

"How are we treating him?" asked Sam.

"As a witness," replied the Chief. "As it stands right now we can hold him for forty-eight hours before we charge him. I've put a call in to Gordon Kline, the Home Secretary to see what the chances are of getting an extension if we need one."

"Ok," said Sam. "Let's hope we don't."

Jenny was as happy as anyone on the team that Joe Reed had voluntarily given himself up, but she still felt uneasy. "I think this might be more complicated than any of us realise," she said.

The Chief smoothed his hair. "Why, Jenny?" he asked.

"Well, this is bang out of character," said the profiler. "The Joe Reed that strutted around on the video and planned the rapes, kidnappings and the murder of two women is ruthless and remorseless. It doesn't add up that he would just walk in here with his hands up."

"Ok," said Sam. "So what's the plan, Chief?"

"First things first," came the reply. "Conduct a standard witness interview, Sam. The usual drill: confirm his name and address and ask him what he knows about the murdered women."

"And where Sharon Daly is," added Jenny.

"Ok," said Sam as he headed for the door. "He might just admit everything."

"I doubt it," said Jenny in a remark under her breath which eluded Sam's ears, but not the Chief's, who eyed her quizzically.

***

Sam entered Interview Room 1, nodding to the PC standing guard inside the door before sitting in the blue plastic chair opposite Joe Reed. He felt excited, thrilled even, finally to have the opportunity to confront the man he'd been searching for so desperately.

"Hello," said Reed.

Sam ignored any pleasantries, "I'm DI Sam Bradbury of the Manchester Metropolitan Police," he said. He explained to Reed that he wasn't under arrest and went on to ask if he had any objections to the interview being videotaped.

"No, of course not," said Reed.

Sam glanced at the mirror behind him and knew that Jenny and the Chief would be glued to the whole conversation. The three of them would review the footage afterwards for body language and anything they missed first time.

"Can I have your full name for the record please?" asked Sam.

"Edward Arthur Jerome," said Reed.

Sam's pen hovered over his notepad that he had laid out flat between them.

"J E R O M E," Sam spelled it out. "Edward, Arthur?"

"That's correct," said Reed.

"Address?" asked Sam.

Reed looked puzzled for a few seconds, his furrowed brow revealing a line of previously unseen wrinkles. "I'm not sure," he replied.

"Not sure?" asked Sam. "Or don't know?"

Reed licked his lips and sat back in the chair and Sam watched as he began rubbing his palms rhythmically up and down his thighs. The pattern of grimy hand marks on his cream trousers suggested this wasn't the first time he had succumbed to this habit.

"Or just won't say?" asked Sam.

"I'm not sure," said Reed. "I don't think I've been very well lately and I can't seem to remember too much."

"Ok, Mr Jerome," said Sam trying not to emphasis the alien surname. "What's your date of birth?"

"Tenth of April, nineteen seventy-seven," said Reed without hesitation.

In the viewing room the Chief scribbled *Edward Arthur Jerome, 10-04-1977* on a piece of paper and handed it to Jenny's researcher Paz, who hurried it away without requiring any explanation.

"I'm sure it's made up," said The Chief.

"Maybe," said Jenny.

There was something about Joe Reed that didn't make sense. His posture was not at all aggressive or threatening, and his body language spoke more of a victim than a perpetrator. Jenny couldn't imagine this man squashing a fly, let alone coldly murdering two women.

"What is it that you want to tell us, Mr Jerome?" asked Sam back in the interview room, his eyes boring into Joe Reed.

"I just want you to make him stop hurting those women," said Reed.

"Who?" asked Sam looking perplexed.

"Joe Reed," said the witness. "He needs to be stopped."

***

The Chief looked bewildered and turned to Jenny. "What does he mean?"

"I'm not sure," said Jenny. "But the man sitting in the interview room isn't the same cold-blooded Joe Reed that we've been hunting."

The door sprang open and Paz burst into the room, holding an A4 print-out in his hand. The Chief took the missive and immediately sent Paz into the interview room with a message for Sam to come out for further instructions, and then he handed the information to Jenny. Jenny read the paper, her brow furrowing as she took in the basic detail.

Edward Arthur Jerome: born 10th April, 1977.

Father: unknown.

Mother: Jane Jerome, prostitute and drug addict; Social services involvement.

Step-father: Daniel P Prince.

Daniel P Prince and Jane Jerome both died in the same car accident, locally.

One step-brother, Declan P Prince, son of Daniel P Prince, died in the same accident.

No criminal convictions and never been arrested under suspicion.

Sam entered the room and Jenny handed him the record, which he read quickly without emotion. "There's something wrong here," he said.

"Yes," said the Chief. "That's not Joe Reed."

"Or he's lying," said Sam. "He might have just picked any name and date of birth he'd come across and he's just playing games."

"Or he could be the wrong guy," said the Chief.

"There might be a fingerprint file for Edward Jerome from his social services file," said Sam referring back to the information. "Let's see if it matches this guy and see where that leads us."

Sam left the room. Jenny and The Chief watched as the DI appeared back in Interview Room 1 to ask the suspect whether he objected to having his fingerprints taken.

"Why?" asked the dishevelled witness.

"Just to help us eliminate you from our enquiries," said Sam calmly. Receiving a shrugged acceptance he nodded to the PC standing at the door, who disappeared to locate a fingerprint kit. Sam sat down opposite Reed.

He looked different from the man in the video, less assertive and with none of the charisma evident on the film. Judging from the musty smell coming from his clothes, the witness hadn't seen water for more than a few days and his beard was beginning to grow unchecked. His blue polo-shirt and cream slacks were crumpled as though he'd been sleeping in them; there was dirt under his fingernails and his skin was grimy.

"You haven't been looking after yourself," said Sam, adopting a concerned approach. "Do you live with family?"

Reed's grey eyes seemed vacant and it took a few moments for him to register the question. "I don't know," he said hesitantly. "I can't think."

"Do you know Dawn James?" asked Sam, as if he were asking Reed if he wanted a cup of tea.

Reed's face darkened and he stiffened in his chair.

Sam pressed home, "Or Robyn Cox?"

Reed squirmed in his chair and Sam let the two names hang in the air, watching his quarry fight a personal battle to stay calm.

"Do you know where Sharon Daly is now?" Sam pressed.

Reed's mouth began to twitch involuntarily and his palms rubbed violently on the thighs of his trousers. Suddenly the witness sprang forward in his chair, glancing from side-to-side as though he might be overheard. "He's got her," said the suspect, almost in a whisper.

"Who has?" asked Sam.

"Reed, Joe Reed," said the witness, before leaning forward still further, his stale breath infecting the DI. "He's going to kill her," he whispered.

The witness sat back in the chair, his body slumping as though the strain of unburdening himself had drained all his energy. Just then the PC returned and nodded to Sam who stood up to re-join the Chief and Jenny in the observation room, where they were studying the results of the fingerprint search.

"So," said Sam. "Does his story add up?"

The Chief handed him the results, and as he digested the information Jenny elucidated. "His fingerprints match with the numerous samples taken at crime scenes and attributed to Joe Reed, but there are no fingerprint records for Edward Arthur Jerome held by Social Service. When the Jerome family were on the Social Services Register there were different rules surrounding privacy, and prints weren't routinely taken as they are now."

"So this Jerome story is crap!" exclaimed Sam.

"It may not be that simple," said Jenny. "The problem is that we can't rule out that he's given us his real identity."

"So?" said Sam. "This is Joe Reed? This is our man?"

"No doubt about that," said the Chief.

"So let's just arrest him and have done with it," said Sam impatiently.

The Chief took the fingerprint information from Sam who stood waiting for an explanation. "Not so fast."

"He's obviously confused," said Jenny. "He says that Joe Reed is keeping Sharon Daly captive and is ready to kill her, but the problem is that he *is* Joe Reed."

414

Sam looked at her. He was confused and he stood waiting for her to say something that he might understand. "So how do we find Sharon Daly if Edward Jerome doesn't know where Joe Reed is keeping her?" asked Jenny.

Sam stayed silent for a few seconds wrestling with the question.

"He's obviously lying," said Sam eventually. "He's concocted this whole story to throw us off the trail."

"So why turn up here?" asked the Chief. "Why would Joe Reed walk in here to hold up his hands and then pretend to be some guy we've never heard of? We've already run some background checks on Edward Jerome and he dropped off the grid ten years ago. Since then he's had no bank accounts, no employment records and hasn't signed on to an electoral role. His last known address was in Smallwood, Birmingham where he appeared on the electoral role for seven years. PAYE records show that he worked in a local car showroom. We've asked the West Midlands Police to make further enquiries, talk to anyone who knew him and his employer and then report back."

"That's going to take time," said Sam.

"Time we don't have," muttered Jenny. "Every minute he's here shortens Sharon Daly's life. If he's here with us who's feeding her? Giving her water?"

"Ok Jenny," said Sam. "So what do you think?"

Jenny leant back against a desk, an involuntary movement of protection against the reaction to what she was about to say, "Right," she began. "What if he is Edward Jerome right now and then Joe Reed when he commits his crimes?"

"What?" asked Sam, "a schizophrenic?"

"Not exactly," said Jenny slowly. "A split personality, which is less common but can be more powerful."

The Chief and Sam leant back against the desk opposite and settled in for an explanation.

"Normally in a case of schizophrenia, the subject displays signs of several personalities competing for the conscious thoughts of the host brain.

Whilst most sufferers can be lucid with the help of drugs, they are generally confused with no real sense of themselves."

"Ok," said the Chief, "and how is this is different?"

"It's his posture and attitude," said Jenny. "The man sitting in Interview Room 1 isn't likely to be murdering anyone any time soon. He's unconfident, shy even. His sense of self-worth is almost zero and he can be persuaded to do things when he isn't sure why he should do them. Such as when Sam asked for his fingerprints and he just complied. So he can be dominated and bullied." Jenny watched Reed through the glass and saw him visibly shrink into himself. "Look at him!" she went on. "He's crapping himself in there. To get Joe Reed in that room we would have had to outsmart him, and he would be arrogant, aggressive and uncooperative."

"So what are you saying?" asked the Chief.

"I'm trying to say that I think Edward Jerome and Joe Reed are two completely separate personalities that exist in that man's mind. Each personality will assume control of the mind at certain times and it's the Joe Reed personality that kills the women."

"Whilst the Edward Jerome personality regrets it?" asked Sam.

"Maybe, yes," said Jenny. "Edward Jerome will only be aware of Joe Reed as someone he thinks he knows, but has never actually met. Perhaps even someone who only exists in his dreams."

"And vice-versa for Joe Reed?" asked the Chief.

"Not necessarily," said Jenny. "One of the personalities will be dominant, and looking at Edward Jerome it's probably Joe Reed's. I don't know why the Joe Reed personality would have allowed Edward Jerome to waltz into Central Park, but I'm guessing something happened last night when he tried to kidnap Emma Jones - something he wasn't expecting and forced him to retreat."

"You're seeing Emma Jones today aren't you?" asked Sam.

"Yes, I was going over to her house this morning to try and get a sense of Joe Reed's emotional state," said Jenny.

"Ok," said the Chief. "Put him back in a cell and give him the best food we can muster. I'll get on to Dr Phillips and see if he'll come over."

Jenny's pride got the better of her and her cheeks reddened. "I could talk to Jerome," she said as non-confrontationally as she could.

The Chief looked at his profiler and admired the ambition that seeped from her every pore. "I just want a second opinion," he said. "If you're right, Jenny, we need all the help we can get."

Chapter 29

The man slowly pushed a shopping trolley around the supermarket aisles. He didn't appreciate being outside his comfort zone and he didn't like the feeling that he had lost control of the situation. He was walking steadily - keeping a check on himself, trying to act as though he were any other shopper out buying provisions for the week. The truth was that anyone looking into his dark, deep-set eyes would have recognised the naked panic you might see in the eyes of hunted prey.

Smoothing his hair, he methodically filled his medium sized trolley with cereal, toilet rolls, a four-pint plastic bottle of milk, in fact any item that was bulky and cheap. He wanted to walk out into the car park with at least five supermarket bags full of groceries. He reasoned that if there were any policemen watching shoppers today in the supermarket on Bury New Road opposite the row of shops where Joe Reed had botched Emma Jones kidnapping, they would overlook him as an everyday shopper and not give him a second glance. Of necessity he had changed his plan from the previous evening, and now he was going over the events in his head to try and think if he had left a trail the police could pick up.

The previous evening when he had seen Emma Jones crossing Bury New Road with her baby the man had known that her encounter with Joe Reed wouldn't end well. He fully expected Reed to murder the woman in the alley and had acted as fast as he could, starting the engine of his blue Ford and driving round the block to the supermarket car-park. Leaving his car, he had crossed the road on foot and stood at the end of the alley where Emma Jones had disappeared just in time to see Joe Reed bolt out of the other end, sending an unknown woman flying and leaving Jones and her son unharmed. After that he'd expected to see Reed appear at the van and drive away, but he didn't. The man listened anxiously as the echo from the alley sent the unidentified woman's voice ringing in his ears as she shouted for the police on her mobile. A quick decision had to be made, so he hurried to Reed's van in the next alley, its engine left idling as he'd instructed.

He got in and drove, knowing it would only take a matter of minutes for the police to respond to the call and he couldn't drive far undetected. Immediately, he made a left turn and then a right, parked the van and cut the engine. The man wound down the driver's window, and as he'd suspected the air was thick with sirens within seconds and he could hear the patrol cars coming towards the crime scene from every direction, exactly as he thought they would. Once the initial commotion was over he started the engine, pulled out onto the side street and turned right, away from the glowing blue skyline to his left. The man drove within the limit, careful not to trigger any of the speed or traffic light cameras as he wound his way through the back streets along a route carefully planned before-hand to avoid any CCTV.

After a heart-stopping drive he eventually pulled up in front of 63 Cathcart Street and got out. Then he opened the garage with his spare set of keys and rolled the van into the building and out of sight.

It had taken nearly an hour to make a journey which would have been no more than twenty minutes on the main thoroughfares. The man had memorised the back roads so he knew when to stop for a few moments well back from red traffic lights and wait for them to turn green so that he could sail through without having to wait like a sitting duck. He knew the key to making it back to Oldham undetected was to wear his seatbelt, stick to the speed limit, indicate properly well before turns, and above all drive in a calm and controlled manner.

This last had been the most difficult part: he wanted to gun the engine and get back to Cathcart Street as quickly as he could. His sense of panic built from the second he began to drive the van, to the extent that when he eventually parked the vehicle in the garage he vomited beside it as he got out, releasing his foul discharge over the wheel and driver's door.

It was dark by the time he reached Cathcart Street and the man used his spare key to enter the house, realising for the first time that Joe Reed's house key was on the ring with the keys to the van, and if Reed did make it back to Cathcart Street he would have to knock on the door to get in. Once inside, the man didn't turn on any lights, but went straight upstairs to Joe Reed's bedroom to spend an uncomfortable and sleepless night monitoring the news on Reed's laptop that he had brought in from the van and plugged in to charge. The man fought off his longing to go down to the basement. He knew that Sharon Daly lay defenceless, and imagined with mouth-watering relish how she would be helpless to resist his basest needs. He wrestled with himself, getting as far as the top of the stairs more than once before turning back, his fear of Joe Reed returning to the house and finding him with Sharon Daly greater than his desire.

The internet news channels told him everything he needed to know and quickly, and he was grateful for the speed with which editors managed to update their stories to keep them fresh. It took less than an hour for the first reports to appear of Joe Reed's unsuccessful kidnap attempt on Bury New Road, and since the stories had clearly been released by the police in an attempt to elicit a public response, the man was confident that Reed hadn't yet been apprehended.

As the night wore on the stories began to take on a more familiar historic tone, using phrases that told the man Reed had escaped capture at the scene, and he realised that his gamble to drive the van away had probably paid off. The police would naturally think it was Joe Reed who'd jumped in and driven it away, and would have concentrated all their efforts on looking for the vehicle. They would have little choice but to study CCTV and erect ever widening circles of road blocks and check-points away from the scene in all directions. The man congratulated himself and smiled, knowing that if Joe Reed *had* taken the van in his obviously highly emotional state he would have been apprehended by the police before he reached the end of the road.

He sat there feeling pleased with himself for having out-thought the police yet again and began to plan his next *'Patrick'* letter in his head, this time taunting the ineptitude of the police at the scene and especially the stupidity of Chief Inspector Mark Ambrose, the biggest buffoon of them all. The man's mood went from elation at having got the van through the police lines and back to Cathcart Street, to a nagging fear of what had happened to Joe Reed. He had seen Reed running out of the end of the alleyway, and since he hadn't returned to the van he presumed that he would make his way back on foot. Using an internet walking-distance tool, he calculated Joe Reed's pace as average and came up with a walking time of two hours and fifty minutes. He then added on half an hour in case Reed had been compelled to change his route because of the strong police presence, but reckoned even so that by now he should have been back at the house.

If he did eventually appear, the man planned to make his exit through the back-door and leave it open, imagining that Reed would eventually go round to the back to look for a way in without his keys. He reasoned that if he slipped away quickly, he would have no need to confront Joe Reed and could make it back home on foot. Reed's bedroom window overlooked the front of the house and the man listened for the slightest noise from outside, leaving one curtain slightly open so that he would be aware of anyone arriving. But all he saw was the orange glow from the street light illuminating the empty road flanked by rows of terraced houses, and when the birds eventually began to sing in the few skinny trees that adorned the street he realised that Reed might not be coming back to the house.

If Reed hadn't made the journey back to Cathcart Street and he hadn't been apprehended by the police, then where was he? He couldn't have gone to Emma Jones' house or followed her anywhere, as the police would surely have spotted him. The man was perplexed: where else was there to go?

***

This morning, as he slid the supermarket trolley down the final aisle toward the tills, the man's mind was racing, scrabbling for some clue to Joe Reed's whereabouts. He couldn't imagine that Reed would go anywhere other than Cathcart Street, and so he decided to go back and see if he was there. If he wasn't, he would wait at the house; it seemed the only logical thing to do. The woman on the till - 'Tracy' according to the tag pinned on her tabard - smiled at him and asked how he was. He stared back at her, taking in her long dark hair and dark eyes. Thoughts of Sharon Daly trussed up in the basement of Cathcart Street filled his mind, and he felt himself stir, his manhood instantly pressing against the inside of his beige, knee-length cargo pants. Tracy continued to smile, her heavily laid on make-up was more like grease-paint and the thick red lipstick made her mouth look unreal, almost doll-like. The man forced himself to produce a smile in return.

"I'm good, ta," he said, and feeling encouraged Tracy began to chatter to the man about how hot it was. She wittered on about how she hadn't known a summer like it for years, and about how the heat affected her legs. The man wasn't listening, though; he was lost in thoughts of Sharon Daly, lying waiting and vulnerable.

The assistant flashed her eyes at him, insisting on packing his groceries. Despite his unprepossessing appearance and lack of reciprocal conversation, she thought she was being interesting, perhaps even sexy, and the man realised she was beginning to flirt with him. He smiled, suddenly struck by the delicious thought that if Joe Reed wasn't back at Cathcart Street when he got there, he'd be able to have some fun with his captive. Tracy smiled back, showing her off-white teeth and tossing her hair in a way that she obviously thought was provocative.

The man collected his trolley to a cheery goodbye from Tracy as he headed for the double doors that opened as he approached, and then he exited the supermarket into the bright sunshine. The air-conditioning in the store had done its job well and he was instantly aware of a wave of heat engulfing him, and of the sun burning his face. Panicking once again he glanced left and right for any signs of the police, but then forced himself to slow his pace when he saw his blue Ford parked at the back of the car-park where he had left it the previous evening. He had watched the car-park when Emma Jones came for her Pilate's classes and he knew that the back spaces were used for some free parking by local residents from the tight rows of terraced houses that flanked the huge superstore. The management obviously chose to turn a blind-eye to their potential customers' minor infringement of the rules; the man had parked amongst these vehicles thinking no-one would find it unusual, and he'd been right. His panic began to give way to a general alertness as he told himself that in his khaki tee-shirt with beige cargo-shorts and sandals with no socks, and pushing a trolley full of groceries he wouldn't stand out. Besides, the police were looking for Joe Reed and this man looked nothing like him.

Gratifyingly, there were no police anywhere to be seen and the man grew in confidence as he approached the car, popped the boot, deposited his groceries and got in to drive away. *'Idiots!'* he thought.

Chapter 30

Jenny couldn't bring herself to go straight home to Peter and the argument that would surely be waiting for her. She sat in her car with the engine on, the air-conditioning oozing cool air against the remaining heat of what had become a sultry evening more reminiscent of Mississippi than Manchester. She wrestled with her thoughts trying to picture herself having a normal evening, even a civil conversation with her husband. What would she do if she went home? Kiss him lightly on the cheek with a cheerful greeting as she flopped in to her favourite armchair for the refuge of some television drama that they might both enjoy? Perhaps Lilly would still be awake and they would sit and play with her, making her smile and enjoying Lilly's life together as loving parents? *'Unlikely'*, she thought and realised, not for the first time since she had discovered her husband's deception, that her life had already changed and their lives would never be the same.

It was the little things she began to grieve over, the things that couples do when they're relaxed and fully at ease with each other: the small kindnesses like the casual touches on an arm or small of the back, or the thought of Peter brushing her hair away from her face as they sat close together talking, their eyes meeting and holding each other's gaze, exploring each other's faces for signs of love, intelligence, the beginnings of a smile. Despite herself, Jenny couldn't stop the thought of Peter's kiss wandering into her mind. When they first met he had kissed her often and without reserve, and she'd been thrilled to have found a man she thought she could know purely based on this one physical attribute. When their lips joined, she imagined that she had a private window into Peter's soul, kissing her every time as if it would be their last kiss. Nothing was ever half-hearted, everything seemingly *meant*. He would slowly open his mouth, coaxing hers open with his tongue, gently at first and then fiercely, as though he would consume her totally. She had relished every second, finding herself working hard with her own lips and tongue to make the moments last as long as possible. She never drew away first, holding his cheek clasped in her hand, listening out for the soft murmur that she knew would come. That sound so easily missed like a whisper on the breeze made her feel wanted and loved.

Jenny had fallen helplessly in love with Peter through his kisses, and every kiss drew her more deeply into that comfortable, warm place that no-one ever truly believes exists until it proves to be a reality, and then they never want to escape from it. She felt herself thrill at the memory and then almost at once she was breathless, as if a punch had landed square on her solar plexus in the sudden realisation that Peter would have kissed Candice the same way. Involuntarily she squirmed to one side, the pain coming fast in excruciating waves as it coursed through her slim body, forcing her to rock from side to side as though she were trying to keep her balance on the deck of a ship that was listing wildly out of control.

Joe Reed, Dr Phillips, Sam and the Chief had kept her mind occupied all day, leaving time only for fleeting thoughts of Peter and Candice and their callous cruelty. But with nothing now to ward off the agony, her mouth opened and an anguished wail escaped her lips. The profiler squeezed her eyes tight shut and every knuckle of her clenched fists was white. Eventually, the pain subsided enough for Jenny to straighten up. A wave of dizziness swept over her, and her long, thin fingers trembled as she gripped the steering wheel, the gold of her wedding ring glinting in the evening sun as though mocking her torment.

Without thinking she put the car in drive and screeched from the car park. There was only one place she wanted to be right now, somewhere she knew there would be comfort without questioning or judgement.

***

Bob Baker made his way to the front door as soon as he heard the tyres of a car roll across the gravelled drive. Visitors were rare after eight pm, and with the open windows at the front of the house ushering in what little breeze the muggy evening would allow, the sound of the approaching vehicle could be heard in the living room.

When he opened the door he was shocked by the vision he saw before him, and instinctively put out his arms to lend support to his daughter, who seemed about to keel over at any moment.

"Hi Dad," said Jenny almost in a whisper, as though the effort of speech would see the last of her remaining energy disappear into the darkening night sky.

"Jenny?" said Bob, alarmed. "Are you ok?"

Without waiting for his daughter to answer he half carried her down the hallway and into the sitting room where she broke free from his grasp, and then stood straight for a moment before depositing herself into the nearest chair as gracefully as she could manage.

"I need a drink," she said flatly.

Bob Baker studied his daughter for a moment undecided whether it really was a drink she needed, or a doctor. Her long dark hair, hanging in threads as if it hadn't seen a brush for a week, seemed dark as night; her face was even more gaunt than usual, the high cheekbones standing out beneath skin that looked drained of blood. Even her smart grey skirt suit was creased and tired looking, and her usually pristine black shoes were scuffed.

"You look like you've gone a few rounds." he said, but without any real humour.

"I feel like it, Dad," said Jenny, without attempting to make eye contact until it was clear that her father wasn't going to budge until she did.

When she did look at him he saw that her brown eyes were circled in red and still moist from the well of tears that had flooded from them over and over again. She quickly looked away again, but the fleeting glance was enough to satisfy her father that the problem was emotional, and she was at least physically uninjured.

"I'll get you that drink," he said.

Two minutes later he was back with a glass of white

wine for his daughter and a glass of red for himself. Jenny took the glass and drained it.

"Hey, that's decent wine!" and Bob picked up the empty glass and went back to the kitchen to refill.

When he returned Jenny had settled back into the armchair and he sat as close to her as he could on the end of the adjacent sofa and handed her the fresh glass.

"Go easy with this one, eh?"

Jenny managed to flash her father an unconvincing smile. "You and your wine!" she said, and deliberately took only a sip before placing the glass on a black leather coaster protecting the polished surface of the low table in front of them.

Bob sipped his own drink and stayed silent as he swilled the liquid around near the rim, interested in the patterns developing as the heavy red wine took its time to settle back into the bottom of the glass. Jenny watched her father perform his ritual and knew he would wait until she was ready to talk. It was obvious that he was already worried, but they both knew instinctively that this waiting game was a necessary prelude to anything that Jenny might reveal. Ever since she was little more than a toddler her father had known that patience was the only way to get Jenny to open up to him, even over the smallest problems she had. They had sat in silence dozens of times, Bob pretending to be engrossed in some task or other, whilst Jenny organised her thoughts and relaxed with the only person in her life that she could trust with a raw open heart. Bob also knew instinctively that this time it might take even longer than on previous occasions and he settled back into the sofa, staring at his glass and waiting for his daughter to speak.

For her part, Jenny usually cherished these moments alone with her father. As if enacting a rehearsed process she would wrestle to form the best words to describe the problem and through painful emotion eventually reveal how she felt.

She knew from long experience that however the words came out her father was always ready to listen carefully and offer encouragement when she floundered, before finding the right way to comfort her. This time was different, though, and she thought even her father's love might fall short. The pair sat in silence for ten minutes or more, with Bob eventually draining his glass before placing it on the table. He was almost ready to give up and offer his daughter a bed for the night in the hope that a good sleep would help her more than he could at this moment when she suddenly cleared her throat.

"Peter's had an affair," she said with an effort to keep the emotion from her voice.

Just then, the harsh words having only just left her lips with not even an opportunity to hang in the air, the sound of car tyres again found their way into the living room.

"Who's that?" asked Jenny, startled and slightly annoyed that having found the courage to begin to talk she had been interrupted.

"It's your mother. She went out earlier on some errand."

Jenny realised that she hadn't even considered her mother, as if the woman's existence was an irrelevance.

"Christ!" said Jenny, suddenly aware of how she must look and longing to reach a bathroom to fix her hair and make-up before her mother saw her. She felt like a teenager caught out by returning parents with a stray guest in the house when she was supposed to be baby-sitting. Hearing the garage door closing and footsteps crunching across the drive, she began to panic - even more so when she realised that there were four feet and her mother obviously wasn't alone.

"Just need the loo," she said to her father, and shot down the hall and up the stairs to the main bathroom just as the front door was opening.

With the door closed behind her Jenny almost began to laugh. The farcical nature of her flight up the stairs simply to avoid her mother and guest wasn't lost on the profiler and she shook her head at her own foolishness. This bathroom was little used, following the installation - chiefly on the insistence of Val - of a state-of-the-art wet room, replacing the tired master bedroom en-suite, with both Val and Bob happy to use the luxurious new facilities. Consequently, Jenny found herself in the unchanged bathroom that she had routinely used as a child and then a teenager, even getting ready for her wedding day in this room. Despite the fact that the fittings were old and worn, housing the traditional 1970's avocado green suite of sink, toilet and bath with a shower over, this room felt like home and Jenny settled down on the already closed toilet seat to collect herself. She could just about make out a muffled conversation between two female voices and supposed her father had probably beaten a hasty retreat to his study to escape his wife's visitor.

Jenny shared Bob's displeasure at the thought of a stranger in the house and the idea of escaping through the bathroom window fleetingly crossed her mind, before she realised how stupid that was, and stood up to make herself presentable.

Ten minutes later after fighting with unruly hair and liberally applying make-up, especially around her swollen eyes, Jenny descended the stairs and made her way towards the voices emanating from the sitting room where her conversation with her father had been so abruptly abandoned.

The profiler stopped outside the door, smoothing the creases from the front of her grey, knee-length skirt before making a conscious effort to lift her chin and force a smile to her lips. Jenny was preparing to stride confidently into the room with a hastily rehearsed idea to give her mother and her companion a hearty greeting before quickly making her excuse to leave. After painting on a smile that had been the most difficult part of the process, the sight that greeted Jenny as soon as she stepped through the doorway wiped the effort away instantly and she stood stock-still, her hands frozen by her sides, her brown eyes wide open with shock. Her mother was sitting in the seat that Jenny had occupied no more than fifteen minutes previously and her guess that her father had left the room had been wrong as he hadn't moved, except perhaps to refill his wine glass which he held with two hands as if to steady the liquid. The third person sitting hunched up as if she had just suffered a blow to the midriff was her sister Candice.

Candice lifted her head and the four of them stared

at each other without speaking or moving for what seemed like an eternity. The quartet was frozen into position as though they were taking part in a game of musical statues caught at the point where the tune had been abruptly cut off and it was a case of the first one to move loses. Eventually Val made a conscious effort to relax and leant back into the plush grey sofa. Her movement unintentionally broke the spell and the two daughters erupted like volcanoes. They babbled at the tops of their voices, gesticulating violently whilst delivering blow-by-blow insults that only meant they effectively cancelled each other out like two negatively charged ions. This made the two women angrier and more vicious as the seconds ticked by.

Eventually, Bob stood up. "I've heard enough!"

The menace in his voice was enough to subdue the two women at once. "Jenny," he said, "Sit down!

Jenny immediately fell silent and made her way to the far end of the room. She sat on a hard, formal chair that had the unintended benefit of giving her height against her sister who continued to sit deep in her armchair. The profiler straightened her skirt and crossed her legs, clasping both hands together and resting them on the higher knee, giving her an air of natural superiority.

"Did you know?" she scowled at her father, her eyes boring accusingly into his.

Bob Baker broke eye contact and looked to his wife who answered for him.

"Your father didn't know anything until a few minutes ago when I came home with Candice," said Val, her voice calm and controlled.

Her mother's attempt at normality set alarm bells ringing in Jenny's mind and she suddenly wished she had made that escape out of the bathroom window.

"But *you* obviously did?" accused Jenny, her voice rising in octaves.

"Not exactly," said her mother. "I had an idea from Candice that something was happening with a possible…" Val paused, struggling to find the right word, "… boyfriend," she said eventually.

"Boyfriend!" screamed Jenny. "How can my husband be anyone's boyfriend?"

Candice began to gather herself and started to speak, but her father stopped her as soon as he heard the first sound escape her lips. "Probably best if you keep quiet for now love," he instructed and glowering at her father Candice sat back in her armchair, frustrated that she couldn't have her say. "Now let's all keep calm," continued Bob. "We're a family, remember."

Jenny shot her father a look that would have turned a lesser man to stone.

"Tell that to *her*," she said almost in a growl, flinging an accusing finger at her sister.

Candice seemed to shrink into her seat, her long dark hair falling over her face to protect herself. Silence followed.

It was as though Bob's mention of family values had thrown the group into deep thought and Val stared intently at nothing, her unfocused gaze fixed on some point in the thick white rug. Eventually Jenny broke the silence,

"Where are Darren and Claudia?" she asked.

A dreadful, creeping feeling had begun to prickle the

profiler's skin that Candice had been to Jenny's house for an argument or perhaps even a rendezvous with Peter and somehow left the children with him.

Val answered for her daughter. "They're with a neighbour," she said, giving Candice a nervous glance. "I got a call earlier. The neighbour was worried because Candice had dropped off the children and was an hour overdue to collect them. I found her wandering outside the flats when I went over there to try and help. I've spoken to the neighbour and they're happy to put the children to bed and one of them will stay in the flat until I take Candy home."

"You didn't mention that," said Bob flatly.

Val put her hand on her husband's knee.

"I didn't want to worry you," she said. "You were in the garden pottering around when I took the call, I just thought it was easier if I went down there on my own."

Bob exchanged a glance with Jenny.

"Seems a strange thing to do," he said, shifting his weight away from his wife causing her to stretch her arm to keep contact.

"So you did know," Jenny seethed, "that's why you rushed over there."

Val retrieved her hand and rested it in her own lap.

"I knew that Candice was having problems and I wanted to help," she said defensively.

"Oh this is great," said Jenny, a mocking laugh escaping her lips.

"This isn't Mum's fault," said Candice through her hair before brushing the locks away from her face and sitting up straight. "I told Mum everything after you came round the other night. I had to talk to someone."

Jenny considered the two women. She had always been closer to her father than her mother and they both knew it. Jenny told herself that her relationship with her mother was perfectly normal. It was one based on the oldest cliché known to woman; you can never please your mother, no matter how hard you try.

Jenny had tried and kept trying. Some of her earliest memories consisted of being given instructions by her mother, either verbal or through example, with Jenny always falling short in her mother's estimation. Jenny's cakes were never baked well enough, her friends were mistrusted and any childhood boyfriends undermined. Her exam results were never as good as some random friend's child's results, and her choice of career was looked upon with an attitude that fell short of derision, but was hardly positive.

Consequently, Jenny found herself playing catch-up with her mother from an early age, going out of her way to please the woman she saw as her role-model, usually without success.

When Jenny became an adult and could consider the relationship from an intellectual point of view rather than a child's eye, she consoled herself with the fact that many women had a similar relationship with their mother. Psychologically it was not unusual for the eldest daughter to be burdened with a mother's self-loathing and perceived life failings. So Jenny treated her mother with compassion, divining that Val used emotional distance as a tool to help propel her daughter to excel where she hadn't. Now, sitting there with her mother and sister, Jenny realised for the first time that her family was split already. Val was undoubtedly closer to Candice: ever since her birth the younger sister had been given all sorts of leeway in matters where Jenny had been forced into a rigid regime. Candice was indulged with any treats she demanded when they were children, and as they got older the rules for Candice were relaxed almost to the point of neglect. It was Candice who came in at three am when she was in her teens, seemingly with none of the punishment that would surely have been meted out to Jenny if she'd defied her mother over curfew times. Punishments for Jenny's misdemeanours consisted of being grounded for seemingly weeks on end, with household jobs thrown in as an added barb of cruelty. Candice's childhood sins, if identified at all, were met with a half-smile, along with a punishment so light as not to be worth the effort at all.

As Jenny watched the two women, it dawned on her that Candice had already been forgiven by her mother for the episode with Peter, Val apparently accepting the betrayal without so much as a raised eyebrow. With her mother displaying affectionate body language to Candice rather than Jenny, the profiler realised that it was with her sister rather than herself that her mother sympathised. It seemed to Jenny she wasn't the only one who had made the connection and she watched in helpless anguish as her family seemed to fragment in front of her. Perhaps re-enforced by the seating arrangements, the four people became two couples; Val and Candice one pair with Bob and Jenny the other.

Jenny spoke directly to Candice as though to test the new status-quo.

"So that's it then?" she asked. "You sleep with my husband and you're forgiven, as always?"

Val didn't react to the obvious side-swipe, but Jenny could tell by her father's reaction, glowering at his younger daughter and slowly shaking his head that not everyone had forgiven Candice.

Silence once again descended, with the atmosphere in the room ever more charged with each passing moment until Jenny at last ignited the fire to usher in the gathering storm. "You're not the only one he's been sleeping with. You know that, don't you?"

"Don't be ridiculous," said Val.

"He told me," said Jenny, a note of taunting creeping into her voice.

"What do you mean, he told you?" asked Val.

Jenny lost her patience with her mother's refusal to allow Candice to speak for herself, "Is it you sleeping with Peter or *her*?" said the profiler provocatively.

If Jenny had spoken to her mother with this degree of disrespect at any other time her father would have stepped in to admonish his daughter and both Val and Jenny looked to Bob to gauge his reaction, but Bob sat silently, watching the scene unfold and it was clear that he was in no mood to intervene on his wife's behalf.

"I mean," said Jenny. "*She* can answer for herself."

"*She* has a name," said Candice bitterly.

Jenny ignored her comment.

"Well, did you know?" she pressed.

"You're just being defensive," said Candice. "He told me I was the one he had always wanted and I fell for it. End of."

"And you believed that?" taunted Jenny, almost laughing between gritted teeth.

Candice stayed silent. "You're just the latest in a long line," said Jenny, "a very long line," and with that she stood up to leave.

"Don't leave," said Val quietly. "Not like this."

Jenny studied her mother. Val prided herself on keeping trim, but as she sat looking up her face seemed thinner than Jenny remembered, pinched even. Her mother's freshly dyed auburn hair was cut a half-inch shorter than usual accentuating the look and making her features almost jut out from her face. The creases around her mother's brown eyes had stretched into heavy lines. "You look tired," said Jenny with sudden compassion, and was surprised when her mother stood up with tears in her eyes. For a split-second it looked as if she would throw her arms around Jenny, but she stopped just short, able only to offer a conciliatory rub of her eldest daughter's upper arm.

Bob stood too, "I'll see you out," he said slipping his hand around Jenny's waist, almost claiming her as his own. He turned his daughter away from Val and walked close to her out of the room and towards the front door. "Will you be ok?" he said once out of earshot.

Jenny snuggled her head into her father's welcoming shoulder as they walked.

"Will you?" she asked by way of an answer.

Chapter 31

Driving home from her parents' house the previous evening with her emotions raw, Jenny had consoled herself with chain-smoking Marlboros and playing Queen's *Bohemian Rhapsody* at almost full volume. She felt as though she was losing control, realising as she pulled into her drive that all the places that she'd thought were safe a week ago were now barbed with pain, embarrassment and humiliation.

Without a word to Peter she had raced straight up the stairs and slept in the spare bedroom. Fortunately an exhausted sleep came quickly until her alarm woke her, set deliberately early so that she could spend time alone with Lilly, who now sat on the floor at her feet in the living room. The child was gathering dolls and teddies together for a make-believe breakfast of scrambled eggs and tea.

Jenny watched her daughter playing, the tot's chubby fingers pouring pretend tea into red plastic cups with saucers before the empty vessels were shared between the toys. Lilly gave each doll or teddy a slightly different voice in which to say a polite thank you as the little girl held the cup to where she imagined the lips would be on the toy she was currently force-feeding. Jenny felt emotionally drained after her confrontation with

Candice and her mother the previous evening, and tried to imagine that the numbness she felt was a normal reaction to watching her child at play. Candice, though, had seemed to feel nothing for anybody but herself, and so perhaps this was how the Bakers normally felt - bereft of emotion.

Jenny had woken dragged down by a heavy feeling of emptiness. Wordlessly fetching Lilly from her bedroom, she made her way downstairs. As she sat watching her daughter entertain her toys Jenny realised that her entire nervous system had become blunted, almost non-existent. Lilly lifted a red plastic cup with a beaming smile that on any other day would have made Jenny's heart leap but the profiler simply took it without speaking, raised the hard rim to her lips and pretended to sip, more as a duty than a pleasure. After a short, dispassionate consideration of her state of mind, Jenny decided that not feeling anything must surely be abnormal and pushed herself into joining in with the tea-party, desperately trying to wrestle some feeling from her emotionally dormant self. Lilly eventually lost interest in the tea-party, her attention turning to a tower of large, colourful blocks. The child knocked the tower down and attempted to rebuild it, only to see the structure collapse after the fifth block had been added. Jenny watched Lilly's determined efforts with bemused pride. Time and again her daughter tried to rebuild the tower; each time it fell she tried again with increased determination. Realising that this game would keep Lilly busy for some time, and shaking her mind free of self-analysis the profiler began to study Ed Jerome's social services file. She was expecting a record littered with problems.

Ed Jerome was the product of a drug-fuelled prostitute mother and it would have made sense if his family felt the brunt of any subsequent emotional turmoil. The first observation that struck Jenny was how strikingly similar Jane Jerome was to the rape and murder victims - to the point where she could be Emma Jones' double. The report told of a transformation in the family when Jane Jerome met and married Dan Prince. He seemed to bring stability and security to the lives of his new family and the Jeromes seemed to find an even keel. The social workers visited less frequently, eventually ending any home visits after the couple had been married for twelve months and there had been no reports of further drug use by Jane. The profiler made a mental note to call the social workers who were accountable for the well-being of Ed Jerome and ask if they had any indication, no matter how small, of whether Jane Jerome had abused her son.

Jenny scanned the notes of the visits made by social workers and was surprised that each careful entry spoke of a happy child in a loving environment.

The absence of any unusual behaviour became increasingly puzzling as she read. If Ed Jerome had grown up to become a killer, there would be tell-tale signs in his teenage years, typically resulting in a criminal record, perhaps even a spell in youth custody. Classically the profile of a boy who would later commit serious crimes might include extreme introspection, cruelty to animals or setting fires. Certainly there would be a record of police intervention over some petty theft or

445

violence towards the would-be killer's peers. But the file detailed a boy who was studious, thoughtful, considerate and caring. He took care of his appearance and according to the file spent most of his time studying or playing sports.

'How could he be so normal?' thought Jenny, an image of the dead eyes of Dawn James suddenly invading her mind.

***

An hour later Jenny was in her car. Emotionally drained or not there was one thing she was certain of, she had no stomach for Dr Phillips this morning. With his prying intellect Jenny was sure the doctor would be able to see her pain and she wanted to avoid any personal questions, especially from someone with the ability to see right through any lies. She dialled Sam.

"Morning Sam, much happening with Reed?" she asked as soon as she was connected.

"Dr Phillips gets here in half an hour and we're going to try and talk to him again," said Sam. "The Chief's getting nervous holding a suspect that we know is guilty without formally charging him and offering him a lawyer."

Jenny considered the problem. "He walked in of his own accord and offered to help with the investigation," she said. "Whether he's charged or not is irrelevant isn't it?"

"It should be," said Sam. "But the law doesn't see it that way. Reed's the main suspect and he should have been read his rights by now."

"What about Sharon Daly's rights?" said Jenny more fiercely than she intended.

The thought of the helpless mother kept prisoner somewhere for yet another night and surely by now close to death crowded her thoughts.

"She has rights too," continued the profiler. "If we charge Reed now and he does ask for a lawyer then he might not say anything else, we won't find her in time and she'll be dead."

"He does have the *right* to silence Jenny," said Sam. "But getting Reed to crack and tell us where he's holding Sharon Daly is her only hope. That's all the Chief is focused on right now, and he thinks the risk is worth it."

"What's the worst case scenario, Sam?" asked Jenny, calmer now.

"Well," he said. "If we get information from him before we charge him it'll be useless. Any barrister worth his salt would have the evidence thrown out of court as inadmissible."

"Really?" asked Jenny. "So even if he's guilty he might just walk out?"

"Not quite," said Sam. "We've got enough forensic, witness and crime-scene evidence to convict Reed whether he talks or not. But the investigation would be scrutinised and the Chief would definitely be hauled over the coals."

"But he's prepared to take that risk?" asked Jenny.

"I suppose he is. Are you on your way in?"

"Almost. I've been studying Ed Jerome's Social Services file. The mother married when Ed was young and the family lived in Cathcart Street, Oldham." She paused, hoping that Sam would agree with the suggestion she was about to make. "I thought I would go up there, have a look around and talk to some of the neighbours. See if they remember the Prince family or Ed Jerome, and try to build a clearer picture of him."

Sam thought for a moment. "I suppose while Dr Phillips is in with Reed, there's not much you can do here," he said. "Ok, fine, see what you can dig up."

"Great," replied Jenny, relieved that she didn't have to face Dr Phillips.

"Do you want me to send Paz to meet you there?" asked Sam.

Jenny thought of Paz, her researcher, and decided that his youthful exuberance would be particularly unwelcome given her emotional state.

"No, I'll be ok. It's a long shot that anyone who lived in Cathcart Street when Ed Jerome was there is still around. That area's seen a lot of change over the years, what with immigration and the loss of local industries. I'm pretty sure a lot of the original residents will have moved away."

"Fair enough," said Sam. "But if you do find a witness who you think has real information, then call and I'll send someone out to meet you."

"Sure" said Jenny, hesitating before she added, "Reed's obviously seriously unstable, but if he does give up the location of Sharon will you call me and let me know?"

"Don't worry," said Sam, "I will."

"Thanks," said Jenny and rang off.

***

The journey to Oldham was uneventful, boring even.

448

Nothing out of the ordinary happened, nothing shocking. Motorists behaved as they should, people got off and on buses, pedestrians used the designated crossing places and the day seemed the same as any other summer's day. But in Jenny's mind the image of a missing woman stuck fast, like the memory of a horror movie. The profiler knew that the longer it took to find her, the more likely it would be that they would be too late.

Eventually she turned into Cathcart Street and drove the full length of the row of terraced houses to stop at the far end opposite number 63.

The day had started cloudy and by ten the sky had become a threatening grey, overcast with a bank of solid rain cloud that extended in all directions. The temperature had dropped accordingly and Jenny regretted her choice of a thin black linen skirt-suit over a sheer white blouse. The profiler sat in her car studying number 63, which looked tired and barely lived in behind its low sandstone wall. A gap opened where a gate once stood, and the space between the wall and the house, barely five feet in length, was strewn with a trail of litter leading to an elevated front door. The door was accessed by two steps, with traces of paint suggesting they had once been red.

Number 63 occupied the end plot in a row of more than fifty terraced houses with a mirror-image set of shabby dwellings on the opposite side of the narrow street. Many of the houses were boarded up or burned out, with perhaps half of the dwellings unoccupied. That left fifty or so doors to knock on and Jenny was encouraged that by virtue of sheer numbers there might be someone who remembered the Prince family, and especially Ed Jerome. She tried to imagine how the house might have looked when the Prince family lived there, deciding that the blue and white stone cladding and replacement windows were probably additions that Dan and Jane Prince had been proud to make. With a son of his own and a stepson and new wife to add to the family, Jenny thought that the house must have represented a good new start for Jane and Ed Jerome, with its red-painted steps, and perhaps a black wrought-iron gate to welcome visitors. The house she was looking at now suggested that more recent owners had been unkind, neglecting the cherished improvements, creating more of an eye-sore than a portrait of a family home.

Jenny's phone rang and she consulted the screen, the caller was her Uncle Ronnie. Ordinarily, she would have been thrilled to speak to him, perhaps discuss the case or just enjoy a catch-up. However, the last time he'd rung Jenny had the distinct impression that her uncle had a hidden agenda. He'd asked questions about the Chief's competence to run the investigation and Jenny hadn't wanted to be put on the spot. She decided to ignore the call and stepped out of her car, involuntarily shivering in a cool breeze making its way down the street and tunnelling between the houses. The summer had so far been unusually hot and sticky and the sudden chill in the air took her by surprise. The profiler was forced to button her jacket as she made her way across the tarmac toward number 63.

Reaching the house, Jenny attempted to peer into the

ground floor bay window. After trying to look through the closed curtains from every angle she realised that the window covering was in fact a thick sheet of some sort of pink material that had been nailed inside the frame, leaving no chinks to see through. Moving to the tired front door, she lifted the letter box lid, which gave her a restricted view of the hallway. The profiler could make out an aged, filthy carpet piled high with yellowing newspapers, leaflets and charity bags, convincing her that the house was most likely empty and she was probably wasting her time.

***

Parked half way up the narrow street stood a bright yellow Vauxhall Vectra occupied by Paula Tripp, who watched Jenny get out of her car and walk across Cathcart Street to number 63. The Manchester Evening News Chief Reporter had followed Jenny ever since she left home that morning, keeping a safe distance as they toiled their way across the city and on to Oldham.

Tripp was becoming increasingly frustrated by the lack of information from the police following the unexpected appearance of a suspect - especially since at the previous evening's press conference Chief Superintendent Ambrose had dismissed her reasoning that the suspect was Joe Reed with an arrogant wave of his hand.

Tripp had often struck lucky from the fact that Gill Spencer, one of her friends, worked as a receptionist at the Manchester Metropolitan Police Headquarters. Gill had tipped Paula off that a man had walked into Central Park, been wrestled to the ground by Sam

Bradbury and was still being held for questioning. She'd given Paula a decent description of the man and although no charges had been laid, Paula thought it was a good bet that it was Joe Reed. The reporter had already written an editorial for that evening's Manchester Evening News with a suitable headline grabber and knew that if she was right, she had the scoop. It wasn't enough, though: Paula wanted more - she wanted the inside story. Leaving a senior reporter at Central Park to cover any further official breaking news from the Police, she decided to follow Jenny on the off-chance that the profiler might lead her in the right direction and she could steal another march on her rival hacks.

On the drive to Oldham Tripp wondered more than once why Jenny hadn't taken the by-pass. It would have cut the journey time by half and she even feared for a few fleeting moments if Jenny was trying to avoid being tailed, and was keeping as far back from the pro-filer's car as she could without losing her altogether. She was evidently wrong, though, as Jenny made the drive at a leisurely pace without any manoeuvres that would lead the reporter to think she'd been spotted. Tripp was pleased to use the cover of the early morn-ing traffic to make her bright yellow Vauxhall Vectra less conspicuous as she stalked her prey. The car and the quirky colour had grown on Paula; she even won-dered if its brightness might have the opposite psycho-logical effect than she had first thought, and in the gaudy car she somehow found it easier to follow some-one almost invisibly.

Paula smirked to herself as she saw the profiler reacting to the increasingly cool morning. Jenny's black skirt-suit and matching black heels looked completely out of place amidst the tired, scruffy terraces. The reporter watched with growing curiosity as Jenny began snooping around the front of number 63. Tripp shifted her position to see the profiler lifting the letter-box, holding back her thick dark hair to peer inside as far as she could.

'They'll think she's a benefits fraud inspector', thought Paula, mentally pouring scorn on Jenny, who was clearly an amateur when it came to fitting in with the local population, a difficult but necessary skill which Paula prided herself on having mastered.

Despite her ineptitude Paula was intrigued as to why Jenny was in Oldham at all; she had obviously intended to come to this specific address. Paula's nose for a story told her things were about to get interesting and she unbuckled her seat belt just as Jenny knocked loudly on the front door of number 63.

***

After leaving the letter-box to settle back to its normal position Jenny stepped back and craned her neck to the front upstairs bay window, more in hope than conviction. Then just as she was about to turn away and try some other doors in Cathcart Street, she thought she saw a shadow pass across the bedroom window and the nets that curtained it definitely twitched.

'So someone does live here,' she said to herself, and in the absence of a bell or brass knocker the profiler rapped her knuckles loudly on the wood of the front door.

Nothing,

Jenny tried again,

Still nothing.

Turning her attention to the letter-box and pulling it apart it as widely as she could she pressed her mouth into the opening. "Hello! Is there anyone at home?" she shouted.

Still nothing came from inside and Jenny rapped a third time. She was just about to give up when she heard slow, heavy footsteps from inside the house, first on the stairs and then proceeding down the hall. The carpet was so threadbare that the footsteps echoed as if the walker was treading on bare floorboards. Eventually the inside lock was turned and the front door swung inwards scraping a fresh, untouched newspaper delivery as it went. During the course of her criminology degree and subsequent training Jenny had learned that a policeman can develop a sixth sense for danger. She had read that many instances have been recorded where a professional has followed a hunch and been proved right, or perhaps sensed a danger that they have cleverly avoided. This policeman's sixth sense was stronger in some than others and was almost never natural. The feeling came from experience gained over years of handling a whole range of potentially dangerous or complex situations. At that moment it was this instinct that was singularly lacking in Jenny when the door opened.

The man standing in the entrance, elevated by the two steps up to the front door seemed harmless enough. He looked to be in his sixties, as shabby and unkempt as the house in which he stood. His clothes were well-worn and grimy, and his scuffed brown shoes were so old that Jenny could make out the impression of his toes through the softening leather.

"Hello," she said, managing what she hoped was an engaging smile. "My name is Jenny Foster, and I'm attached to the Manchester Metropolitan Police Serious Crime Squad."

The man stared at her with dark unblinking eyes, and assuming that he probably needed more reassurance before he would speak to her, Jenny quickly produced her identification from her bag and held it up for the man to see. The man stared at his visitor; without warning his hand darted from his side and snatched the profiler's ID wallet from her hand, then without a word he glanced at it and thrust it in to his trouser pocket. Jenny was taken by surprise at the speed of the man's movements and she noticed how powerful he looked for someone who was probably in his sixties. Over six feet tall with broad shoulders and muscular arms, he took a step forward and with the added height of the elevated step he towered over her.

"I wanted to ask you a few questions about a previous occupant of the house," said Jenny, the words beginning to sound child-like in her head. "How long have you lived here Mr...er?"

At that moment the clouds opened and the threat of rain became reality, with heavy rain drops beginning to pelt down. The man craned his head out of the door to look both ways up and down the street, as if assessing the severity of the sudden storm.

"You'd best come in," he said and moved aside for Jenny to pass.

*** *

Watching Jenny at the door of number 63, Paula couldn't help but burst out laughing when she saw the old man snatch the profiler's ID out of her hand.

'What *is* she doing?' she said to herself in disbelief, and chuckled as Jenny eventually disappeared inside the house. The rain was beginning to spatter her windscreen and Paula didn't particularly want to get wet, but she'd suffered worse than a soaking to get a story and something told her that Jenny wasn't here and out of her comfort zone for nothing. Summoning her resolve, the reporter popped the boot, got out of the car and retrieved her handbag-sized umbrella, wrestling with the mechanism to get it up before the rain turned her stylish blonde bob into a sodden mess.

Locking the car, Paula Tripp made for a gap between the terraced houses leading to the ginnel which she knew would run down the back of the row. On her way across Cathcart Street she counted the front doors between the gap and number sixty-three, calculating that she would be at the back-yard of the right house after twelve back gates. Paula ducked as she moved quickly down the cobblestone alleyway. The rain bounced a foot high off the stones all around her as she passed high walls, some topped with broken glass set into concrete to deter unwelcome visitors. The reporter counted off the green gates as she went until eventually she reached the twelfth and stopped for breath. There was no sign on the weathered gate to confirm that she had counted properly until she realised that she was at the end of the alley and she must therefore be outside the last house in the row, which she knew was right. Trusting her luck she tried the gate, silently congratulating herself when it began to move inward and then, unhindered by a latch, she slipped into the yard beyond.

**

Jenny heard the door close heavily behind her as she stepped into the hallway of 63 Cathcart Street. For the first time she began to experience a vague sense of uneasiness, quickly shaking it off to concentrate on the fact that her host still had her ID Wallet in his pocket. She could hear the rain beating down outside even through the closed door and she was relieved to be under cover, even though the place didn't look fit for habitation. She glanced back at the man for reassurance that she was going the right way as she stepped down the hall and into what she imagined was the sitting room.

All thoughts of why the man had taken her ID or even of why she had come in search of 63 Cathcart Street in the first place disappeared at the sight of the room. It was hard to imagine how anyone could survive in such a filthy, cheerless environment. The only piece of furniture was an old wooden dining-chair and wallpaper hung from the walls as if they were weeping. The smell that hit the back of Jenny's throat was almost unbearable; struggling to find the source of the stench, she noted all the old pizza boxes and chip wrappers strewn across the floor. The room was bathed in a dark pink glow from the light passing through material nailed to the window frames. Consequently, Jenny found it impossible to imagine either the original colour of what was left of the carpet, or what had made the multiple stains that covered it.

She turned to the man, the look of shock on her face revealing her realisation that something was horribly wrong. "I'd ask you to sit," he said, a smile crossing his thin lips. "But you might get your skirt dirty."

Now that Jenny looked at him again, he suddenly seemed taller, younger, more powerful, little resembling the scruffy old man who had answered the door a few minutes earlier.

"I'll need my ID card back," she said firmly, deciding to dispense with any niceties and try to regain some control.

"Oh, aye….all in good time, Jenny!" he said stolidly, and his use of her Christian name sent chills through her body.

She remembered telling him at the door why she was there, but his familiar tone, together with his domineering attitude put her on the defensive. "I did mention that I'm with the Manchester Metropolitan Police Serious Crime Squad didn't I?" she said.

The man's eyes were keen and restless, going over Jenny's face and body as if assessing her worth. "You look a lot like her," he said, more than a hint of malice lacing his words.

Jenny at last began to sense that she was in danger and turned her professional eye on the man standing before her. It was clear that he was confident, intelligent and strong-minded and Jenny realised that he also had an agenda. "Like who?" she asked, keeping her voice as calm as possible.

"I know exactly who you are *Jenny Foster*," said the man. "Oh aye, I've watched you parading yourself across the telly like you're worth summat, and I've read all about you online and in the papers. You're the Manchester Metropolitan Police secret weapon; the so-called *criminal profiler* who's been recruited to analyse and catch Joe Reed."

Jenny stayed silent, finding herself staring into the man's face.

"Come on," he jeered, "Face it! You're out of your depth. You've got no idea what you're dealing with, have you?"

"What am I dealing with?" asked Jenny.

"Me!" said the man.

Before Jenny could react he slapped her hard across her right cheek.

His hands were large and rough and the blow sent Jenny spinning across the room, coming to rest with her back against what was once the fireplace. In the movies that Jenny often watched men, even if they were criminals, seldom hit women. On the odd occasion that they did the assault was usually followed by a show of remorse.

Not this time: real life was different. Now the man came swiftly across the room, took a clump of Jenny's hair in his right hand and pulled her head towards the floor. She was powerless to resist as she grabbed his wrist and found it immovable. As if in slow motion she watched with growing fear as the man's foot left the ground to deliver a devastating kick to her nose, which exploded sending a searing pain across her face. She battled to stay conscious through the pain as she choked on her own blood, but before she could retaliate the man half dragged her to the only chair, quickly securing her to the wooden frame with rope that seemed to appear from nowhere.

"Let's see how the great Chief Inspector Ambrose talks his way out of this one," he whispered in her ear as the bonds tightened.

***

Paula Tripp made her way across the concrete floor of the back-yard, the only real feature of which was a smouldering pile of clothes, papers and a charred laptop that had been stacked high and then set alight. With the sudden rain having dampened the fire, there was now more smoke than flames and Paula used it as a screen to reach the back door, which she found ajar. The rain continued to beat down around the reporter; her flimsy umbrella was beginning to prove inadequate as an effective defence against the volume of water falling from the sky and a growing wind forced the metal arms to bend and flip it inside-out. With a curse she tossed the brolly onto the smouldering pile and turned her attention to listening hard at the crack of the door.

Paula could hear a man's voice, mocking and confident, punctuated by the odd word or two from Jenny and she instinctively knew that Jenny was in trouble.

Cursing herself that in her haste to follow the profiler to the house she had left her mobile phone in the car, she was torn between going inside to see if Jenny was safe and simply turning away and leaving her to it. After all, she reasoned, Jenny had no idea she was there, and wouldn't be at all pleased to know that she'd been followed. Besides, Paula could still hear DI Sam Bradbury's angry words over her recent attempt to get some leverage against Jenny ringing in her ears, and she wasn't in the mood to have another strip of flesh torn from her. Tripp was just turning to make her way out of the yard when she was stopped in her tracks by the unmistakable sound of a loud and unexpected slap. Paula had heard women being slapped by men many times. She had stalked celebrities who routinely used physical violence against the women they were supposed to love. The sickening sound was unmistakeable. There was a rustle of clothes, followed by a loud, thudding slap as worn skin connected with softer tissue and then a gasp of surprise as the victim succumbed to instant shock at the violation.

Paula had stepped in a few times in her career, usually to her detriment and always without thanks. Despite all that, she knew she couldn't turn a deaf ear, and hearing a further blow land her resolve hardened and she prepared to go in.

At first she hesitated, frozen by fear and indecision, but then finally she burst through the back door, steeled to confront whatever situation greeted her.

Chapter 32

The Chief had already taken two calls from his superiors before nine am.

The first had come from the Deputy Commissioner's Office as a general enquiry as to how the case was progressing, predictably followed by a second call direct from the Commander. The latter conversation hadn't gone as planned, with the unsettling outcome that senior investigators from Scotland Yard would be boarding the next train to lend support to the investigation. As a hardened political animal the Chief knew that *lending support* effectively meant *taking over* and he feared that the independence of the Manchester Metropolitan Police would be compromised, almost inevitably resulting in an erosion of the team's confidence in him as their leader.

During the first call, the DC had held back from making any criticism of the investigation itself, and even the Chief's insistence that he wasn't ready to charge the man in custody had been met with a passive response. The Commander's attitude, however, had been altogether different. In no uncertain terms he told the Chief that he had until the next train arrived from London either to formally charge the suspect or apply for Home Office leave to detain him further. Realising that decisions had already been made over his head, the Chief had taken the news without argument, returning the telephone receiver to its cradle slowly and gently as if to give the caller the an impression of acquiescence.

As a dogged natural survivor, the Chief had learned over a long and mostly successful career that when a Chief Superintendent was trumped by his superiors it was too late to try and influence decisions already made. The conclusion was obvious: either he cracked Joe Reed, or Ed Jerome or whatever his name was in the next few hours and found Sharon Daly, or he would be put out to grass before the month was up. Sitting in the observation room of Interview Room 1, the Chief and DI Sam Bradbury watched from behind the two-way mirror as Dr Phillips entered the room. Ed Jerome had been brought up from the cells some fifteen minutes earlier and left alone for the time deemed necessary to create pressure prior to a major interview. The suspect had already started to fidget as the psychologist walked in, escorted by a uniformed officer who remained at the door. Dr Phillips took his time to sit down opposite his quarry, keeping the width of the desk between them and placing an impressive pile of files to the right hand side of the desk. Taking the top buff envelope, he slowly drew out a black Mont Blanc pen from his jacket pocket and laid the file out flat on the table top between them. Ed Jerome studied every move that Phillips made and was clearly becoming agitated.

"I see they gave you a shower and a change of clothes," said Dr Phillips, looking at Ed Jerome for the first time and taking in his new attire, which consisted of a royal blue paper jump-suit.

"Yes, everyone has been very kind to me," said Jerome. "Why wouldn't they be?"

After innumerable counselling sessions the psychologist was an experienced interrogator and was calmly prepared, as instructed, to challenge everything the suspect said.

"I don't know," said Ed vaguely.

Dr Phillips took in Ed Jerome, focusing on the detail that he could actually see. A recent shower and accompanying shave had made him look younger. Somehow the physical presence of the man sitting there didn't suggest the childhood victim of abusive parents - one who had eventually suffered some psychological trauma strong enough to make him kill.

Jerome was suave and attractive with a physical presence that in other circumstances would easily have been capable of dominating the room. His grey eyes were bright enough to belong to a movie star and with his black hair groomed back from his face they seemed to penetrate to the heart of whatever they looked at. Despite being thirty-four, the suspect had no wrinkles and the absence of lines around his eyes and mouth when he spoke or reacted would lead anyone he met to assume he was at least three, if not five years younger. The blue jump-suit was too tight around his broad shoulders and Dr Phillips could see that Ed Jerome was in pretty good physical shape, obviously watched what he ate and maybe took regular exercise.

These observations were at odds, however, with Ed Jerome's mental state.

He was clearly submissive, with the natural position of his chin almost resting on his chest, and any eye contact was fleeting, almost apologetic. He kept his hands locked together at his groin to comfort himself, and even so they shook continually as if he were a man waiting for a blow to be delivered at any moment. Ed Jerome's comment that the Police had shown him kindness showed a subservient nature and Dr Phillips was finding it increasingly difficult to believe that the same man was secretly a monster. However, it was his job to unearth the truth and he pressed on.

"Tell me Ed," said Dr Phillips. "What happened to Dan Prince and your mother Jane?"

Before the interview Phillips had discussed with the Chief and Sam the fact that the deaths of his mother and step-father and his brother Declan were undoubtedly the trigger or stress factor that sent him into his current psychological state, eventually leading to his crimes. The suspect's fidgeting became worse and his hands parted to begin rubbing the tops of his legs in an auto stress relief pattern.

"And Declan," continued Dr Phillips, speaking as he would to a ten year old child. "You must miss your step-brother? I bet you got up to some tricks when you were both younger?"

Ed Jerome stayed silent, his mouth beginning to twitch almost as violently as his hands rubbing against his trousers. Eventually Dr Phillips realised that his subject wasn't going to answer the question and decided to relieve the stress and try to get Ed Jerome to open up, and at least start talking about something.

"Ok," he said, "we'll come back to that. Tell me about

your time in Birmingham when you worked at the car showroom. Did you enjoy it?"

The question took Ed Jerome by surprise. He slowly stopped fidgeting, making an attempt to recall any memories.

"Remember?" asked Dr Phillips prompting recall. "You lived in Smallwood, Birmingham at the time and the job at Evan's Cars lasted a while?"

Ed Jerome's memory sparked into life. "I was their best salesman," he said beginning to sit straighter, a shadow of confidence crossing his tortured features. "I loved that job; everyone was friendly. Me and Ted Evans the boss used to go to the Eagle after work - shoot pool and talk about cars."

Dr Phillips let him pause, allowing his memories to develop without interruption.

"There was a girl who worked there too," continued Jerome. "Younger than me, a blonde. She had a great laugh that lit up the pub. Angie her name was."

"Did you see her outside work?" asked Dr Phillips, allowing his own face to mirror Ed's reminiscent smile.

"Once or twice," said Jerome. "We went to see a film once. Er, Rocky Three I think it was, with Sylvester Stallone. She was like that, loved a good action movie."

"Do you keep in touch?"

"No," said Jerome quickly, his face beginning to darken. "I haven't seen her since the day I left Birmingham."

"Why did you leave?" probed the doctor. "You seem to have fond memories of your time there?"

Ed Jerome thought for a moment, as though taking great care to construct an answer. "I felt a bit funny after the accident," he said. "I needed to get away."

Dr Phillips consulted his notes. "You left a month after the accident. Why wait so long?"

Jerome began to look uncomfortable. "I wasn't *waiting* for anything," he said. "I left when *he* told me to."

"Who?" asked the doctor in as matter of fact a way as he could.

"I….I don't know," said the suspect and began rubbing his trousers again. "I'm so confused," he added, his face dropping into his spare hand.

At that moment the door opened and Sam stepped into the room, caught Dr Phillips' eye and gestured for him to follow. In the observation room a few minutes later Phillips was clearly angry.

"I was getting somewhere," he said sharply. "Your timing couldn't have been worse, Detective Inspector."

Sam ignored him and turned to the Chief, who handed his DI a file. "There's something we didn't know until a few minutes ago that might be relevant," said Sam. "I think that there's more than meets the eye to the accident that apparently claimed the lives of Dan, Jane and the son Declan."

"Ok, go on!" said Dr Phillips, his attitude quickly becoming professional again.

"I didn't want to make a judgement until I had all the facts," explained Sam. "The accident happened on a quiet road with no other vehicles involved. There was no need to look any further at the time and the local Police put it down to a tragic accident. But I've had a forensic accidents team re-examine the circumstances and they're not convinced it was an accident at all."

"So you think..." began the Doctor, but Sam cut across him.

"Hang on," he said and produced some still images from the scene. "It was assumed the car they were travelling in lost control, went through a low hedge and hit a tree on the bank of the River Irwell, and plunged into the water.

The occupants of the car had multiple injuries and were probably dead before it hit the river. But look at this." Sam pointed at the first image that portrayed a bend in a country lane lined with hedges. "There's not a single skid mark on the tarmac."

"So no involuntary reaction to brake?" asked Dr Phillips.

"That's not all! No one seemed to have been wearing a seat-belt, hence the state of the bodies."

Sam produced a still image of what was presumably Jane Prince, her face a pulp of flesh barely recognisable as human.

"How fast was the car travelling?" Phillips asked.

"It's hard to tell with no skid marks. But Forensics say that judging from the damage to the tree, the car was doing between forty-five and fifty miles an hour."

"My God!" said the doctor, clearly shocked. "So what you're saying is that the driver didn't try to brake or swerve, just drove at speed straight into a tree?"

"Basically, yes."

Dr Phillips thought for a moment, staring through the one-way mirror at the suspect. "So you think Ed Jerome had something to do with it - and maybe his first crime was to wipe out his family?" he speculated.

At this point the Chief intervened, to deliver the most dramatic part of the new theory. "It's possible," he said, "but there's something else. Witnesses say that Dan,

Jane and Declan Prince got into the car in Cathcart Street and drove away, hence the reason it was decided they were all in the vehicle when it hit the tree."

Dr Phillips sensed a 'but'.

"The truth is," continued the Chief, "that only one body - Jane Prince's - was recovered from the car; then a second body from the river, Declan Prince."

"The currents quite strong in that part of the River Irwell apparently," said Sam. "It wouldn't be too unusual for a car crash victim to be swept out of a vehicle on impact, especially if they aren't wearing seatbelts."

"So where was Dan Prince?" asked Dr Phillips.

"His body was never recovered," the Chief told him. "The local Police assumed, after an extensive and costly search that it had sunk to the bottom somewhere. They closed the file on the basis that it was too expensive to drag the whole river."

"There was no reason to," added Sam.

***

Back inside Interview Room 1 a few minutes later Dr Phillips tried to formulate a plan. Somehow he must bring out the Joe Reed side of Ed Jerome's personality. The Chief had made it patently clear that without a breakthrough soon Sharon Daly would become the killer's third victim. The only strategy the psychologist thought might work was to pile pressure on Ed Jerome, question the legitimacy of everything he said and try to back him into a corner. Ethically, Dr Phillips thought that any such psychological games were at best questionable and would most likely be dangerous, but he

470

felt justified in view of the fact that Sharon Daly's life was probably now resting in his hands.

He sat down with an air of purpose and no preamble. "So Ed, let's begin again where we left off."

Ed Jerome looked up wearily, black rings were beginning to form around his eyes and Dr Phillips thought that a medical doctor would probably be a better idea than an interrogation, but he pressed on regardless. "Joe Reed: How do you feel about him?"

Behind the glass in the observation room Sam snorted with frustration.

"I hate him," said Ed Jerome. "He hurts people and he's cruel."

"You know that he's a killer?" said the psychologist in a level tone, and waited for a reaction, but nothing came except silence. "Well?" he pressed. "You do understand that Joe Reed has been responsible for the deaths of at least two women and there's a third woman still missing?"

Ed Jerome glared at his inquisitor, a look of indignation on his face. "I left notes," he said pleadingly. "I asked for help." And he began to cry like a small child.

"Who were the notes for?" asked Dr Phillips.

"You!" said Jerome through his sobs. "I left them for you, so you could stop him."

Just then Sam burst into the room, obviously no longer able to contain his frustration and hurled his body at the table. The Detective Inspector almost threw it off balance with the force of his hips, scattering files across the room.

"You *are* Joe Reed, aren't you?" he growled, his voice

already at a level that Dr Phillips would have deemed inappropriate.

Ed Jerome seemed to shrink into his seat, instantly pulling his knees into his chest to make himself as small as he could against Sam's fury.

Sam leaned closer to the shaking suspect, "Stop playing games with me," he snarled. "Tell us where Sharon Daly is!"

"That's enough," said Phillips, alarmed at the sudden brutality of the questioning.

Sam ignored him and pressed ahead, leaning over Ed Jerome in an attempt to penetrate the man's psyche. "Your step-dad, Dan Prince? We know that he didn't die in that accident," he said vehemently. "There were only two bodies recovered from the *accident*, your mother and Declan Prince. Dan Prince wasn't there and probably wasn't even in the car when the accident happened was he?"

Ed Jerome unfolded his limbs and stared blankly at Sam,

"Did he escape?" roared Sam, pressing home the advantage that he thought he'd levered. "I think *you* set up that accident with Dan Prince and the two of you have been giving us the run-around ever since. The rapes, the two-year disappearing act, the abductions; you must have had help, no-one as pathetic as you could have pulled all of this off alone."

"Please!" cried Dr Phillips, choking on the revulsion that he felt for Sam and his tactics. "This is absurd!"

Just then Ed Jerome stood up. His chin thrust high he seemed taller than before, prompting Sam to take a pace backwards and the uniformed officer at the door to become instantly alert. "You don't know anything," he said, his voice unwavering, mocking almost. Now it was his turn to crane his head toward Sam who, despite his experience, found himself cowering back.

"About what?" asked Dr Phillips, his training as a psychologist taking over, keeping him calm and focused.

The suspect stopped and studied Dr Phillips as if he were seeing him for the first time. His burning eyes, grey and bright, seemed to pierce right through the doctor, who suddenly felt naked and alone under the power of their gaze.

"Sit down!" commanded Dr Phillips who knew that showing weakness at this point would end in disaster and professional control was his only weapon.

"Sit down, Mr Reed!" he said again with as much authority as he could muster.

The suspect eventually complied, slowly and deliberately, swinging his legs out to the side of the desk to cross them at the knees as though he were at a social gathering and wanted to show his dominance.

"So, you're Joe Reed" stated Dr Phillips. "Can you tell us where Sharon Daly is?"

Reed studied the Doctor with a grin. "You think you've got it all worked out don't you? Just because I'm sitting here, you think it's over?"

Sam, now recovered, moved to stand a foot or so from the desk and motioned the uniformed officer to do the same. "Listen, Reed," he said, his years of interrogation experience telling him that he needed to get the upper-hand. "It's *you* who's confused. It's *you* who's in a police station answering questions and it's *you* who's going to end up behind bars for the rest of your miserable life. If I were you I'd start co-operating, and fast." Joe Reed sat nonchalantly surveying his captors, and the blue paper jump-suit, designed to strip a subject of his individuality, suddenly seemed oddly fashionable. Reed positioned himself cross-legged with his arms folded, daring either Dr Phillips or Sam Bradbury to challenge his dominance. "I want a lawyer," he demanded, keeping constant eye contact with Sam, who he instinctively knew was the more senior person present.

"Do you have your own or should I provide a duty solicitor?" asked Sam.

Reed smiled.

"I'm surprised you're smiling," said Dr Phillips. "You know it's over don't you?"

"Nothing's over," said Reed. "Nothing's ever over."

The doctor sensed that the suspect might want to talk, perhaps boast about what he had done.

"Did you enjoy killing Dawn James?" he asked, in the sort of tone usually reserved for asking for a loaf of bread.

"I said I want a lawyer," replied Reed with a distant smile.

"I'll arrange a duty solicitor," said Sam and nodded to the constable at the door, who promptly left the room. Reed leant back in the chair, the plastic easily flexing in response to his weight.

"So, Mr Reed," pressed the doctor. "Was Dawn James the first woman you killed? How did it make you feel?"

"Ask my lawyer," said Reed and laughed at his own thin joke.

"How about Dan Prince?" asked Dr Phillips. "Did he enjoy killing Dawn James?"

Reed's smile disappeared and his eyes grew dark and instantly threatening.

"Dan Prince is dead," he declared coldly. "You can't play games with me."

Sam and Dr Phillips looked at each other, their eyes searching, trying to communicate without speaking. A few minutes ago, they had discussed the accident which claimed the lives of the Prince family, and there was no concrete evidence that Dan Prince had died in the accident along with his wife and son. From the evidence they did have they had concluded that Dan Prince and Joe Reed were a team, working together. Sam dug into a file, producing the scene photographs of the accident and laid them on the desk in front of Joe Reed. He took a few moments to study the pictures, before shock began to register on his face.

"You've mocked these up," he said throwing the stills across the desk in Sam's direction.

"In what way?" asked Sam, pointing at the pictures, sensing that Reed didn't understand or agree with the content. "There's the car, your mum Jane and your brother Declan. The body of Dan Prince was never found, because I assume he was never in the car?"

Reed's face hardened to stone and he shook his head angrily.

"You and Dan Prince are working together aren't you?" asked Sam. "Where's Sharon Daly?"

"That's impossible," said Reed almost to himself.

"What is?" asked Dr Phillips. "What's impossible?"

"Dan died in the accident," said Reed, his face a mass of confusion.

"How do you know that?" asked the doctor, relying on his training to ask simple, to the point questions.

"I just know," said Reed, his guard visibly rising. "Now where's my lawyer?"

***

The Chief, Sam Bradbury and Dr Phillips were sitting in the observation room.

A duty solicitor had been on-site dealing with another client and was available immediately, causing a necessary suspension of the interview whilst he consulted his new client away from the interview room.

"That's it then," said Sam. "Let's charge him. We've lost."

The Chief said nothing, his gaze passing through Sam and to the wall beyond.

"He might still talk," said Dr Phillips. "We had him confused with the accident report and he'll want to know more details. Surely we can use that information as leverage to the whereabouts of Sharon Daly."

"Not a chance," said Sam. "Once we charge him, the brief will tell him to say nothing else."

"Even at the expense of a life?" asked Dr Phillips incredulously.

"In the eyes of his lawyer he's innocent," said Sam, "Unless Reed suddenly has a pang of conscience and volunteers the information, we're screwed."

"Well, he might!" said Phillips, growing more agitated. "At least we have to try."

The Chief broke his silence. "No point. We have a duty

now to charge him with the murders of Dawn James and Robyn Cox."

"That means we have to tell him that anything he says will be taken down and may be used in evidence against him," said Sam redundantly.

"So his lawyer will tell him to say nothing," added the Chief.

Dr Phillips rallied. "So that's it! We just forget Sharon Daly and wait until we stumble across her body?"

A look of tired sympathy crossed the Chief's face. "It's out of our hands now anyway," he said.

"We can't just abdicate responsibility," said Phillips, almost beginning to plead. "We've got to keep trying."

"I'm not abdicating responsibility, Mike," said the Chief, resorting to using the doctor's Christian name to help him connect. "A team of senior detectives from Scotland Yard will be here within half an hour to take over the investigation. It's their call now."

"I see," said Dr Phillips, and slumped back into his chair.

The tension in the room was palpable with the three men staring into space. They had resigned themselves to defeat when the door swished open and Paz, Jenny's researcher, burst in without knocking. "I'm sorry sir," he said as soon as he saw the Chief. "I mean, I'm sorry to barge in, but I've found something that I think you should see."

Paz handed the Chief a file and waited for him to read it, almost dancing with excitement. The Chief passed the file straight to Sam, who in response to the researcher's enthusiasm quickly began to pore over the contents.

"What is it?" asked Dr Phillips.

"It's Patrick," said Paz. "I've found out who he is."

"I assumed it was Reed who sent the letters under a pseudonym," said the doctor, recalling the mocking letters addressed to the Chief, one of which Sam was reviewing as they spoke.

"I'm not convinced," said Paz.

"Go on," said Dr Phillips, growing impatient.

"Well, we think that Dan Prince didn't die in the car accident," said Paz, "or should I say, Daniel *Patrick* Prince."

"That makes sense if Prince wrote the letters," said Sam. "But we're still not sure about his connection to Joe Reed. Reed thinks Dan Prince is dead so they couldn't be working together."

"Unless?" said Dr Phillips, his mind sparking into action.

"What?" asked Sam impatiently.

"Hear me out," said Dr Phillips. "Ed Jerome is working in Birmingham, pretty steady and happy in a car showroom. He's put his past behind him, which may have included some kind of abuse by Dan Prince or perhaps his mother, or both."

"Ok Mike," said The Chief, "so he ups sticks and leaves after the accident to join up with Dan Prince?"

"Why would he if Dan Prince had abused him too?" and the psychologist paused a moment to formulate his thoughts. "Just a theory. Dan Prince engineers the accident killing his wife and son. I know the reason's unclear, but bear with me. Then he contacts Ed Jerome in Birmingham posing as Ed's step-brother Declan."

"Why would he do that?" asked Sam sceptically.

478

"He wants to manipulate Ed Jerome, he wants to use him to play out his fantasies," said Dr Phillips.

"It's a wild theory," retorted Sam.

"Perhaps; but look at the evidence. Jane Prince has long dark hair and so have all the victims, even the early ones that were raped. They all have a similar physical build to Jane and they all have children too. Also, all of them are about the age that Jane would have been when she married Dan Prince."

"So?" said the Chief trying desperately to grasp Dr Phillips train of thought.

"So, after they're married Dan Prince abuses Ed Jerome and his own son Declan with Jane either participating or at least complicit, probably in a similar way that Joe Reed abuses his victims."

"What?" asked Sam. "Suffocation, torture, sodomy?"

"Exactly," said Dr Phillips. "Now, what if Ed leaves home to go to Birmingham and escape the abuse. Jane would lose her reason to keep quiet about any abuse meted out by Dan Prince to his own son Declan."

"What - Dan Prince snaps and kills them both?" asked Sam.

"Precisely," said the doctor, his theorising emboldening him to press ahead. "But Dan Prince needs to keep going, he's a sexual sadist. Jane may have told him she wasn't prepared to hide his abuse of Declan anymore. Or perhaps Declan was even enjoying the sadism. Many victims experience a kind of acceptance of their situation and some end up accepting the abuse and can't perform properly without it."

"So what you're saying is that Dan Prince contacts

Ed Jerome posing as Declan Prince, his comrade in abuse?" asks Sam.

"And motivates him to punish Jane Prince over and over?" asked the Chief.

"That's how I see it," said Dr Phillips. "It's a pattern of abuse instigated by Dan Prince and covered up by his wife Jane and then later adopted by his stepson Ed Jerome, also known as Joe Reed."

The room fell silent, contemplating the implications.

"So we need to find Dan Prince then," said Sam eventually.

"I may be able to help there," said Paz.

"Ok," said Sam. "Go on."

"Well, as we know, there aren't any property ownership or tenancy records for Ed Jerome or Joe Reed. But 63, Cathcart Street was sold just after the accident that claimed the lives of the occupants."

"We know that," said the Chief.

"Yes, *but*," countered Paz, "the new owner sold again quite quickly to a Mr Patrick King."

"Daniel Patrick Prince, Patrick King. That's more than just a coincidence," said the Chief.

"It's the money too," said Paz. "That house was paid for in cash."

Sam stood up as if his seat had suddenly become electrified.

"Christ!" he shouted, grabbing at the Chief's arm.

"What is it, Sam?"

"Jenny!" he shouted. "I let Jenny go to Cathcart Street this morning."

Chapter 33

Once inside the house Paula Tripp should have been frozen with fear. Instead, adrenalin coursed through her body providing courage and strength and she pressed ahead, positioning herself at the door between the kitchen and the living room.

The reporter scanned the kitchen worktops, desperately searching for something that would give her an edge - anything she could use as a weapon. The kitchen was ancient and looked like it hadn't been used for years. The powder blue doors of the units were either missing or hanging from their hinges, and the worktop was filthy with accumulated dust and grime in the way that only time and neglect can achieve.

Paula took a few steps backwards and gingerly began opening drawers, being careful to stay as silent as she could whilst rooting through the contents of each one. Eventually she found a small paring knife at the back of the final drawer. She turned the rusty blade over in her hands, cursing her luck.

Paula gathered herself together, but despite the unexpected chill of the day and the breeze blowing freely through the back door and around the kitchen, beads of sweat began to develop on the reporter's forehead. The black stained handle of the small knife began to feel slick in her hand as the enormity of what she was about to attempt dawned on her. She suddenly felt like a small child confronted with danger and trying to defend herself with a toy. Padding back to the internal door, she closed her eyes tight and pressed her body against the frame, taking a moment to listen to what was being said beyond. The voice was male and clear, despite being muffled through the door.

"So, Jenny Foster," the man mocked. "Criminal Profiler, what am I going to do?"

Jenny stayed silent.

"You probably know by now how wide of the mark you've been; aye, and just how stupid and incompetent you are?" he said, malice lacing his words. "I bet you profiled that Joe Reed was a loner, on the edge of society, someone that'd get caught easy and fast?"

Paula heard no reply from Jenny as the man went on taunting his captive. "Your DI Sam Bradbury didn't have a clue that there were two of us, and he hasn't got a clue where you are now!" the man snarled.

Now at last Paula heard Jenny's voice, clear and calm, her preceding silence probably used to give her a chance to think, "Joe Reed's at Central Park," said Jenny. "And DI Bradbury knows exactly where I am."

The man laughed. "Nice try *Jenny*," he said. "You'll have to do better than that, Lass."

"He gave himself up yesterday," said Jenny, keeping her voice calm. "He presented himself as Ed Jerome and gave this address. That's how I knew to come here."

The man didn't answer and Paula sensed that Jenny had struck a chord.

"That's bullshit!" she heard him say eventually.

"They'd not send you on your own. You're hardly a response team."

"Can I have some water?" Jenny asked, trying to buy time and deflect the man's malice. "I can hardly breathe through the blood."

"Seeing if there's any compassion already Jenny?" asked the man, tutting loudly. "Shouldn't you at least wait until we've formed some kind of relationship?"

It was obvious to Paula that the man was smiling as he spoke.

"You need to remember your training, Jenny," he taunted. "Think, Lass! What were you taught to do if you were ever in this situation? Hmm?"

"Connect with the assailant and try to find some common ground," said Jenny flatly, playing along with the man.

"So?" he hissed. "Connect!"

There was silence for a few seconds before Jenny began to speak.

"Well, you're obviously not Joe Reed," she speculated. "We have him at Central Park. So, who are you?"

"Can't you work it out?" asked the man. "Who could I be?"

Jenny recalled the details that she'd read in Ed Jerome's Social Services file.

"Well you can't be Declan Prince, you're too old. If you are from Ed Jerome's past you must be Dan Prince?"

"Go on," said the man.

"But Dan Prince died in a car accident according to the records," said Jenny. "Did you cause the car accident that killed your wife and son and make it look like you were a victim too?" Jenny paused. "If that's true, then you must have got back in touch with Ed, whom you know you can manipulate, and persuaded or perhaps even forced him to rape and kill for you?"

"Very good," said the man. "You're brighter than I thought."

"Can I have some water now?" asked Jenny, "there's blood dripping into my mouth."

Paula panicked: if he agreed to get Jenny water he would come her way.

The reporter quickly slipped across the kitchen and out through the back door leading out to the yard, closing it behind her. The man didn't appear in the kitchen and Paula crouched for a few moments, cursing that she had been so easily seen off. She should have waited behind the door from the sitting room to the kitchen in case he went for water and she could have surprised him. She could have used the knife to hold him back, but instead she'd run out like a scared child. She realised now that the kitchen was redundant and if the man was going to get water for his captive, he would probably have gone to another room or even upstairs to a tap that was more frequently used, and where there might be a glass. Tripp wrestled with thoughts of what she should have done; she wished she could just burst into the room and try to get Jenny away from the man. Hating herself for her cowardice, she crept back into the kitchen and then slipping through the door and keeping low, she took up her previous position at the door frame.

Paula stood for a few minutes straining her ears, only to be met with silence.

As the silence deepened she pushed gently on the door,

which opened enough for her to see that the room was empty. Cursing herself, the reporter stepped through and into the sitting room where the first thing she saw was the blood spattered on the empty chair and more blood gathered in large droplets under the legs. The presence of blood made the danger concrete and the reporter's stomach churned. She stood like a statue holding her breath as she listened for any signs of life. Hearing nothing, she eventually forced her limbs into action, crossed the room and made for the hall where she spotted an open door. The light from within the hall showed her some steps leading downwards and she waited, listening intently. The reporter looked nervously up and down the hallway for signs of life, but nothing stirred.

Gripping the paring knife she moved to the doorway leading downwards.

The wooden steps were steep, and peering to the bottom she could make out a pair of black heels that she recognised as belonging to Jenny. The profiler was obviously on the ground and Paula wrestled with her fear, trying to decide what to do next. She wanted to go down the steps, face the man and rescue Jenny. But her fear was driving her to run back through the house, down the alley, get to her car and call for help. The reporter's bravery and confidence were waning, her legs quivered and her limbs were stiff with a numbing terror. She decided that going down the steps wasn't an option. Staring at the small knife in her hand, she realised that the man would be too powerful to overcome with such a ridiculous toy. Reality dawned and she knew she should have gone back to her car to call for help as soon as she was certain that Jenny was in danger. She made a concrete decision, and turned to go.

Before she could take a step, a pair of strong hands gripped her shoulders from behind. Paula involuntarily opened her hands and dropped the knife, watching helplessly as it clattered down the staircase. The hands held her in their grip for what seemed like an eternity; stale breath wafted across the back of the reporter's neck and her skin prickled.

"Who the hell are you?" asked the man's voice and before she could answer he turned her around to face him, clamping a rough hand on her throat, almost lifting her off her feet. He was in control.

Paula's arms seemed to be stuck rigid at her sides. She kicked her toes, desperate for grip on the ground, but the man ignored her struggles - merely studied the reporter with dark eyes. She tried to plead with the man, but his grip on her throat tightened making speech impossible, and all she could manage was a strangled cry as he suddenly shifted his weight forward and threw her body down the stairs.

Paula hit every step.

She felt the hard wood connect first with her left shoulder, then her back, before her feet hit half way down. The grips of her sensible black shoes took hold and the momentum of the fall tossed her forward to complete the journey with her face buried in carpet. She lay still: shock had shut down her broken body and she was terrified to move. Automatically she mentally examined her frame for damage; her left shoulder felt numb and she was afraid that her back was broken when she felt a searing pain stabbing between her shoulder blades. Paula had fallen directly over the knife that had preceded her, and as the man reached to haul her unceremoniously to her feet she sub-consciously scooped up the blade in her hand.

Paula wanted to bring the knife up and spear her assailant, but before the thought had properly formed he spun her around and clamped his arm around her neck. Pulling her arm back with his other hand he took hold of the small knife and without a word of warning plunged the knife into the reporter's sternum and let go of her.

Paula Tripp fell in a heap on the floor, and as she fell the air left her body, like a tyre ripped open by a nail. Time seemed to freeze as the carpet loomed towards her and the reporter's body almost bounced as it folded in on itself on impact. She clutched at the knife still buried in her chest and brought her knees up to withdraw into a protective ball. She didn't pull at the handle of the blade, her sensible reaction being to leave it there and shield herself from any further attack.

As she lay on the ground shock turned to panic as she felt herself descending into unconsciousness. As if a hole had opened up in the floor, she began falling uncontrollably. Tripp's final thoughts before her brain shut down against the pain and shock did not lead her back to her family and her childhood home in Tarporley where her parents still lived and where she had spent most of her life. Instead her mind recalled the face of Don Chapman, her editor at the Manchester Evening News, and she wondered how she would be remembered.

**

Jenny Foster saw the whole thing. Dan Prince had un-
tied her from the chair in the sitting room then half
carried, half dragged her to the basement where he
had quickly sedated her with a fist to the stomach before throwing her to the ground like a rag-doll. Jenny
hit her head hard on the floor, her brain buzzing with
the threat of unconsciousness, but then the violence
of Tripp's bone-crunching fall sharpened her muted
senses. She watched in mute dismay as the man easily
overpowered Tripp and plunged a knife into her chest,
before letting her body fall to the ground like a mario-
nette with all its strings cut at once. Confusion reigned
in Jenny's numb brain, at a loss as to why Paula Tripp
had suddenly appeared, battered and bleeding in front
of her.

Paula writhed uncontrollably with pain, eventually coming to rest facing Jenny in a tight ball, her eyes
glassy with fear. Jenny tried to call out to her, desperate to know how and why she was here. But the words
wouldn't transfer from the profiler's brain to her
mouth and she watched silently, in the grip of an icy
horror as Paula Tripp lost her battle with consciousness, her eyes rolling to the back of their sockets before the lids closed. Jenny saw the handle of the knife
protruding from her breast and the blood pooling beneath her and realised that she would probably never
open her eyes again.

The basement stank of human waste and death. Jenny
rolled onto her side, waves of nausea flowing through
her body as her own injuries stabbed at her with a dull,

paralyzing ache deep in her stomach. Panting quickly to restore some form of regular breathing pattern, she focused on her surroundings, trying to make sense of what had happened. Then her eyes lighted upon a naked woman lying to one side of the room. Cruel knots bound the woman's hands to her feet making movement all but impossible. Her long, dark hair was matted with filth and burned thick and red into the small of her back was an angry number 3. Slowly it dawned on the profiler that the woman must be Sharon Daly and she was fleetingly elated that the missing victim might be still alive.

"How does it feel knowing you'll be number four?" asked Dan Prince, his voice mocking, loaded with intent.

Jenny had almost forgotten that he was still in the room.

He hauled her to her feet, and facing him Jenny was horrified at the life-force that shone from his face. His eyes were alive, almost dancing inside their sockets, his cheeks were flushed a deep red and his mouth was set in an expression of pure pleasure that engulfed her in a wave of nausea. Prince began tearing at Jenny's clothes and she felt her black skirt drop to the floor. She was powerless to resist her attacker as her arms were thrust in turn above her head and she watched her shirt and black jacket thrown to the ground. The blow to Jenny's nose coupled with the bang to her head were causing the profiler's brain to spin uncontrollably, gathering momentum like a washing machine in its final cycle, and now Dan Prince threw her to the ground.

She watched, silently, helplessly as he crossed the room to a box and rummaged inside, returning after what seemed a lifetime. She vaguely heard the clank of chains and felt a cold sensation on her neck as Dan Prince wrapped it in a thick, black leather collar, buckling it tightly from behind. Jenny began rasping for breath as her throat competed in vain with the tightness of the leather. She felt Dan Prince kneel on her back to pull her arms behind her, quickly securing them with rope. Her back arched as Prince took more rope, tying the profiler's feet together before linking the rope from her wrists and pulling tight.

"Comfortable?" asked Prince, jerking Jenny's hair so that she was forced to look at him. Her eyes opening and closing involuntarily and the spinning in her head gathering pace, she heard Prince speak as if through a dull curtain. "Let's get you settled," he said.

Jenny felt her face being forced down into the carpet, her cheeks and forehead burning as they rubbed against the harsh pile. Suddenly, a searing, unbearable pain gripped her entire body. She was unable to move against her bonds and even though the anguish brought instant clarity to her mind, she couldn't pinpoint where the agony had begun. It was as though her entire lower body had burst into flames, each lick of the fire a searing new pain added to the last. Even through the blood that continued to seep from her nose Jenny caught the unmistakeable and sickening smell of burning flesh. The ordeal seemed to be endless, jab after hot jab causing her to buck against her bonds, which only tightened with each spasm. The agony was unbearable, seeping through her entire body and carpeting her brain. Suddenly, she felt Dan Prince's weight lift from her body. The intense agony subsided into a raw burning sensation that came in endless waves from the top of her buttocks, and the inexorable spinning in her head returned.

The last thing that Jenny Foster, Criminal Profiler heard was the sound of Dan Prince unbuckling his belt behind her and then a clear plastic bag was pulled over her face, before she fell into the ink of unconsciousness.

Chapter 34

DI Sam Bradbury loathed hospitals and hated anything medical, especially the smell of sterile corridors.
Nurses clad in blue uniforms with their hair pinned into tight buns or ponytails scurried purposefully across
the shining tiled floor. Patients queued for everything,
waiting to see doctors, buy a newspaper, eat lunch or
even use the lavatory and as Sam strode past them he
was relieved that he wasn't amongst their number.
Reaching the elevator Sam stepped in and pressed for
the basement, taking the opportunity to use the mirror in the lift to straighten his paisley tie and brush im-
aginary dust from the lapel of his grey suit.

The basement level was quiet compared to the lobby
and as Sam paced the corridor the rubber on the soles
of his shoes squeaked his noisy progress.

Eventually he reached a frosted glass door and stopped
to compose himself before entering. The absence of
life in the long corridor enveloped it in a welcome
cloak of silence and the DI waited for a few moments,
concentrating on his breathing, calming his nerves to
prepare himself for the sight that would greet him inside the room. Eventually he let out a deep sigh and
pushed through the door marked '*Manchester Royal
Infirmary, Mortuary*'.

Frasier O'Connor, the Chief Medical Examiner came from behind a desk fitted with microscopes and strode toward Sam as he entered. "Morning, Sam," said the coroner in his thick Scottish accent and extended his hand to be shaken.

"I've only got a few minutes," explained the DI. "I wanted to see the body for myself. Make myself believe that last night was real."

"I understand," said O'Connor. "It's this way," and he led Sam through autopsy rooms reserved for the dead. Stainless steel examination tables stood bolted to the grey, heavy-duty rubber floor, ominously waiting for their next subject; bright, stainless steel instruments stood in trays on sterile surfaces, and Sam's depression grew with every step.

O'Connor stopped at a door marked 'Private. No Unauthorised Entry' and ran his fingers through his grey hair.

"Ready?" he asked. Sam nodded and the pair went through the door.

The room was brightly lit, with the only furniture being a row of six more unoccupied stainless steel tables. The coroner moved to the opposite wall with its row of floor to ceiling doors, each one labelled to show that they could house four names each.

O'Connor selected a door in the centre and pulled open what turned out to be a full height drawer. When he pulled on the handle the drawer slid effortlessly and silently out into the room. It contained a single body shrouded in a white sheet.

***

Returning to the lobby of the Manchester Royal Infirmary ten minutes later, Sam consulted the scribbled note that he'd retrieved from his pocket. It read 'ICU Ward 12.' The DI spotted a florist, called in for flowers, and then he took the lift to the second floor. It buzzed with activity and Sam found himself hugging the edges of the corridor as he passed by the wards. Eventually he reached Ward 12 and pressed a bell to be admitted. A white-uniformed nurse peered at him through the glass, sternly gesturing for him to use the hand sanitizer that was fixed to the wall in a red square plastic bottle. Sam did as instructed and smiled at the nurse, who remained impassive as she buzzed him in before turning away to carry on silently with whatever task Sam had interrupted.

The ward was quiet, the odd cough breaking a dead silence as Sam peered into the private rooms, until eventually he stopped outside Room 8, straightened his tie again and walked in.

"Hey stranger," he said as he made his way across the room and took the only seat next to the head of the bed. "The nurse called me to say you'd woken up. How are you feeling?"

The patient in ICU Ward 12, Room 8 wrestled with her body until it sat up straight and tried to smile through gritted teeth. "I'm ok," she said in a voice that sounded hoarse and rasping. She took Sam's hand and pressed it.

"Thanks," she said.

Sam returned the reporter's squeeze and the pair looked at each other, the moment passing slowly between them. "No thanks necessary."

"The doctor says I'm lucky to be alive," said Paula Tripp, grimacing through the pain. "The knife he stabbed me with wasn't good enough to puncture my breast bone."

"I know," said Sam.

They were still holding hands and Paula squeezed hard, "Tell me what happened," she said, "no-one seems to know anything."

"The doctor says I can only stay a few minutes. I just wanted to make sure you were ok. You need rest."

"No, please!" said Paula. "I need to know everything now."

Sam knew from previous experience that Paula was stubborn, and if he was in her position he would probably want to know what happened too. "Ok," he conceded. "I'll bring you some water and then I'll tell you what happened."

Paula let go of Sam's hand and watched as he busied himself filling two water cups and retaking his seat.

"You've got company in here," he began. "Sharon Daly is alive, just down the corridor. The doctors say that she'll make a full recovery, physically at least."

"And Jenny Foster?" asked Paula, the thought of the profiler igniting unexpected emotions of friendship and camaraderie.

Sam's head bowed and Paula caught her breath at what she knew would be DI Sam Bradbury's next words.

"She didn't make it," said Sam. "She died in the basement at Cathcart Street."

Tears sprang into Paula Tripp's eyes as she remembered seeing Jenny on the floor before she was stabbed. "What was she doing there?"

Sam's mouth twisted as he struggled against the onset of his own tears. "It was my fault. She told me she was going to Cathcart Street, but none of us knew what was waiting for her. I thought it would be a good distraction for her - a way for her to be useful gathering background information on Joe Reed."

Paula bit her bottom lip, and the pair sat in silence for a few moments, contemplating their roles in the chaos. "Who was he?" asked Paula eventually. "The man who stabbed me I mean? I thought you had Joe Reed at Central Park."

"That was the piece of the puzzle we were missing," said Sam. "Dr Phillips put it together. Paz researched the owners of Cathcart Street and we realised that a man called Dan Prince probably owned it. To cut a long story short, he was Joe Reed's step-father and drove Joe Reed to kill. That's how we knew that Jenny might be in immediate danger."

"So it was Dan Prince who…" said Paula, trailing off.

"Wounded you and killed Jenny, yes," said Sam.

"What happened to him?" asked Paula, her eyes flitting to the door as though he might burst in at any second to finish the job.

"He's downstairs in the mortuary," explained Sam. "When we realised Jenny might be in serious trouble I called in armed response and they stormed Cathcart Street. Prince was shot dead."

Paula Tripp's face contorted into a grimace. "Are you sure it was him?" she asked illogically.

"We're sure, don't worry," comforted Sam. "I've just come from the mortuary now. I wanted to see his body for myself."

"Ok," said Paula, an obvious sense of relief passing across her face. "And Joe Reed? I assume he's been charged?"

"He's being processed," Sam told her, a look of concern crossing his face. "He'll be referred to a secure psychiatric unit for assessment. The pressure we put him under hit him hard. When he realised that he was being manipulated by Dan Prince he retreated into a shell."

"Manipulated?"

"It's a complicated story, but Joe Reed hated his mother Jane who'd allowed her husband Dan Prince to abuse him from boyhood. Reed was being driven to kill by someone he thought was his step-brother Declan who had shared the abuse, but it was actually Dan Prince who was controlling him. Dr Phillips thinks he may never recover."

The pair sat in silence again for a few moments. "How did Joe Reed fall for that?" asked Paula.

"Dr Phillips worked out that as children Declan Prince and Joe Reed suffered abuse at the hands of Dan Prince, probably the same abuse as Joe Reed handed out to his victims.

"What?" speculated Paula, "and Joe Reed's mother just let Prince do it?"

"Yes," said Sam. "I've seen situations like this before and more often than not, the mother is just as much a victim as the abused child."

"Because she feels trapped or even beholden to the man?" said Paula.

"Dan Prince was obviously a powerful and controlling figure," mused Sam. "Jane Prince probably never set

out to hurt her son, but she was living a squalid existence as a prostitute single mother. Dan Prince had tak-
en her and her son in. She must have felt as though she
had no choice but to go along with anything he did."

"Bastard!" said Paula under her breath.

"Then when her son left home to get away, Jane
wouldn't go along with it anymore," continued Sam.
"Dan Prince rigged a car accident, killing Declan and
Jane and faking his own death to gain anonymity.
Then he posed as Declan to coerce Joe Reed to kill for
him."

"It all sounds so far-fetched," sighed Paula.

The pair descended into silence, each contemplating
the secret horror that a family can endure.

"There was a secondary location," said Sam eventually.
"Dan Prince didn't live at 63 Cathcart Street. He had
a flat a few streets away where he kept surveillance on
Joe Reed and the house. We found video clips of the
murders and rapes and..."

"And what?" asked Paula.

"And a video was being recorded of your ordeal in the
basement too."

Paula felt the pain of the knife wound and Sam read
her mind.

"Sorry we weren't quick enough," said Sam.

"At least I'm alive," said Paula and finding DI Sam
Bradbury's hand pressed it as firmly as she could.

***

Peter Foster hauled himself sweating from his lover
and flopped onto his back, satisfaction glowing in his
face. The woman next to him propped herself up on

one elbow to face him and began tracing out her name in his chest hair with a long manicured nail. "That was incredible," she said.

Peter smiled and propped his hands behind his head to give her maximum access to his chest. The pair lay silently for a few moments, the woman contemplating how to extend the affair, Peter contemplating how to remove the woman from his marital bed with the least amount of fuss possible.

"Does this mean we can be together?" she asked, gazing at him with her big brown eyes. "From the first moment I saw you I knew this would happen, I knew we would end up together. I think it's destiny!"

Peter knew he had made a mistake taking his au-pair to bed in the first place, but she'd made it obvious that she was fair game, and he was always loath to pass up an opportunity.

He began speaking to his erstwhile lover as though she were a recalcitrant child that had asked too many times for something that was bad for it.

"Destiny? What do you know about destiny?" he scoffed.

Tricia wouldn't be put off so easily, "so it was just sex you wanted?" she accused, "I felt more than that and I *know* you did too."

Peter studied her with seeming amusement before he began to speak again, condescending this time, reminding Tricia of conversations she'd had with her grand-father where he offered advice without ever truly understanding the problem.

"You're young," said Peter, "whereas I'm not."

"What difference does that make?" asked Tricia, anger

beginning to surface in her voice at the realisation that she'd probably already lost the battle.

"Well," he continued soothingly, "you would be wasting your youth, and we have nothing to give each other except this."

"We'd be marvellous together!" exclaimed Tricia, feeling as though she were being backed into a corner from which escape would be impossible.

"No we wouldn't," said Peter firmly, and began stroking her hair as though attempting to calm an overexcited puppy. "We'd be leading separate lives. I would want to do the things that older people want to do and you would want to do the things that younger people want to do."

"Rubbish!" retorted Tricia. "This is beginning to sound like an excuse."

"Not an excuse," said Peter, "stark reality."

"Not my reality," she said softly, and moved to kiss him.

Peter returned her kiss with none of the passion they had shared earlier, and Tricia drew away with only the memory of his cold, unresponsive lips on hers.

"If we went out for an evening together for example," he went on, "I would want a sophisticated dinner in a quiet restaurant in good company, where I could talk and try to be interesting; whereas you'd want to go to a bar or nightclub to be with other young people, and dance and laugh and have a wonderful evening just being young."

Tricia pulled herself away and drew the sheet up her lithe, tanned body, suddenly embarrassed to find herself naked and vulnerable.

"Piss off," she said flatly.

The sound of the front door bell saved the couple from a full-blown argument. Peter slipped out of bed and into the en-suite leaving Tricia to fulfil the role for which she was being paid, and she quickly dressed and headed for the stairs.

After several calls upstairs from Tricia, each one more frustrated than the last, Peter Foster eventually strode into his living room only to stare in disbelief at the sight that confronted him. His erstwhile lover and au-pair Tricia stood propped against the mantelpiece, her bed-ruffled hair tied back in an unkempt pony-tail. Her eyes burned into Peter with a mixture of irritation and fear at the presence of his other two guests, who had both stood up when he came in.

"I'm Chief Superintendent Mark Ambrose and this is WPC Collins," said the tall, uniformed officer extending his hand. "Please, I think you should sit down."

Peter drew upon his boardroom experience to gather his wits. "Yes, I know who you are," he said. "Why are you here?"

"Please…" said the Chief, gesturing to one of the sumptuous grey armchairs and sitting down himself.

Peter shrugged, arranged himself in the chair and waited for his visitor to speak.

"There's no easy way to tell you this Mr Foster," began the Chief. "Your wife Jenny has lost her life in the line of duty."

Tricia screamed, her knees giving way beneath her, before WPC Collins, standing behind the Chief moved quickly to support the au-pair and move her gently into an unoccupied armchair. The Chief paused, emotion haunting his long thin face.

The two men stared at each other for a few moments, the Chief unable to gauge Peter Foster's reaction before continuing, deliberately and slowly.

"Jenny was following a lead to a house in Oldham where she was exposed to a dangerous psychopath." No reaction, and so the Chief carried on. "An armed response unit attended at the scene, but unfortunately they were too late to save Jenny's life."

Peter remained silent, his eyes glazed over, staring into nothingness.

"I'm very sorry, Mr Foster. The medical staff did everything possible at the scene."

Peter cleared his throat. "Did she suffer?" he asked, looking from the Chief to WPC Collins.

"The coroner's report will be detailed and thorough," said the Chief diplomatically.

"The details will be released at the formal inquest, which is normal procedure when an officer is killed in the line of duty."

"Jenny wasn't an officer," stated Peter flatly. "In fact, she wasn't qualified to be following up leads at all," he continued, anger rising in his voice.

"It's difficult for me to say any more," said the Chief calmly. "The investigation is on-going."

"Was it Joe Reed?" asked Peter, a measure of control obvious in his voice. "Was it that bastard?"

"I really can't talk about the details Mr Foster," said the Chief. "There will be an internal investigation."

"Well if you can't tell me any more," growled Peter, "I think it best if you just piss off!"

Once the door had closed behind the police officers, Peter took a sobbing Tricia into his arms. The young girl's tears fell lightly onto Peter's shoulder, and as he rocked her back and forth the shadow of a smile crept across his face.

The End

More Titles from Percy Publishing

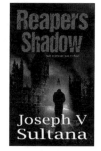

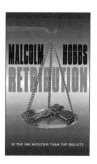

The Middle Man
by Philip J Howard

MrH was 'The Middle Man' for some of the biggest underworld factions in the world of crime. For over twenty five years he was the link and negotiator to the deals. From an eighteen year old kid to middle age there is nothing in life he hasn't seen. His motto is "let nothing in life surprise you" Here is his true view of events that took him to deaths door and almost beyond to eventually changing his life around and making him the renowned Film and TV Director he is today.

A book and film being produced in 2015.

Ray Quinn – Will be telling his story, the highs, the lows, the record contracts, the money, the life.

This book will be published in Early 201

PERCY
PUBLISHING

Visit www.percy-publishing.com for more information.

Facebook: www.facebook.com/percypublishing

Twitter: @percypublishing

To Contact I D Jackson
Find him on FaceBook